THE DOWNFALL OF RAYMOND RAINBOW

ABOUT THE AUTHOR

Michael J. Milford was born in Guernsey in 1938. During the war he lived in Halifax in England. He returned to Guernsey in 1945. He served in the British army and the merchant navy between 1954 and 1965. He also lived in Australia for a few years. He has written numerous poems and articles for the local newspaper. He is married to Joan and lives in Guernsey. This is his fourth novel, his other three were: *The Hypnotist*, *The Mansion*, and *The Ernie Prettle Story*.

THE DOWNFALL OF RAYMOND RAINBOW

MICHAEL J MILFORD

Matador
9 Priory Business Park,
Wistow Road, Kibworth Beauchamp,
Leicestershire. LE8 0RX
Tel: 0116 279 2299
Email: books@troubador.co.uk
Web: www.troubador.co.uk/matador
Twitter: @matadorbooks

ISBN 978 1838590 581

British Library Cataloguing in Publication Data.
A catalogue record for this book is available from the British Library.

Printed and bound in Great Britain by 4edge Limited
Typeset in 11pt Minion Pro by Troubador Publishing Ltd, Leicester, UK

Matador is an imprint of Troubador Publishing Ltd

ACKNOWLEDGEMENTS

Once again, I want to thank my wife Joan with the typing and spelling, for her continual support in my endeavours to be a writer, and for her patience when I insisted on her hearing the latest chapter. I'd like to say thank you to all my readers who enjoyed my other books, and gave me the inspiration to continue writing.

Special thanks to my publishing company for the work they put in, in producing this book. Not forgetting my editor for correcting my many mistakes

This is a work of fiction, names of characters, places and incidents are either the product of the author's imagination or are used fictitiously, and any resemblance to actual persons living or dead, events or locales, is entirely coincidental.

ONE
Monday

On a site in a seedy part of the city stood a long wooden building; it had seen better days and was once a church hall, but now it belonged to a man called Edward Bail. He had spent his time and money on the premises and transformed it into a modern gym with the sole intent to make the sport of karate, his 'passion,' a recognised pastime, a sport that young and elderly people could participate in.

He was dedicated, there was no doubt about that, and he went out of his way to train his members to achieve the highest grades in competitions up and down the country, and was a member of the judging committee that would award higher grades called 'Dans'. He was also a married man and worked as an insurance agent, but an unfortunate downturn in the insurance business had made him redundant so he found himself in hard times, and was having second thoughts in keeping his club running, the money was drying up and the bills were not being paid. It was not a normal thing for him to be in his gym on a Monday afternoon, but one of his members needed just an extra bit of training for an upcoming competition and grading, so he was helping out as he did on many occasions, when not looking for work.

It had been a heavy workout in the gym that afternoon, and Raymond James Rainbow was sweating profusely. He was determined to achieve his next higher grade in his favourite sport of Karate that he had been studying for the past few years, on as many nights as his job allowed. He bowed to his opponent, picked up his towel and made his way to the showers. He knew he had to get a move on because he had a very important date with his girlfriend that evening in his apartment, where he intended to ask her to marry him. He towelled himself down catching his reflection in the full-length mirror; he was happy with his physique that he had worked hard and long to attain. At thirty-five years old he was in good trim, and life was good, he felt great. He had been very lucky in life, and as an only child he had been spoiled by his mother mostly, but his father, who had a prominent position in society, had also done a lot to see that his son got the right education, and was taught at a young age the right thing to do to be successful in life. He had had an idyllic childhood, and had been no trouble at all to his adoring parents. At present he had a brilliant job, a beautiful fiancée and his future was mapped out, like a golden field of daffodils, with certainly good things on the horizon, he had worked hard to make it this way.

'Good workout today Ray,' his training colleague and club owner Eddie commented as they both got dressed, after an invigorating shower, 'You've certainly improved in the last few months that's for sure, you gave me a hard time in today's session, some of your moves were so fast you were like lightening, man, I'm glad we're friends I would hate to be your enemy.' Both men laughed. Ray held out his hand.

‘I think I may have damaged my hand, it bloody well hurts like hell. I hope I haven’t broken it’, he rubbed it gently; ‘I might have to give it time to heal, miss a few sessions.’ He looked at his watch; it was time to go home, he had an important date.

‘Got to get going, got to fix a nice meal, and try to impress my future wife, didn’t I tell you Ed, tonight’s the night I go down on one knee and with chocolates in one hand, an engagement ring in the other and ask her the age old question.’

‘You’ll never get away with it, she will see right through you, will you tell her that you are a born killer just ready to pounce on anyone who dares to get in your way? Will you tell her that you have death waiting within your deadly hands?’ Eddie said, jokingly. Ray went into a Karate stance and made the sound of a hissing snake; he stared, his eyes wide open, and his arm flew with the speed of sound towards the face that was laughing, stopping just before contact by a fraction.

‘Hell that hurt,’ Ray held his hand and the pain showed on his face. He looked at his palm and massaged it. ‘I’ve got to get a bandage on it when I get indoors. Here take a look at this gem, it’s a beauty.’ He handed a small box to his fellow athlete. ‘Go on, open it, and take a look.’

Eddie opened the lid and squinted in the poor light; he walked to the window for a better view. ‘This must have set you back a pretty penny, it’s a beautiful ring,’ He remarked glancing over his shoulder.

‘She’s worth it,’ Ray replied, ‘every cent; she’s my pride and joy.’ At that moment the door of the gym opened and two members of the karate club came in for their workout.

'Hi Ray, how you doing? Hi Eddie, did you manage to get me that new karate jacket you said you'd get for me?' Brian Stevens enquired.

'Yes it's in the office, I'll get it for you,' Eddie replied. He went to the office, 'Received it yesterday, special delivery,' he said as he disappeared at the end of the gym.

'So how did the workout go Ray? you should be almost ready for your next Dan by now, you were pretty hot last time I saw you perform,' Brian said as he opened his locker, and put his bag inside.

'Yes, just a bit of tweaking to do then I'll be wearing that black belt, been training long enough I guess I deserve it, a lot of work and sweat has come out of here.' He pointed to his body, looking in the full-length mirror and flexed his muscles, he certainly loved himself.

'Well, all I can say is good luck to you; you deserve it that's for sure.' Brian looked towards the office that was at the far end of the gym and said, 'Eddie's taking his time getting my jacket; maybe he's checking the accounts, he told me that he's got some financial trouble, and there's been some talk about putting the subs up, or even closing the club down, did you know Ray?'

'No, I wasn't aware of anything like that, it's something that he's never talked to me about, but that's not surprising we're not the closest of friends in fact I would say he's more of an enemy than a friend, sometimes he riles me up so much, I could just chop him to bits with my karate blows,' Ray replied as he shook his head. 'I must admit I find Eddie sarcastic at times and at other times he seems jealous or at least envious but money problems, never a mention, let's hope the club stays open long enough for me to get that new black belt. The test is on the cards for next month. Then I won't care, I'll soon find another club maybe nearer to where I'm proposing to live when I get hitched, anyhow just have to wait and see, things can change in a split second. If the truth was told we need more membership in this club, twenty-two members are not enough to keep this place going'. He looked at his watch once again. 'Got to get going lads, it's my first day of my holiday today, going away tomorrow for a short break, don't know where yet somewhere sunny I expect, I've left it to my lady to decide where, it's six twenty, enjoy your workout I did mine earlier because I'm with the other half tonight supposed to be making a meal for us both, but I've hurt my hand on that fucking dummy over there, broke my finger I think, He showed the lads his reddish-looking digit.

'You won't be able to use that finger tonight,' Steve joked. The two men looked at one another and burst out laughing. 'I like your outfit Ray', Brian Stevens remarked, 'its good quality designer stuff, quite expensive I would expect'.

'Yeah only the best for the best I say, my girlfriend bought it for my birthday, she's a darling, anyhow when you're as good-looking as me it's only right to dress well, don't you agree?' all the men laughed.

At that moment the weekly cleaning lady, Mrs Vera Turnbull, who had been cleaning the office, left with a cheery goodbye, as two more lads came into the club followed by two more. Ray talked briefly about the karate contest that was coming up then picked up his bag and slung it over his shoulder and with a wave went out the door, to race home; he didn't even say goodbye to Eddie and was running late with a good thirty minutes walk through the city, and the sun was going down. He had left his car at home, he walked whenever he could.

As he hurried along the shutters were coming down on some shop fronts, and shop assistants were happily putting on theirs coats after a hard day dealing with the public, and wondering what they would have for their tea.

The dark dingy alley called 'Baker' was a shortcut to his apartment; he rarely took this way, because of the garbage bins and the derelicts of the city that would do their drug deals in the tenements' doorways. He was aware that the time was running away, and he was late, as he walked quickly along the high street, as the evening dusk was setting in. People were hurrying home after a long day at work, heads down in a world of their own. He turned right off the busy street into the narrow alley and glanced up at the dirty sign that said 'BAKER ALLEY' in big black letters, then turned an acute left just a few metres in; the decision to take this shortcut was to change his life beyond anything that he could ever have imagined.

The darkness hid this neglected area from his eyes. What he didn't know was that this act of taking a different route home by turning a corner would change his life, as he had so far enjoyed, into a bad place. He thought he heard voices ahead of him coming from the side of a large garbage bin; he inadvertently kicked an empty beer can that went clattering along the tarmac disturbing some rats having their early evening meal of a half-eaten hamburger. The smell of neglect and decay hung in the air like a garbage tip. He passed litter bins, and litter lay in heaps in the corners of doorways. A dirty bulb in a broken wall case cast a dull light on a few overflowing garbage skips that had escaped from being emptied. He walked on; as he approached a big skip he was surprised for a moment when out of the blackness suddenly a very burly figure of an unshaven man appeared and stood right in front of him stopping him in his tracks. The tramp took hold of Rainbow's neck with his big hands and held him in a vice-like grip, as though he was trying to choke him; both men staggered as Rainbow tried to get out of the clutches of this assailant.

'Jesus Christ, help me out, give me a ciggy,' the man blurted out.

'Sorry mate, don't smoke,' Ray said, escaping from the vice-like hold and stepping sideways. The man stepped sideways as well blocking his way once again.

'I need a smoke for fuck's sake,' his hand went up to his chest, and made a sound as thought he was in severe pain. In the semi-darkness Ray sensed he was in a bad place, a dangerous situation, the maniac might have a gun or a knife; he felt the adrenalin kick in.

'I've already told you, I don't smoke, now make way, we don't want any trouble now do we?' Ray's voice took on a threatening tone.

'Give me something to take this pain away, help me, man.' His voice was now very menacing. Ray could see that this encounter was not going to end well. He had had that kind of experience before. He took a deep breath and spoke slowly, emphasising every word, he felt his anger rising. He was getting pissed off.

'Listen, my friend, you don't know what you are getting yourself into believe me it will be worse than trouble itself, now for the last time step aside, and go about your business, and I'll be on my way and I'll forget what you just did, I might as well tell you now I'm a—'

Ray couldn't finish his sentence as the man lunged towards him once again; he saw the fists flying towards his head. He side stepped the blow and went into a karate stance, then with the edge of his hand he hit his assailant with a lightening chop to his throat right on the Adam's apple. The man collapsed to the ground grasping his throat, and lay between two garbage bins. Ray was also in agony as the pain shot through his body, his hand swelling and throbbing. He heard the man gurgling and gasping for breath.

Ray bent down over the prostate crumpled body,

'I told you I don't smoke, I told you didn't I, I warned you, and you ignored me didn't you?' The man was now fighting for his life, fighting to breathe, and in great distress. 'You shouldn't go around attacking people, you never can tell who they are, or what harm you can do, I hope you have been taught a lesson, *don't accost people*.' He emphasised the last words. The man's eyes opened wide as though he was searching for a way out, then he pushed himself up to the sitting position, muttered something Ray couldn't understand, then fell back cracking his head on the tarmac, the sound reverberating along the alley. A muffled sound that sounded like a curse was emitted, at that point the man stopped breathing. Ray slapped the man's face trying to get him to breathe, he tried to massage the throat, and it felt soft and mushy. He noticed blood seeping from the corner of the dead man's mouth; he ripped the shirt apart, and buttons flew everywhere making a clattering sound like a machine gun on the side of the bin. The tattooed eagle on the chest of the corpse seemed to cry out in despair in the dim light of the alleyway, as he pumped the chest. Panic was setting in; it was welling up inside his stomach, he felt sick, 'Why did you do it? I didn't mean to hurt you, you should have listened, and you don't know who I am, what I do.' Rainbow muttered, almost in a pleading way.

The distant sound of police sirens made him stop the fruitless task of trying to resuscitate the man he had just killed. He got to his feet, looked behind the bins to make sure there were no witnesses. The alley would keep its secret. He set off towards his apartment that he could see in the short distance. What he didn't know was that the police were not too far away on the high street. He half ran out of the alley onto the main street, his home just across the road. He saw no one as he approached the main door of his apartment block. He let himself in and raced up the four levels to his home that he shared with a parrot called Pedro that swore a lot. He slipped his key into the lock, and let himself in and closed the door behind him standing there for a full minute, shaking his head, not believing what had just happened. He glanced at his watch; it was just on seven o'clock.

He went to his drinks cabinet and poured himself a stiff drink, a double whisky, adding a drop of water from the tap in his bathroom. He needed to calm down; he felt that he could explode at any time. He looked in the mirror above the basin, where he placed the drink. His face was strained, 'What have I done?' he said aloud. 'What the fuck have I done?'

'What the fuck have I done?' screeched the parrot from his cage in the other room. For a split second Ray was startled at the intrusion into his thoughts; he opened the tap, and ran the cold water over his swollen hand, it was hurting and throbbing, he felt it gently but couldn't feel any bone out of place. After drying his hands, he took a sip of his drink then returned to the lounge, looking towards the parrot, 'Fuck off,' the parrot shouted flapping his wings. Normally Ray would have laughed but on this occasion the parrot got no reply. He went back to his cabinet, stopped, and drank the remainder of his drink. He refilled the glass, with a single this time. He went to the table that was placed opposite the window and sat down to think, to sort out what had happened to him and to try to fathom out what could be done to alleviate the situation. Looking out of the window he could make out the alley in the distance; all seemed quiet, the moon shone its light across the area casting dark shadows, and it seemed to be trying to hide some ghastly deed. For the next five minutes he was lost in deep thought, then looking once more at his watch he noted the time, it was 7:08. He knew one thing; he certainly wasn't going to prepare a meal now, not with his injured hand, and his appetite gone. Another thought occurred to him; he jumped up from the table and changed his clothes putting them in a black plastic bag for disposal at a later time. His girlfriend Charlotte would be arriving soon, although he didn't want any company at this time, he needed space on his own, to think. The whole evening had been spoilt because of some lowlife. He moved with his drink to the settee. What had happened to his life? It had been a good one up till an hour before, then one wrong turning? One misjudgement of a situation and turmoil now descended like a deluge of rain. If only he had continued along the high street as he always had done in the past, things would be different; if only it was possible to rewind like a video tape.

He sipped his drink, his mind in overdrive. He relived the confrontation over and over again in his mind. He had defended himself from a dangerous robber. He might be lying in that alleyway now, dead. He had too much to lose if he handed himself in, even if the authorities understood his predicament, they might say it was an overreaction, undue force. He couldn't take that chance, he realised he had done wrong to leave the scene of a crime, he had heard it many times in the past but it had been done, and there was no going back now. He held his head in his hands, his energy ebbing away like a receding tide.

The knocking at the door made him jump, his nerves on edge. *It wasn't Charlotte, she had her own key, and so who could it be?* He thought. He got up clumsily knocking the side of the coffee table with his shin. 'Fuck' he said out loud, 'fuck,' the parrot replied. He looked through the door's spy hole to see Eddie his karate colleague standing there. He opened the door.

'Eddie, what the hell are you doing here? I only left you a short while ago; surely you don't miss me that much?'

'Raymond, oh Raymond, what have you done? You should be ashamed of yourself, never let your girlfriend know you did this, she would disown you, that's for sure. It's unforgivable.' He pursed his lips and shook his head, hands on hips. 'I know something about you, you can't hide it from me, so don't even try, my friend.' Ray was shocked and taken aback as he faced the now intimidating man. 'Is the lady here yet? I always wanted to get a look at her,' he said looking past Ray into the apartment.

'No Eddie she's hasn't arrived yet so get to the point of your visit, and how did you know that I lived here? I don't remember ever giving you my home address.'

'I know a lot about you but what you did just less than an hour ago is real bad, you should be ashamed of yourself.'

'Oh yeah, and what would that be? Maybe you could enlighten me before I die of boredom, I'm sorry to be sarcastic, don't mean to be, but I've things to do, you know that, so for the second time, come to the point of this visit.' He felt his stomach knotting, as he eyed this man with suspicion. Did he know? Had he witnessed the assault, was the game up? Thoughts flashed through his brain.

'Don't you know what you have done?' Eddie continued. 'You have a poor memory that could compromise you in the not-too-distant future.'

'Oh come on, stop fucking about, and tell me what's on your mind.'

'Stop fucking about' was screeched inside the apartment.

'Sorry,' Eddie blurted out, 'I didn't realise you had someone with you.'

At that moment the sound of police sirens filled the area. With his hand cupped to his ear Eddie remarked, 'Someone's in trouble, someone's day has come, some poor dog has had their day, as the saying goes.'

'It happens all the time, that's life, now please Eddie for the last time tell me why you're here, and tell me what you know about me that's so bad before I get to the end of my tether.'

'Well that's gratitude for you, I do you a favour and you talk to me this way, maybe I should just forget it.' He went to walk off, shaking his head.

'What favour, Eddie, what favour? I'm sorry but you do go on a bit, and you know I'm busy at the moment, so please my friend get to the point of your visit.'

Eddie stopped in his track, and turned around, his face stern-looking, 'What I know about you is that you are very forgetful, do you remember telling me what you were going to do tonight, your special evening, something you were going to ask her, didn't you tell me you were going down on one knee to propose, how can you do that now with what you have done?' he gestured with his hands.

'What the hell have I done, tell me now, then go Eddie, go, because, my friend, you are beginning to grate my nerves.'

Eddie put his hand deep into his pocket of his tracksuit and produced a small box. 'No one can get engaged without one of these.' He opened the lid and Ray recognised the ring immediately, the very one he had shown at the club and forgotten when he had left.

A wave of relief rolled over his whole body like a wave on a sandy beach, and it showed on his face as he took the ring, closed the lid then put it in his pocket. 'Thanks, Eddie, I must be getting forgetful.'

'Hold on there must be a reward somewhere in this case, a drink perhaps, a donation towards the maintenance of the club, I could even blackmail you, you know, a few pounds to keep my mouth shut.' He made a zip movement across his mouth. Eddie was trying to defuse a tense situation that he could see developing, so was only joking.

'I've just paid you back, I've saved you from a beating,' Ray sneered.

'How's that, who's going to beat me up?' Eddie remarked.

'Well I was, but I changed my mind, so you're very lucky and that, my friend, concludes our time together today, and you have been paid in full so I'll see you at the club next week.' He went to close the door.

'That's gratitude for you, I go out of my way to help you out and all you can do is talk to me in a threatening way. Well let me tell you, you won't see me again, because I've just banned you from my club for ungentle manlike conduct; you can pick up your stuff that's in your locker, and leave the key in my office, and I won't be representing you at this year's karate shows, or appraisals, you'll have to apply for your forthcoming tests for your next Dan yourself, you can't get away with talking to me like that, I don't care who you are, I wonder what your colleagues would say if they had heard your threats.' Eddie was fuming, 'There's only one more thing to say and that's goodbye.' With that, he turned around and went down the stairs and out of the building.

Ray shut the door with a slam, 'Fuck you, you asshole,' he muttered as he went to the window, 'Fuck you, asshole,' the parrot repeated. He looked out into the blackness of night towards the alley. The flashing lights of the police and ambulance competed with the solitary light that normally lit up that area. *So they had found him and quite quickly because some bodies were not found for days, and sometimes weeks,* he thought.

Soon the body would be on the way to the city morgue then forensics would be called in. He stood back from the window and looked at his killer hand; it was still hurting, but not as bad as it had before. He once again got another drink, his fourth since he had arrived home; he was feeling the effect, his mind ready to explode. The parrot cage swung from side to side as the parrot flapped his wings, 'Bastard, bastard,' the bird screeched. He went over to the cage.

'I've had enough from you, time for you to go to sleep, so goodnight.' He put the cover over the cage as the parrot said, 'FUCK YOU.'

Eddie had made his blood pressure rise; he felt a shooting pain in his stomach. He returned to the table and looked out over to the flashing lights of the crime scene, in the alley, and waited for Charlotte.

TWO

Tony Waybee, drug dealer, thief, convicted criminal, was busy just two streets away from where Raymond Rainbow sat in his window seat. He had almost run home after his close call. He entered his little dingy basement flat, and lit a paraffin lamp that had been his only source of light since he had had the electricity cut off for non-payments of the bills that still lay in a pile, with others on a chair in the corner of the room. He went to a cupboard and opened a beer, as he picked up a stack of old newspapers, and with a sweep of his hand, he swept the clutter that was on the table on to the floor. He found a pair of scissors, then sitting in a rickety chair he set about scouring the papers for suitable words for a very important letter; cutting out letters and words, he laid them in front of him. It hadn't taken him long to decide on this course of action, total revenge was needed, nothing but. His encounter with near death was still very prominent in his head. He had been very lucky to escape it, he was positive of that fact. He swore under his breath, he had never done anything like this in his crime filled life before, but had seen it in films. He had put on rubber gloves and using tweezers, he pasted the words onto a sheet of paper forming a letter with a demand for money. He was adding a new crime to his portfolio, the crime of blackmail. He scanned the letter to check that he had used the right words, he then put the letter in an envelope making sure not to lick it, he knew of DNA. *Can't take any chances*, he thought. He was high on adrenalin and he was very excited after all he had been through, an experience that had been new to him, he had seen a killer, and stranger still he knew the killer well.

He had been on the wrong side of the law since he had been a teenager, but had never tried his hand at blackmailing; now he thought this was a way to get out of the country and maybe to start a new life away from the villains he mixed with, he had to get clean. This very day he had seen his best friend killed, murdered, almost in front of him, in front of his eyes. As he sipped his beer he realised he had been very fortunate not to have been discovered as he hid in the rubbish bin. His mind recalled how he got to be in the alley at that time of day. Tommy, his best pal since they had met four months before, Tommy had said he was from out of town, and because of a mental breakdown had left his job as a lorry driver and come down from the north for a change of scenery. They would meet in the café and talk, and then they would try to score, get some drugs, and see what robberies were going to take place. Tommy liked to talk to the top drug dealers, but he was very secret about taking his own drugs; they never took drugs together. He remembered how it had started. Him being in the alley at that time of day, normal drug dealing started much later in the night. No it hadn't been for drugs, but for boots. *A bloody pair of boots had nearly been my downfall*, he shook his head at the thought. It had all started when they had come across 'Bootsy Harris', a local crook, at the off licence just off the high street, that very afternoon, with once again, a new pair of boots, that he tended to show off by wearing trousers that were shorter than they ought to have been. He had a fetish for boots, all kinds black, brown, suede, platform at one time.

'New pair of boots, I see,' he had pointed out.

'Yeah nice aren't they?' Bootsy had replied looking down at them with glowing pride.

'You must have hundreds of pairs of boots by now,' Waybee had said sarcastically

'No not really I've got a few hanging around just in case they come back into fashion.' Bootsy laughed out loud then continued, 'I chuck away loads of pairs when I get new ones, I dump them, that's what I do,' he said with conviction.

'Tell me where, tell me where,' Waybee had joked, 'I need another pair, these are fucked as you can see.' He lifted his foot up to show the hole in the sole.

'I put a nice pair in a big black bin in Baker Alley half an hour ago,' Bootsy volunteered, 'go get them, they don't empty the bins for a few days, they will fit you you're the same size as me, nine, isn't that true? You can have them if you want them, a gift from me, but you owe me one, don't forget, I've always liked that silver ciggy case you have, and now you don't smoke any more maybe you could let me have it,' he turned and shuffled away with a bottle of rum in each pocket of his jacket.

'Thanks,' Tony said, 'thanks for your generosity, you're very kind, I'll think about it,' but he hadn't meant it. He was being sarcastic. He had a dislike for him because he knew that he sold drugs to kids, and had at one time been convicted for sexually abusing a child. He was a dirty bastard, lowlife.

Yes, that was how it had started, Tony mused as he continued to sort out the bits of paper cuttings for the letter. He took it out of the envelope again, he wasn't too sure of the wording; he had to get it right. A tear formed in the corner of his eye as he remembered what had gone down. Anger welled up inside him. *That bastard will pay, that's for sure.* Rainbow would be punished, that was a certainty; he snipped out the word SAW and laid it on the letter then pasted it in.

He remembered making their way to the alley and finding the bin with no trouble. Tommy being the bigger man had helped him into the garbage bin to look for the boots; it had proved to be difficult in the semi-darkness. Bootsy had said he'd dumped them in an almost full bin, and should be easy to retrieve; he had been rummaging around inside the bin when the confrontation had taken place. He had frozen as he saw what was happening through a crack in the bin. He saw the face full on, he recognised the man; he had met him many times before.

When silence descended, he had managed to get out of the bin with difficulty, smelling to high heaven, with a pair of laced boots around his neck; he cut his hand on a tin can as he dropped to the floor landing on his friend's bare chest, leaving boot imprints. The body exhaled from the impact. He got to his feet then bent over his friend. 'You OK, Tommy? Tommy,' he pushed on his chest, although he had never done first aid before, he felt he had to do something for his friend. He tried mouth-to-mouth resuscitation but it was too late, his friend had been dead for the last ten minutes. He took the watch off his friend's wrist and relieved him of his wallet. He had left the alley running and passed two men who were walking into the alley; he kept his head down till he emerged into the high street just in time to see the flashing lights of the police car and the ambulance attending an accident of an old lady who had been run over at a bus stop. He wondered if he should report the killing there and then, but on second thoughts decided not to, because he had thought of a better idea.

He relived the incident over and over again in his mind as he put the finishing touches to the blackmailing letter. He finished his second beer, put the tweezers and paper paste with the gloves in to a sideboard drawer, slipped on his coat, picked up the letter, turned off the paraffin lamp, and went out into the dark night to deliver the letter by hand; he knew where the bastard lived. As he was leaving his flat, he realised that the boots he had got out of the bin had been left behind at the scene of the crime, and his fingerprints would be all over them; he would have to retrieve them and fast. He remembered the boots falling off his shoulders as he attended to his friend. He hurried along the high street, relatively quiet now with most of the shops closed. He looked into the alley but a policeman barred his way and there was a lot of activity around the skip bins; it was obvious that Tommy had been found. He gingerly walked away, towards the apartment where he knew the assailant lived. In the lower ground floor area, he went to the post box that was attached to the wall and with one last look, pushed the letter in. He left as quickly as he had arrived, and soon he was back in his hovel. Nobody had seen him, at least nobody he knew, the two men in the alley had not seen his face, that fact he was sure of, but once again it had been a close shave.

He lit the lamp once more, and made a cup of tea, and then sat at his table; he took his boots off. 'For Christ's sake when is my luck going to change?' he muttered as he threw the boots across the room breaking a small mirror in the process. 'Fuck there goes another seven years of bad luck, when will it all end?' He realised that he hadn't eaten all day; the pang of hunger reminded him so. He put on a different coat and his boots again, and combing his hair he left to get some fish and chips just a short distance away.

As he waited in the line in the chip shop a voice broke the quietness that prevailed. 'Tony, you bastard, where the fuck have you been in the last few days? Big Joe Bananas has been looking for you; He wants to talk to you about your so-called friend.' Tony glanced over his shoulder, and recognised the scar-faced man as a petty crook who hung around the big boys doing small jobs, and running errands for them. He also was in with a local gang who revelled in the name 'The Animals.' Tony didn't like him very much; he had had trouble with him in the past.

'Yeah, which one, you know I've got lots of good friends, I'm well liked, you know.' Tony volunteered with a false laugh.

'The big one, the big ugly fucker, the one who has been throwing his weight around just lately, the one who goes over the top, it seems to me, to prove what a villain he is.'

'You're not talking about Tommy are you, you can't be referring to him, he's a great guy, you don't like him because he duffed you up, the night you got pissed and got heavy with him. Remember?' The man nodded as the two men shuffled towards the counter.

'Yeah I do remember, I was pissed; he wouldn't have done it if I had been sober that's a certainty.'

'What can I get you gentlemen?' the man behind the counter asked.

'We're not together, I'm not with him,' Tony said with a strong conviction almost sneering. 'I'm here on my Jack Jones; I'll have one bag of fish and chips. And one of those small bread rolls,' he pointed to a plastic container on the end of the counter. 'I haven't eaten all day, bloody starving.' The server didn't answer; he just turned around to get the order.

'You've been with him today, I know that because Bootsy said he talked to you this afternoon, so where is he now? I've got a message for him from the big boys, they seem to have a bee in the hat, or should I say bonnet, there's a rumour that the man has been telling porky pies, because there's no sign of all them guys he said he knew. He told big Joe that he was in with the gang up north, so Joe put the feelers out to find these people; it seems no one up there has ever heard of them, they seem to be non-existent. So the boss wants an explanation and he wants it soon, do I make myself clear?' It was evident there was no love lost between the two men.

'Bootsy was right, I was with Tommy today for a short while, he said he was going home and before you ask, no I don't know where he lives, he never told me, we would meet mostly in the café.' Tony handed over a ten-pound note and took the change without a word as his fish and chips were put on the countertop. He turned to leave the shop.

'And what can I get you, sir?' he heard the server say to the scar-faced man.

'Fuck all, I wouldn't eat the shit you put up in this joint, go back to where you belong, you don't belong over here, Paki bastard.'

'We're from India sir, not Pakistan, and I was born here, just down the road so I'm as local as you are.' the server protested. He bent behind the counter and produced a baseball bat. The lowlife made a hasty retreat. 'Tony,' he shouted down the street, 'hold on a minute,' he ran to catch up. 'I'll meet you in the café tomorrow morning at ten, maybe your friend will turn up then I'll give him the message from the big man.' He put out his hand offering a handshake.

'Sorry I can't shake hands, I've hurt it, cut it this afternoon.' He held it up to show the wound. 'Gotta go now before my chips get cold, if I see Tommy I'll tell him but I doubt if he will take any notice of me; goodnight Ted.'

'What a tosser,' Tony mumbled to himself. As he got to his flat, he put the fish and chips on the table and for the next half hour ate them with a beer. He wondered what big Joe was on about, as far as his friend was concerned, they had always got on well, anyhow whatever he had against Tommy was now of no significance, now that Tommy was no longer in this world. How could he tell the cops what he had witnessed? They would never believe him, never in a month of Sundays. Then like a bolt from the blue he realised he had no alibi. He had been seen with the deceased on many occasions, and on the very day of his demise surely the police would be around to see him very soon, he had to go out to get himself an alibi, or he could see prison as his home for a long time to come, and he certainly wasn't going back inside again for something he didn't do.

Tommy's body would now be in the morgue and the police would be looking into the killing. He went to the bathroom and swilled his face with cold water, put the fish and chip paper in the overflowing dustbin in the backyard. As he came back into his room he remembered what Bootsy had said to him that very day. He went to his bedroom and in a side drawer near to his bed he found the silver cigarette case he no longer used. He looked at it and remembered the happy times he had had when he smoked, and more so the woman who had given it to him as a gift; he wondered where she was at that moment. He closed it and put it in his pocket; this, he thought, would clinch his alibi. He decided to go over to see Bootsy before he went to bed, with his gift; all he had to say to the police is that they spent all evening together, if he was asked.

He left the flat, the moon had gone, and it was drizzling, the dark clouds gathering, with a slight nip in the air. With his head down, he hurried the twenty minutes' walk to where he thought his alibi would be; he didn't know exactly where he lived, but he knew his boozer, he knew that dear old Bootsy liked his drink. The pub was empty apart from an old couple talking quietly in a booth in the corner of the dimly lit bar. Tony approached the barman who was sitting on a stool at the corner of the bar, listening to music on his headphones, and doing a crossword. 'Can I get a drink here?' Tony said sarcastically.

He shouted the request out louder when the bartender didn't look up. The old couple in the corner looked up breaking their conversation for a moment then went back to their whispering, as though they were planning a bank robbery. The barman jumped up with a start as though he had been woken up, or surprised to be where he was in the pub. He whipped the plugs out of his ears, and threw the pen on the desk. 'Sorry mate, I was away, do you know a four-letter word for a Russian ruler? Or a five-letter word for a—'

Tony broke in, 'It's not quiz night is it? I don't answer any question on the grounds that it might show how clever I really am, but I'd like to ask you this, if you feel like working, I would like a pint of your best bitter. But don't put yourself out.'

The barman knew that the man in his bar was the unpleasant kind, so decided immediately that all pleasantries would end. He had met similar types of this ignorant lowlife on many occasions so it was no good trying to be nice.

'Pint of bitter coming up,' he said reaching for a glass, and putting it under the pump. He took the money, gave the change without another word, and went back to his crossword and music. Tony took his drink and sat near the big window that looked out onto the street, he took the cigarette case out of his pocket and looked at it as he sipped his beer, remembering a time in his life that was worth the living. She had gone to live in Spain, and when he got the money from that prick Rainbow, he would be going to Spain to try to make amends for the asshole he knew he had been when they were together. Ruby would take him back, and with all that money he was going to get, he was sure it would happen soon. His thoughts were interrupted for a moment when he heard raised voices coming from the corner booth. He looked towards the couple and they looked back then looked away again. He slipped the case back into his pocket as the door opened and let in the coldness and dampness of the night into the bar. The two men were loud and excited.

'Police all over the place, arrests taking place, chaos.' Tony overheard the men talking at the bar. He got up with his drink and went closer to where the men were standing, and pretended to look at a painting that hung over the empty fireplace; he stood there for a few minutes straining to hear the conversation. But it was in vain; the men picked up their drinks and went to a table at the far side of the pub.

'Seems to be a lot of trouble around these parts?' Tony said to the barman, who was now wiping a glass. 'Seems like it.' he replied reluctantly, as he wasn't willing to get into a conversation with this type of customer. Not after the earlier encounter. He went back to his work.

'Did you hear what those guys over there were talking about?' He pointed to the table where the two men were sitting deep in conversation.

'I don't listen to people's conversations, can't help you there,' the barman said in reply then left the bar to go out the back on a pretence task, his dislike for this customer intact. Tony looked around the bar, and then finished his drink. He went to the window, looked out and down the street; it was dead, and it had started to rain, he couldn't wait much longer for his alibi friend. If the police were all over the place, as he had heard, they might come in at any minute, he surmised. He went back to the bar, and shouted out, 'Anyone serving here?' There was no answer, so he shouted again. The barman poked his head through some drab curtains, two bottles in his hands. 'Yeah, want a refill?' he said putting the bottles on the shelf.

'No, just a question, do you know Bootsy Harris, an ugly-looking bastard, who comes in here, he drinks in here so I've been told, has he been in tonight?'

'Haven't seen him tonight, but they might know.' He pointed to the old people over in the corner. Tony looked over; the couple were still hunched together deep in conversation. 'They were here when I came on duty tonight, they would know.'

'Why do you think that they would know if he was in here?'

'Because that's his mum and dad, that's why, 'Do you want a refill?'

'Didn't I just tell you, NO, you deaf?' Tony said with a sneer.

The barman picked up the glass, and turned away, he had met some nasty customers in his life but this one took some beating, he thought as he returned to his crossword.

'Do you know where I can find Bootsy Harris?' he said as he approached the table.

'Who wants to know, what's he been up to now?' the old man shook his head from side to side. 'If you're from big Joe for money our Barry owes, well tell him he'll get his money back next week, Barry has said he just needs a bit of time, but he'll pay up, our Barry always pays his debts, tell big Joe to be patient.'

'Tell him yourself, I'm not here on any errand for big Joe I've got better things to do, I just want to see him on a private matter, so have you seen him tonight? I need to talk to him, it's urgent, I have to contact him, do you understand me?' The old woman stood up, and staggered slightly. 'Who the fuck do you think you're talking to you asshole, fuck off, we'll tell you nothing, piss off,' the woman's face contorted in anger, her voice raised. 'You're not the one that beat our Barry up are you? Well try it on me.' She lifted her scrawny fists.

What Tony didn't see was the barman flicking his fingers to the two men sitting at the far side of the bar; they were up like a shot, and walked across the bar. 'Having aggro Beth?' Before she could answer the burly man said to a very surprised Tony, 'Out, get out, you don't cause trouble in this bar, no sirree, get out now unless you would like to have your supper in hospital.' The two men squared up to a frightened bully.

'I just wanted to know where Bootsy is, that's all,' Tony spluttered as the two men threw him out onto the wet pavement outside the pub. The barman poured the two men free drinks, and went to talk to Mr and Mrs Harris; they told him that Barry had done a runner and left town till things quietened down. Tony cursed all the way home; it had all been fruitless, Bootsy had let him down, he would remember to give him a dig next time he saw him. He sat at the table and continued on his passion.

When at home and not robbing people or house-breaking, he was building a model cargo ship, complete with a hold for cargo, and remote-controlled. He had been building models since his school days, he loved it just as much as a good score of his favourite drug, and he would finish it in the next day or so. What a different day it had been, what a day can bring, the changes, the surprises. And there was another one waiting for him as he opened up Tommy's wallet; an identity card fell out, there was a photo of Tommy, but the name on the card was Robert Jennet, detective sergeant of the Wigan police force.

THREE

Charlotte was a beautiful woman, she was madly in love, and had been for three years and tonight she was expecting to hear the words women in love, love to hear. He had told her he had something important to ask her on their last date just a few days before. Could it be the proposal she had been waiting for? She felt excited as she walked along the high street; the shops were just closing for the day with shutters coming down and workers going home to their lives away from the working day. She passed the entrance to Baker Alley without a glance, and then stopped for a moment to see the ambulance driving away, taking someone to hospital. The onlookers were now dispersing as the police were redirected to another emergency in Baker Alley. She was tempted to go in the alley as other people were now doing, to see what had happened, but her curiosity subsided, as she caught sight of the apartment block where her loved one lived, and she didn't want to keep him waiting. From a distance she thought she recognised Eddie coming out of the block; she had met him a few times at karate tournaments, and at other times when she had picked her Raymond up from the club.

At last she reached the block, she saw a man post a letter in Raymond's post-box but he seemed to be in a hurry and she didn't see his face that was hidden in the shadows of the evening. As she entered the foyer, she picked up the envelope that had MR RAINBOW embossed in big bold letters that seemed to have been cut out of newspapers and not too long ago, as one letter was coming unstuck. She put the letter into her handbag and started to climb the stairs to the top floor. She glanced at her watch; she was running late; she was also excited and very eager to see what Ray had to tell her, before they set off on a week's holiday, somewhere in the sun, he had promised, and set for the very next day. The holiday was a must; she had been very busy in her job as a legal secretary, they both needed time to unwind, especially her boyfriend. He had been studying for promotion at his work, and training every evening, and some weekends for months it seemed, for his black belt in karate. Her head was full of these thoughts, as she let herself into the apartment. She slipped out of her coat and hung it up in the small hallway, taking the letter out of her bag; she entered the apartment to see Ray sitting at the window, looking out into the dark night.

'There's a lot of activity in town tonight,' she volunteered as she placed the letter on the coffee table. 'Brought this up, saw the man post it, he seemed to be in a hell of a hurry, I also thought I saw Eddie Bail leaving, has he been up here? What did he want?'

'Hold on darling please, one question at a time.' He stood up and met her smile; he kissed her lightly then sat down again at the window. 'I forgot something at the club, and Eddie returned it, first time he's been here, don't know how he knew where I live, can't remember ever giving him this address.'

'Maybe he looked it up in the telephone book, or you gave it when you registered at the club. Does it really matter how he knew, you got whatever you left at the club back; what was it anyhow? It must have been important for him to leave his club to return it so soon.'

Ray just smiled, and looked at her, then said, 'It's a secret, and I will tell you later but for the moment get yourself a drink, we need to have a talk.' She smiled, and then noticed him rubbing his hand. 'What have you done to your hand, it looks swollen?' She leant over to take a closer look.

'I've broken it I think.' He lifted it up to show her.

'How did you do that?'

'Hit the bloody stud on that dummy we used in the club, I've told Eddie that old dummy needs replacing. The club is deteriorating fast, needs an influx of new money that's for sure, parts of the building are falling down, other parts need painting; I'm thinking of changing clubs and soon.' He looked at his hand again. 'I've put it under the cold tap, it was throbbing before, but it's not so bad now, the cold water must have soothed it a bit.'

'I think you might have to let a doctor look at it before we go on our holiday,' she suggested as she got up to go to the drinks cabinet to get herself a drink, 'want a refill?' She picked up his glass before he could reply.

'What activity were you on about?' he said as he watched her get the drinks; he glanced out of the window again. It was now raining hard, the pitter-patter hitting the window pane. He was happy; the rain would erase any footprints and wash away any other evidence that might convict. Police forensics don't like heavy rain on a crime scene, he had read once in a crime novel.

'Activity, what activity are you on about?' he asked again. She brought the drinks back to the table, just as the sky lit up with lightning, striding across the blackness of night.

'I was lucky to get here before this storm; looks like I'll be staying the night now, aren't you a lucky thing?' She kissed him on the head as she put the glasses on the table and sat down opposite.

'Activity, what activity?' he repeated.

'Oh yes, that was on the high street as I was coming here tonight, someone told me that an old woman had been knocked over near the bus stop, by the very bus she had been waiting for, now that's strange, to be knocked down by the same bus you're waiting for. I didn't see it, I just saw the ambulance leaving the scene, then there was more activity as the police rushed to that alley, you know the one, where the junkies hang out, maybe they were doing a bust, who knows? Everyone around here knows that that alley has a bad reputation.'

'You can say that again,' he agreed taking a sip of his drink. 'Here's to a nice evening and a good holiday; we really need the break.' She lifted her glass to clink his. He looked out of the rain-soaked window into the darkness of the night, and deep inside the crevices of his mind, he was trying to understand why he had taken such drastic action on his assailant; there must have been another way he could have handled it. That instant flash reaction, as quick as lightning as Eddie had said in the club, was it the stress of his job, or was it the pressure of months of studying, years of reading, writing, staying home with no social life? It had been noticed. His colleagues at work had told him to get a life and get out more. He needed to rein in, ease down, or a mental breakdown was coming.

'Ray, Ray, to a nice night,' she raised her glass again; 'you're not listening to me, are you? You look vague, what's up, is it your hand?' She looked concerned.

The windows rattled as the sudden storm showed its anger. Ray got up to pull the curtains together, something he rarely did; there was no need for curtains on the top floor, Charlotte had put them there because she had said it made the apartment more homely, a woman's touch, he remembered she had joked. He picked up his glass, and clinked hers. 'To a nice night, sorry, I have a lot on my mind at the moment.'

'You had something to talk to me about, you said.' She smiled demurely.

He looked at her, her smile lit up the room, like a beautiful summer sun. He loved her very much, and had done so since that meeting three years before. It had been love at first sight. How could he lose her, and his career, his life, just because of a mistake, a moment of madness, just because of a reprobate, a low-down scum, a piece of dog shit that had encroached on his almost successful life, with the prospects of lots of better things to come, promotion at work, marriage to a beautiful woman, a new house in the countryside, an idyllic lifestyle, and now it could be in jeopardy. His world was now in tatters, on the brink of disaster. He had to have time to think this one out. He tried with great difficulty to be normal; as she spoke to him her words flew over his head as he once again relived the encounter in the alley.

'Raymond what's up with you, you're not hearing a word I'm saying are you? What did I just say? Tell me.' She spoke to him as though he was a naughty child.

'Sorry, love, I've had a hell of a day at the gym, been training too hard, been pushing too hard, I need a break. This holiday has come at a right time for me, I'm mentally exhausted, and my promotion is on the cards, and that would be more money if I got it. The interview went well but it could go either way, that's another worry. I should know soon, like I said the money should come in handy for our big day.'

'Big day, what big day, are you proposing, are you asking me to marry you? Don't say any more the answer is yes, I accept.' She laughed out loud.

'I was going to make us a nice meal tonight but everything went haywire after I hurt my hand, and then I was late in leaving the club, don't feel like doing much now. I feel a bit woozy, can't take any painkillers either with the amount of drink I've had, I just feel like going to bed, but I've got something for you, hope you like it.' He got up and went over to the cloak stand and went through the pockets of a coat for the ring then he realised that he had put the ring in his trouser pocket when Eddie had given it to him. He felt a little foolish, but he didn't show it as he returned to his excited girlfriend. He picked up a red plastic flower which he had taken from a vase of artificial roses that stood on the mantelpiece, and placed it in his mouth. He got down on one knee and opened the small box; the diamond glinted as he took it out and gave it to her.

'Will you?' He hesitated. 'Will you?' he repeated. The flower fell in front of her; she picked it up and held it to her heart.

'I will treasure this flower and keep it forever, and to answer your question, you know I will, I've been waiting for you to ask me since the first time we met, I love you, my Raymond, and soon I'll be Mrs Rainbow; fancy that, I got my Rainbow in the end, I'm sure there'll be a pot of gold waiting for us.' She slipped the ring onto her slim finger and looked at it. 'It's beautiful, Ray, it's beautiful.' They kissed and clinked glasses once again.

'I've done my packing, have you managed to do yours yet? Or should I do it for you as I normally do?' she inquired. 'It won't take me long, you never want to take much, it's always a tee shirt and jeans that you want to wear all week if I didn't tell you off.'

He gave a half laugh. 'What would I do without you, my darling? I would be a scruffy lout. You know I like to chill out when I'm on holiday, not having to wear my working uniform. It's good to dispense with collar and tie for a while, so yes my love just throw a few things in the old rucksack, and I'll get us a bite to eat. I was going to take you to our favourite restaurant, but because of my hand and the weather we'll eat here instead. And there's another surprise for you: I've got a bottle of Champs, so we'll open that, OK with you? Oh yes and there will be music.' He pointed to the music deck next to the drinks cabinet.

'All that sounds wonderful, I'm looking forward to this short break, a week's better than nothing; one thing I want to know is, when will we get married? Have you got a date in your mind, or do I have to wait until Mr Right comes along?' She laughed out loud at her own joke, and got up to start the packing in the bedroom.

'Rainbow is Mr Right,' she ventured with emphasis.

He frowned then hesitated, 'Yes, I think I'm your man,' he joked back.

As she entered the bedroom she stopped and turned around. 'When I finish the packing maybe we should celebrate our engagement with a bit of old-fashioned hanky-panky, after all you know I want a big family and I'm very broody at the moment after seeing my friend with her brood today, so get ready, my future husband, I want a bit of sexual intercourse with my champagne.' She gave him an exaggerated wink and disappeared into the bedroom. He shook his head and smiled; for the moment his worries had departed into the back of his mind.

But not for long; he picked up the letter from the coffee table, and slit it open with a gold letter opener shaped like a dagger. He opened the letter, glancing around to the bedroom not wanting Charlotte to see it. He went into the kitchen part of the apartment; he read it over and over, not believing what he was reading. This was impossible, there was no one there to see what had happened; he had looked around the alley, the bins. He remembered looking; there was no one around, no one. The bedroom door opened 'Will you be taking the black rucksack or the blue one?' she shouted out.

'Charlotte I don't care, any one, it don't matter to me, any one.' He emphasised '*any one*'.

'Sorry I asked, Mr Grumpy, won't be long now, another ten minutes, don't forget to put the champagne on ice,' she went back into the bedroom shutting the door. He went back to the letter; he laid it on the kitchen table. It had been made up of newspaper cuttings with some words lopsided, some big letters, and some small, it read:

> I SAW YOU KILL TONIGHT but £10 000 will STOP ME TALKING TO THE FUZZ I'M not joking WILL be in contact soon get the MoNeY I no Joke

He put the letter back in the envelope and put it in a safe place in a drawer in a bureau. Then he got the bottle out of the cooler, put it in an ice container; he was doing things now like a robot would, with no thought, his mind on overtime. He almost jumped out of his skin when the phone rang in the hallway. He lifted the receiver cautiously. He listened carefully not saying a word, his face full of anguish. At last Ray said, 'Yes I understand I'll be in tomorrow, see you.' He replaced the receiver.

'Fuck,' he said to himself; he heard the parrot say the same, under his cover; he wondered how to explain all this to Charlotte. She came out of the bedroom, 'Who was that on the phone?' she enquired as she sat on the settee.

He sat next to her and clasped both her hands in his; he looked her in the eyes,

'Don't know how to tell you this, darling, but they want me to go in tomorrow; something big has come up, there's been a murder in town tonight that must have been all the activity you were talking about in Baker Alley, the gang wars have started up again the boss reckons. So the holiday will have to go on hold for the time being, I'm so sorry, love.' He could see the disappointment break over her face like a wave breaking on a shore. He bent forward and kissed her, 'We'll go on a longer one when all this is over, I promise you, and maybe we'll go on that cruise that you told me about up to Norway.'

She sighed, 'let's hope this is not the beginning of a bad patch, you know, a bad time, bad luck, and just when we get engaged; why can't they get someone else on this job, why you? It's always you.' She was inwardly fuming.

'The boss did say that he wants his best men on this one, and I guess I must be in the category of his best men; there's a meeting at nine tomorrow morning.'

He got up and went to the kitchen, picked up the champagne and two glasses from a top cupboard. 'We must be positive, and look on the bright side, things could be a lot worse.' He popped off the cork, and poured the champagne, his mind not believing a word he had just said. 'To us and our future,' he raised his glass, 'now what are we going to have to eat?'

FOUR
TUESDAY

She was still sleeping when he left for work; he had made a cup of coffee but with the appetite gone he didn't eat anything; he had looked at the blackmail letter once more before tucking it in a book in his library. He had slept badly, slipping in and out, and at times he sat on the edge of the bed just looking at Charlotte deep in a world without worry, lying there without a care. The night had been a long one; he got out of bed before the alarm went off, showered, and got dressed. At six o'clock he had heard the garbage men collecting the rubbish and sprinted down with the bundle of clothes.

'Will you get rid of these old clothes for me, and this is for your trouble,' he had said, a five-pound note changed hands. In reflection it hadn't been a great celebration for their engagement, things he was going to say and do didn't materialise as he had visualised. They didn't even have sex as she had said she wanted; the disappointment of not going on holiday had put a dampener on the whole proceedings. The night would never be forgotten, the night he killed a man, and the same night that he got engaged. He took an aspirin with a glass of water, gave his future wife a gentle kiss on the head, and left the apartment, quietly shutting the door. He checked his letter box but there was no mail, then he went out to meet the day. He walked along the high street, a new day was beginning, shops were being opened, and the smell of coffee hung in the air, as though inviting people to start their day with a caffeine intake. The smell of newly made bread seemed to challenge the coffee's domain, but failed, as both smells intermingled and seemed to walk hand in hand to enhance the early morning air. People wrapped up in their own worlds went about the business of the day. Raymond made his way towards his place of work; as he passed Baker Alley, he decided to revisit the site, turning left into the alley. It seemed very different in the daylight it wasn't as threatening as it had appeared on the previous evening in the gloom of night. Police tape was still in place around the bins, it fluttered in the slight breeze. At the far end of the alley a policeman was talking to a lorry driver, and pointing to one side, then the other. Raymond stopped at the spot where he remembered the man was lying, and looked around the area. He was sure he hadn't left anything that could incriminate him in any way; he went over things in his mind again and again, he had got rid of every stitch of clothing he had been wearing the night before. Being awake during the night he had given the bag of his clothes to the early morning bin man, and saw with his own eyes the bag get placed in the back of the garbage lorry and disappear into the darkness with thousands of discarded things to end up in an incinerator. For the first time he saw that the bin near to where the incident had taken place had an inch crack down one side as though it had at one time been bursting at the seams. He looked around to see the policeman coming towards him, shouting, 'Keep away, keep away from there, can't you read DO NOT CROSS POLICE LINES?' As the policeman got closer to where Ray was standing a look of recognition came over the cop's face.

'Oh sorry, sarge , didn't recognise you from back there, I was just telling that bin driver that he can't take the bins away at the moment, not until forensics have finished with the scene of this crime. He's not too happy, he said he wants to finish early because he's taking his missus shopping this afternoon; wish I had a job like that, where I got every afternoon off,' he laughed out loud, and adjusted his helmet.

'You could always resign or retire, have you ever thought of that, and then you'll get all the time in the world off.' He knew what he had just said sounded sarcastic but continued, 'Haven't forensics concluded here? They're a bit slow; this happened last night, didn't it? Someone got done over here the boss told me, some junky, no doubt.'

'Daylight, sarge, daylight,' the constable repeated, 'because of all the garbage that's fallen out of the bins as you can see,' he waved his hands, 'they are coming back this morning with some of the lads to do a thorough search of the area; if it was a gangland killing to do with drugs you never know what will turn up.'

'Have you heard if the victim has been identified yet, was he someone known to us?' Rainbow said, looking around the area.

'No, his name hasn't been released yet, but something fishy is going on, there was a lot of whispering in the station this morning in your department, you'll find out when you get in, I heard there's a meeting of the top brass at nine.' He glanced at his watch. 'It's twenty to nine now,' he said, as he heard footsteps heading his way; it was the driver of the garbage lorry.

'Have you heard anything yet?' the bin man demanded. 'When can I get on with my job? I've got to take the missus out shopping this afternoon. Oh hello again,' the bin man turned and spoke to Rainbow, 'thanks for that bag of things you gave me this morning, the trainers fit like a glove, so to speak, and the shirt's a beauty, funny what people throw away, good gear, the pants are designer too, fit enough for a wedding,' he joked.

Ray composed himself, and then slowly replied. 'Sorry mate, not me, I've never seen you in my life, I've never given you anything, you're mistaken, leave this area, now, there's a police investigation going on here.' The driver went to say something, but Rainbow interjected.

'Go before you get yourself in trouble, *now*,' he emphasised.

The driver moved away muttering under his breath, 'Only trying to do my job.' He got into his lorry and drove off, watched by the two policemen.

'Sorry I was a bit sarky, Charlie, I've had a heavy night, better get down to the station to see what's going on, see you later.' Rainbow said, and then left the Alley.

The storm had left a distinctive freshness in the air, and the sun was bright and warming as he walked swiftly to work. He felt mentally drained because of the lack of sleep and the drinks he had consumed the night before. He kept thinking that if only he had continued down the high street the night before instead of going through Baker Alley, he had never used that route before, only on one or two occasions, when he had been in a rush, and in daylight, he remembered. If only; those two words, *if only* the clock could be turned back; regrets, the lives of people were full of these, he concluded. Before, life had been so good, with promises of a very bright future, with a pending promotion on the cards, his forthcoming wedding to a beautiful-looking woman, his karate tournaments, new home in a nice country setting. He had worked hard to get the good things in life, he had tried, then in just a second of madness everything had changed, and now his life was on the brink of disaster. He would have to put his every effort and all the determination in his body to find a way out of this dilemma. He had done wrong, now he had to try to live with it. As he turned the corner towards the police station, he glanced at his watch; it was five to nine. He said hello to two cops he recognised, and stopped for a moment.

'Been a killing in Baker Alley, near to where you live, Ray, have you heard?' The patrol cop remarked as he got into the car. 'Just going down there now, to scour the place. It's all secret at the moment but this isn't just another of those gangland killings, it's something bigger, much bigger, it's all over the station, you'll soon find out. All the big boys are all over the place, yeah, something big.'

'I found out just now, I came down the alley and saw Charlie Bright, he was having trouble with the bin lorry driver who wanted to take all the "could be," evidence away to the bloody tip, sometimes I wonder about the public.' Rainbow pointed his index finger at his temple and frowned. 'Anyhow, got to go, got a meeting in a minute, see you later.'

There were at least four top brass policemen at the nine o'clock meeting with detectives that hadn't met one another before. The chief inspector saw Rainbow walk in, and introduced two detectives from up north, who had driven down through the night; they had an interest in this important case that Rainbow was soon to find out about. The Northern detective put his hand forward to shake hands. Without thinking, he took the detective's hand, and the men shook hands. The pain shot through Rainbow's arm, and for a moment, he thought he might pass out; the shock showed on the faces of the policemen, who all seemed to take a step back.

'Sorry I didn't think that my grip was that firm, are you OK?' The burly detective said with a slight smile. He took a step forward and put a hand on his shoulder to apologise again. The other cop resisted the handshake. As Ray held his hand with his other, he explained how he had injured it at the gym the day before. The men took their seats and the meeting began.

The chief inspector began by introducing the team from the North by name as he read them out from his notes on a clipboard that he had on a small bare table; the men nodded to one another as they were announced.

'Gentlemen, I have called this meeting this morning, because of something very serious that happened here in our town last night. For those who haven't heard the hard facts yet, a killing took place in an alley called Baker Alley, just off the high street, at approximately 6.50pm. Now I know that some of you will be surprised that a killing of another gang member that you've all been acquainted with at one time or another in your careers, holds so much importance now.

We have all been down this road, and between us in this room, it's been said that when one gangster kills another then there's one less for us to deal with, one less junky in this world.' There was a ripple of laugher. 'Gentlemen, this one is no laughing matter, I want you all to pull out all the stops to find the perpetrator of this crime because this isn't just another gangland murder. No, it's very different and I have to tell you now, that what I'm about to disclose to you must be top secret, yes, gentlemen I repeat, top secret.' There was some mumblings. The inspector hesitated for a moment then continued. 'The man who was killed last night was one of ours; he has been identified as Detective Sergeant Robert Jennet, an undercover agent of the highest order, who had been working for months to bust the drug dealers who have been operating in this area for years.' Raymond Rainbow felt his heart stop for a moment, then race, like a dog at a racetrack. His face drained of blood and he felt sick.

'He was closing in on the top dogs in the cartel, and I'm sure that this was a killing that was commissioned by the highest vermin in the drug game. He may have blown his cover, but somehow I doubt that; Bob was too clever for that, he was a damn good actor, and I've been informed he played the part well. The commissioner had been informed of the agent's misdemeanours, and realised that to infiltrate into these gangs he had to prove himself to a certain degree and that's what our undercover man Robert Jennet did. He was involved in… ' The inspector looked down to his notes and flicked a few papers until he came to the right one, '… 'Four burglaries, three street robberies and five minor assaults on other villains mostly, plus drug scores; most of the victims have been secretly compensated. Agent Bob was so convincing at being a criminal that he infiltrated the drug cartel, and we were on the verge of some big dealers arrests, till something went wrong, and last night he lost his life in the pursuance of his duty as a policeman; we will find his killer, this is the promise I have made to the commander-in-chief. Any questions so far?'

The detective from up north indicated that he had a question by raising his hand.

'Yes,' the inspector said, pointing his finger at the man with a flick of his wrist as though he was caning a schoolboy for some infringement in school rules. 'Yes, you,' he said.

'Has it been established how Robert died yet, sir?'

'It has, an autopsy was performed last night, and I have the report here.' He picked up his clipboard. 'Death, it appears, was caused by a blow, or blows to the larynx, or Adam's apple to the likes of us.' He indicated the Adam's apple as though the men in the room wouldn't have known where it was located. 'Other tests need to be performed, and we should have the full report in a few days' time, a week at the outside. May I also say that it appeared that whoever did this, robbed the victim and no identification or monies was found on the body, and his watch was missing. His next of kin, his wife, has been informed, but no information must be leaked to the papers at this time, until investigations have started, and there is no time to lose, so I'm going to split you up into two-man teams; there may be more clues when forensics have finished the work at the scene, they should be finished by midday.'

Rainbow felt really sick, he felt that everyone in the room was looking at him, for a moment he felt like shouting out, 'Stop this now, stop this madness, it was me, I did this, I killed him.' He could feel the sweat globules begin to form in the middle of his back, wetting his shirt, and on his forehead running down his temple.

The inspector noticed how Rainbow was acting, fidgeting in his seat, and looking quite ill. 'You OK, Sergeant Rainbow, you look like you are going to faint?' All eyes were on him now, and he realised at that moment just how a guilty man felt when cornered.

'It's so hot in here, sir; can I be excused for a few minutes to get a bit of air?'

'Good idea, we'll all take a thirty-minute coffee break, and I'll get the teams sorted out. Bates, open the window it is hot in here,' the inspector ordered, as the detectives left the room to go to the station's cafeteria.

The fresh air was invigorating and Rainbow welcomed it like a long-lost friend. He sat down on a low wall, just outside the front entrance of the station, and put his head in his hands for a moment, despondent. He wondered if he could pull this one off, it went against all that he had been brought up to believe in; he wasn't a criminal, he had always been a good copper and always upheld the principles of law. His years in the force hung on a thread, and he was frightened that his life as he had known it, was about to come to an abrupt end. He had to pull himself together, or all would be lost.

'You OK?' he heard a voice say. He looked up and one of the detectives from up north sat down beside him and lit up a cigarette, inhaled deeply then coughed.

'No good for you I know, but at times it's needed to calm the nerves especially at a time like this. We were summoned to get down here late last night when the boss found out that one of our boys, Robert, who was undercover from our CID, was involved. He was a good cop, I knew him well, first class, yeah first class, did you get to know him?'

Rainbow turned to see a fresh face of a younger man in his twenties, well built with jet-black hair, and an air of confidence in his voice.

'No I didn't know him,' Rainbow replied, 'but I wish I had met him, he sounds like someone I could have got on well with; sometimes operations of this nature are top secret, and only the top cops are in on them. I think all undercover operatives should be known to their fellow officers in case they meet up in the course of investigations.'

'I tend to agree with you, I arrested one of our undercover blokes once, got a hell of a bollocking; how was I to know he was one of us? I can't read minds, I'm not clairvoyant, I said that at the time, I remember we laughed about it later, but it wasn't so funny at the time; you feeling better now? It was warm in there.'

'Yeah I'll be OK, I think we had better go in, by the way, I'm Ray, Raymond Rainbow, detective sergeant, some people say I've got a colourful disposition and others say something else,' he smiled.

'And I'm Detective Constable Derek Banner based in Wigan.' Both men shook hands as they walked back into the meeting room.

The inspector came into the room; all the men stood up.

'Be seated, gentlemen, I hope you are all refreshed now, they say the coffee is good down the canteen here.'

He smiled as he picked up a piece of paper, and flapped it in the air, as thought he was swatting a fly. 'These are the teams I have come up with, with the help of my colleagues; it's the best of the best. I have a belief that this case will be solved, and in record time, but before I announce the two-man teams, I want to say that a well-known criminal was seen leaving town last night, who has been seen in the vicinity of Baker Alley on many occasions including yesterday afternoon. I believe Police Constable Collins spoke to him, about looking in bins and dislodging the garbage in the bins, unto the roadway; he was seen getting on the 8.30pm bus to London. He is known by most of you; his name is Barry Harris or 'Bootsy', his nickname, because he has a fetish for boots of all descriptions. Whoever did this crime will have gone to ground like the rat he is but make no mistake, gentlemen, he will be hunted, and in the end he will get his just reward of being behind bars for the rest of his life, where he belongs.'

Rainbow gulped, as he listened intently, wishing that the meeting would come to an end; what he didn't know was there was worse to come. The inspector continued talking. 'The first team will be Detective Constable Barns, you will be with Detective Constable Harris; you are not related to Bootsy are you, Detective Harris?' he said joking, everyone laughed.

'No sir, Bootsy is no relation of mine, maybe a far, far distant cousin,' he joked back, and everyone laughed again.

'The second team will be DC Willis and Weston,' the two cops looked over the room at one another and nodded acknowledgment.

'My third team is Detective Constable Smith and Detective Constable James; I want you two to concentrate on the city centre. But you will also report to the leader of all the teams at least once a day before the end of your shifts. The rest of you, carry on with the work you are currently on, but keep the ear to the ground for any snippet of information on this case. On my last team is a detective none of you will have met before, only briefly this morning, he's from up north in Wigan, and he came down here because he's got a special interest in this case, this detective is… stand up, detective, you said your name was I believe, Banner but I think we know differently, don't we?' The inspector gave a knowing smile. 'Now's the time to let your secret out, the floor is yours.'

The young detective stood up and turned to face the table, then said, 'Thank you, inspector, for this opportunity to introduce myself, my real name in Derek Jennet, my older brother Robert was the victim last night.' There were looks of surprise, and muttering from the detectives. Rainbow felt he might have a heart attack. Derek paused for a moment then continued. 'I looked up to my brother, he was my hero, he was a good cop, he at one time wanted to be an actor, I now wish he had taken up that profession. He would have still been here, but on the other hand he loved to help people, and loved his job of putting criminals away.' He paused once again, looked at each cop in turn then said with purpose, 'I will put all my expertise into finding the killer or killers of my dear brother, for his memory's sake.'

All the policemen applauded, and Rainbow found himself doing the same; he felt sorry for his fellow officer, but he felt sorrier for himself. After the clapping died down, the inspector finalised his briefing by announcing that the leader would be Detective Sergeant Raymond Rainbow, and all the teams were to report their findings to him personally, and his partner would be Detective Derek Jennet, the brother of the deceased.

FIVE

Across town, Tony Waybee had got out of bed early; he had a lot of things planned for this day. He had composed another letter the same way he had done the night before, now it was time to get his operation going, he wanted the money and soon. He had a plan for a new life, and it wasn't in the area he was now in. He put the finishing touches to his model boat, and after a quick wash and a cup of tea, he decided to go to the river to test it out; it would be crucial to his plan. But first he had to get the letter into Rainbow's letter box, and that was dangerous, because there was no way of knowing when he would come home.

Tony knew Rainbow the copper well, he had been arrested by him before on trumped-up charges quite a few times in the past; he hated him with a vengeance, and was determined to make him pay for his past behaviour and also for what he had done to his friend the previous night. He had disregarded the identity card he had found in his friend's wallet as a forgery because he knew better, there was no way that Tommy was a copper, they had spoken many times, and Tommy had made it perfectly clear that he hated the police. After all, he himself had had a police identity card exactly the same, with his name and rank, before he had got rid of it. Detective Sergeant Anthony Waybee, crime squad, they had both had a good laugh over that.

Old Freddy the forger had made them as a joke one day as the three men had been talking about fake documents and passports, he remembered; it had been Tommy's idea for Freddy to make up the fake police identity cards, and if anyone accused him of being a cop he would show the card, and then laugh at the reaction he got from all the villains he knew. He remembered the day Tommy had showed it to big Joe Bananas the gangster, when the big man had suggested he was, then accused him of being, an undercover policeman; he then explained that the cards were not real and that Freddy the forger had made them. Big Joe said at the time that he had almost shit himself. They had used the cards to rob places, and to get into late-night illegal gambling dens, where the drug dealer roamed. The reason why he had been surprised when he had seen the card was because Tommy has said that it was best if they destroyed the cards because if the police ever arrested them and found the forged cards they would put pressure on to tell them who the forger was, and as Tommy had said, he was no grass. So he had burned his card, and he thought Tommy had done the same.

His friend had been a great actor, and he had made a good living, ever since they had teamed up together. The times that his friend had been unfortunate to have been arrested then released without charge were the times that his friend would rant and rage at the bastards, as he called the police. And Tony found no problem about the fact that no one remembered him up north, after all, crooks don't give information on one another, it's the law of the underworld, so if the big drug dealers like Big Bananas couldn't find out who his friend had mixed with up north, so what? He had to be careful, he knew, because it wouldn't take long for the police to pick him up as a suspect; no matter what happened in the town, the police were always on his back.

He put his model boat in a canvas bag, and then went out to meet the day. As he walked towards the river he hoped that he wouldn't meet anyone he knew he had no time for petty talk, he had grander things on his mind. With head down he walked swiftly towards the river and the little pier where he had tested many of his boats before. The controlling device had been fully charged in the model shop just a few days before; he was satisfied that things would go well, his plan would he successful.

The slow-flowing river glistered in the morning sunshine. Apart from an odd few old fishermen trying their luck from the banks, he had the rickety pier to himself. On the opposite bank just fifty feet away, thick bushes and trees lined the water's edge and rose up to a hillock descending on the other side of the river's bend. Fifty yards upriver a footbridge spanned the slow-moving water. The wooden planks creaked under his feet as he surveyed the area. The sun burned his slightly balding head as he went down the steps at the end of the pier that were used for getting into boats, used mostly by the local rowing club, and the odd motorboat that ventured around the bend in the river. Leaving the duffle bag on the top decking he picked up the boat and descended the steps; placing the boat in the water, he noticed how well it laid, the balance just perfect. He positioned the boat in between two stanchions and made sure that it wouldn't drift away. He knew what he was doing, he had done it all before, but this time he had to make sure this would be his best launch yet; it was planned for the next morning, today was just a practice run. When he was satisfied he climbed the six steps and retrieved the bag; he slung it over his shoulder and made his way up the riverbank to the walkway over to the far side of the river, up the slight incline on a well-trodden path to the top of the hill. From this viewpoint he could see the pier with ease, and around the bend in the river. *Just the perfect spot*, he thought as he opened the duffel bag, and took out his remote control unit, which he set on a rock. Leaving the device he walked down the other side of the hill to the water's edge and found a place where he could bring his boat in, on the other side of where the pier stood, out of sight of anyone that was now around the bend of the river. He looked up the river and saw the familiar bridge that went back into the city centre. Walking back up to the top he realised just how much he was enjoying this game.

The sun was high in the sky, the flowers were blooming, and he hadn't taken any drugs for five days now; a feeling of well-being came over him, planning revenge was a good thing, he was enjoying the moment. He picked up the control and pointed it towards the boat hidden in the shadows of the old pier. The boat put its bow out into the sunlight as though deciding whether to go or not, then decided that it was safe and chugged away up the river around the bend. The trial was going well, he was timing this trial from beginning to end, and it had taken four minutes forty-eight seconds. He put the control in the bag and made his way down to where he had expertly docked his model boat; the trial had passed all of his expectations, now he felt satisfied. Placing the boat in the bag, he made for the bridge, and for the pint he had promised himself.

It was getting near midday. He got home; left the bag and the boat intact just inside the door, then completed the letter that he had started earlier. It didn't take him long, he felt excited at this new game he was playing. He glanced around his dingy home and felt happy that soon he would be leaving this way of living for good, once the cash was in the bag. He slipped on his cleanest dirty shirt and left for his promised pint, and to post the letter.

As he passed the apartment block he made sure that nobody saw him enter the foyer and was in and out in a flash. Then he made his way to The Beggars Arms pub, a pub he had never frequented before; he didn't want to meet anybody who knew him, questions could be asked, and he had too much to think about, so he intended to keep a low profile. He ordered a pint of bitter and a cheese roll, found a corner table away from the lunch time crowd , and sat down to think out his strategy. The letter had been easy to construct; he wondered if £10,000 was the right amount to demand, maybe it should have been £20,000, but the unfortunate thing was there was no one he could ask, he didn't know any other blackmailers; the thought made him smile. He ate his roll, took a sip of his beer and for the moment felt fine, things were going to plan. But his well-being was short-lived. The scar-faced man sat down in the chair opposite without an invitation and placed his half-full glass of beer on the tabletop with a heavy hand that made customers look in their direction.

Tony felt slightly put out; he didn't want any company and certainly not this character.

'Caught up with you at last, you fucken' dimwit. I've been looking for you all morning, you've took a lot of my time, and I've got better things to do in my life than to chase a prick like you. Where the fuck have you been? I've been to the café, I told you last night that I would meet you in there at ten o'clock; you had better have a good fucken' reason for not being there, or you're in serious big trouble, so come on shithead, tell me, or do I have to do all the talking, and I'm warning you, talk, and make it good.'

'Teddy my friend, slow down, you're frightening the customers, and the bar staff,' Tony Waybee said waving his hand up and down above the table.

'And you am I frightening you? Cause if I was you, l would be shitting myself.' Ted said, his face contorted in anger as he tried to control his temper. 'Where is he, you moron, where is that asshole you call your friend, the one you were sucking off?' He was now pointing his finger, with fury in his voice.

'Take your trouble outside, there'll be no fighting in here; if I hear one more raised voice the police will be summoned, gentlemen, please take my advice, and behave.' The bartender was small in statue, but the way he spoke with calmness in his tone of voice, and the threat of the police made the message sink home immediately.

'Sorry I didn't mean to shout, forgive me, it won't happen again, look we're friends.' Ted offered his hand to Tony who shook it reluctantly. The bartender returned to his bar talking to customers who had reported the disturbance on his way.

'I'll catch up with that idiot later, the jumped-up wanker, now where were we up to?' Ted said with a snarl.

'You were asking about Tommy but as I don't know where he is at the moment, he could be floating about in space for all I know, I saw him yesterday and he said he was heading home, that's all I know. Oh and by the way, I don't do that, suck men off, not my thing, so I'm asking you nicely, don't ever say that to me again.'

Ted drank down the remains of his beer and placed the glass on the table and looked directly at his adversary, then with venom in his voice he spat out, 'and what would you do if I said it again, and again, and again, what would you fucken' do, you asshole?' he said, pointing his finger into Waybee's face.

'This is what I would do,' Tony said quietly as he stood up and reached into his pocket. At that moment there was a sort of swish as the Stanley knife went through the air, like Concorde going through the sound barrier. Waybee left the bar through the side door and disappeared around the corner, and into the crowd of afternoon shoppers.

The scar-faced man sat there for a moment, unbelieving, until he saw the blood falling onto his trousers and down the front of his shirt; he put his hand to his face to try to stem the blood flow, stood up, and fell over two tables, knocking drinks to the floor amid the screams of the women in the pub.

Half an hour later Ted was in hospital getting stitches in a seven-inch slash to his right cheek that would match up with the one on his left cheek. He was already planning vengeance; that Tony Waybee would be paid, just like the piper.

*

Charlotte woke gently and glanced over to where her loved one had lain; she remembered the soft kiss she had received as he had got out of bed to go in to work. She stretched out and hugged his pillow she could smell the aftershave that he had worn the night before. Her slowly waking mind remembered the champagne they had shared; she had wanted to have sex to celebrate their engagement but he had resisted her advances even when she had come out of the bathroom completely naked with only her knee-length boots on, didn't seem to turn him on; even the parting of her lips did nothing to arouse him. She had been slightly hurt by his rejection, after all they had been having full sex three times a week for years, and earlier on in their relationship every night, but last night was different, somehow he looked worried at times. She threw the duvet back and laying flat on her back, caressed the sides of her curvy figure, massaging her full breasts, she tweaked her nipples till they were hard, they tingled to her touch, her hand went to the mound of blond hair between her legs and she began to caress the moistness that happened when aroused, her actions became faster and faster as she thought of her lover's big penis that she had loved to have inside her, and also the time he wanted her to take it in her mouth. She laughed as she came to her climax; she got out of bed and took a shower. She made coffee and toast and went down to pick up the post.

Raymond her fiancé was in a meeting at the station when she called him on her telephone. He had been brief, and said he would come home for lunch; he said nothing when she had told him another letter, just like the one he had received the night before, was in his post-box, and she was going to see her mother after lunch.

'Sorry about that,' he said as he returned to the meeting, 'that's the price you have to pay when someone loves you, they always want to know what you are up to, where you are and what you're doing. I'm sure you have all had it at one time or another.' All the detectives agreed, with nods and laughs. 'Now gentlemen you all know what to do, report anything to me no matter how small you may believe it to be. I'm off to the morgue to see if the coroners can shed any light on how he died. See you when you've got something to report and take care, it's a wicked world out there.' The policemen collected their papers together and left the room to try to catch the killer of one of their own.

The first stop had to be forensics, then the city morgue; he knew how the deceased had died, but he had to follow protocol, carry on as normal, a certain code of practice as in all cases, as the top brass would have said, *modus operandi*. But he also knew he had to become the good actor, just like the deceased had been. He had to play out each set, and put on a convincing account. It had gone this far now, there was no turning back, he had decided that he wasn't prepared to let the life he had worked so hard for go down the drain for a mistake he had made. He had put in too much, so now he would have to put his every effort to getting rid of the curse that had descended on him.

'Take notes,' he said not looking at his new partner. The detective fumbled like the TV detective Lieutenant Colombo to find his notebook and pen.

The morgue attendant adjusted his glasses as he read out the probable course of death. 'It's been established that the deceased died of asphyxia caused by blows or a blow to the larynx or oesophagus. A post-mortem has been performed on the cadaver, and no diseases were found, the man looked super fit. But we are still doing some further tests, sorry but it's not clear just yet, a little vague, but we are very busy at present, all this paperwork,' he complained. 'What we do know is somebody had jumped on him, because the prints of boots were on his chest, and whoever did this had been walking in powder.'

'Powder? What kind of powder?' Rainbow asked, looking around the morgue wondering if the man he had killed was in the fridge. The clinical antiseptic smell irritated him; he had to hurry with this part of the pretence, he had never liked seeing the dead, no matter who the villains had been.

'Cocoa powder, the kind used to make the drink, it was all over him, with the imprints of footwear on his chest; as I have already told you, the killer used him as a trampoline. The windpipe had been crushed by the savage blow.' He adjusted his glasses once again, and put the papers in a drawer behind a desk. 'And that, gentlemen, is all I can tell you at the moment; if you want to see the body he's in the top one over there,' he pointed to a metal filing cabinet. Rainbow pulled a face and shook his head. 'I don't know if you want to see him one more time but you identified the body, didn't you?' Rainbow inquired, although he already knew the answer.

The young cop's face looked sad as he declined the offer of seeing his brother again.

‘Thanks for that, Graham, could the blow you describe have been caused by falling on his throat maybe from a height, maybe hitting the side of a container or maybe he fell from one of those bins, wasn’t he rummaging in the rubbish?’ Rainbow enquired.

‘No I’m afraid that’s not the case here; he was punched or struck with the hand because we found no traces of anything,’ he hesitated and cleared his throat, ‘like a brick; say he had been hit by a brick or say a bit of wood, then residue of the object like brick dust, splinters and so on would be on the body, but on this one it was clean; as I have said it was a blow or a karate-type hit.’

Rainbow’s stomach formed knots the second that word ‘karate’ was mentioned; his blood pressure rose, he felt his face flush, and hoped that it wouldn’t be noticed as he turned away from the two men, indicating to his inside jacket pocket. ‘Vibrating bloody phone, excuse me for a moment.’ The phone was not vibrating, he had lied; he walked out of the theatre, went to the water dispenser in the corridor, and poured himself a plastic cup of water.

Forensics were brilliant at the work they did, they had helped to solve many a crime in the past; how they could come to the conclusion about how the man had been killed so soon worried him; he drank the water down and returned to the room.

‘Sorry about that, I didn’t realise I was so important.’ He was trying to be normal with his little joke, because in his head there was a thunderstorm playing havoc with his mind. ‘So is that all you can tell us on this case, did you get that down?’ he asked his colleague, asking both questions at once.

'It's all down here word for word, but I would like to ask a question please: did you determine the time of death, and could you say if he suffered? Did you know he was my brother?'

The attendant looked surprised at this statement, because he hadn't been on duty when the detective had earlier identified his brother's body; he realised that he could have used his words better when talking about the deceased, rather than using words like 'cadaver'. He would have been a bit more sensitive in this situation, but the guilt feeling soon dissipated, then he volunteered a surprising piece of information that surprised Rainbow once more.

'Time of death is always hard to determine, but I would say between six and seven o'clock and he died within a few minutes of the offending blow. In my professional opinion whoever did this didn't mean to kill, because the deceased had slight bruising to the chest, as though his assailant had tried to resuscitate the heart, you know what I mean, get his heart going again, then he gave mouth-to-mouth as well. We have that DNA on file now, and my boss is putting them through the system as we speak, so my guess is we will have the culprit in custody real soon; and that's all I can tell you at this time, so I must get on, I'm up to my neck in a mountain of work and it's nearly lunch so I will bid you gentlemen good day.'

'Thanks again, Graham, have a nice day,' Rainbow said, and both men walked out in to the sunshine. 'I hate going in there; it's not that I'm squeamish but there's no way I could do their job cutting up people, all the blood and gore, no not my cup of tea I'm afraid.' Rainbow blurted out without thinking of his partner's feelings, then realised what he had said and apologised. 'Sorry, my friend, I forgot; at the moment you must be feeling bad to know your brother is in there, but don't worry we'll catch whoever did this.' He placed his arm on his shoulder to console the sad-looking detective.

'What do you make of this karate business, could that have happened? One of the other officers told me you were into this sport; could a karate expert have killed my brother?'

'Well that's a very good question,' Rainbow said, 'and I'm going to tell you the truth, I can't see anyone in the sport doing this kind of thing; we are taught to control our every move, see this.' Then with a flash his hand shot towards his partner's face with the speed of a bullet train, then stopped just one inch away from his face.

'Bloody hell, sarge, you don't have to demonstrate, you frightened the shit out of me.'

Both men laughed, one nervously.

'See, control, it's called, the application of controlled aggression. I can't see anyone in this sport doing this; I'm sure this is a gangland killing. Don't worry it'll be sorted one way or another, now I want you to interview the two people who found your brother, find out who was the one who gave mouth-to-mouth, I overheard someone say that they saw someone running away, anyway, see what they have to say, and I'll see you tomorrow afternoon at the station. I've got some other business to attend to tomorrow morning, it's been ok'd by the chief,' once again he lied, 'and this afternoon I have other things to do, I may just pop into a few karate clubs just to gently look around maybe a bad apple got into the barrel, if you get my drift. I'll just mooch around, and don't worry, we'll get the bastard.' Rainbow tapped the young detective on the shoulder and they went their different ways. He looked at his watch; it was twelve noon as he made his way home for lunch, and the letter that was waiting for him on his coffee table left by Charlotte before she left to go and see her mother.

He fed the parrot and filled the water tray; the parrot flapped its wings shaking the cage from side to side, feathers slowly falling to the floor.

'What do you know, Polly, anything new?'

'Fucken' big tits, fucken' big tits, aaaaarrrrr, craw, craw,' the bird screeched.

'Language, I've told you about your language before, you need your mouth washed out. Now behave and have your dinner.'

'Fuck off, big tits,' the parrot turned his back to look in his little mirror. Rainbow sat at his table with the two letters he had just retrieved. The first letter, he retrieved from the book where he had left it the night before, and placed them side by side.

AT 12 NOON TOMORROW WE WILL REPORT YOU TO YOUR FRIENDS

TO STOP THIS HAPPENING BRING £10 000 TO THE OLD PIER ON THE RIVER AT 10 O CLOCK SHARP TOMORROW MORNING YOU WILL SEE A MODEL BOAT underneath THE PIER FOLLOW INSTRUCTION THEN STAY ON THE TOP OF THE PIER FOR HALF AN HOUR YOU WILL BE WATCHED SO IF

> YOU DO ANY THING beyond wHat WE have told you you will be saying HELLo to a prison senTENCe this is not a joke

He studied both the letters; it seemed there was more than one blackmailer; the first letter had said 'I SAW YOU', the other letter said 'WE'. At first he had thought that the sender was foreign because of 'I NO JOKE'; it was baffling. The new letter had been made up of cuttings from newspapers and magazines. He made some coffee and a sandwich, he glanced out of the window, the sun burning bright in the sky warmed the hearts of most people, but Rainbow's heart was heavy. There was nothing he could do, he would have to go to the bank and draw the money out, how he would tell Charlotte where the deposit savings for their new house had disappeared to, he had no idea.

The rest of the afternoon and evening, Rainbow just let slip away with sleeping and thinking, trying to see a way forward, but failing.

SIX
WEDNESDAY

The phone rang early and woke him from a deep sleep; he rolled over, and for a moment wondered where his girlfriend was; he looked at the bedside clock and saw it was 7.30. It was Charlotte who was asking when they could expect his arrival that morning. He adjusted the pillow and lay back, and then switched the light on.

'Look, darling, I've got a lot on this morning, so I'm glad you woke me. I was dead to the world, could have slept for ever, feel so tired now. I would love to stay in bed all morning, but as I've told you I've some very important things to see to, very important, but I'll drive up this afternoon. How's the battleaxe getting on anyhow?' He laughed out load as he heard Charlotte's protests; he held the phone away from his ear and threw his legs out of the bed. 'See you this afternoon, sweetheart,' he whispered. 'I have something big for you to feast your eyes on, you might want it for your supper.' It made him laugh once again as he heard her giggling on the other end of the line. He wished that life was always like this laughing, but now he had to face reality.

He had a quick shower after he had masturbated; the power shower had triggered off a reaction in his head, the warm water caressing down his back reminded him of the times he had had sex with Charlotte and he could picture her standing in front of him, the water hitting her breasts and running down to her navel then into the forest of hair between her legs. He remembered when they were having it doggy fashion the water hitting her back, and her squealing with delight as he thrust her with his truncheon as he liked to call his penis. He smiled as he recalled those happier times. Coffee was brewing as he got the money that he had taken out of the bank the day before, and put it in his inside pocket of his jacket. He had toast and marmalade and glanced at yesterday's newspaper, and there it was on the second page, just a small piece that he had missed the night before:

> Police were called to Baker Alley on Monday night when two members of the public came across a male in his thirties lying between two garbage bins. 'He had been beaten up badly,' said Mr Gray, one of the persons who had come across the body. 'It looks like another gangland killing,' a police spokesman said. The police had a busy night with road accidents and fighting in the city centre. Later on another communication from the police said the man from the alley was pronounced dead on arrival at the hospital; his name was being withheld until next of kin had been informed.

He tossed the paper onto the table, and glanced at his watch; it said 8.33. He looked at his bank statement: fifty thousand, four hundred pounds of hard-earned money they had both saved for their deposit on the house of their dreams, and now the amount had gone down to forty thousand, four hundred pounds. He hoped this was just a one-off demand, but with his experience in these blackmailing cases, there were more demands by the blackmailer as time went on. They had to be caught, and it had to be himself that did the catching, but how he would deal with them once they had been caught? He could only surmise at the moment, but getting rid of them for good popped into his mind, would he kill again? It might have to come to that if there was no other way out. He tried to shake the thoughts from his head as he put on his shoes. Taking one last look at the letters he put them in his pocket; he had no choice, he would comply with the instructions but would write a letter of his own and put it in with the money. He got out a page from his writing pad and wrote:

> 'It was an accident it's not what you think you saw, but I am paying you this one and only time, because this is a penance I feel I must pay. I hope you will take the money and enjoy it. I'm not in any judgement in what you are doing, so I hope we can put this unfortunate thing to rest once and for all, and after today, say goodbye.'

He reread his letter once more. The letter was attached to the money that was still sealed in the plastic container. He said goodbye to his parrot as he left the apartment, the parrot didn't reply, but that was nothing out of the ordinary as the parrot sometimes didn't talk for days then he would have a fit and swear continually for hours at a time, to the amusement of all who were in earshot of him. Once again Rainbow looked at his watch; it was 9.30, he still had plenty of time. He had to be at the pier at ten o'clock, so a walk beside the riverside was decided upon, he may see the speedboat that would collect his money and get the registration number. He knew it was all wishful thinking, but it passed away the time as he walked along the bank towards the pier.

*

Tony Waybee had also been an early riser; he had had a fitful night in anticipation of the payment he expected to get on this beautiful summer's day. And the fact that he expected the police to call on him over the slashing of Ted Sims in The Beggars Arms. He was too excited to eat anything so with his duffle bag in tow, he had left his basement hovel for his favourite café and a cup of tea. It was eight forty-five. The café was full of people who had travelled into the city from the outskirts by train or bus, who just wanted a booster of coffee to get them started in the long day they all expected, in the offices, the banks and other trades. Tony sat with his eyes on a big red and white clock that was placed right up on the wall behind the counter, and sipped his very hot tea. He saw a gang of four men come into the café that he recognised as a gang that belonged to big Joe Bananas. 'Bloody hell,' he muttered under his breath as he went to turn away from their looks. A pock-faced young man stopped at the table.

'No good trying to hide, Tony my friend, your hiding days are now in the past, we have found you.' He made a gesture with his hand toward the other three men who had stopped just in front of the counter. 'The last messenger who was sent out to contact you has ended up in hospital, now we are hoping that his slashing had nothing to do with you. You will have to assure us now that you had nothing to do with that, and I'm going to give you plenty of time to get your answer together. You have ten seconds from now.' The man's face was flushed and unfriendly, and anyone could see that this was not a joke; he spoke in a soft tone but still very menacing, he flicked his finger at the other men in a sort of a dismissal, and said in a demanding way, 'I'll have coffee, and two bacon and egg sandwiches.' The men went to the counter, and he pulled up a chair.

'Well I'm waiting for an answer, did you do our Teddy over, and was it you who marked his face? And why haven't you done as you were asked, to come to see Big Joe? You must know he can be very nasty if anyone crosses him, remember what happened to Maltese Joe last year? He thought he could take over in these parts, but he was mistaken, yes my friend, he made a big mistake in fucking about with the boss. You are aware that he has disappeared? So the time is up, did you duff Ted up? And if you did I'm afraid to say your days on this earth are very few. Do I make myself clear?'

Tony took a sip of his tea, looked the young would-be gangster in the eyes, glanced over to the other men who were now at another table near the door then said, 'If you stop fucken talking for a minute then I will answer your questions, but can I say this before I start. You and your boys, because that what you are, boys, plus your boss don't worry me one little bit, to tell you the truth, I would be more worried if I had found a bit of dog shit on my good boots, so don't come the big man stuff with me now do you understand?' Tony pointed his finger in the face of the hood with a sneer on his lips. The man shifted uneasily in his chair; he had heard of Tony's reputation. It had been said he was fearless and had been inside many times. And although it had never been verified, there was talk that years ago he had killed some gangsters on the east side, but was never brought to task for it because the police were pleased to see someone else clean up the criminals. Whatever, no charges were ever brought against the burly crook that was Tony Waybee.

'Now we understand one another, and you've zipped it, I'll tell you what I know. First off, I haven't seen Ted this week; you say he was slashed, where did this take place, was it in town? Because I thought he was out of town.'

'It was in The *Beggars Arms pub* on Clayton Street yesterday early afternoon,' the young hood, said, emphasising the name of the pub. 'People in the bar gave a description that fitted you to a tee, like ugly bastard... only joking for fuck's sake, Tony calm down, I'm only joking.'

'Look my dear friend I've no time for joking so I'm going to say this only once then you can fuck off, because I've got things to see to, I'm busy. I've never been in a pub or any bar called, The Beggars Arms, I haven't seen Ted for a while, and tell your boss that I will go to see him as soon as I can find the time, but if it's anything to do with Tommy tell your boss I don't know where he is either; he may have left town. Now fuck off.' Both men stood up from the table at the same time, Tony towered above the young crook, and for a moment they stared at one another but the young one desisted and backed down.

'Can I get you a cup of tea, or an egg sandwich, Tony?' he offered.

'No, for fuck's sake, *no*, I don't dine with morons.' Tony sneered, turned and walked out of the café. He didn't look at the three other young crooks who were now chatting up two girls who were sitting at an adjacent table. The time was dead on nine fifteen.

He hurried towards the river, the hustle and bustle of the city held him up at times. Traffic lights seemed to be on red at every junction, and people seemed to get in his way as he weaved his way through the throng of shoppers and school children in lines of two abreast going to a museum, or park. He realised he was running late. He swore under his breath as he swerved from side to side. He stopped at a stationery shop, and asked for some white chalk, the kind they used in schools on the blackboards; the young assistant had to ask her supervisor where the chalk was kept, because she hadn't remembered ever selling any. In the end he settled for coloured crayons and placed them in his bag then joined the mass of people going about their business.

At last he saw Queens Avenue, just five odd houses that stood on the edge of the river in an idyllic setting. He came to the end of the avenue, and there was the peaceful river just meandering its way to the small lake on the outskirts of the city. He saw the pier a hundred yards away, and went towards it. Just two fishermen sat on the banks near the small bridge. Just as he approached the pier a man walked out from the trees and just beat him onto the pier. He put his bag on the wooden decking and got his fishing rod out and started to assemble it.

'Just my fucken' luck,' Tony mumbled.

'Good morning,' the man said as he heard the wooden boards of the pier creak under the weight of the big heavy man that Waybee was.

'Hi, sorry to have to tell you but you won't catch much here, the fish are up around the bend, and not only that, this pier is mostly used for people with model boats, and sometimes canoes pull up here; there's a lot of activity just around here.' He opened his hand and spread them indicating the area. 'It's good for fishing up there,' he pointed towards the bridge.

'Thanks for your advice,' the fisherman said, 'but I've fished from here before, and I found it just fine and may I add, caught lots of fish, so I'll stay here. I really don't care about people with model boats, they have the whole river and lake to sail their silly boats on, so good morning to you, stand back I'm going to cast out.' It had started slowly at first but took up speed, and now Tony's rage burst in his brain, like a rocket on fireworks night.

'I don't think we are on the same page, so I'm going to try my best to make you understand me. I have to meet someone of great importance in my life on this very pier in half an hour, and we need privacy, so I'm asking you in a nice way, go and fish up near the bridge, please do this thing for me, will you?'

'Fraid not,' the man turned to face his adviser. 'I'm here to stay until at least midday; go, sail your boat elsewhere if that's what you're doing.'

Stars in abundance burst, then blackness descended in his brain as he fell to the floor, hitting his head on the deck of the pier, which swayed for a moment like a drunken man. He lay unconscious as Tony descended the steps on the side of the pier. He unzipped the bag and copied exactly what he had done the day before, set the boat in the water in between two joist cross-pieces that held the structure together with an exit to the river. He wrote a message on the boat then when he was happy climbed the steps to the top. The prostate man was just coming to and groaning, his face bloodied, nose broken.

'What happened?' he kind of pleaded, as he saw a face near his.

'Our heads clashed,' Tony said with no feelings, 'get up, you're bleeding and your nose could be broken, if I were you I would go and get some medical care, I'll help you get up.' He got the man to his feet and stuffed his gear into his bag; with a coloured crayon he wrote another message on the wooden plank, and then helped the dazed would-be fisherman away from the pier towards the bend in the river onward to the city. With a gentle push he sent the wounded man along the river path.

'Take care, go to the hospital, and forget that we spoke, and in future fish elsewhere,' Waybee warned. The man stumbled off holding his nose with a blood-soaked handkerchief, trailing his bag on the ground.

Tony looked at his watch; it was ten minutes to ten, he was running late. He had hoped to be set up long before this, he started to almost run. He crossed the footbridge ignoring the good mornings that the two fishermen offered, and walked up the hill to the rock on the top of the mound. The birds were singing; the sun was climbing the blue cloudless sky; after a bad start to his day he hoped that things would go well from then on. He got to the rock and looked out towards the pier, and then in the distance his saw a solitary man walking along the bank towards the pier. He took out his control unit, sat on the rock and waited.

*

Rainbow saw the pier from a distance and saw the two men on it then walking away in different directions but he was too far away to see their faces. The first thing he noticed as he approached the old pier was the blood drops on the wooden decking, then the message, it simply said, GO DOWN STEPS AND SEE BOAT FOLLOW INSTRUCTIONS. The arrow pointed to the steps. Rainbow took a quick glance around then gingerly descended the steps; he saw the boat. It was a well-made cargo boat with a bridge, and a hold where the cargo went; he saw the note attached, he ripped it off. It read, 'Put money in hold and go up and wait half an hour you are being watched.' He took the money out of his pocket and put the package in the hold of the boat, it fitted perfectly; he looked at the back of the boat and saw that it's name was Betty, and it was registered in London. There was another badge with the word BICK within an emblem. *Must be the make,* he thought; he then went back up the steps to wait, as he had been told to do. As far as he was concerned he hoped that this was the end of this episode. He looked at the blood once more when he heard a whining of a motor coming from under the pier, then he saw the bow of the boat poke out into the river, it turned left and chugged away; he watched the boat disappear around the bend in the river, and he said goodbye to £10,000 of his and Charlotte's hard-earned money.

*

Tony was happy so far, he held the controls and he was controlling his model with an air of expertise and things were going well. As the boat went around the bend in the river he took one more glance at his enemy standing on the pier, and started down the hill, still controlling the boat. The pier was now out of sight on the other side of the hill. He didn't see the young boy who had now tagged along with him.

'Give us a go, mister, I can do that, I can control the ship, please mister give us a go.' The boy looked up at him with pleading eyes.

Tony was surprised at first, because he was concentrating so hard on his task of steering the boat to his side of the bank, that he hadn't noticed the boy's approach. As he looked down to the boy he didn't see the swan with six of her young, swimming to the bank with the boat bearing down on the young ones. Somehow a male swan appeared from nowhere it seemed, and he was closing in for the attack. The boat was forty yards from the shore.

'Later, you can have a go, later, when I bring my boat in, but please leave me alone while I'm bringing her in, there's an important cargo aboard,' he said with a sigh. The boy nodded then mouthed 'OK' and followed him at a fair distance down the hill towards the water's edge.

Tony saw the swans when he looked up from the boy and could see trouble brewing. He put the full speed on the control and the boat shot forward, the bow wave travelling towards the baby swans. The waves soon had the cygnets bobbing up and down trying to keep up with mother. The big male swan swam alongside and raised his neck and with a spring-like action, pecked at the bridge and made the boat nearly turn turtle. Tony fought with the controls and tried to zigzag out of trouble, but it was in vain; the attack started again, this time with his wings that sent the boat back into the middle of the river, water splashing over the sides.

'Fuck it, fucken swans,' Tony muttered, forgetting that the boy was just behind him.

'I'll throw stones at them, I've got a good aim, I've done it before, mister, I'll chase the buggers off, watch this.' The boy picked up a few stones, and threw them at the swans hitting the male on the head, before Tony could say anything.

They had reached the water's edge at the bottom of the hillock, the water lapping at their feet. Tony looked at the power meter on his console and to his surprise it was flashing low. He realigned the control and turned the boat back to the shore; the swan made one last attack before another stone hit his head, and he swam off in the direction of his wife and babies; but he had done his duty in protecting his kind, and now the enemy was sinking just ten yards from the bank, to Tony's dismay. He saw the boat go down just like the Titanic did. Bow first, and then it slid into five feet of water.

'Fucken' hell, just my fucken' luck,' he shook his head in frustration and fury. 'Please God, what have I ever done to you, for fuck's sake?' he shouted, looking up at the heavens.

'I'll get it for you, mister, I'm a good swimmer. Let me get it,' the boy said excitedly. 'If you let me have a go I'll get it back, I can see it there, and it's just under the water, look.' He pointed as he took off his shoes and shirt and dropped his trousers to his underpants. He entered the water and waded out before Tony could say anything.

'Be careful boy, don't slip, yeah I can see it.' He bent over putting the boy's clothes in a neat pile and watched as the boy stood near the sunken boat; he saw the boy squat down in the water and thrash around, then the boy dived in the river, and five seconds later came up with the boat in his firm hands. He stumbled back to the water's edge spitting out water. 'I got it mister,' the boy said still excited, 'see I told you I could swim didn't I? I told you.'

'You did, and you were great, get dressed, look here use this towel.' He handed the boy a towel that he had in the bag he used for wiping his boats when they came out of the water. He emptied the water out of the boat then retrieved the package; there was a note attached, but the water had made the ink run and the note was unreadable. He shook the water off the package, jammed the money in his pocket, and put the boat in the bag with the console. The boy finished dressing, his hair sticking up in the air crying out for a comb. Tony offered a comb then said, 'Thanks for your help I'm very grateful to you so take this money and be on your way,' he handed the boy five pounds.

'No, mister, I don't want your money I want to have a go at controlling your boat, you promised me, you said I could have a go later didn't you, didn't you?' he repeated. The boy stood arms akimbo, and waited for an answer. For a moment Tony was stuck for words then said, 'Look I haven't got the time just now, but we'll do it another day and maybe bring a picnic if your parents permit us doing that, OK?'

'I ain't got parents, no mum or dad, and what's a picnic? Can I be your friend? I like to sail boats but I've never done it, please mister let me be your friend, I saved your boat didn't I?' Tony was taken aback at the cheek of the boy, and his blackmailing tactic; he had indeed saved the boat, if the boy hadn't frightened the swans off when he did the boat might have sunk in deeper water, and the money would have been lost forever, so he knew that he owed the boy something more than just a fiver. He looked over the river and saw three men rushing along the towpath. He turned to the boy and asked for his name and age; the boy said his name was Ben and he was ten years old.

'OK this is what we'll do, you can be my friend, but because I'm a lot older than you I will be the boss, and you must do everything that I say without argument; do we both agree to that, and Ben you will call me Uncle Tony, is that OK by you?' he held out his hand. The boys face lit up with a sunshine smile that would have made an early morning ray of sunshine ashamed of its performance.

'Yes, thank you, yes,' the boy repeated.

'We must go now,' Tony said in a whisper holding back the tears that suddenly came from his boyhood memories of a father that was never there for him and a mother who was always drunk. The two new friends walked along the bank towards the bridge hand in hand with the delighted little boy looking up at his new uncle; he was happy.

*

'That's him, that's him!' the man shouted as he approached the pier. 'He's the one who hit me.' Then as the three men came closer he realised that he had made a mistake and the man on the pier wasn't the same person that had assaulted him just twenty-five minutes earlier.

'Don't move, stay where you are, police,' the plain-clothed detective shouted thirty feet away from the jetty. Rainbow turned around and recognised Detective Constables Willis and Weston coming towards him with a bloody-faced man in tow. Rainbow glanced at his watch, it was time to leave, and the time stipulated was up. He had kept to his part of the deal, had paid in full, and hoped that would be the end; he felt a bit of admiration for the way the blackmailer had received the money. He had investigated many blackmailing cases in the past, and ransom payments, but transfer by model boat, this was the first, and he would award top points for originality. *The blackmailer must have a great imagination*, he mused. Recognition dawned on the faces of the two detectives as they set foot on the pier. 'Hello there, sarge, didn't recognise you from down there; met this guy stumbling around, and he said he had just been assaulted so we are investigating, he's just said it was you that hit him. Sorry, sarge, this man says that you assaulted him,' he looked at the bloodied man.

‘No it wasn’t him. The bloke who did this,’ he pointed to his nose, ‘was bigger and his head was clean-shaven,’ the man said with difficulty. ‘I was trying to fish here, just here, look that’s my blood.’ Once again he pointed to the spots of blood on the pier.

‘Did he have a model boat with him? Did you see which way he went after he assaulted you, did you notice?’ Rainbow asked, the three cops looked at the man waiting for a reply.

‘No I didn’t see a boat, all he had was a bag, a duffel bag. Yeah that was it, a duffel bag, but I didn’t see any boat, he was a nasty kind, look what he done to my nose, he broke it, he knocked me out, see that, my blood.’

‘Yeah, you just said,’ Rainbow ventured; he looked at the other cops and instructed them to get the man to hospital, and then to continue with their inquiries. They left the area and disappeared down the towpath that ran alongside the river. He walked up the river to where the fishermen were trying their luck.

‘Nice morning, gentlemen, nice weather for a spot of fishing. I’m police, there’s nothing to worry about, I’m not going to ask you if you’ve got your fishing licences, or anything like that, I’m just wondering if you happened to see a guy pass along here about say half an hour ago?’

‘You don’t need a licence to fish this part of the river,’ the fisherman pointed out, ‘it’s open to the public; to answer your question there was a bloke who passed here about half an hour ago he was in a hell of a hurry, didn’t have the time to say what a nice day it was, went over that footbridge over there.’ The man pointed across the river.

'Thanks, sorry to disturb you, hope you catch something for tea, did he have a duffel bag with him, did you notice?

'Didn't see a bag. 'Harry,' he shouted along the bank to his fellow fisher, 'did that bloke who passed in a hurry this morning, you know the one who didn't answer you when you said good morning to him, and did he have a bag?'

'Yeah he had a duffel bag slung over his shoulder, went over the bridge, why who wants to know?' He cast out to the middle of the river and frightened two swans and some little ones swimming on the far side of the river making their way upstream.

'Thanks once again, and get a licence, wouldn't want a fine, would we now?' Rainbow went over the bridge, and up the path he saw the rock with cigarette butts in the ground, he could see the pier, he could see how the blackmailer had put the plan into action, he could see how the trees and the bushes had hidden the man from his view from the pier, it had been a well worked plan, well executed. In the meantime, while Rainbow was talking to the fishermen and walking up to the top of the hill, Tony was sitting in a burger place munching into a cheeseburger and his little friend was drinking a milkshake, and eating a load of French fries.

The boy explained that he lived in a children's home and he had run away that very morning. Tony admonished the boy but gently, warning him of the dangers that lurked in the streets of the city. He made the boy promise that he wouldn't ever run away again, and in return once a week they would meet and go sailing boats.

'Will I be able to bring my helicopter and fly it? It flies well, and I'm an expert in controlling it with a control like you got, for your boats.' The boy made a turning movement with his hands.

'Of course you can, we'll have lots of fun with our boats, and your' copter.'

Tony escorted Ben back to the children's home and handed the boy over to the head of staff, which seemed very grateful, and said that she would get the permission that was needed to take the boy out once a week. The two new friends shook hands, and the boy hugged him, and then said, 'Can you be my new dad now?' That brought a tear to Tony's eyes. 'I'll run away again if they say I can't come with you,' the boy shouted as he was led indoors. Tony made his way home to count his money, with a new idea forming in his head.

SEVEN

Eddie Bail opened the club door; he was early because he had some painting to do. The karate club was falling down bit by bit so a painting job would at least brighten the place up until money could be found to get some repairs done. He entered his office and threw the morning papers on his cluttered desk, and put the coffee pot on. He went out and got the paint and brushes ready, cleaned down the area that needed to be painted then went back to his office, and poured the strong-smelling coffee that was bubbling on the small electric stove in the corner of his office. He loved the smell of coffee; it reminded him of when he was young and living in the country with his mother and father and his two sisters, his mother always had coffee on the brew and as a boy he drank gallons of the stuff. He added white powder called Coffee-mate and four heaped spoonfuls of sugar; he liked his coffee sweet. He sat at his desk, the aroma hit his nostrils and he sipped the liquid and felt a satisfaction splash on to his mind like a wave breaking on a sandy distant shore. He flicked the paper open and something caught his eye, he shuffled his chair so that he was in a more comfortable position, and read the headline. 'KILLING IN CITY SLUM'. It continued underneath. 'At approximately six forty-five on Monday evening an unidentified man was murdered in Baker Alley in the city just off the high street, if anyone was in the high street at that time on Monday and saw anything that might help the police, the number to call is printed at the bottom of the page.' The man was in his thirties and his name had not been released until his next of kin had been informed. The man had been struck a karate-type blow to the throat, a spokesman said. The victim was taken to hospital, but was already deceased. Eddie sipped his coffee, with his hand cupping his head. Monday, he thought, at about six forty-five, that was the time that he had left the club to return Rainbow's ring that he had forgotten. He remembered getting to Rainbow's apartment at seven fifteen, or thereabout. The distance from the club to the high street, walking, was roughly half an hour, even if someone went the long way around. That would have put Rainbow in the vicinity at the time. He wondered if Rainbow had taken a shortcut through the alley, he wondered if he had delivered the karate blow the papers had mentioned. He had seemed very agitated when he had gone round there to deliver the engagement ring, he seemed on edge, he had threatened him, he remembered. He drank the remains of the coffee and washed the cup; he left the office and started the painting job.

The sun was burning hot and at its zenith, it was midday, and Eddie was sweating freely with smudges of paint on his face and hands, his shirt sticking to him. He decided to continue later in the afternoon when it was a bit cooler and he had had a rest and a bit of lunch. He put the paint away, cleaned the brush and fixed his lunch on a small portable electric cooker, which he kept in the corner of his office next to a small sink. Beans on toast, fried egg, bread and butter. He sat at his desk and enjoyed the meal and the solitude. He washed up, and lay on the little single bed that folded down from the wall. He lay there thinking of the cleaning duties that he had to attend to later on in the day; it was a shame that the cleaning lady was not coming in after what had happened to her, she had been very nice and she had always done her duties to his satisfaction. When she would be back, if ever, was anyone's guess. Things were going from bad to worse, he thought, as he drifted off to sleep in the quietness of his office.

Clanging woke Eddie from a deep sleep, he looked at his watch; it was three o'clock, he had slept for two hours. He heard the clanging again and swung his legs over the side of the bed and went off into the gym to see what or who was making the noise.

Rainbow turned to face Eddie, his locker was open, and he was putting his gym clothes into a bag.

'I've come to collect my things, I wish you would reconsider my membership, Eddie, I'm sorry for speaking to you the way I did the other night, I don't know what came over me. Maybe the engagement thing got to me; I can't explain it, as you know I'm not normally that cranky.'

'You threatened me, remember, you said that you had saved me from a hiding, remember? You know, Ray I don't deserve to be treated like that after all I've done for you over time. The times I've stayed on here at this club to help you with extra lessons, when I should have been home with the wife, the time I opened the club on Sundays, my day of rest, just for you to get in some extra training. I could carry on and on, and you know it, Ray, I've been bloody good to you, and you know it, don't you?'

Rainbow offered his hand, his left hand, in a gesture of renewed friendship; a heart-rending look crept across his face, like a shadow does as the day is ending.

'Eddie I've been an asshole, I'll say again I'm sorry for my ungentleman like conduct, I can only promise you that I will never speak to you like that again, and this is not creeping to you just to stay in this club, because I've been put forward for a place at Acme karate gym.' He lied but at that moment turned to look into the locker.

Eddie took his left hand and shook it gently.

'Still getting trouble with your right hand I see, it's still puffy,'

'Yeah I'm going to get it looked at later this afternoon, in fact when I leave here, I think I have broken a bone in it, now don't ask me the name of the bone because I haven't a clue.' He tried to make a joke, tried to break the tension he felt. It was very rarely that he buckled down to anyone, let alone Eddie, who he really didn't have a great deal of liking for, no matter what he had done for him in the past. But it would be a shame to throw all the training down the drain when the tournament was only a short time away. And the club was close to home.

'Put your things back in your locker, and we'll forget about the incident; after all, you must remember, Ray, I have a black belt second Dan, and you don't know what would happen if we got into a real fight now, do you?' With that Eddie took up the karate stance and went to attack, his right fist flew towards Rainbow's face like a bolt from the blue.

Rainbow was taken by surprise at Eddie's display but the training he had put in over the years took over, and his reaction was as fast and blocked the blow that was meant to stop just an inch from his face, in the control that Eddie had intended, but he had used his right hand once again. Rainbow's face contorted in agony as he felt the pain go through him and he felt sick for a moment.

'Fucking hell, Eddie, what the fuck you doing, we've just shook hands.'

'Fucken' hell, Ray, I was only joking; I didn't think you would block. It was a controlled hand blow, I only did what you did to me the other day, remember just before you left for home; sorry man, there's me saying that word again, now one last time I'm sorry. Finish what you're doing there and I'll put the kettle on and we'll have a cup of coffee in the office then we'll have a talk on the tournament, and you can sign a new card for your subs, I destroyed your old ones.' Eddie left and went to his office.

Rainbow swore under his breath as he massaged his hand and put his things back in his locker then locked it and made his way to the office. He noticed the rusty barbells and the worn-out mats, how dingy the old club looked; it certainly needed a facelift, a money injection.

'Pull up a chair, Ray, the coffee is almost done, now the tournament's in Allchurch on the fifteenth of next month; it will last all day, so we will have to get a hotel for the night. You're ready for it; you'll get your next Dan, that's a certainty, so I wouldn't lose too much sleep in worrying about it.' Eddie settled down behind his desk and poured the coffee into two mugs; the bag of sugar had the top cut off, and a spoon was standing in the sugar, as though showing off.

‘Help yourself to sugar,’ Eddie said after he had settled in his seat as though he was about to chair a board meeting. He indicated to the newspaper that was still lying on the desk, and took a sip of his coffee, making a slurping noise.

‘See the papers, Ray, seems there was a killing the other night at the same time that you were on the way home, you didn’t do it, did you? You must have been near that area, according to this,’ he pointed to the paper then picked it up.

Rainbow was instantly annoyed at this accusation and his face showed it.

‘You’re not accusing me of the killing, are you? You must be out of your fucking little mind, now if you’re joking I’m telling you now, it’s in poor taste, so stop now. If you want to talk about the tournaments, or the club, then I’m all ears, but I haven’t time for this kind of bullshit; for your information I’m in charge of the case, I’m looking for the perpetrator of the crime.’ He glared over the table to where Eddie was smiling.

‘Hey, hey, slow down, you’ll be having a heart attack, I was only saying with my fucking little mind, you see there you go again within a few minutes of us shaking hands and supposedly making friends, you start to call me names again, now do you consider that as good friends? Come on, Ray do you?’

‘I don’t find it too funny to be accused of killing someone, nor would you so can we talk about something else, because I have to leave. I’m supposed to be going to see my mother-in-law this afternoon. Charlotte’s upset, she thought we’d be on holiday this week, somewhere in the sun,' He glanced out of the window. 'I know it's sunny here but we're meant to go away, to catch the sun elsewhere.' He laughed but feebly.

'I didn't mean any harm but I thought you might have seen something on your way home, after all it's on your route, you passed the place where the crime happened, at roughly the time it took place, in the alley.'

'See there you go again, you are just surmising, you're just delving into the realms of conjecture, that's all you're doing, you don't know which way I went home do you? So I'll put you right, my inquisitive friend, I didn't walk down the alley that night I walked along the high street, past thousands of people. It's very rare that I go home down the alley anyhow. It's a shortcut but not that much of one.' He finished his coffee and felt satisfied at his explanation; he moved to get up and go.

'So you saw that unfortunate accident on the high street at about the time you were passing?' Eddie remarked; standing up and taking the cups to the sink he glanced out of the window, and saw a car pull into the car park at the rear of the club.

'Yeah I did, the ambulance was called and the old woman was taken away, she was knocked over at the bus stop by the very bus she was waiting for, now there's a strange thing, life's like that sometimes, you never know what's around the corner.'

'You actually saw the woman then? You know, after she had been knocked down?'

'Yeah I actually helped to put her into the ambulance.'

'Did you speak to the lady when you put her into the ambulance?'

'What's this? Third degree, are you in training to become a detective? I thought that it was my job to ask questions; of course I spoke to her, she was in a stable condition.'

Eddie put the cups away after washing and wiping them, then said, 'Did you know the woman, had you ever seen her before that night at the accident scene?'

'That's fucking it, I've had enough of this,' Rainbow shouted out. 'No I didn't know the woman, never seen her in my life, I don't know every woman in the city you know. Why all the questions? Is this the new club rules because if they are, then I'm out of here?' Rainbow was getting really agitated.

'Come in.' Eddie shouted when there was a knock on the door. The door opened and an elderly man came in and shook Eddie's hand, ignoring Rainbow. Eddie extended his hand towards Rainbow, 'This is Ray, he's a member of this club, and may I add also a sergeant detective in our city police force.' The elderly man reached forward to shake hands. 'Nice to meet you, I hope I haven't come at a bad time, it sounded that you were in the middle of an argument, or maybe I've come at the right time, eh,' he laughed out loud.

'No,' Eddie said, 'we were just discussing, but no disagreements, we're friends aren't we Raymond?'

'Of course we are, bosoms pals,' he said, sounding sarcastic.

'Nice of you to take time to come in, I was sorry to hear about your wife's accident, I was shocked when I found out, how is she?' Eddie said to the visitor.

'She won't be coming in to do any cleaning for a month or so, so I was passing by and I thought I would pick up any monies owing; will her job be open when she's better?' The old man caught his breath as he spoke then stopped for a moment, then continued after a cough. Rainbow listened intently. Realising he had made a mistake and that surely his lies had been exposed, he felt very foolish. He felt he wanted to disappear, to run as fast as his feet could carry him.

'She loves her job here; she's always on about it, only the other day...'

Rainbow, who had been standing by his chair, broke in and interrupted.

'Sorry gentlemen, but I must be on my way, sorry to hear about your wife's troubles, I know her well, and we have had many laughs over the last couple of years. I last saw her when she left here two nights ago; I hope she gets better soon.' He made for the door.

'Hold on a minute there was one more thing,' Eddie said.

'Yeah it was two nights ago,' the old man continued, 'after leaving here after her cleaning that she decided to step under a number two bus down the high street at six forty-five, or thereabouts, then it was a hospital stay for her; as it so happens it was only a sprained ankle, and a few bruised bones, she'll be up and around pretty soon I hope, because I don't like making my own tea; it's funny but you start to miss them when they're not there.' Rainbow had stopped listening to the old man after he found out that it was the cleaning lady who had been knocked down at the bus stop and he felt panic in his head.

Once again he was shocked; he knew that the lie he had just told had been exposed and it was written all over the face of his adversary.

'I believe we must have a little talk, Ray, so hang around and I'll get some more coffee.' Eddie said as he put some money in an envelope and gave it to the old man as he left the office without a goodbye.

The coffee was made in silence, as Rainbow searched his mind for some way out, but could find none. Eddie placed the coffee on the table and sat in his seat once again and looked at Rainbow then spoke. 'That old gentleman was Roy Turnbull, the husband of the club's cleaning lady who we all know as Vera; you do remember her, surely, our cleaning lady?' It was a sarcastic remark, and Rainbow sensed it.

Eddie looked hard at the unhappy detective then came out with the question.

'Did you do it, Ray? It's quite obvious to me that you were in the alley at the time, you've lied and you know you have, so have you got an explanation for me, because I have a strong interest in this case. You can confide in me, after all we're friends.'

'It's self-defence, Ed, self-defence.' He repeated. 'Yeah, we are good friends and have been for a long time as far as I'm concerned, so OK, we've have had our differences in the past but as the song goes, too few to mention, so I guess now is the time to see how strong our relationship is, are we really friends? Or will you tell my superiors, after my explanation, we shall see.' Rainbow put on the best sad look he could muster then told his story, of how he had been attacked, and how he had defended himself just the way that Ed had taught him, how he had tried his best to resuscitate the assailant, and how he had panicked. He had been beside himself with grief, how sorry he was to have taken a life.

As he was relating the story, a tear ran down his face; he was a good actor. Eddie passed over a pack of tissues, the hard man reduced to this. Rainbow felt sorry for himself now that Eddie knew that he was a killer. Eddie shifted in his seat; for a moment he felt sympathy, but fought with his conscience. Surely it was his duty to society to report any misdemeanour to the authorities, especially a crime of this nature, a murder or any unlawful act.

'I believe you,' Eddie said, as he put his hand on Rainbow's shoulder, 'I can't see you doing this on purpose, especially in your capacity as a policeman; no doubt your attacker was some lowlife, and the world won't miss scum like that, so this is what I will do for you: I will forget we've had this talk this afternoon and your secret will stay in this room, and I will suggest that because we are good friends as you have pointed out, we should work together to make this club a success. As you are aware, this is my life, and I love my club, but I can't keep the place going without the infusion of some money for the roof, and some repairs that are needed badly. Now I know that you have a bit of money in the old bank, and if you put some in here, the club could carry on, and everyone would be happy once more. I know that in your mind, being a copper, it might sound like blackmail, but that's one game I have never had time for, so believe me there's no pressure on you to participate in it; what's your views, Ray?'

Rainbow's mind was whirling; he felt like ending it all by sending Eddie to the pearly gates, but soon dismissed that idea.

'I want to thank you Ed for your understanding; you'll never know how sorry I am, I can't for a minute tell you how grateful I am to you for helping me like this. You do realise I'm sure that this could be the end of my career, my life as I know it. You are the only one who knows the truth of what happened that dreadful night, haven't told anyone else, not even Charlotte, no one. So I would like to take up your offer in the club, how much would you want to get things going?'

Eddie took a pad and wrote a few things down then looked up and said, '£10,000 would be a nice figure to get things going, but I would want the money in my bank account by tomorrow at the latest, because I have a builder I know who is available in the next few weeks or so, and he could start on the roof as soon as possible. I know it only leaks when it rains but it needs to be done.' He laughed at his joke about the rain, so did Rainbow but he didn't find it that funny, and it was a false laugh; he was in no mood for laughing.

'Ed, I need a bit longer to get the money together, the money is in a joint account, and I need to make an excuse to Charlotte for her to agree to release it; give me three days, did you want cash or will a cheque do?'

'Just cash, no cheques, sometimes they bounce.' He burst out laughing once again. Rainbow didn't see anything funny, and gave a false smile.

'Well, now that's out of the way, better get back to my painting again, gonna give me a hand, partner?' He emphasised the word 'partner'.

'Sorry Ed, I've got things to do down at the station; I'll be in touch, don't worry.'

Rainbow was seething inwardly and walked through the club and out into the car park; he glanced back and if looks could have killed, Eddie would have been very dead.

EIGHT

Detective Constable Derek Jennet had been busy since the last time he had been with his partner. He had found out that his brother had regularly reported his findings to the top brass every time he had got himself arrested, and the name of Tony Waybee was well known to the head of operations, along with Big Joe Barnsom, alias Joe Bananas because of his love for eating the fruit most of the time. It was also known that big Joe was a leading drug dealer, but it was his masters that the police were after, and his brother, alias Tommy, had been undercover and on the verge of exposing the top dealers when he had been killed.

A visit to Waybee's home was on his agenda, when he found out that his brother used to hang out with this petty crook and had done so for the last few months. That morning his first call had been to interview the two men, who had reported finding his brother in the alley, and he had been told how they saw a man leaving the area and how they had shouted for him to stop but to no avail. It had been too dark to recognise him. They said that they did not give mouth-to-mouth to the man on the ground as they concluded him to be already dead; it was at that time that they called the police. They also pointed out that they had given this information to a policeman on the night of the incident. He had thanked them both for their help, and left to try to find out more.

He was told the names of other well-known crooks and villains who operated in the area. Edward Sims, Barry Harris, alias Bootsy because of his fetish for stealing boots from stores and in the shops in the city, plus many more would-be thieves that he would interview at a later date. He had been told that Ted Sims was at his dwelling after being released from hospital.

'Cut myself while I was shaving.' Ted Sims had replied to the question, 'I'm a clumsy bastard, never any good with a forking razor, and to answer your other question about Bootsy, I believe he left town two or three days ago; is there any reward for this information?' he had asked. He knew that Tony Waybee was in town on Monday afternoon, because he admitted that he had seen him with that other asshole Tommy, whatever his name was, and they had admired Harris's boots near the off-licence, because Bootsy had told him so as he bumped into him after the incident. The detective had kept his cool when he had heard the disparaging remark about his brother, and just gave a certain look a copper gives at the request of a reward. Being professional he thanked the crook for the information he had received, and left the house. He went looking for Tony Waybee but there was no one at home so he had decided to return later in the day. In the meantime he would go and visit a few karate clubs to see if he could smell out a few bad apples that may be lurking in a barrel, just as his partner had pointed out. He drove in the club car park just as Rainbow was getting into his car.

The two detectives were surprised to see one another so soon; after all, Rainbow had said that he was going to see his girlfriend and his mother-in-law-to-be that afternoon. Derek wound down his window as he pulled up beside his superior then got out of his car to join his colleague in the front seat.

'Hi there, sarge, didn't expect to see you here, I thought you were up with your—'

'I know what you thought, but you were wrong,' Rainbow interrupted. 'What are you doing here? Did you do what I told you to do? Check out who gave mouth-to-mouth to your brother? Check out the two who were in the alley?'

'Done all that and more, I've found out that a certain Anthony Waybee, commonly known as Tony, was a close associate of my brother's and they spent a lot of time together, and I have been around to his house this afternoon but no sign of him; a neighbour told me he had gone out but would be back later, so I thought I'd go see him later today.'

'Well you've done a good job of wasting police time, why would we be interested in knowing about another police officer who used to hang out with your brother?

'No, sarge, you got me wrong, the bloke who was my brother's associate was a crook who tagged along with Robert when he was undercover with the made-up name of Tommy. Apparently they were together every day. I've found out they were together on the day my brother was killed, because a character called Edward Sims said he saw them together on the very day. Sims also told me where my brother lived, so I took it on myself to go around, to see if there was anything of importance in his room; it turned out that it was a seedy guest house owned by a Mrs Trotter, Mary, she was very accommodating and said that her lodger was a quiet nice man who paid his rent regular, and was no trouble at all; she had been concerned when he hadn't returned on Monday night, and still wondered where he had got to. I had to break the bad news to her and she shed a tear. She let me into his room; it was sparse with a single bed, a wardrobe, and a table with a single chair. I went through his things and packed up a few items that belonged to him. There was nothing to show that he was undercover, basically he just slept there, but one thing I found out, he was on medication for high blood pressure, and heart tablets, so he wasn't as fit as the pathologist had said, he was certainly under a lot of stress. I have the name of his tablets in my book.' He read them out: 'bisoprolol' and 'amlodipine',

'Hell, you have been busy, sorry about that misunderstanding earlier on,' Rainbow interjected. 'Tony Waybee… somehow it rings a bell, somewhere in here,' he pointed to his head.

At that moment Eddie came out of the club and approached the cars, paintbrush in his hand.

'You're still here? You could have helped me to do a bit of painting in the time you've been chatting; I thought you told me you were busy? You could have gone and got our business sorted by now. I hope you weren't bullshitting me, Ray, you know me, I don't like shirkers, I'll report you to the board of directors, you know what I'm talking about.' Behind the smile was the menace that was prominent in his voice.

'This is my partner, Detective Constable Derek Jennet, and this is my karate instructor, Eddie Bail,' Rainbow volunteered. Both men shook hands through the open window of the car.

'Seems like you have a few partners then, you said you were busy.' He turned to Derek. 'Fancy joining the club? We need a few more students, don't we Ray? Maybe you can persuade your partner to join.' He turned to go back into the club.

'I'll do my best, Ed, I'll do my best,' he repeated. 'To Tony's, whoever, I'll follow you,' Rainbow instructed his colleague.

They pulled out of the club car park; he glanced back and saw Eddie wave his paintbrush in the air with a false smile on his face from the office window, and a feeling of sickness welled up inside his body, coupled with an acute hatred for him.

It only took the detectives twenty minutes to get to Waybee's address; they parked in a nearby car park and walked to the flat.

Tony Waybee had got home after taking the boy back to the children's home, and had taken an afternoon nap. The knock on the door woke him. He looked out the window and saw two guys in suits, and thought that it was about time the electricity company sent someone to see him concerning his bill, as they had promised three months before. He answered the door, and on seeing Detective Sergeant Rainbow standing on his doorstep his heart sank quicker than his model boat had earlier on in the day.

'Anthony Waybee, are you Anthony Waybee?' Detective Jennet said in his best policeman's voice.

'Who's asking? Who wants to know?' he said in a defiant way.

'Me, you must remember me, we met many times haven't we Tony?' Rainbow said with a sly smile, going to his inside pocket, with the intention of showing his identity card.

'Oh it's you. Yeah I remember you, you fixed me up good and proper many times in the past, and I had noffink to do with the crimes you got me for, well I ain't done noffink wrong this time either, I've been straight for years.'

'Can we have a word with you about a friend you have been hanging around with for the last few weeks? A man known as Tommy, do you know of such a man?'

Tony felt relieved as he heard the question; he thought that his blackmailing days had come to an abrupt end, and he had been rumbled so soon.

The day was slowly slipping away and a chill had descended on the ground where the sun had been playing all day. Rainbow felt a chill come over him and a pang of hunger hit his stomach as he realised he hadn't eaten since the toast and marmalade he had had at breakfast.

'Yeah I know Tommy, he's a good friend of mine, but I'm not grassing on him, so if he's done anything against the law, then that's down to him, noffink to do with me.'

'When's the last time you saw him? He's done nothing wrong we just want a few words with him that's all,' Jennet asked, in a matter-of-fact way.

'I was with him on Monday afternoon, but then we parted, and he said he was going home, and I haven't seen him since. Look I want to go out, and seeing I ain't done noffink wrong, and I don't want my friends seeing me talking to you lot, so I would like to say goodnight to you two honourable gentlemen of the law if you don't mind.'

'Can we come in then out of this chill for a chat we won't be—'

Tony interrupted Rainbow and said, 'Only if you've got a warrant, I don't let you lot in my home without one, it's been known that you lot have planted things in the past, so unless you have a warrant the answer is a definite *no*. I know the law; you might think I'm thick and you have said that to me before, haven't you Detective Rainbow? Remember the last time you done me, you called me thick, just because I told you that I can't read or write. You took the piss out of me.'

'OK, we haven't got a warrant, but we could get one soon enough, and about this thing about planting, I hope you're not making any accusations,' Rainbow was getting riled up and wanting to curtail this, after all he was only pretending to be investigating to placate his colleague, he had to be seen to be trying to do something to try to solve a murder case that he already knew about, and was trying to hide.

'Sorry I didn't mean you about the planting, I don't know anything more about Tommy, he left me to go home, that's what he told me. If you don't believe me ask Bootsy Harris, he'll tell you, but I guess you have asked him already?'

The detectives looked at one another, and then Jennet spoke. 'Do you know there was a murder in Baker Alley on Monday night? And where you were on Monday night?'

'Fucken' hell, I knew it, I'm being done again for a bloody murder now, well let me tell you this, I wasn't any where near Baker Alley that night nor have I been there for weeks or months, I was here, home on my own.'

'I suppose you're going to tell us you were watching TV that night,' Jennet blurted out.

'No, I'm not saying that at all, I wasn't watching TV because I've been cut off, and I haven't got an electricity supply at the moment. I thought you two were the electricity men, come to talk to me about it, then I open the door and you are here accusing me of murdering someone, and I know you, Detective Rainbow, I know you don't really believe I did it, you know better, don't you? Sure I've been in trouble in the past but only petty things, but murder never, not me, I wouldn't hurt a fly, and to answer your question, no I didn't know there had been a murder in Baker's.'

'Don't you read the newspapers?' Jennet inquired.

'No I don't, I can't read, remember?' Tony answered looking at Rainbow. 'Ask him.'

'That will be all for now, Waybee; don't leave town, we may want to talk to you again and we would like to say that we are sorry to take up your time.'

The detectives walked back to their cars and Rainbow got into his colleague's car.

Tony closed the door and lit the paraffin lamp; he was relieved, he jumped for joy, he had come face to face with the very person he was blackmailing, and he was in the clear, he didn't have an inkling. He celebrated with a can of beer, and decided to go out for a few more pints later that evening, but at present he was very happy to have pulled off the money call and he had had another idea to generate more money. After all, £10,000 was nowhere enough for the plans developing in his mind. The flight to any foreign country was expensive and Brazil or Argentina was the flavour of the month. He adjusted the wick on the lamp, pulled the curtains and set to work on another demanding letter.

Jennet spoke first, after taking out his black book and getting a pen at the ready.

'What do you reckon, sarge? He looked a shifty sort to me, very nervous and defensive.'

'I've had lots of dealings with him in the past,' Rainbow said, 'and I've put him inside a few times but I've never known him to be involved in any violence, but you never know what people are capable of; can't read into anyone's mind and like the old saying goes, you can't judge a book by the cover.' He realised he was being profound, and felt that he had spent enough time on this wild goose chase; he hoped that he had shown interest in this case, but if the truth was known he wished it would all go away; he knew he was in a bad place, he was being blackmailed, not once but twice. He felt nausea deep in his stomach as he had done earlier; he could hear Jennet saying something as he was writing things down in his black book, but he wasn't listening, it was a drone in his head. He felt a fool when he thought of his admittance to that prick Eddie about what he had done; he had been caught out on the lie about his seeing the accident but now he realised he could have got around it with another lie. After all was said and done he was a good liar and always had been, he could have said that he was joking and had stopped for a coffee or better still admitted to a secret affair that he was having with another woman in the city, any lie or excuse, but to admit that he had done the killing even if it had been in self-defence was beyond a joke. He had to rethink and sort it out; he wasn't going to spend his savings on a run-down club for an idiot like Eddie Bail, there was no way. That money was for his new house with Charlotte.

'Sarge, sarge, you OK?' He heard Jennet say, and was jolted out of his deep thoughts.

'Yeah I'm tired, it's been a hard day you know, I've not eaten since breakfast, I'm starved, I'm off home before I lose more weight, I was supposed to go to see my fiancée and her mother; she will think I have left her, that's the trouble with policing, you get caught up in the cases you're on and if you're not careful it takes over your life, and in no time at all the years go by, and you find yourself alone, or in an old folks' home rotting away. You know Derek I'm seriously thinking of getting out, you know, resigning; I'm sure there's other things in life to do than sit in cars trying to solve crimes that are at times unsolvable. Yeah, I've about had it.'

'Oh come on, sarge, don't go before this one is over, this case needs your expertise, and I need you to find my brother's killer. We need to find the bastard and fast, there's a killer out there somewhere, and you know I have this feeling; I believe we are close to the capture of the culprit, that Waybee knows more than he's saying, call it a copper intuition or whatever you want but he knows more than he's saying, and I am going to keep a copper's eye on him. He knows the gangsters in this city and I'm after his knowledge, I won't let up until I've avenged my brother's killer.'

'Yeah, I understand your feelings, if I had a brother who had been killed, I'd feel the same; anyhow we'll carry on tomorrow, if you can go to every karate club in the city, see what you can find out, and report back in a couple of days. In the meantime, I've got things to sort out, OK?' Rainbow opened the car door and got in his car, waved and set off towards Charlotte's mother's house.

On his way he popped into the station on the pretence of getting a report. Barns and Harris had already gone home after getting nowhere with their inquiries, Smith and James were 'still out there somewhere' as the desk sergeant had put it. Rainbow was informed the detectives Willis and Weston were in the canteen, and had been for the last hour, drinking coffee and trying to piece together the bits of information they had found out.

Rainbow got a coffee from the machine, which was temperamental. It gave him two extra sugar portions, and one extra milk; he sat down at the table and said, 'so what do you know, have you solved the case? I hope so, and then we can all go home.'

'We have a description, sarge, a man, a bulky man, not very good-looking, in his forties, not well dressed, jeans with trainers, bad temper, not a nice kind.'

'Very well done, lads, you found the killer's profile, now we can make up a photo fit; all the other detectives on this case were not needed, it seems.'

'No, not the killer, sarge, the bloke who hit Mr Wiley, and broke his nose this morning on the pier, he pointed out five different people on our way to the hospital, some nutcase he was. Apart from that there's very little to report. Oh yes, there was just one thing we found out, one of the local crooks left town on the night of the Baker Alley killing, just after eight, went up to London on the eight-thirty bus, yes that's right.'

He flicked through his notebook. 'To tell you the truth, sarge, the underworld are keeping stum over this one; no one wanted to know, something big is coming down, it's in the air, you can feel it.' The detective looked at his colleague for corroboration, but there was none forthcoming, so he put his book back into his coat pocket.

'Carry on with any snippets of info you get, but go and see if there's anything else on the warehouse robbery that happened last month; see the janitor again, and also that guy who was sacked from the company, we didn't get around to interviewing him, he was away on holiday if you remember, his name was Johns, or something like it, Toms maybe; right I'm off to see my future wife.'

The three detectives left the police station to go their various ways. The night had finally arrived, and as he drove to see his woman, he realised it had certainly been a long and different day. But he had got through it, although at times it had been hard. The time he saw £10,000 of his savings sail away around the bend in the river was horrendous but admitting to Eddie what he had done was the worst.

After an hour on the road he finally pulled into the drive and as he got out of his car, Charlotte came running out of the house, and flung her arms around him kissing his neck; he glanced at his watch, it said 9.02, and then they went indoors.

NINE
THURSDAY

Tony Waybee was once again up early. He had had a few drinks the night before and he had formed a new plan in his head that he meant to implement as soon as it was possible. He dressed in mostly unwashed clothes, and had a quick wash in cold water.

Today he would go and pay his long disputed electricity bill, now he could afford the one hundred and eighty two pounds, thanks to the copper he loathed. He left his dwelling at eight and went to the café he used; he ordered a full English breakfast that consisted of eggs and bacon, beans, black pudding, fried bread, bread and butter and a mug of tea, and devoured the lot, talking to nobody. He sat at a corner table near the counter that was used mainly by the staff, but they allowed him to use it because he had been a good customer since his electricity had been shut off. He left without paying because he had an agreement with the owner that there would be no trouble in the café, and nobody would try to get the so-called protection money that had been tried on from time to time, from out-of-town gangsters. He had made it quite clear that he would deal with anyone who tried it on. He was the café's minder. He hurried through the side streets toward the children's home and entered the big front door.

A familiar-looking woman was sitting behind a desk, and she was on the telephone. She must have been talking to one of her family because when she saw him enter and approach her desk she said, 'See you tonight, darling.' She replaced the receiver, and looked up to hear his requirement.

'Good morning, nice day, but the weather is in for a change so I understand,' he said, trying to be as nice as he could be. He knew that ordinary people responded better if you were nice, as opposed to villains who only responded to the power of violence. 'I need your help please,' he continued, 'I brought a boy back yesterday who had absconded, I made sure he came to no harm, it's a dangerous world out there,' he waved his hand towards the exit. 'One of your staff told me that it would be OK to take the boy out for a few hours, you know, to the park, feed the ducks maybe, get an ice cream. It's hard on young children who have no parents to show them the way in this wide world, they need someone to guide them on the road to wisdom. I didn't have any parents, so I know what it is all about. The boy's name is Ben, he's a lovely little chap, about this high,' he indicated with a flat hand, 'four foot maybe.'

'Have you got an appointment, Mr…? She said. Her eyes were piercing.

'No I didn't think I needed one, the person I saw yesterday said she would get the clearance for me to take the little boy out, that's why I'm here now.'

'Everyone who comes through that door,' she pointed her finger, straight and thin, at the main entrance, 'needs an appointment.' She swung her chair around and walked to some filing cabinets and sifted through some files.

Tony waited for her to return, but she carried on looking at papers and files taking them out, and then putting them back again. Tony waited patiently. Ten minutes passed by. He wondered how he knew her, she looked liked someone he had known, but couldn't put a name to.

'Excuse me, but how long will you be? I have another pressing engagement to attend to this morning.' he said in a controlled way, but his temper was awakening, it had one eye open. *If this was a man he would be decked by now*, he thought.

'Oh, you're still here? I thought we were done, I've told you, you need an appointment, without one you're not seeing anyone, so good morning.' She seemed to slam shut the filing drawer; the sound echoed through the reception.

At that moment a door opened from an adjacent room and the person he had spoken to the day before entered. 'What was that bang, Mavis, it sounded like thunder; I hope we're not going to have a storm, I'm preparing to take the children to the park this morning. So we don't need bad weather, or the children will be so disappointed.'

'No,' Mavis said, 'it was that faulty filing cabinet drawer again, it needs replacing, I've put in a request, but when it will be replaced, heavens know,' she sighed.

Waybee noticed that the woman was the very same one who had taken charge of the boy the day before; she turned to face him and recognised him straight away. She smiled.

'Hello again, fancy meeting you so soon, I've put your application in the in-tray, but I was hoping you would pop in, because I need a little more information about you. I have, forgive me, forgotten your name for a start, will you come to my office and I'll take down a few particulars?' She indicated her office as she looked through the window. 'Nice day to take the kids to the park,' she said to Mavis.

'He hasn't got an appointment, that man hasn't got an appointment,' Mavis blurted out.

'Mavis, he doesn't need one, he is a friend of this children's home, its fine, don't worry, I'll take full responsibility, this way,' she said to Tony, and they went through a door that led to her office. Tony gave Mavis a smile denoting that he had won the day; she sniffed and sat down, ready to give someone else a hard time. Then it dawned on him the woman receptionist was Mavis Sims, the sister of Ted Sims who he had slashed and fought on many occasions; luckily it didn't seem that she had recognised him. He hadn't seen her for years; after all, he had been in prison for long periods. He would avoid her in future; he believed she still held a grudge. At one time years ago Mavis and his wife Ruby who was now living in Spain were good friends. He was led upstairs along dingy corridors to the back of the home to a small untidy and also dingy room that was an office. The woman told him to sit opposite her as she fumbled in a drawer for the appropriate forms.

Tony was reluctant to give his details as he knew that the police would never allow a crook with his form to take children out, and although he had no sexual inclination toward children in any way whatsoever, permission would not be granted. He had beaten up many child abusers in prison in the past, and paid the price for his love for little kids. He decided to give false information; when she told him the application would take several months to come through, she explained that the police were slow but thorough with applications of this kind. In several months' time he expected to be on a golden sandy beach on some foreign shore under a palm tree drinking Bacardi, and his arms wrapped around a beautiful young blond; these thoughts made him happy for a moment as he gave false information to her questions. No, he had never been in prison. No, he had never been in trouble with the law. Yes, he was married, and had a good job as a foreman for a firm making furniture in a warehouse. The only true thing he imparted was his first name, Anthony. He gave a false surname: Brinks. She looked up and smiled, then took the application form and placed it in an out-tray. 'That's it, Mr Tony Brinks, that should do the trick,' she said with a smile. 'I'm sorry it takes so long but all good things are worth waiting for, don't you agree?' She smiled again.

'Certainly do, but I'm very patient, I realise I can't take the boy out on my own but with your kind permission, I would like to join you on your trip to the park; you see, I promised him I would be with him when he flies his model helicopter, and I hate to let people down, especially kids. I like to keep my promises; they have been let down too much in life already.' He was hoping that he was being emotive enough to sway her if she was in any doubt. She smiled once again and said, 'I have no objections to you joining me and the children in the park, I'll go and get them. I have already told them to get ready; they are very excited. Will you wait for us outside, and don't say anything to Mavis on the way out. She's not too happy, someone slashed her wayward brother the other day across the face with a Stanley knife while he was having a drink.'

'I'm sorry for her, there's a lot of nasty people out there in the world, I won't say a word,' he said. He just glanced at her as he passed her desk; she was on the telephone once again, and saw him pass, but didn't look up.

He left the building and waited at the gates, he didn't have to wait long before he heard the excited chatter of kids coming from behind the back of the home, a column of twenty children in twos snaked out with a carer in front and one bringing up the rear.

Benny's face broke into a smile when he recognised Tony, his friend, and in his young mind, a father figure. He broke ranks and ran up to hug this slightly embarrassed man.

'Benny, my boy, you OK? You look smart in that shirt, let me carry that bag; is that your helicopter?' The boy handed over the bag, and felt proud as he took the hand of his new dad, the Carers looked pleased as well, the whole assembly made their way to the park. The park was just a short way from the Children's home and in fifteen minutes the children were getting together in little groups to play well-played games of old.

Tony and little Benny sat under a tree in the shade and slightly out of hearing range.

'Let's see this helicopter then, I want to see you fly it.' The boy sat down and took the helicopter out of the bag; he made a few adjustments, then got the control console out and switched it on. Placing the control on his lap he turned on the power, and fixed on the joystick.

'Watch this,' the boy said with enthusiasm in his voice.

The helicopter rose slowly but surely and lifted into the air with a whirling sound; at fifty feet it flew across the park with swoops down over the children playing.

'Bring it back here, right here,' Tony jumped up from his sitting position; he pointed to the ground right in front of the boy.

'That's easy,' the boy bragged as he brought the joystick back; the helicopter swooped down, and landed precisely where he had indicated, right on the spot.

'Well done, you are a very good pilot, you're an expert, and I can see that.'

'I'm a marvel; I'm a bloody marvel,' the boy laughed.

'Language, watch your language don't let the teachers hear you say words like that.' Waybee admonished.

The boy looked up from his console, and said, 'Sorry, Dad, but that's what the teachers said, I was a blinking marvel, see I said blinking, is that OK, Dad?'

The boy's blue eyes sparkled in the sunlight that caught his face, he was a lovely little boy, and Tony was warming to him like a father would. 'Yes that's OK, blinking is fine. Now can your helicopter carry a load like a small book maybe? Hold on there I'll show you what I mean.' He walked a short distance to where a carer was lying on the grass reading a book. 'Sorry to bother you but can I have a loan of that spare book you have there?'

'Is he getting on your nerves? He tends to you know, he's always on about getting a new mum and dad, he drives the staff mad sometimes, but funnily enough he didn't mention anything about a new dad yesterday; first time for ages; maybe he thinks you will be his new father?' She smiled and handed over the book she had next to her on the grass.

'Yeah he started to call me Dad and we only met yesterday down on the river; didn't I tell you he wanted to have a go on my model boat? But I didn't have time; that's when I brought him back. No, he's certainly not getting on my nerves, in fact the opposite, he's very likable, and the book is a little experiment, we both want to see if the copter can lift a load, that's all. It's just an experiment, and a bit of fun, we're both having a great time.'

'Well you have another half an hour before we have to go back to the home for the children's lunch so make the most of it. It could be months before you see the boy again; I've told you how slow the authorities can be.' She returned to her book. He noted the sternness in her voice and as he walked back to the boy he noted the bun in her hair, and guessed she must be a spinster; she had that air of assertiveness about her. The boy had just launched his toy once again skywards as he sat down.

'Bring her in, Captain; I want to see if she can carry a load.' He showed the boy the book, and as he was bringing the aircraft down to land, got a piece of paper out of his pocket and wrote a few words on it. He laughed to himself as he attached the book to the undercarriage with an elastic band he had in his pocket.

'OK, Mr Marvel, let's see if you were right, see how good you really are. I want you to deliver that book,' he pointed, 'to that lady lying on the grass over there; deliver that book to her, Mr Marvel.' He laughed out loud.

'Easy-peasy, just watch this,' the boy was full of enthusiasm, his little body rocked from side to side with happiness; it was great to have a dad to play with. What he had missed in life was now here by his side, and he wanted to hold on to it for ever. His concentration was intense as he pulled the joystick back; the helicopter rose into the air with hardly any effort as it flew across the sky in the opposite direction of the carer. The boy made the craft swoop and turn, fly high then drop towards earth as though it might end up crumpled in a crash. Then the boy turned to Tony and with a smile on his face said, 'Going in to engage target, Roger and out.'

The helicopter came out of a dive and straightened up, hovered over the lady, and slowly descended to just three feet from her. The boy looked towards Tony for the praise he knew was due to him; he felt he had performed well.

'Well done, Captain Marvel, now bring her home.' They looked towards where the carer was and saw her gently take the book off the craft and read the brief note, it said:

> THANK YOU FOR THE LOAN OF THE BOOK, HEREBY RETURNED BY FIRST CLASS POST, BY AIR. Tony, Ben.

She lifted the book in one hand and waved it in the air.

'Mission completed, bringing her home,' the boy giggled as he brought the aircraft back, but not before one last loop the loop. It landed gently and he cut the motor down, and then looked up, 'What do you reckon on that then, Dad?'

'That was great; you certainly have the skilfulness I was looking for. Now Benny I have a mission for you tomorrow morning, well both of us really, it's an important and dangerous mission, but it means you running away from the home in the morning, can you do it? I'm not allowed to see you again for weeks or months, until I get proper papers and the authority from the people in higher office. They are very slow in these matters, and what I've got in mind needs your help and it must be done tomorrow, no later than ten o'clock sharp.'

The boy sat wide-eyed as he tried to understand the important part he had to play. 'I want you to meet me at the trees over there at ten o'clock dead on,' he pointed to some undergrowth of bushes and plants on the edge of the park with an entrance and exit to the streets beyond. 'No later, or the mission will be lost and the enemy will be the winner, this I can say is top secret no one, and I mean no one, can be told of it. Do you understand Captain, am I making myself clear?'

'Yes sir, you are as clear as crystal,' although he wasn't quite sure what crystal was, it was a saying he had heard some teacher say once. 'Do I have to bring my helicopter?'

'Yeah, the copter is an essential part of the mission, so make sure you oil the propellers tonight, and make sure the battery in the console is fully charged up.'

'They are called blades, not propellers, silly,' the boy pointed out knowingly.

The carer who had been reading the book was talking to the other carer and her voice broke the ring-a-ring o' rose's game the children were now playing.

'Right children time to go have some lunch, get together in twos now. Benny come along,' she ordered. The children obeyed and got in columns like a well-trained army platoon would.

The boy put his aircraft in the bag, hugged his new dad and said, 'I'll be here at ten sharp, top secret,' he pulled his fingers across his mouth as though zipping it, smiled and said, 'Thanks for a nice time this morning, Dad, see you tomorrow, I love you, you will always be my dad now.' Tony turned away, tears welling in the corner of his eyes. He thought it strange how a little boy could bring these feeling in him that he had never experienced before; he had never had any children of his own, she had never wanted any, Ruby had been too busy enjoying life, and even if they got back together again, she was too old now. But for a moment he felt that he may have missed out on some wonderful experiences in his life.

They all left the park, after he had posed alongside the carers and the children as Miss Butters took some photos with her new camera. He gave Ben a wink as they parted company, he looked back as he walked away and Ben was looking back as well until they turned a corner. He hurried home to finish off his demand letter.

*

Charlotte had let him sleep in; after dinner the previous evening, they had sat on the veranda, and he had told her of his thoughts of quitting the force because of the pressure he had found himself in just recently; maybe he should try something else but he hadn't come up with anything tangible. He had exhausted himself with over an hour of sex, every position he knew, with a passion that came from nowhere, as though he would never have it again. She felt sore between her legs as she thought of the fun it had been, but then she wondered why he had resorted to vulgar expletives, like, 'Take the prick up your fanny,' 'Let's fuck like rabbits,' and 'I want to come on your face, and in your mouth,' things he had never said before, she somehow didn't object at the time, as she also had blurted out at one time, 'Fuck me hard,' just before she came for the third time, but she found it strange that he had been like that. She had certainly enjoyed it, and at one time became concerned when her moans of sheer ecstasy had become louder and louder as her mother had very good hearing. It was one o'clock when he came down the big winding staircase to face another day that he was beginning to dread.

'Sleep well, my love?' she asked as she made the pot of tea. 'Want some lunch?'

'No,' he replied, 'I've got to show my face at the station, see what's gone down, I should have been there this morning but if anyone asks, I'll say I've been on some enquiries, they don't normally want to know what I'm up to.'

'What case are you on now?' she enquired as she passed him a cup of tea.

'The Baker Alley murder case,' he muttered, 'they wanted me on it.'

'So all that activity on Monday night was a murder? And just before you got home? You were lucky, it could have been you; now I think of it, you pass that way often on the way back from your club, you missed it by minutes—'

'Not on Monday I didn't, I took the long way around the high street, anyhow I don't come home that way, and if I have in the past it's been very rare.'

'Alright darling you don't have to defend yourself to me, I just thought you may have gone that way that's all, I don't like to think that you could get hurt when it's so close to home.'

'I'm not defending myself, and being in the police force there's always a chance that I might get hurt, so don't worry about it.' He realised that he was getting angry so decided to get ready and make the effort to go into work, but if the truth was known, he would have preferred to go back to bed.

He drove at a steady pace. He was in no way in a hurry to get to the station. The desk sergeant looked up as Rainbow walked in the front door.

'The chief wants to see you Ray, he was in a bad mood, he said that you must go right up, but that was at nine this morning, he may have calmed down a bit by now, after all he's had lunch and as we all know he's always better in the afternoon after he's had his lunch.' The telephone rang and it was the inspector.

'Yes sir, he's just come in now, yes sir, I'll send him up straight away.' The sergeant pulled a face, and indicated with his finger pointed upstairs. 'Still in a bad mood it seems, tread carefully, Ray.' Rainbow nodded and then climbed the stairs and gave the door a light knock.

'Come in,' said the gruff voice; the inspector looked flushed in the face. 'Oh Rainbow, it's you, I thought you had left the force, thought you had retired,' He could hear the sarcasm in his voice but he didn't care, as he meant it. 'Where the hell have you been? Sit down; I have a few questions to ask you, what the hell are you up to?'

'Sorry sir, I don't know what you are referring to,' he stumbled as he spoke.

'Don't know what I'm referring to? Now come off it, sergeant, you know perfectly well what I mean; first off, I set up teams, now teams work together, not on their own as your ex-partner is doing, I say 'ex' because as I can see, you haven't done any work together since the meeting the other day.'

'Sorry to disagree with you sir, but we did go to see a Mr A Waybee, and interview him for maybe an hour,' he lied. 'Then we spent a further hour discussing the case in Detective Jennet's car.' He lied about the length of time again.

The inspector was getting red in the face; he picked up some papers and waved them in the air. 'I see here that you sent Willis and Weston to investigate a case that had been solved, the Bridgetown warehouse robbery. Don't tell me you have forgotten that the janitor was in on the robbery, and is now serving time and Johns, the man who went on holiday, died while surfing. That case is closed. Yet you send them on a wild goose chase; why?' He looked at Rainbow waiting for an answer.

'Sir, there's a perfectly sound explanation to your question, I didn't send them to the warehouse to enquire about the warehouse case, of course I know it has been wound up, I simply told them to go around the warehouse at Bridgetown and see, and maybe talk to, the villains who frequent that area.' Once again he lied through his teeth.

'And what about Barns and his partner, and Smith and James, what have they found out? They have told me that they haven't seen you since the meeting, and I was told that you were seen down by the river where people sail their model boats, now please don't tell me you were sailing boats on the river, when you're supposed to be investigating a murder that happened right on your doorstep almost; you live just off Baker Alley don't you, Sergeant Rainbow?' Spittle was flying out of his mouth like a garden hose with a break in it.

'No sir I wasn't sailing boats, I was following tips and talking to people who knew the deceased, Robert Jennet, who was known as Tommy in this vicinity and undercover.'

'There you go again, sergeant, you are just reiterating what I already know, I want you to work with the team I put together, and solve this case as fast as possible; my boss is on my back, and he wants answers, so pull yourself together, and get me some results, or I'm afraid I will have to pull you off this case and give it to someone else. You know this is not good for your promotion prospects, so get to it, you have until next Monday, five days including today.'

Rainbow went to speak but the inspector stopped him in his tracks. 'I don't want to hear any more excuses, get your team together and start again, get some results, that's all.' He ended abruptly.

'I'll do my best sir,' he said as he left the room. The inspector didn't reply.

Rainbow went to the canteen; he needed a strong coffee. The desk sergeant was sitting at a table, so he joined him.

'You were right, he was in a foul mood, he gave me a right rollicking; maybe his wife said no last night, he's real mad, even accusing me of playing with model boats, and fucking about on the river; as though I would.' Both cops smiled at the thought.

'I warned you,' the desk sergeant ventured, 'he even had a go at me for drinking a cup of tea behind the front desk, there's a canteen downstairs, he said, then that was when he told me to send you up as soon as you came in. I hope he stays in his office while I'm on duty.' He sipped his coffee, then put more sugar in the brew, and stirred it, then tasted it again. 'That's better,' he said, looking in the direction of his colleague.

'Have any of the lads been in yet? I have to have a talk to them, they have been talking behind my back, the inspector even knows where I sent them and what I told them to do; maybe he should run it, he warned me that he would take me off the case if I don't get anywhere before Monday. Maybe I should have admitted that I did it, after all he pointed out it happened on my patch right next door to where I live.'

'Did you do it, Ray? It's possible you know, you go home that way you could have hit the assailant as an impulse, because everyone in the station knows that you are an expert at karate, and there's your injured hand; you said you did it at the club, but did you?' The desk sergeant shrugged and smiled.

Rainbow laughed out loud after he had a fit of choking and said, 'Well I'll be fucked I've been doing all this work, and you have solved the crime just sitting here drinking coffee. I had better go and see the inspector again and tell him what you have just done, you're a fucking genius. I'm off the case as from now, but I was with my fiancée at the time of the killing. And Eddie was there when I injured my hand in the club so I'm afraid your theory falls down; come to think of it you would never make a good detective, better stay behind the front desk.'

'Hold on, Ray, I was only joking, don't be so defensive; I never wanted to be a detective, I've always been happy on the beat then when I was promoted the desk job suited me fine, so I didn't deserve that nasty comment, I will accept an apology.'

'I apologise, I was only joking as well, you would make a good gumshoe, as they say in America, or a detective as we are known over here.'

'So did you do it then, was I right, or what?

'Of course I did, but don't tell anyone will you? After all, we're friends aren't we?' they both laughed.

The door of the canteen opened and the inspector walked to the counter, he turned and said, 'You're still here, Sergeant Rainbow? I was on the understanding that this is a busy time. Shouldn't we be in the field?'

'Yes sir just on my way.' With a wink he left his colleague who had a smile on his face.

On arriving at the apartment block he stopped for a moment to watch the gardener planting some seeds, then entered the foyer. He saw the letter immediately and seeing the cut-out letters on the envelope, he knew it was another demand. He went back outside and spoke to the gardener but the man had just started the job a few minutes before he came home and had seen no one come into the block; he said he was sorry he couldn't help.

Ray went up the steps cursing under his breath before even opening the letter. On entering his apartment he went directly to the desk and with a letter opener opened the letter; he laid it on the table, and read the contents.

GO TO KINGs Park tomorrow FRidAy AT 10 0'Clock in the Morning with £10 000 We made A Mistake LaSt time should HaVe been £20 000 this is the LasT time We will want any money from you Be sharp and Sit under the tree IN the centre of the park and wait for fUther instrUCtions If You don't turn up Or Play anY tricks yor boSs will find Out What you did Remember I saw you. Wrap monNY in Brown bag celotape

The letter was badly composed and crumpled.

'Fucken' hell,' he muttered. He went to the bank straight away to get out another £10,000, leaving £30,400 left in his account. He went to Kings Park to find the tree that he had been instructed to sit under the next day; he sat and surveyed the area. The day was ebbing away, as he made his way back to a lonely apartment.

TEN
FRIDAY

The morning broke with heavy showers at first, and then as the rain drifted away the wind took over, and bent the newly planted flowers in the garden outside the apartment. With a heavy heart Rainbow left to make the appointment. The money, in crisp twenty-pound notes, was still in the cellophane wrapping; £10,000 of hard-earned money was slipped into a brown paper bag then Sellotaped up. The house deposit was now gone; how would he explain the money loss to Charlotte? He had no idea at all. With collar up against the wind, he walked toward the park. He had written another letter to the blackmailer pleading almost for a meeting to discuss the situation further, but it was a fruitless proposition and he knew the blackmailers were not going to expose themselves, but this state of affairs had to have an end soon as he would run out of money, and with the money Eddie wanted for the club he could say goodbye to the house that he and Charlotte wanted. Something had to break and soon.

Tony Waybee was also on his way to the park, head down, collar of his overcoat high. He was in no mood to see the same tossers that he had met in the café two days before. He missed his breakfast because he was too excited, and his appetite had taken a holiday.

He walked at a steady pace adjacent to the park; the wind was gusting, and he wondered if a toy helicopter could fly in this weather. He saw the boy turn the corner, he was running and as he approached he could see that the little boy was distressed.

The gateway to the park was just ahead of them as they approached one another.

'In there,' Tony shouted, 'in that gate.' It was an order just like the army. The boy disappeared through the gate and was standing near some bushes as Tony entered the park.

'They're after me,' the boy spouted out, 'they saw me climbing over the wall, Mr Jenkins and Miss Butters shouted at me to come back, they shouted that they would get the police on to me,' he volunteered; he had been crying.

'Calm down, a pilot has to be composed, be professional not crying like a baby, now stand to attention and say, "Reporting for duty sir".' The boy wiped the tears from his face, stamped his feet together as he had seen the soldiers do and stood to attention; he gave a salute.

'Reporting for duty, Dad, sorry,' he corrected himself, 'sir.'

Tony saluted back, and then he noticed that the boy didn't have his bag with him.

'Where's your helicopter? Where's your bag?' Desperation was making an entrance in his head. 'Don't tell me you forgot your helicopter, you silly boy.'

'I dropped it as I was running from them just around the corner up there.' He pointed.

'I don't believe this,' Waybee muttered under his breath. 'Look, you stay here behind that bush, and don't move before I tell you to, do you understand me? Behind that bush, I'll go and see if I can find it.'

'I'm sorry, Dad, I'm not silly am I? Sorry to let you down.'

'No you're not silly, do as your told, be back soon.' He saw the boy squat behind the bush then he left the park and walked up the road to try to retrieve the main item to his plan.

At the other end of the park Rainbow was approaching the entrance. He glanced at his watch; it was fourteen minutes to ten o'clock, he was in plenty of time. He glanced up at the sky; the greyness promised nothing but further rain, his life seemed to have no future; his life seemed to be grey like the sky. The sunshine of life had been his for the taking, now there was nothing to look forward to. How he was going to get out of this mess, he had no idea, but the grey thoughts that were forming in his mind were turning black, and they made him feel very uneasy. He had never considered himself to be a killer but if he got his hands on the vermin who was doing this to him maybe extermination might be an answer to his problem. He continued to the rendezvous. He saw the solitary tree in the middle of the park, and walked across the wet grass.

Tony had walked around the corner and he saw the bag discarded on the side of the road up ahead. At that moment, as if from nowhere, he heard his voice being called out.

The carer he had met at the school was running from a side street, with a fat older man in tow. 'Mr Brinks,' she called out, 'Tony, fancy bumping into you this early in the morning, he's done it again, he's done it again,' she repeated.

For a moment Tony was taken aback at what she had called him; he had forgotten the false name he had given at the interview at the home.

'Done what? Who's done what? Please calm down, who are you talking about?'

'Benny has run away again, I hope you didn't put him up to this, last night he couldn't sleep, kept on about a secret mission he was going on, he wouldn't stop talking, kept the other children awake most of the night, have you seen the little blighter?'

'Miss Butters, I didn't put him up to anything of the kind, do you think I would jeopardise my chances of seeing the boy in the future by telling him to run away, why would I take the risk? There's not a chance. I haven't seen him, and I'm very busy, but I will put aside my business to help you look for him; now do you believe me?'

Mr Jenkins nodded his approval, and said, 'If you find him, Mr Brinks, will you bring him back to the home? I'm getting too old for this game; the little bugger is always on the run. I doubt if he will make it in this world, most probably become a robber or something like that or escape from prison, and be on the run again,' he laughed at the thought. Tony didn't find it that funny. He looked up the road to see a man stop near the bag with a dog; the dog sniffed, then cocked his leg and pissed over the contents that were just poking out; he saw the man kick the dog, then bent down to pick the bag up and look inside. Tony saw the look of satisfaction creep across his face.

'You two go that way,' he pointed to a side road that led away from the park area, 'and I'll search this way. If I find him I will bring him back to you, good luck.' They disappeared down the side street. Tony walked quickly to the spot where the man with the dog was; he was about to walk away with the bag.

'Excuse me, you've got my bag there, I dropped it earlier,' Waybee said.

'Prove it,' the man challenged, 'prove it,' he repeated.

'There's a helicopter and a console in that bag, so hand it over please.'

'No I won't, you can see what's in there from where you're standing,' the man said defiantly.

'Give me back my property now; I don't want to have to take it from you pal.'

'I'll set my dog on you so watch out; Brutus, bad man,' he commanded the dog. The dog growled showing his teeth, and strained at the lead.

Oh fuck, here we go again; can't anything go right for me? Flashed in Waybee's head.

Tony kicked the dog full in the face, and the dog howled in pain and cowered behind his master, Tony reached for the bag, and at the same time butted the man in the face, blood sprouting out of his nose onto the pavement,

'Glasgow kiss for you pal, wise up.' Tony turned around and hurried away leaving the man staggering across the road, with the dog straining at the lead.

'Benny,' he shouted as he passed the bush. The boy popped up like a jack-in-the-box as though he was playing a game of hide and seek a smile on his face.

'Is the mission on now, Dad? You've got the bag, I see. Sorry I lost it.'

Tony looked at his watch; it said two minutes to ten. 'Yeah it's on but we must be quick so keep up,' he told the boy as he made his way through the bushes and the trees to the edge of the park where the open space took over and the grass started.

He peered out from behind a stout tree, and looked over to the lone tree that he had sat under just the day before. There was a person standing there, too far to make identification. It was dead on ten o'clock; the time had come. He attached a note to the undercarriage with the rubber band and when he felt satisfied, stood back.

'Mission on, Captain, fly the copter to that tree over there where that man is standing, and land it in front of him, just like you did yesterday, and no loop-the-loops this time, mind you. This mission is very important and it's worth £10 for bags of sweets, so, Captain, to the controls and let's go into action.' The boy's excitement mounted as he fixed the helicopter for flight.

'This is wet, and it smells,' the boy said holding up the console.

'Wipe it with this handkerchief and let's get going,' Tony commanded.

'Yes sir,' the boy said as the copter took flight. It rose in the air then veered off to the left away from the target. 'Hard to control,' Benny remarked as he fought with the controls. 'It's the wind, it's too windy for flying today really, and I've never flown my helicopter in this kind of bad weather before.'

'Now you bloody well tell me, you said you were a good captain, an expert pilot, and a good pilot should be able to fly in any weather, so concentrate on the job.'

'I am, I am,' the boy pulled the joystick back, and the aircraft started in the direction of the tree, but the gusts of wind made the flight seem precarious.

'Land it near that tree over there, where that man is standing.' Tony's heart was pumping and sweat goblets were forming on his brow although there was a nip in the air. He felt like cheering as he saw the helicopter descend a few feet from the tree. The man stepped forward, and bent down to carry out the instructions that were written on an old piece of notepaper. And after a long minute he stepped back and went under the tree just as a shower of rain tumbled from the angry skies.

'Bring her home, Captain,' Tony ordered.

'Yes sir, airship on the way,' the boy shouted, showing enthusiasm. He pulled the stick back, and the craft rose slowly as though fighting to get airborne.

As the helicopter gained height it veered to the left again but this time the craft was losing control, the rain and wind was making it difficult, and the boy fought with the console. The craft flew high then seemed to hover for a minute, and then it shot over the spot where they were, carried by the wind, and came down in the trees with an almighty bang.

'Sorry, Dad, I couldn't control it, the lights on the console have all gone out, look.'

He held the panel up to show it, but Tony had disappeared into the bushes to try to retrieve the crashed helicopter.

'Look around,' Tony shouted in desperation to the boy, 'look around find the damned thing,'

They both ran around like headless chickens, looking up then down, searching.

The raindrops hit them in the face and the rain was beginning to seep through their clothing. Ten minutes passed by, and Tony was becoming desperate; there was nothing on the ground, no wreckage. The helicopter seemed to have disappeared like the aircrafts did in the Bermuda Triangle. He ran to the edge of the tree line, and looked over to the tree and tried to get the line of trajectory, the flight path; he pointed to the tree with his finger, and looking up he brought it toward the tree line in an arch-type movement, trying to determine where it had crashed. Twenty minutes had gone by. The boy stood by his side, looked up and burst out crying.

Tony looked down, the boy's wet hair straggled his face.

'Don't cry. It's not your fault that the mission failed, it's this bloody weather.'

'What was the mission? What was I supposed to do?' the boy spluttered.

'I just wanted to see you fly your copter that's all, and you proved you could, it was this bad weather that spoiled it.' Then he had a thought. It was that bloody dog pissing on the console that fucked it all up; he deserved that kick in the face.

'I'll get you a new helicopter as soon as we meet again; you had better get back to the home before they call the police, don't say that you saw me otherwise I will have to go to prison, and I won't be able to see you again, so let's keep it our little secret, OK Captain?' Tony glanced up and looked across the park towards the lone tree and saw the man coming towards them across the grass. The half-hour wait that had been stipulated on the note was over and the man was coming closer. 'Let's go, come on, run, let's get out of this park,' Waybee commanded. At the gate he bent down to kiss the little boy he knew he would never see again. 'Now you go straight back home, and don't mention me because I would certainly get into trouble, and they won't allow us to meet again, be a good boy now, and don't worry about the helicopter because I'll make sure you'll get a new one.' He hugged the child once more and watched him disappear down the road.

He hurried home to dry off, and to drown his sorrows at losing £10, 000; it was obvious that using toys to receive blackmail money had its pitfalls. With the boat sinking, and then the helicopter crashing Lady Luck had never been walking hand in hand with him, but at least he still had the first ten grand.

*

Rainbow walked across the wet grass where he had seen a boy and a man standing, but when he got to the tree line they were gone. He went into the undergrowth and looked around, and picked up a white piece of cloth; it was a handkerchief, he discovered, and it had the initials AW in one corner. He slipped the handkerchief into a little plastic bag that he always carried with him in case some evidence was picked up; he also found the console that had been disregarded in the frenzy to find the crashed aircraft. He slipped it into a plastic bag also. He had seen the helicopter fly into the trees, he had heard the bang, but followed the instructions to the letter to stay at the lone tree for thirty minutes. He left from the same exit as Tony had just a few minutes before. As he walked down the street towards the station the sun came out for a moment as though shooing the grey skies to one side.

The desk sergeant looked up and told Detective Sergeant Rainbow that his teams were in the meeting room, and he had heard that a press meeting was arranged for two o'clock.

Rainbow took his wet coat off, and hung it near a radiator on the back of a chair to dry. 'Now gentlemen what have you come up with, if anything? To tell you the truth, I'm finding this a difficult one. Let's start with you two, Detectives Barns and Harris, what have you found out? And make it as brief as you can, we need to have lunch before the two o'clock press call, so be brief, gentlemen.'

Barns spoke first, 'Well we have had the same luck as you, sarge, we've spoken to lots of the local villains in the city, and apparently the deceased was well liked, and was accepted in the underworld; it seems they didn't know of anyone who would want to kill him.'

The way Detective Barns emphasised the word 'kill' made Rainbow's inners shudder.

'And what about the karate clubs; what did you find out, Smith?'

'We didn't find out anything, sergeant, because you didn't say we should go to any clubs. I and Mr James here have mostly been with forensics.'

Detective Jennet spoke up, 'It was me you told to see what I could find out from the clubs, and I did, I visited five altogether but no one could help, most said what you told me, sarge, that they can't see a karate person doing this kind of killing. All the people I interviewed had alibis for that time on Monday evening, the time of the murder.'

That word, it was beginning to bother him again; guilty feelings came flooding in like a neap tide. The clock on the wall ticked on and it was twelve noon.

Willis looked at some papers, then said that one name stood out more than others from the associates that Detective Jennet had in the underworld; this man's name had been mentioned time after time. The man's name was Anthony Waybee, and they were going to interview him next, maybe later on in the day after the press conference.

Rainbow listened intently; there was something on his mind, something was tormenting him, but he couldn't put his finger on it. Then, like a premonition, or a copper hunch, he remembered seeing those initials AW and he verified it by going over to his coat, and retrieving the plastic bag with the handkerchief in it.

'Thanks for your input, keep trying, I'm sure something will break soon, I'll sort out Tony Waybee; come to think of it, I remember putting that bastard away in the past, in fact we interviewed him just a few nights ago, remember Derek? He wouldn't let us in because we didn't have a warrant; well, we are going to get one, and today we're going to pay him another visit. Have your lunch now and I'll see you at the press conference at two.' All the detectives stood up and went to get their lunches.

Jennet sidled up to his boss and said, 'He's going home today, the coroner has released the body for cremation, so my brother will be going home to Wigan and I've been given permission to go with him on his last journey. Sorry, sarge, so I won't be coming with you to see that crook Waybee, but I should be back after the funeral.'

'Don't worry, do what you must, and please represent me at the funeral. See you when you get back; we might have made a breakthrough by then, with a bit of luck, and give your family my condolences.

'Will do, sergeant, and thank you.'

The press wanted to know what the name of the deceased was, but the chief inspector said that they were trying to trace the next of kin but there was some difficulty in that area; enquiries were in progress, and someone soon would be apprehended. A good team of the finest detectives were on the case. He could hardly tell the truth, that an undercover man was the deceased, because the information that had been received from Detective Robert Jennet had revealed that a big drug import was emerging very soon, and he didn't want the gang to get wind of any undercover man that had infiltrated into their organisation. It was very doubtful that his cover had been blown.

This was a random killing he was sure, because he knew that Robert had made a few enemies in the lower echelons, as he tried to prove himself to the top crooks and drug cartel. The next bulletin would be after the weekend on Monday. He said he was sorry that he had no more information at this time. He then closed the meeting. The inspector didn't speak to Rainbow, but a dirty look passed the space between them as the men left the room. Rainbow got the search warrant; it was just a formality, then he took the console and the handkerchief to forensics, and handed them in for fingerprints. He then left the station, saying goodbye to his partner Derek Jennet once again as he got ready to take his beloved brother on the long journey back home to Wigan.

*

The boy had arrived back at the home dripping wet to the carer's disapproval. After a forced bath he was captive in his room, and he sat on his bed crying.

He had been threatened that if he ran away again the application that his friend Tony had put in wouldn't be sent, and that he would never see him again. He was forced to admit that his helicopter had crashed in the park, and he had lost his control panel.

The boy vowed to get revenge on Miss Butters and Mr Jenkins when he was big. He wished he had flown his copter better, he had never had that trouble with it ever before. His time would come. He went to sleep, and at teatime the morning events were slowly drifting away; after all, he was going to get a new helicopter as soon as he saw his dad again, he had been promised, and he trusted his dad, because he loved him. What the boy didn't know was that the application was still in the office, in the out-tray.

*

It was late afternoon, and Tony had just woken up from his afternoon nap. He answered the door to the electricity men, and paid the money he owed on the promise that his electricity would be switched on the next day. He apologised for the aggro over the bill, but it wasn't meant, and the men left with one more dispute solved. He got ready to go out to celebrate, but was inwardly unhappy about the loss of £10,000 in the failed attempt in the park that morning.

He vowed to go back the next day for a more thorough search of the park. The loud knock on his door stopped his thoughts, and he peered through the window to see his enemy, the 'filth', as he called the police, standing on his doorstep. He cursed under his breath, and wondered if he should just pretend to be out. Maybe Rainbow had twigged on about the blackmailing; after all it was the second time in as many days that he had paid a visit.

Tony decided that he wasn't in the mood for talking, and hid behind the settee. The knocking got louder, and Rainbow shouted through the letter box, but Tony just sat it out until the quietness returned. After five minutes he peeked out into an empty street, and decided to go out the back window that led into a small yard, which had filled with rubbish over the years, since the back door had been blocked up. Eight stone steps took him up to the alley behind the house. He made his way to the café to have an evening meal, then after, a few drinks in his local pub.

Rainbow swore under his breath as he walked away from Waybee's house; he knew he was home, he had seen the curtain move from the corner of his eye, but he knew that it was only a matter of time before they met up again. The thought did cross his mind that if Waybee had always hung around with the deceased, as it had been established by the other detectives, then he may have been with him in the alley on that fateful night, maybe lurking in the shadows. Just because he himself hadn't seen anyone didn't mean to say that there was no one there. Maybe it was Waybee that was the blackmailer? And then there was the handkerchief he had found in the park; could it belong to… it was starting to fit together. *Waybee and his friend were looking for a drug fix in Baker Alley, they had been drinking maybe, and while Waybee took a piss behind the bins his so-called friend tried to prove himself once more. He had picked on the first passer-by, and that passer-by had been me.* That was it; it sounded feasible; now it had to be proved. He was relieved to see there were no more demanding letters in his letter box as he entered the block. His intentions were to have a shower and a change of clothes then he was off for a weekend of love that he had missed out on by having to work.

The parrot was quiet; although it was a relief not to hear the parrot squawking, he was a bit concerned because he had been unusually quiet in the last few days, and he hoped that the bird wasn't ill. He made a cup of tea and sat at the window to drink it, before the long drive to be with Charlotte.

He made sure the parrot's water tray was full and there was a good amount of food in the cage. 'Goodbye you bastard,' he said to the bird in his best parrot impersonation but the parrot just dropped his head, ignoring the food and the water. 'If you're not talking to me then fuck you,' Rainbow said as he left the room; the parrot remained silent. He drove through the city and when passing the high street he stopped at the red lights. He saw two thugs that he had put inside for a bank job a few years back; at first he was surprised to see them out of prison so soon, but time flies, he thought. They went into a bar that was renowned for the lowlife that frequented it. He took a left and parked the car in the car park at the rear of the pub. A couple were in a corner, just outside the back entrance, being very amorous; he had his hand up her skirt, she was moaning loudly.

'Take it elsewhere, not in public; there may be priests or monks around,' Rainbow said as he approached the back door.

'What's it to you mister, fuck off, mind your own business,' the rough-looking man blurted out with a sneer. He pulled his hand from under the woman's skirt and squared up, hands clenched.

'It's got fuck all to do with you, knob head,' the angry woman blurted out, 'we're old enough to do what we want, you fuckin' jealous? You don't look like a fuckin' monk to me so piss off, before I set Harry on you.' Rainbow placed his left hand on the man's right clenched fist, then in a flash, his right hand onto the elbow, and then with a thumb movement he dug it into a pressure point that sent the thug into spasms of acute pain. He squealed like an injured animal; the woman's anger disappeared like a magician's rabbit into a hat, and she looked on in disbelief as her boyfriend held on to his very painful arm.

'No I'm not a monk, but I'm a karate expert, first Dan, and I'm also a detective sergeant in this city's police force, so I'll tell you one last time, take your lovemaking some place else, and not in a public place; this is my authority.' He flashed his identity card. The attitude of the pair was amazing. He took hold of her arm, then apologised profusely, 'Sorry sir' the woman said as they both staggered out of the car park. He watched them leave, shook his head then entered the pub.

Rainbow had never been in this bar before; it was an old-fashioned pub with a longish counter with tall stools. The windows needed a wash, and the drapes were moth-eaten; he didn't think much of the décor as he approached the buxom barmaid with a deep cleavage, her sweater was so tight he imagined her breasts fighting to get out for a breath of air. Her hair was tied in a ponytail. She caught his eye and smiled.

'What can I get you, sir? She asked. She had a tooth missing, and a bruise that was just fading from her cheek; she picked up a pint glass before he could answer her.

'Just an orange juice, I'm on duty, there's no problem; I'm looking for two men who just walked in a few minutes ago, have you seen them?' He flashed his ID card.

'They're in the snug bar over there, I hope there's no trouble, I'm trying to make a go of this pub; it had a bad reputation, and since I've been here I've been getting rid of the bad people who used to drink here, see this,' she pointed to her bruise and her mouth. 'Got this in my effort to clean this place up, but I'm winning the fight,' she gave a toothy smile as she poured the juice; 'On the house,' she waved her hand, and went to serve another customer. He picked up his drink, took a sip, and went into the little snug bar. It was nicer in the snug, there were booth-type slide-in seats, with small light fittings above them; the small counter had just four stools. The two men were sitting in a booth drinking pints of beer, deep in conversation. Rainbow did a theatrical surprise jump back as he looked around the bar. The men also were surprised to see a copper in the bar; no cops had been in this public house ever before to socialise, they only came in to arrest people, so it was a surprise to see a policeman they both knew drinking in their domain. He walked over to the booth.

'Well what do you know, you never can tell when you're going to come across old comrades, acquaintances from old, long-lost friends, I thought you were still working for the government, you know, doing time, for our Queen and country, sorry lads but I'm surprised to see you out, it only seemed like yesterday…'

'Good conduct, that's what it's called, I did the crime, I've done the time, I'm clean now, so you've got nothing on me, or him,' he nodded his head towards his friend.

'Shove up; I just want a few words, it won't take long.' The man slid across the seat reluctantly, and Rainbow sat down. The three men knew one another well, it was Detective Constable Rainbow who had arrested them six years before for a robbery, and had got a conviction that sent them to jail for ten years apiece. Rainbow sipped his drink, the two men felt uneasy to be drinking with the fuzz; they hoped that their associates would be doing other things at this moment, and keep away from the pub. They certainly didn't want to be seen socialising with the police, some villains just wouldn't understand.

'I'll get to the point; you remember Tony Waybee? Well I'm having dealings with him at the moment, and I was wondering if you knew something he did in the past that I could get him on? Now don't get me wrong, I'm not for one moment asking you to grass on him, because I know the underworld's code of not grassing on your mates, but you must know that he's no mate of yours, he never did you any good, on the contrary, my friends, more harm.'

'What's he done now? I haven't seen him since I got out of the nick; I keep away from those people who I used to mix with years ago now I'm on the straight and narrow. I've even got a girlfriend, and a kid on the way, and a job on the bins is in the pipeline, so I don't know nothing.'

'What about you? What do you know?' Rainbow asked the other man who hadn't said a word at all; he had just looked around the bar disinterested, sipping his beer.

'No comment,' the man said.

'What do you mean, no comment, can't you understand the question?' he said mockingly.

'No comment,' the man replied without expression.

'You need to get a life, my friend; you can't go on in this world saying "No comment".'

'No comment,' the unfriendly man replied.

Rainbow shook his head and with a slight smile turned away to speak to the other man; he told how, although Waybee had committed no crime that he knew of, he was being awkward in not letting him into his house without a warrant, and had been disagreeable at other times. Now if he had something on him then he may have a bit of leverage when asking future questions. 'What do you reckon; can you help with anything?'

'Nope, can't help you there, ask Bootsy Harris,' the man said quietly with his hand over his mouth, 'they used to hang around together; him and Waybee, they used to be close years ago, they done a few jobs together, but I guess you already know that don't you?' Rainbow didn't answer, just nodded then drank up his drink and was about to leave when someone he recognised walked into the bar and came up to the booth.

'There you are, Billy,' the man said, 'I thought I'd see you in here, you got it, the boss told me that if I saw you around to tell you that the bin job is yours if you want to go in to see him on Monday morning at nine o'clock; it's a good job, you get lots of perks and the pay's not bad, OK you have to be up early to start early, but then you're used to being up throughout the night when you were a burglar, remember, or was it a cat burglar?' He burst out laughing, but when he saw the reaction on Billy's face he stopped abruptly like a car hitting a brick wall.

'Bloody hell Billy, it was just a joke, on the bins the lads have lots of banter it's not meant, it's just a joke.'

'You shouldn't say things like that, you never know whose listening, joke or no joke, and it's not funny.' He pointed his finger at the man. Then he pointed it at Rainbow.

'Let me introduce you to Detective Sergeant Rainbow of the city police.'

Surprise dawned on the bin man's face, like the sun in the morning, and then recognition dawned.

'It was a joke, I didn't mean it, it was just a bit of banter, that's all.'

'Don't worry about it,' said Rainbow, 'I didn't hear what you said anyhow, don't mind me, carry on with what you were saying to Billy boy here, I promise I won't repeat what you have to say to anyone; anyhow I'm off duty now, this is just a friendly get-together, ain't that right?' he directed the last question to Billy's friend. 'No comment,' was the reply. The bin man sat at the last vacant spot at the table without being invited.

'What do you want me to tell the boss? Are you interested or not? As I was saying, the pay is good and there's a lot of perks, you'll be surprised what people throw away, I've had loads of picture frames, loads of dirty mags,' he laughed again.

The man who had been saying 'No comment' whispered in his friend Billy's ear, then stood up to leave;

as he went to go Rainbow said goodnight, thanked him for his company and said that he hoped they would meet again. The man stopped and looking straight at the cop then said 'No comment' and went out of the bar.

'What a strange fellow he was; I didn't find him very talkative, is he OK in the head?' Rainbow said half laughing.

'He's perfectly OK in the head, got a degree in science, and a Bachelor of Arts degree while he was in the nick, but he has one beef and it's a big beef, he hates pigs, not my words you understand. He never talks to the filth, as he says, because of the injustice he was dealt out on the robbery case he got ten years for, something he never did, and I know that to be true because he was with me on the night of the robbery, and I didn't do it either.'

'Tell that to the judge, not me. It wasn't me that put him away, there were other officers on the case at the time, if I recall correctly. Anyhow, it seems he came out of it OK; now he's a learned man, most probably cleverer than me; anyhow, when you see him again wish him the best of luck from me, and if I can help him with anything then I would be happy to do so. Do you guys want a drink? I'm buying.' Somehow a feeling of guilt crept across Rainbow's mind as he got up to get the drinks.

'Not for me, I'm driving,' the bin man said, 'can't afford to lose my licence.'

Rainbow returned with a pint and another orange and sat down.

'You know, sometimes the law gets it wrong. It's like anything in life, human beings make mistakes, we do some things we regret, sometimes we rectify them immediately, and at other times what we have done is done, and cannot be altered, no matter how we wish it could be, but we have to live with it. Get on with life.' For a moment he felt like blurting out what he had done; he wanted to get it off his chest. He sighed.

Both men looked at one another then Billy spoke. 'Tell your boss I'll be in on Monday and thank him for the opportunity; as you say, the pay is good and now that I'm on the straight and narrow I need a good job with, as you've said, lots of perks.'

'Yeah, there is, I even get people chucking away gear like this tee shirt I'm wearing, look,' he lifted his shirt with the sort of pride a schoolboy would show when bragging to his friend about something he liked. 'Also these trousers, they fit like a glove,' he glanced down with pride.

Rainbow recognised the bin man at last; it was the very same man that he had given his bundle of clothes to on Tuesday morning, and had denied doing so in the alley, but it seemed the man hadn't recognised him; he thought it was time to leave. He glanced at his watch; he was surprised that he had been in the bar for almost an hour.

The bin man continued. 'You're not into boats are you, Billy? You know model boats.'

'Why do you ask?' Billy enquired.

'Well, it's because I got a three-foot one yesterday in the garbage, it's well built, sturdy. I don't really go in for models, but this one was too good for the tip, so I want to sell it; it's in the car now, I only want a fiver for it, it's even got a name on it, now what was it?' he frowned. 'I know, it had a little tag on the stern, yeah, I remember now, it was registered in London and the name was BETTY. Do you know that bully-boy Tony Waybee? It was in his garbage bin, wrapped up in loads of cut-out newspapers.' Rainbow was soon on the way to see Charlotte, with a model boat in the boot of his car.

ELEVEN

She was thrilled to see him, and had some good news to impart: the estate agent had been in contact, by telephone, and the vendors of the house they had fallen in love with on the outskirts of the city, a beautiful rural setting, would become available soon as the contracts could be exchanged, and the other bit of good news was that the bank had agreed to the loan as soon as the £50,000 was deposited. She insisted in celebrating the good news with a bottle of the finest champagne that had been bought for them by his parents, and there was the third surprise from Charlotte with the news that his parents would be visiting over the weekend for a celebratory meal. Apparently his father was on a week's holiday from his high-status job as a High Court judge, and had said to Charlotte that they would come down on their way to Cornwall for their week's holiday. 'After all,' he had said, 'it wasn't every day that his only son and future daughter-in-law bought a house.' He also said that he and his wife were looking forward to the wedding. Nausea welled up in Rainbow's stomach as he listened to her enthusing about the house, and the wonderful life they were about to embark on.

They sat on the veranda on comfortable wicker chairs and drank the champagne; he emptied his glass and quickly refilled it, his mind on overtime. He saw her lovely mouth, her lips moving so voluptuously, but her words were lost to him. He felt sorry for her, how could he tell her? How could he let her down? She had worked so hard for her dream. The night was balmy; the full moon sent a glow, a certain blush that made her radiance shine. Her smile, her white even teeth; she was the essence of beauty, and he was about to lose her. He had killed a man, would she have the forgiveness and love for him if she knew? He wrestled with these thoughts.

She went into the house to get another bottle of wine as he wiped away a tear. He was convinced he had one of his blackmailers, and he would get it out of Waybee who the other one was, but he still had to get something on him; a counter-blackmail maybe! Waybee, he was sure didn't have the brains to do it on his own.

And there was Eddie Bail to sort out; there was no way he would give any more of his money away. Murderous thoughts had just raised their ugly heads again.

Charlotte returned with the new bottle of wine and they replenished their glasses.

'Who were you talking to in there? I thought we were here alone,' he enquired.

'Oh, that was Michelle, she was upstairs on her computer, she came down for a drink, she's taking a bath now, and I'm going to follow her in half an hour's time.' They clinked their glasses. 'To the good life,' she said as she raised her glass.

'Yeah,' he replied.

Michelle was Charlotte's twenty-three year old sister. She, like her sister Charlotte, was very beautiful, and had a wayward character that was endearing. The woman was oozing with sex; she had long ago taken a fancy to 'darling Ray' as she called him, and she was always teasing him whenever she had a chance. Once, about a year back, he had been in the house alone and she had been larking around and trying to kiss him so he grabbed her playfully and jokingly fondled her ample breasts. She had stroked the outside of his trousers when she saw he was getting aroused, they rolled around on the carpet in front of a roaring fire, he put his hand up her dress pulled her knicker leg to one side, and fingered her off, but that had been a while back. They had kept their little secret until now, whenever they were in one another's company she'd give a knowing smile, as if saying, *I remember*. He was very fond of her.

He came back to reality as Charlotte told him he looked tired and weary and they should have an early night after they had eaten. In the meantime she was going to take a bath as soon as her sister came out of the bathroom. She left him on the veranda with a new drink, outstretched in the wicker chair; he flicked off his shoes, and sipped his drink. Five minutes passed, as he thought of the day's events: his being parted from another ten grand, the meeting at the station, and the revelation, the shock of finding out who his blackmailer was; he would deal with him after a good night's sleep. His mind somehow drifted back to Michelle and the day of the romp. He didn't see her standing just in the shadow of the doorway; she startled him, and he straightened up.

She was standing in a pink robe, her hair wrapped in a white towel with a belt that just held her robe together; her breasts were firm and they were mostly exposed. She took a few steps unto the veranda, and stood looking down at him.

'I see you are aroused again, darling Ray, it seems that you are pleased to see me.' She tossed her head with a laugh; the towel flew across the veranda to the floor. 'Seems like you have a bulge in your pants; he's trying to get to me; is it this he wants?' She opened her gown exposing her beautiful curved body; the hair between her legs seemed to glint under the moonlight.

'Michelle, your sister could come down any minute, pull yourself together please; I'm in enough trouble as it is,' he feebly protested.

'No she won't be down for at least half an hour, she has just got into the bath, so I have time to give you your celebration gift on getting your loan.' She smiled and knelt down in front of him; her hand went to his zipper and pulled it down. She undid his belt, it was so fast, he had little time to resist; it popped out and like a soldier, it stood erect, seven inches of throbbing gristle. She took it in her hand, and slowly pulled the foreskin back then she looked at him and smiled. 'Don't tell my sister, will you?' She put her mouth around the rim, and pushed it into her mouth; she moved her head up and down while he lay back and took deep breaths. He felt good. There's a saying, 'A stiff prick has no conscience,' and Ray at that moment was conscience-free. In and out it went; she looked up, her eyes wide, and then taking it out of her mouth said, 'You're a naughty policeman, aren't you?' She laughed then continued sucking him; her left hand went under her gown, and she fingered her moist warm intimate part till she shook with delight. He said he didn't want his spunk to go onto his trousers, she smiled once again and said, 'That's no problem,' as she held it in her mouth until he shot his semen, and she swallowed it. She wiped the end of his truncheon, as she affectionately called his member, with her gown, stood up and gave him a quick kiss on the mouth. 'Happy celebration,' she laughed, and ran back into the house.

He stood up, and wiped his mouth with the back of his hand, did his belt up, sat down again, took a sip of his drink and smiled to himself. His conscience came back suddenly, and paid a fleeting visit. Did he really deserve his Charlotte? He had been unfaithful on more than one occasion. She had been a virgin when they had met, he thought of the privileged life he had had, a good education, a good upbringing in a good home, with loving parents, and a good career in the police force. He looked up at the moon. A cloud that seemed to have lost its way tried to devour the moonbeams, and for a moment the light went out, casting blackness over the earth. He refilled his glass, and his mind drifted to his colleagues who he had sent on wild goose chases, getting nowhere on a case that could never be solved, because only he knew the truth. His hand had healed up, and he decided there and then, sitting on that veranda, to give up the sport he had loved; it was a dangerous game when the participants were unstable like he was. He heard chatter coming from inside the house and the two sisters came out with another bottle of champagne and three new stemmed glasses. Charlotte spoke first, 'Michelle wants to drink to our success on getting our loan and to give you a kiss, since she hasn't seen you for a while,'

'You wicked policeman, where have you been? You're not avoiding me are you? Soon I'll be your new sister-in-law,' Michelle said in a mocking way. 'I was thinking maybe you could do me a favour. Remember, I've done you a few favours in the past,' she hesitated then said, 'like the time I… gave you a lift back to your home when your car broke down, and Charlotte was too ill to take you, you do remember don't you?' His mind remembered all right; that was the night, just a few weeks before, they had had full-blown sex with foreplay in the car, which had lasted an hour or more.

He laughed and said, 'Yeah you'll make a good sister-in-law, what's the favour? I'm open to anything you want, and I'll do my very best,' he put on an Elvis-type voice, when he said 'I'll do my very best,' Elvis was Charlotte's favourite singer.

'Introduce me to one of your friends at the station, the tall dark one I saw you with last year, he was dishy, what was his name? Harry Weston if I'm not mistaken.'

'I'll do my very best,' he said again to more laughter. 'Now let's open that bottle, and I'm getting hungry it's about time we had something to eat.' He popped the cork, which shot up in the air. 'I don't pop my cork for just anyone,' he joked as he poured the champagne; he looked at his fiancée from the corner of his eye and felt sorry for her ignorance about her sister and his deceit; she was too good for him, he decided.

They drank to success then gathered the things scattered around, and went into the house. Charlotte prepared the evening meal, as they waited for her parents to join them after their day's outing. Michelle went up to her room to write a few emails.

*

At the same time in a plush house on the outskirts of the city, Big Joe Bananas sat behind a desk smoking a cheroot; his perfectly tailored suit fitted him well and made him feel like a million dollars, the only things that spoiled his appearance were his pocked face and disjointed nose. It was quite clear that his face had taken a battering in the past, and by the way he talked, he was in no good mood. There were things on his mind he wanted clearing up and soon; the big boys from out of town demanded it from him. Now his impatience was in full flow. The biggest drug deal he had ever encountered in his criminal life was imminent, it was worth millions of pounds to the syndicate, but there was only one thing stopping the deal going through, and that was a man called Tommy Crawly.

He had wanted to talk to him all week, but no one had seen him around. The last time he was seen was on Monday afternoon by Bootsy Harris, and he had been with Tony Waybee near the off-licence in the city. Bananas wanted to ask Tommy about his claim that he came from up north, and was in with a big gang up there; he had asked people who lived up there, but no one had ever heard of him. Big Joe had his suspicions. Tommy Crawly had also said that he was in on some big bank jobs and robberies, but once again, no one had heard of him, and some of the bank jobs that he was supposed to have done apparently never took place. Big Joe Bananas wanted answers, and he wanted them now; he had been trying to bring Tommy in for questioning all week, but so far nothing.

Big Joe had instructed some of his minor crooks to inform villains like Ted Sims and Tony Waybee to tell Tommy Crawly to come up to see the big man, but so far, fuck all. Big Joe had a feeling that not everything was above board; he even had a sneaking that Tommy was an underground agent that had slipped in to the organisation, and used that idiot Waybee to get in. Joe was fuming as he ranted and raved at the two sidekicks who sat with him in his office in his magnificent house that came from the profits of a life of crime.

'Scotch,' he ordered from the giant of a man he called the Butcher, because of his tendencies to cut people up with a knife he had bought at a boot sale, which had once belonged to a Ghurkha solider. The other sidekick was as big or bigger, and Joe called him Buster because he seemed to get pleasure in busting noses, and breaking legs. And although they weren't their real names they answered to them.

'Join me, gentlemen,' Joe said, more as an order than a request, as the Butcher poured the best whisky that money could buy into crystal glasses. Joe looked at the grandfather clock that ticked silently in the corner of the office. The pure white carpet was wall to wall, and the place had an air of opulence and luxury.

'Where the fuck are they? This is freaking me out, I can tell you. Butcher, get me an aspirin.'

'Not while you're drinking, surely, boss?' the big man suggested.

'Thanks for your concern, Butch, but you don't know what's going on in my head so get me a FUCKING PILL NOW,' he shouted. The bruiser got up and looking at his colleague made a face as if to say, 'Here we go again,' because they both had seen the boss's manic rages in the past, and accepted the situation, because the pay was good, and at times there was very little to do.

At that moment a big car pulled up in the driveway, and the three men went to the window. The driver put his thumb up to indicate that he had been successful in bringing in four youngish-looking men as he had been ordered to do.

The men got out of the car, and gingerly made their way to the front door.

'Go get them, and bring them in, and tell James to get the first aid kit, and leave it outside the door,' the boss instructed. 'Butcher, you stand by the door and push each one in here to show them we mean business.' Butcher stood, arms folded like bouncers do, and put on his mean face. Joe went to the console and put a classical record on the turntable, and turned the volume down to a quiet level; it made it seem as if calmness prevailed in the room, but it was just a prelude to the violence about to take place.

The men were shoved into the room one by one, and stood in a line, like soldiers on parade. The men looked at one another with trepidation; they had heard of Big Joe's reputation and felt some apprehension. Big Joe sat behind his desk as the door was shut, and the bruiser took up his position behind the men. Joe looked up and said nothing, he just stared at them; they said nothing, and so it went on and on. The men felt uncomfortable as the silence continued apart from the sound of the classical music coming to a crescendo. At last, after five long minutes that had seemed longer, the man at the end of the line spoke in a soft tone.

'You wanted to see us, Joe?'

'Say good evening, don't you fucking morons have any manners? You're supposed to say good evening when you meet people of my calibre, and you in the middle, take your filthy hands out of your pocket you asshole, where do you think you are?' Before the man obeyed, Bruiser thumped him in the back of his head making him turn around to protest, but before he could open his mouth another punch hit in the face; blood seeped out of his nose.

'Lets fucking start again,' Joe said, shaking his head and grimacing.

'Good evening, Joe' the men shouted out in unison.

'Now that's better, good evening to you as well, it's better to start on a good footing, that's what I was taught, so gentlemen let's get down to business. If I recall, and tell me if I'm wrong, I asked you in the nicest possible way to get someone I want to have words with to come here to see me, and I've been waiting patiently, may I add, and fucking waiting, and now my patience has run out, so I want you to tell me why you haven't done what I told you to do? Who is the spokesman in your motley gang? I want to hear a story, and it had better be good, put the music on again,' he pointed. The man at the end started to turn around to do his bidding. 'Not you, you tosser,' Bananas shouted, 'I'm not talking to you, get into line, you prick.' Butcher went to put the music back on, hitting the side of the man's head, knocking him to the floor.

'Get up, you piece of shit, get up,' Joe shouted. The youth scrambled to his feet, holding the back of his head.

The bigger one of the line-up spoke at last and told the story of seeing Tony Waybee in the café and passed on the message, but hesitated when he came to the part when Waybee had said that Joe Bananas could go to hell, and he would come in his own good time.

'Why are you hesitating, what did he say? Talk up, or you are going to get fucked, I believe Butcher likes young boys, don't you, Butcher?' Butcher smiled, and rubbed his hands together in mock delight.

'He said you could get fucked,' the youth said, with a slight smile, 'and that you or your mob didn't scare him, and he would see you when he had the time. As far as Tommy is concerned none of us have seen him around for a while; there is a rumour that the guy who was killed on Monday night in the alley was him, but no name has been put out by the newspapers yet. We've tried, haven't we, lads? To see as many people who know Tony and Tommy. We even saw scar-face Ted Sims in hospital because he was slashed again; another rumour said it was Tony who slashed him. Ted hadn't seen Tommy either; we tried our best, boss.' The rest of the lads all agreed.

'Right I believe you,' Bananas said, 'but next time I give you a job make sure you report back to me sooner, do I make myself clear? So this time I'm going to let you off easy, just remember who the big cheese in this city is.' He nodded to his henchmen who systematically punched each man in the face, and some were even nutted.

'You, you asshole, you spilled your blood on my white carpet,' Bananas screeched, 'so you owe me for the cleaning, have the money here by tomorrow morning, it will cost you £300, and here's a thank you for doing it.' He flicked his fingers. The two sidekicks delighted in knocking him out. The men left carrying him out, and had to walk back to the city. It had been an ordeal for the four young would-be gangsters. And they all vowed to get the instigator of their plight, and that was Tony Waybee.

TWELVE
SATURDAY

The day dawned with a promise of a pleasant day, as the sun peeped up from the horizon, as though surveying the land. The birds were up early, and singing in the trees in the park. All the kids from the home were getting ready for breakfast and were excited to be going to their favourite place of play, the central park. Benny Sparrow was very happy because he had a mission, and the mission was to find his crashed helicopter, with a chance of repairing it; there was also a chance that he might meet his adopted dad. He had promised not to run away again on the threat that the carers wouldn't put the application through to the authorities for him to meet his dad on a regular basis, and he wanted to find his console that he had inadvertently lost in their haste to leave the park that windy and rainy day. He put on his old trousers because he had a plan he would keep secret; this mission had to work, he wanted to impress his dad after he had let him down so badly, when he lost control and crashed.

It was ten in the morning on this fine day that the children left for the short expedition to the park.

*

Rainbow woke with a start from a nightmare that had him in court facing a judge who had just said the words, 'I sentence you to life in prison for the crime of murder.' He was soaked in sweat, as he looked at the sunbeam crossing the room through a gap in the curtains. He looked at the side of the bed that Charlotte had slept in, but she had got up in a mood as once again he had deprived her of sex. His excuse was that the champagne had gone to his head, and also down below, to the very thing she desired. He remembered trying to make a joke about his limp member not wanting to play, and the little soldier just wanted to go to sleep, he even flopped it around just to prove the point. She had not been amused at all, and had remonstrated with him implying that he didn't love her anymore, and that they hadn't had sex for nearly a week. She had turned her back on him; he wondered if she was in a better mood as he got up and dressed. He had to report in to the station, and go and sort out his adversary, Mr Waybee. She wasn't downstairs; there was no one around. The dinner party the night before had been a hazy affair; he was mostly thinking about how he was going to sort out his troubles, and felt guilty about what had taken place on the veranda with Michelle. She had always come on to him ever since he had met her sister way back; he had tried on numerous occasions to resist her advances, but had failed every time. She had continued giving him sly looks, and at times winking across the table; at other times he was sure that Charlotte noticed her sister's flirting, it was embarrassing. Her mother and father were mostly on about their trip. He had been happy when the party came to an end, and they had retired, but not before Michelle had given him a kiss and slipped her tongue into his mouth, brazenly with a laugh. Charlotte had said something to the effect that he seemed to get on very well with her sister and she was pleased. He remembered saying that she was fine but he found her a bit childish at times, then they had got into bed.

He made a cup of coffee and some toast and sat at the table contemplating what he intended to do. No one had surfaced and Charlotte was nowhere to be seen so he left a note saying that he would return in the afternoon, adding as a postscript that he was looking forward to seeing his parents at the get-together meal. He drove to the city to face the day.

*

Benny was stuck in a tall tree in the park, and couldn't get down. He had asked for permission to go into the trees to find his console, and the carers told him not to be long. He promised and went into the trees and bushes as the other children played together, skipping, tag, and some of the boys had a rough and tumble, Benny had searched high and low for his console, to no avail, as unbeknown to him, it was in the forensic lab with other items taken from the alley crime scene: the four buttons from the torn shirt, and the handkerchief Rainbow had found in the park.

He had climbed the biggest tree, from bough to bough, higher and higher, till he could see the kids playing in the distance. He shouted and waved, but nobody noticed him, he looked around and went out on a branch that lowered with his weight and got on to another branch that belonged to another tree. As he grabbed the limb the branch sprang up out of his reach; he looked over to his left and there nestling in a hollow was the battered remains of his helicopter; for a moment he was delighted at his find. The mission had been successful; all he had to do was retrieve it. He inched his body over the thinning branch and grabbed at the protruding limb, and nearly fell to the ground. He clung on, his fright starting to take over; tears welled up as he looked down to the ground that seemed to be a mile away to the little boy. His shoes came off as he tried to get a grip on the bark of the tree; slowly but surely, he made his way to the hollow and there it was, his pride and joy, crumpled. He lifted it out of the hollow, and it was then he saw the package attached to the undercarriage. It dawned on the boy that this must be the mission his dad meant and that his friend, the man under the tree in the middle of the park, had sent him the package; it must have been a game they were playing. He placed the package into his shirt with the intention of giving it to his dad when he next saw him. The boy felt elated, until it was time to get down from the tree. He looked down; there was no safe way, he was thirty feet in the air, he became frightened as he thought he would have to stay up there forever. He shouted out but nobody heard him, so he waited then shouted out again. After being in the tree forever, it seemed to the boy, he heard faint calls then as they got closer he shouted down, 'Up here, Miss, I'm in the tree.'

'Get down from there, Ben Sparrow, what do you think you're doing up there joining the other sparrows?' Miss Butters joked, but it was a feeble joke, the other carer didn't laugh.

He looked like he was in a precarious position; it was easy to work out that without the help of a ladder, the boy was going to stay up there for a long time. 'I want to go to the toilet, Miss; can I pee in the tree?' the boy shouted down.

All the other children laughed out loud, some pointing up without any sense of the danger that the boy was in.

'Get your parachute on and jump,' one boy shouted, amid more laughter.

'Forget the parachute, just jump,' shouted another boy. All the children laughed apart from one little girl who had taken a shine to Benny, and at the age of eleven was totally in love.

'Get him down, Miss, before he falls,' she pleaded, as the girl wiped tears from her face. Miss Butters ordered the children to go back on to the grass part of the park, because they were getting boisterous and kicking leaves in the air.

'No don't pee, hold it, we're going to get you down. Mr Jenkins has just called the fire brigade; they are on their way, so just hold on.' The boy held on to the tree, but peed in his pants.

Rainbow was driving past the park when he inquired as to what the fire brigade was doing in the park unloading ladders, as there was no sign of a fire or smoke.

'Rescuing a kid who got stuck up a tree, not the first time, won't be the last,' the fireman said in a matter-of-fact way, as he slid the ladders off the wagon. Rainbow felt excited as he parked his car in the car park close to where Waybee lived. He lifted the boot, and took the bag out that contained the model boat called Betty.

Tony was just about to go out, he was going to see Big Joe Bananas to see why everyone he met was telling him to go and see the big man. He had never run for any man, not even the screws in the nick had made him run; he would see him in his own good time, not before. Now that time had come; he had nothing to do this Saturday morning.

He jumped out of his skin at the loud knock on the door, and without thinking of looking out of the window, opened the door.

'This is not Avon calling, nor am I selling encyclopaedias, I'm not a neighbour who wants a loan of a cup of sugar, or a door-to-door salesman, I'm just an ordinary copper who wants some answers to a few questions, so will it be all right to come in? Or do I have to get a warrant to enter your dwelling place, Mr Waybee sir?'

'There's no need to be sarcastic, I don't do that, not my thing, and do you know that sarcasm is the lowest form of wit? Yes, to answer your question, you do need a warrant. I Think I told you that before now so good morning to you *sir*,' he emphasised the word with a sneer and went to shut the door.

'Hold on,' Rainbow said. He went to his inside pocket and produced the document. 'Maybe I should read it out to you; it may take some time. And also I've got a gift for you in the bag.' He looked down at the bag, looked up again and gave a wily smile.

'You'd better come in then, but you ain't got anything on me, I'm telling you now, I'm as clean as they come.'

The musty smell of the room drifted like a morning mist across a dark ravine, because the room was dark and damp, and found a way to get up Rainbow's nose. He found it very unpleasant as he placed the bag on the floor next to the table. Then, without asking, he sat down and looked at the models hanging from the ceiling, aeroplanes and model boats on a dressing table on the far side of the room.

'I see you like making models; did you take that up in the nick? It seems you're a dab hand at it.' He pointed around the room, 'Take a seat,' he demanded. Waybee sat down opposite him at the table.

'Yeah, I like making models; is there any law against that? Because I'm sure if there is you're going to tell me about it. I hope you haven't come here to lecture me, because I'm busy, I was about to go out this morning, so whatever you have on your mind get it out of the way, as I have said I've got things on.' He looked at Rainbow with hate in his eyes.

'I was going to ask you about the killing that you were involved in?'

Waybee's face changed to acute anger mixed with a pang of fear that ran up his body like a rat up a drain. 'What fucken' killing? I don't know anything about no murder,' he was red in the face, and he started to splutter.

'The murder of Randy Colbert, that gangster in Churchtown four years ago, I've got information to believe that you were involved along with Big Joe Bananas and his mob, so you'd better start to explain what you know about it.'

'That case was closed; no one was ever convicted, so why has it come back to life now? It's always me why me?' Waybee spluttered.

'Because I've opened the case again, and for your information a case is never closed, and I'm coming after you, do you understand? I have someone who would be willing to testify against you.' Rainbow was lying through his teeth.

'And I have something on you, too, and I will see…' Waybee stopped; realising he had said too much, he looked away and fidgeted in his chair.

'OK that's it; you're going down for a long time. I will ask for a life sentence; you know me, Tony, I don't mess around, so what do you know about me? Tell me.'

'I know you can be a bastard, if you don't get what you're looking for, you've proved it in the past, so if you forget to pursue this case of Randy Colbert, because I'm sure you know that he was scum, the lowest form of life. He messed around with kids and sold drugs to juveniles, to be honest with you he wasn't better than a piece of shit, he deserved to die, but I didn't do it.'

'But you were there when the killing took place; that makes you an accessory to the fact; even that will get you life. So tell me what you know about me, or are you going to start blackmailing me? I mean you could ask for, let's see…' He put his hand to his head in mock thought, 'say, £10,000 then maybe set up a scheme like…' he looked around the room and pointed to a model ship, 'one of those boats, get me to put the money in the hold, and sail it on the river out of my sight, say around the bend in the river where you could pick it up and get away.'

'That's a stupid idea. That boat is not big enough for what you think, it doesn't even float. You've got a vivid mind, you should write a book.' Waybee blurted.

'Maybe this might do the job better, it's bigger, and it floats, because I've seen it float.' Rainbow bent down at the side of the table, took Betty out of the bag and plonked the boat on the table. Tony had surprise written in capitals right across his face.

'Do you recognise it?' Rainbow said with a raised voice. 'You should, you dumped it just a short while ago, and now it's mine because I bought it from your bin man last night in a pub in the city. He informed me that it was wrapped in newspaper cuttings, you know, newspapers that had words and letters cut out. Now for your story, you asshole, because I know you're the blackmailer. Who's in it with you, what's his name? Tell me his fucking name.'

Tony knew the game was up; he had to admit it and hand the money back, well, part of it, he still had it in a drawer in his bedroom less the £200 he had paid out on the electricity bill and other things. Waybee looked down at the floor, he knew he was caught, he was in deep trouble; in his criminal mind it was a fair cop.

'There's no one else involved, there's only me, honestly, I saw what you did to Tommy on Monday night,' he said with menace in his voice and a pointing finger, 'I was with him, we had gone to Baker Alley to get a pair of boots that a bloke I know called Bootsy had dumped there in the afternoon. He told us, that's me and Tommy that they were in a bin, a black bin. You must know that that reprobate Harris has a fetish for small boys, as well as boots, he's got hundreds of pairs, all over his place so I've been told, he's been in and out of nick more times than I've had hot Sunday dinners he's a right moron he's a—'.

'Get to the point!' Rainbow shouted. 'I'm getting madder by the second; who is your sidekick in your fucking blackmailing game? Tell me now, or you're in for a fucking beating.' Rainbow stood up and grabbed Waybee by the throat, giving him a chop to a pressure point on the side of his neck, his fury once again out of control. Waybee cried out like a lonely coyote in the darkness of the night, as he grabbed his neck and collapsed to the floor. Rainbow went to the sink and got a cup of water and threw it in his face.

'Get up, you bastard, I don't want to know about anything unless it concerns the reason why you thought you could blackmail me, now start again and stick to the point.' Waybee got up still looking angry, but on this occasion there was nothing he could do; his bullying tactics were of no use in the situation he found himself in.

'So you were in Baker Alley on Monday evening and…?' Rainbow put both his elbows on the table and stared at his adversary.

'We got to the bin where Bootsy had said the boots were, and Tommy gave me a lift up; while I was in the bin I heard him talking to someone, sometimes he would get funny with people for no reason, and pick on them like trying to prove himself. I was deep in the bin, so I peeped through the crack in the side of the container and I saw…' At that moment Waybee hesitated.

'Well go on, what did you see? Spit it out, there's no one here, only me and you, so who did you see in the darkness of the early evening?'

'By the light on the wall opposite I saw *you*, I saw you with Tommy; I heard you talking to him, "I told you I don't smoke," you said, then you ripped his shirt open, and I remember the rattle on the side of the bin as the buttons flew through the air, you downed him, then you started to—'

'All right, you saw me defending myself, so what? Haven't I got the right to do that? What would you do if someone attacked you? I know you, Waybee; you would fill them in, wouldn't you? So now what are you going to do, report me? Fucking hell, do you honestly believe that they would take your word against mine? You bastard'. He jabbed his finger in waybee face, 'a fucking ex-prisoner, crook and a suspected murderer under investigation? Wise up, you fucking idiot.'

Waybee just looked down with a sorrowful look on his face, and then offered both his hands in a way to accept handcuffs. Rainbow looked stern, and then with a sigh he said, 'I want you to listen carefully to what I have to say.' He paused.

'There is a way out for you, and for me in a way, and you would benefit in more ways than you could ever wish for, so get us a beer, I'm sure you got some, and I will put a proposition to you.' The beer was on the table in glasses before Rainbow could say Jack Robinson. 'Now, I know of your love for Bootsy Harris.' Waybee made a face.

'So what if I suggested to you that you testify in a court of law that it was him you saw that night in the alley? He's a scumbag and he's the one who told me that it was you involved with the killing of Randy Colbert, so you don't owe him anything and the paedophile should be inside anyhow. You'll be doing a service to the community's children. That would get me off the hook; so to speak, my bosses want this case solved. I can't exactly hand myself in now, can I? Now if you do this for me, I could show my gratitude to you in various ways; first off, I wouldn't arrest you for blackmailing me, I would let you keep some of my hard-earned money, but most of all, I would get off your back as far as the murder of Colbert is concerned.'

Tony sat there listening intently; he took a swig of his beer. It sounded like a good proposition to him, he had hated Harris for years and had been in trouble many times because of his big mouth; he had no allegiance to a beast like him. The children had to be guarded. Then for a moment his boy Benny came into his mind; maybe he could get Rainbow's help to see the boy again, maybe help with his application.

'Well, what do you think, Tony?' He realised that he had called him by his first name for the first time. 'If I arrested the bastard, will you testify in court, we can both work out a story, and who knows maybe we might become friends?' Rainbow laughed out loud. 'Who knows? I could invite you to my wedding, or go on holiday together one day; you're not a bad kind of a guy really, deep down. What do you say?'

'I'll do it; yes I'll do it!' Waybee shouted out with enthusiasm and relief. 'And it will save me the trouble of giving him the pasting he deserves; when will you get him arrested?'

'I'll pick him up this afternoon; does he still live in the Fingle estate?'

'Yeah, still lives with his mum and dad, right mummy's boy that wanker is.'

'I know your feelings for him, but don't worry, he'll soon be out of your way behind bars; anyhow, forget him for now, I might want you to do a job for me but I'll let you know later, when the time is ripe; of course you will be paid for doing it. Now tell me how you extracted the money from me in detail with your blackmailing scheme, don't leave anything out.'

Tony explained how he had only got the £10,000 from the first time at the river, and went to the bedroom to hand it over; less the £200 he had spent. He went on to explain how he had crashed the helicopter in the park, never mentioning the boy's involvement. Rainbow couldn't help but admire the ingenious way that Waybee had gone about getting the money. *A model boat and a helicopter, a clever plan indeed*, he thought.

'So the money is in the park somewhere in the trees or undergrowth? I suggest you get yourself down there and find my money; you can keep five thousand of it as a token of my appreciation for your help in solving the case in Baker Alley.'

Rainbow drank the remainder of his beer, stood up and offered his hand; they shook hands, first time ever. 'Let's hope that our new relationship works out and we both benefit by it. To conclude, I just want to make it plain, I didn't mean to hurt your friend and I'm sorry but he did throw a punch at me.'

'No he didn't, I forgot to tell you, Tommy fell down and hurt himself a few days before and was taking pills for muscle spasms that would occur from time to time, his arm would involuntarily shoot forward, which might look like he was throwing a punch; it was a muscle spasm, that's all. I never saw him once hit anyone; sure, he acted tough but violent, never.'

Rainbow kept his feelings well hidden as he replied, 'It looked like a punch to me; let's move on. What happened after you saw me leave?'

'I jumped out of the bin and gave him mouth-to-mouth but it was too late, he was gone, I couldn't feel a pulse. I took his Rolex watch off, only imitation, and found his wallet, they were no good to him anymore, and that's it.'

'So who jumped on his chest? Because whoever did had cocoa powder on his boots; there were foot marks on his bare chest, did you do that? And why would you?'

Waybee was surprised to hear what the copper was saying. *They didn't miss much*, he thought. 'I jumped out and landed on him, unintentionally, the cocoa powder must have got onto my boots in the bin, and there were lots of things in that bin, lots of garbage.'

'Have you still got the boots, watch and his wallet? I think I might need them for evidence.'

'Hold on, I thought you said we were friends; you're not going to pin this on me?'

'Slow down, you have my word as a copper; don't you trust a copper's word?'

'Now that's a good question, do I trust a copper's word?' He put his hand to his temple and thought for a while, then said, 'I m afraid I can't answer that on the grounds that it might incriminate me.' Both men burst out laughing, and then the detective explained how he would take the boots to Harris's home and plant them. He continued, 'And the story would be that you were with Tommy, and you were going to the alley to see if any of the gang were hanging around; you stopped to buy a newspaper and planned to meet your friend in the alley. You bought a newspaper, and Tommy went on into the alley; as you came towards the bin, you saw Harris jump out of the semi-darkness and got into a fight, ripped his shirt and jumped on Tommy's chest. It was then that you approached, and Harris ran off. You then gave mouth-to-mouth, and the reason you didn't report it was because you were frightened of what the mob would do to you for grassing, got it? Stick to that story, and we will be on the way to a better life, and that paedo will be inside, case closed, right? Go get the boots and the other things, watch and wallet, and my money then I'll be on my way.' Rainbow ordered. 'Then get down to that park, get my money back. You can keep the boat, I've no need for it; accept it as a gift from me to celebrate our new friendship, and no more using it for illegal money transfers, understand?'

With his £9,800 in his pocket, and the cocoa-powdered boots, watch and wallet in a bag, Rainbow left to arrest the one and only Bootsy Harris.

Before the detective was out of sight, Waybee was having second thoughts about framing Bootsy Harris; somehow in his mind it just didn't fit right.

THIRTEEN

After leaving Waybee's place, Rainbow drove past the karate club and was surprised to see scaffolding going up. It seemed Eddie was spending his money already. *He's in for a big fucking shock*, he thought, as he made his way downtown to the notorious Fingle estate where Harris lived.

He stopped the car at the entrance of the run-down row of post-war houses; children with broken trousers were playing in the street outside houses with broken windows, garbage that littered most front gardens, and plastic bags and paper were stuck in the fencing. Some gardens had old settees in them where women with cigarettes dangling from their mouths chatted in the afternoon sunshine. He asked two young lads who were riding their bikes on the pavement if they knew where Bootsy Harris lived.

'One pound each for information,' said the bigger boy who had holes in the elbow of his shirt, 'one pound for me, and one pound for him,' he pointed to the younger boy who looked up in admiration at his forward friend, and they volunteered to escort the car to the house. Rainbow felt in his pocket and gave the boys the money; to their surprise, the easy money. They had tried it out before but it had never worked. They looked at the money and smiled at one another.

'Never heard of him, we don't live around here, find him yourself, mister,' the elder boy said as he dropped the money in his trouser pocket, after spitting on it as he had seen his father do on many occasions when he had found money behind the sofa or other various places.

The boys disappeared around the corner before he could get out of his car.

'Future criminals, little bastards,' he mused, as he drove on into the estate and asked a woman walking her unfriendly dog, who growled at him.

'Number 37 next street, what's he been up to now? He's always in the clink, he's a bloody nuisance, I believe he may be out because I saw him a while ago heading for his pub, but he may have got home by now. I've seen him stagger home more than once, I live on the other side of the street, so I tend to see him come and go. My Bert, when he was alive, told me he was a bad 'un, so I try to avoid him, but sometimes you can't help bumping into him. Once he asked if I wanted to go for a walk with him; well, as you can imagine, I said I wouldn't go out with him if he was the last man on earth. Then the cheeky bugger asked me to go to the pub with him. *No way*, I said. His mother and father are no better; I think that there's something missing up here.' She pointed to her temple. 'No not my type of people; if you ask me, they all should be in a mental home, not on a nice estate like this one; they are the kind of people who give us a bad name, isn't that right, Fido?' The dog growled once again. Rainbow wished he hadn't asked her, her chatter was like a rasping on the brain; he wondered if Bert had died to get away from her.

'Who wants to know?' she said. 'Anyhow, you look like police, are you police? Because I don't like the police, tell me now, are you the law? Bert was put away once for something he didn't do, and he told me never to have anything to do with them, he used to call them pigs and the filth and names like that, so if you're the police I'm not telling you where Mr Harris lives so there, tell him, Fido.' The dog showed his teeth and growled once again.

'Detective Sergeant Rainbow, city police, did you forget, you've already told me where he lives, number 37 you said, and one more thing, hope you have a licence for that mongrel; someone will be around to see it shortly, the police are not pigs or filth, so your Bert was wrong, what's the first thing you do if you're in trouble? You call the police, don't you? I'll be seeing you again, madam,' he threatened, and then drove off.

'What a nasty man, what do you think, Fido?' she said, as she wondered if the dog had a licence.

Rainbow had short shrift at the Harris house to his question.

'Not home, down the pub,' Mrs Harris had said, as she slammed the door in his face. He realised he wasn't getting far and he was becoming hungry, so decided to go to the station for a bite then he would go and arrest Harris later; after all, he wasn't going anywhere.

*

Benny sat on his bed with his broken helicopter, trying to put it back together again with superglue. He had salvaged every bit; it had crashed into a hollow of the tree but sort of imploded, and although crumpled it was mostly intact, though the blades were bent.

He had thoroughly enjoyed his morning adventure in the park, the thrill of being rescued by a real live fireman, who had allowed him to put on his helmet; he vowed to join the fire brigade when he was a man. The package was hidden in the back of his locker behind his neatly folded clothes. He would give it to his adopted dad as soon as it was possible. His carers had been relieved as he was carried down the ladder on the shoulders of a burly fireman, who Miss Butters took a fancy to, and after the ladders were taken away, she followed the fireman all the way out of the park deep in conversation on the merits of being a fire-fighter, and forgetting her charges momentarily; she even waved as the fire truck pulled away. In the meantime Benny was the centre of attraction, as the rest of the kids gathered around him as though he was a hero. Benny was over the moon at the attention he had received, and made a few more friends. Mr Jenkins wasn't so benevolent and scolded the child, and warned him that if he climbed trees again without permission he would be banned from any more outings for a specific time. Benny just pretended to listen and put on his sad puppy face before Mr Jenkins put his arm around him to console the boy when he thought he might cry. It had been a nice day so far as he mended his helicopter and wondered when he would see his dad again to hand over the missions package.

*

Tony Waybee had had another beer when Rainbow had left to arrest Bootsy Harris. For a time, sitting at his cluttered table, he wondered if he had done the right thing in agreeing with the proposal to put Harris in the dock. It was true that he had no love for Harris, but to put a man in prison for life was something else. He sat there for almost an hour trying to come to terms with understanding what he had agreed to, but what was the alterative? Rainbow would try to pin Randy Colbert on him; he hadn't killed Colbert, but he had been there along with other members of Big Joe Banana's gang, when he was in with them as a member. He had seen how vicious Bananas had been: he had broken Colbert's legs and crushed his head in with a hammer, and it was after that incident that he had left the gang to pursue a career in crime on his own. He had kept a low profile, and very rarely mixed with any of them, when he had met Tommy. It was him who wanted to get into the gang. He had warned Tommy of the way Bananas kept order in the mob, but Tommy had insisted on meeting the top dogs, and he had introduced him into the gang. As he sat there drinking his beer he wondered if Harris was in custody yet. He finished his drink and threw the can across the room aiming at an overflowing trash can. It missed and clattered onto the floor with the other bits of trash, then he decided to go out for a drink; it was possible that he may hear about Harris's arrest if he went down to the pub that Harris drank in, called The Black Kettle.

Fifteen minutes later he walked to the pub. It was hot and humid; he felt perspiration on the back of his neck.

He looked down at the pavement where he had ended up the night he had been thrown out, and then peeped in the door. There were quite a few customers sitting at the tables. There was no sign of the two assholes who had thrown him out; he felt slightly apprehensive as he approached the bar. He noticed that the same barman was serving drinks, the same barman that he'd been sarcastic to; he hoped that he wouldn't be remembered but just in case he decided to be as nice as he possibly could.

'Hello boss, I was wondering if I could get a beer. I'm sorry about the other night, I didn't mean any harm, I was a bit stressed out, my grandfather had died and I wasn't feeling myself, so I'm sorry once again, it's hot out there and I'm dying of thirst.' He laughed a sheepish laugh. 'If you need any help with the crossword?'

'What's your poison then?' the barman said without any feeling.

'Thanks, just a pint of bitter then please.' The barman poured the drink without another word, took the money and went to serve another customer. The sun streamed in to the bar, and he found a table in the corner with a view of the street outside. He found it amusing as his thoughts wandered, and smiled to himself as he started to think of his Ruby, and wondered what she would be doing now in the sunshine of Spain. He imagined her in a bar just like he was, sitting with a drink; was she thinking of him? Just like the way he was thinking of her. He would go to meet her as soon as this business was over with; after all, he wanted to start a new life, and it had been on his mind for quite a while now. His thoughts shut out the chatter in the pub. Fifteen minutes passed and he looked up and saw Harris staring at him from the bar; he hadn't seen him walk in, he was with Ted Sims who had a plaster on his face. 'Fuck,' Waybee said under his breath, as the two men approached his table.

'My fault, my fault,' Scar-face said, before Waybee had a chance to say anything, 'don't worry I'm not here for revenge, I was a prick, and I'm man enough to admit it, so do you want to shake on it, and we'll let bygones be bygones?' He held out his hand; Waybee shook it but was apprehensive. Sims pulled up a chair, 'Bootsy, get three beers in, I'll pay, look,' Scar-face said, holding out the money. He handed him a tenner, and without a word Harris went to the bar.

'Just come out of hospital a couple of days ago, doctors said the scar would be only about three inches, my cock's bigger than that,' Sims joked.

Waybee didn't know what to say; he was lost for words, so replied briefly with, 'Well that's something.'

'I don't hold a grudge. I had time to think while I was in hospital, I shouldn't have said that you were one of them, you know, sucking cock and taking it up the Khyber, so I'm sorry once again.'

'Well forget it then, remember what you just said, bygones, I don't want to talk about it again, so apart from that,' he pointed to Sims' plaster 'what's gone down?'

'What's gone down? I'll fucken' tell you what's gone down, my friend, the fuzz are all over the place, they came to see me, they enquired about my face, I told then I cut it when I was shaving, I'm no grass, so your secret is safe with me, don't worry'.

'I'm not fucken' worried, get off the subject, you're on it again, one minute you're saying forget it then you're bringing it up again, now don't fucken' mention it again, or you can fuck off, and get another table.' He could feel his blood pressure rising. At that moment Harris arrived with the drinks and placed them on the table, clumsily spilling some of the beer on to Waybee's trousers.

'You awkward twat, you're all fingers and thumbs, watch what you're doing, look what you've done.' He stood up and pointed to his wet trousers.

'Oh shit, what a catastrophe, what a fucken' disaster,' Sims said sarcastically, 'it's not the sinking of the Titanic, it's just a little beer, anybody would think you're fucken' drowning for fuck's sake. Sit down and shut up, it's fuck all compared to this,' he stuck his finger on the plaster on his face. 'Nothing compares to getting fucken' slashed in the face by a prick like you.'

The table went up in the air, and the glasses smashed on the floor as Waybee and Sims fought like cat and dog, swapping blow for blow. Harris was knocked out with a single blow that had missed its target and he lay crumpled in a heap under the table as the battle raged. Other customers in the bar joined the affray as the windows were smashed and chairs were used as weapons, blood spots stained the walls and curtains, and the police were on the way.

*

Detective Sergeant Rainbow had just finished his lunch, and was drinking his coffee when he heard the commotion coming from upstairs, but wasn't unduly worried. It was a common thing for a station to be quiet one minute then all hell would break out suddenly, like that sudden summer storm. He finished his drink, picked up his plate and cutlery and put them in the sink, as was customary, washed his hands and went up the stairs. Shock was the right word to use when he saw the three men standing at the table counter, bedraggled, with blood dripping on to the station floor coming mostly from Sims' face, which had split open again; he couldn't believe his eyes.

'Fighting, in the public bar, The Black Kettle,' the desk sergeant answered the question from Rainbow. Waybee just opened his hands and shrugged, then looked to the floor. The three men were put in the cells for the weekend with the possibility of a court appearance on Monday; the charges were causing a disturbance by fighting in a public place. For a moment Rainbow was at a loss as to what to do next; he was in no position to arrest Harris, he had already been arrested. Then he had an idea: he would continue with his investigations, and go to Harris's house to plant the incriminating evidence, but he had to have a witness, so after the men were taken to the cells he asked the desk sergeant if any of his detectives had reported in, but there had been no progress. Rainbow was pleased about that, but how long would it take to put two and two together and work out something that might have them pointing the finger? After all, the killing had happened almost next door to where he lived, it happened at the time he was on his way home from his club, he had suffered from an injured hand, all it needed was for Eddie Bail to open his mouth, and it would be his end. Yes Rainbow's end. He had to get things moving; the top cops were getting restless at no breakthroughs in this high-profile case, and the press wanted a name to put to the dead man; it had been pointed out that it was highly irregular not to name a deceased.

*

Detective Constables Barns and Harris were sitting in a coffee bar in the city pondering on a thought: that they should call it a day. They had got absolutely nowhere with their enquiries, no one knew anything about the killing in Baker Alley. If ever there was a brick wall then this was it, and it was solid. Everyone they had painstakingly interviewed had a cast-iron alibi for six thirty or thereabouts on Monday evening. Barns had come up with a great idea that they both agreed with, and that was to call it a day and go home. They were on their third coffee when the call came in to tell them to meet Sergeant Rainbow at the Fingle estate, number 37, at three o'clock.

As Rainbow entered the estate he saw the two boys who he had encountered earlier standing on the pavement, looking at their bikes. He pulled up alongside.

'So we meet again,' he said. The boys looked up, and with split-second recognition jumped on their bikes and rode away fast. The older boy shouted over his shoulder, 'No we don't.' Rainbow just laughed quietly to himself, and drove to number 37.

A car was parked outside the pebble-dashed council houses at number 37 and he pulled up behind his colleagues. A woman shouted from an upstairs window as the detectives got out of their cars.

'Can't park there, that's where my husband parks, so move out,' she commanded.

'Police, lady,' Rainbow shouted back. The woman retreated without another word.

The cops smiled, walked up to the door, and gave it a lusty knock. Rainbow quickly explained the reason for this call, pretending that he had information to believe that the occupant of this house, a Mr Harris, had been pointed out in his enquiries as a suspect in the case they were investigating. The door slowly opened, and a frumpish pony tailed woman appeared.

'Barry's not here, he's gone to the pub, I told you before, now piss off,' Mrs Harris shouted with the venom in her voice like that of a viper.

'I'm Detective Sergeant Rainbow, these are Detectives Barns and Harris,' he pointed. 'Are you his mother?' he enquired.

'Yes, and he's not here, he's in The Black Kettle pub, I told you, he's not here,' she seemed as though she was ready for any confrontation that the police would give her; she had had dealings with them on numerous occasions in the past, and they didn't frighten her in any way.

'Sorry to inform you, Mrs Harris, but your son isn't in The Black Kettle, he's in custody at this present time for a breach of the peace, causing an affray in a public place.'

'That's a lie, my boy don't cause trouble to anyone, he's never had a fight in his life, he wouldn't, he couldn't, he's got trouble with his—'

Rainbow interrupted her by putting his hand up to her face.

'The judge will decide that when he appears in court on Monday, but for now we have authority to search his room, I have a warrant here,' he lied. He did have a search warrant but it was for a different house, Waybee's house. He went to his pocket indicating he was about to show it, he hoped his bluff would work; it did.

She opened the door to the policemen, and indicated her son's room. Rainbow told Detective Harris to have a talk to the suspect's father, who was in the front room watching a football match, and the other officer was told to talk to Mrs Harris while he looked the room over. He shut the door and went to a drawer that was adjacent to the back window; he took the watch and the wallet that he had obtained from Waybee and placed them under some clothes, then went to the window and opened it slightly.

One minute elapsed. He came out of the room and made an excuse that he had left his notebook in the car. He opened the boot and collected the bag that contained the boots he had got from Waybee, then he went around the side of the house, and slipped the bag through the slightly open window, then returned to the front door; it had taken him just two minutes. He returned to the front room and indicated that he had retrieved his notebook then went into the bedroom once again. He retrieved the bag, placing it into the wardrobe, and it was all set. He opened the door and called for Barns to help him search the room.

'What are we looking for, sarge?' Barns enquired.

'I don't know really, remember the killer stole a watch, it was a Rolex if I recall, anyhow look around for anything, you never know what will turn up.'

Both detectives looked around the untidy room. Rainbow allowed Barns to search the drawers while he pretended to look in the wardrobe.

‘There seems to be nothing in here,’ Rainbow said as he rummaged around in the top shelf, ‘he was a scruffy bastard; are all Harrises like this?’

‘I wouldn’t think so, James is a very tidy cop,’ he pointed to the door indicating his colleague in the other room; he opened the drawer and moved the clothes aside.

‘Look here, sarge,’ he pointed to the watch, ‘and it’s a Rolex.’

Rainbow left the wardrobe open, and went to the drawer, gingerly picking up the watch. He looked at it, and placed it in a plastic bag noting in his book the time the item was found and by whom. ‘Well done, Barnsy boy.’

‘And there’s a wallet also,’ Barns pointed out, handing the wallet over to his boss, he held it in his fingertips and opened it up and there was a picture of Tommy Crawly who Rainbow knew was really Detective Robert Jennet.

‘Got him at last, and he’s in our nick at the moment, couldn’t be a better result, yeah,’ he punched the air. ‘That’s it, done and dusted,’ he turned to leave and pretending not to notice the bag at the bottom of the wardrobe, he looked down.

‘What’s this?’ He looked into the bag. ‘Look here,’ he said, ‘boots with a film of brown powder on them; didn’t forensics say something about foot marks on the deceased’s chest where he had been stepped on? I believe something to do with a powder substance?’ He pretended to think for a moment. ‘That’s right, cocoa powder, there was cocoa powder on the body that they believe came from boots. I’ll get these to the lab right away. Well done, Barns, good work in finding the watch and the wallet.’ The men returned to the front room.

'Mrs Harris, I am taking these items to the police station,' he showed her the two plastic bags. She looked over the objects that Rainbow held in his hand, plus the boots in the plastic bag.

'They're not Barry's,' she protested, 'they don't belong to him, he's never owned a watch in his life, I don't know if he can tell the time properly, and those are not his boots, he would never wear boots that dirty,' she blurted out as she looked in the bag.

'Well they were in his room, he concealed them in a drawer under clothes, and can you tell me where he was on Monday evening at around six thirty?' Rainbow took out his notebook, and felt for a pen just as he had seen his American hero Lieutenant Colombo do in the television series.

'He was here, he didn't go out all day, isn't that right, Bert?' She looked toward her husband who was beginning to drift off at the boredom of it all, after all this was not the first time that the police had come to see if Barry could help with their enquiries or some other enquiries about burglaries and break-ins. He was, to say the least, fed up.

'He was here with us, never left the house all day, we watched TV together, and why do you ask?' Bert sat up straight, and picked up the console, switching the set off.

'A murder took place in Baker Alley on Monday night, well, early evening to be precise, and now we have reason to believe that your son had something to do with it.'

'Fuck off, are you out of your tiny mind? Barry wouldn't do anything like murder, he loves people, always has, he didn't do it, so if you're finished here I want to get my Bert's tea, the door's that way,' she pointed, 'and by the way, my boy didn't start the trouble today, I bet he was just roped in, as what has happened before. He'll get off with it; you just mark my words.' Bert put the football back on and put the volume up. The policemen left for their cars, hearing the front door slam behind them.

'What did you find out, Detective Harris, anything of importance?' enquired Rainbow.

'Arsenal are top of the league and Jimmy Swanson, whoever he is, is getting a million-pound transfer, and that my grandfather was a second cousin to Bert's grandfather.'

'What about you, Barns?'

'Nothing at all really, she was nice to me, before you came back she only spoke briefly, and asked me to take her son some of his medication. I advised her to take it to the station herself, because I wouldn't be allowed to, she wasn't too happy.'

'At least we have a result; the killer robbed his victim, that's been established, so we'll see what forensics have to say. There will be no fingerprints on the wallet but who knows what they will find? Let's keep this thing under our hats for a while; there are a few other points I have to finalise. Good work, lads, see you back at the station, I'll wrap this up and then we can all go home.' The police left the Fingle estate with twitching curtains all the way down the street.

FOURTEEN

It seemed surreal to Rainbow as he drove through the slow-moving traffic. It seemed that he believed that he was building a case against a totally innocent man, but Rainbow was starting to believe that Harris was really guilty. He was happy with the way he had handled Tony Waybee and he had got nearly ten thousand of his money back, there was a chance that the other lot might materialise and the blackmailing had stopped. There was only that asshole from the club to sort out; there was no way he was going to subsidise a club that he would never use again, since he had decided to stop doing the sport of karate.

He pulled into the station's car park at the same time as the others, and the three detectives walked in to see the chief inspector. Commonly known at the station as 'Sarky' Ryan, because of his sarcastic nature, he was standing at the desk talking to the desk sergeant. On seeing Rainbow, the chief's face took on an air of anger.

'Upstairs to my office now,' he demanded, 'not you two, make yourselves scarce.'

The two officers went down to the canteen feeling a sort of relief. The boss looked liked he was in a very bad mood. Rainbow followed like a lapdog and entered the room. 'Take a seat, Detective Sergeant, or maybe I'm wrong, maybe you're not a sergeant, maybe you're not a detective, maybe you're not even a policeman any more, but whatever you are, there's one thing that stands out a mile, and that is that you're not doing your job very well.' Rainbow fidgeted and felt very uncomfortable for that moment. The chief continued picking up some papers. 'There's a killing of one of our top undercover agents who was about to blow a hole in a big drug haul, and with you on the case, with may I add, seven other detectives, what have you come up with? Now please excuse the expletives. Fuck all,' with that the chief threw the file on to the desk with a force that blew other papers on to the floor. 'So if it's not too much trouble, please tell, tell me why there's no breakthroughs, not even a snippet, have you seen that fucking gangster? You know, that reprobate they call Big Joe Bananas, because he's only five foot two, he's easily found, he runs that betting shop near Browtown, we know it's only a front to his drug dealing; have you been to see him yet? If not tell me why not? Anyone who's got a bit of brain would have had him in the same night of the murder, for fuck's sake man, get a grip, or how can I put you up for promotion? How can I convince the police board that you are a fit copper to be an inspector? I had more faith in your ability than I believe you deserved, to put it bluntly, you fer… fer…' the chief stuttered then said, 'let me down.'

Rainbow sat silently and waited for the tirade of abuse to die down; he knew better than to interrupt the chief when he was in this kind of a mood. There was silence for a minute, as the chief stared with eyes as wild as an ocean gale. 'It's six days today since the crime, and so far not one fucking clue, so you've got until Monday to come up with something, just a little clue, just a lead, something to work on, something I can tell my chief constable to keep him sweet, and off my back.'

'I haven't been to see Big Joe yet, sir,' Rainbow ventured, 'but it's next on my list, and I'm sorry you feel that way, I can assure you I have put everything into this case, I haven't slept well for a few days and remember this was supposed to be my vacation time, I was going to take my fiancée on a cruise to Norway. I also lost DC Jennet who had to go back with his brother, the deceased, for the funeral; my team has also been at it from dawn to dusk every day.'

'Bollocks,' the inspector shouted, 'no more of your excuses, I've seen your team in the canteen many times, at one time I thought they had left the force and had taken up new professions as canteen assistants, there's not a scrap of information in here that shows that they have contributed to solving this case.' Once again he threw the papers on the desk.

'Sir, I'm sorry to say that although I hate to disagree with you, there has been some information we have gained; today, for instance, I interviewed a certain Mr Anthony Waybee, who came forward with information that on the night of the murder he saw a person fighting in the alley with the deceased, and I interviewed him this very day, this morning in fact. He told me that with an identity parade he is certain he could identify the man. Then on another tip, myself and detectives Barns and Harris went to number 37 Fingle estate to search a suspect, Mr Harris, and I have some items for forensics to look at, that's where I was going when I came back here, sir.'

'Well OK, bring them in for questioning, all I can say is we need results and fast, catch this murderer, progress has been so slow, I'm at my wits' end, and the higher authority has said that if there's no breakthrough in the next twenty-four hours then I have got to change the teams, it's out of my hands; do you understand Sergeant Rainbow? Tuesday I'm afraid is the deadline, then the case goes to DS Jones, you have less than forty-eight hours. I'm giving you an extra twelve hours, that's it. Call all the men back, there's no weekend off until this case has been sorted, I want all on deck, no time to sleep or eat, or shit, all effort on catching that fucking criminal, he's out there somewhere. You know, Rainbow, I have a feeling that the killer is not too far away from where I'm sitting now, and I bet you he's shitting himself right now. Get the reports from forensics, on my desk as soon as possible; tell them to prioritise, this could be the breakthrough we've been waiting for.'

The inspector gave a smile of satisfaction as he felt his anger slowly subsiding. Rainbow was different, he felt like he had just had a hiding, being called a criminal was like a blow to his head, it was time to interview Harris and he knew exactly where he was.

He refrained from telling the inspector that both men were already in custody. 'So what are you waiting for, Sergeant Rainbow? It's time to put some colour back in to your life,' he waited for a reaction to his play on words, and when none came the inspector looked across his desk. 'Didn't you get that, Colour, Rainbow?'

'Yes sir, very clever, but my mind's on other things.'

'Hopefully this murder case,' the inspector injected his

last bit of sarcasm before he ended the interview. 'Go out now and solve it, sorry, last chance.'

Rainbow nodded and left the room, then went down to the canteen to get a bit of caffeine in his bloodstream. He now understood the situation, he had to do something, and he couldn't allow Detective Sergeant Jones, who he had never got on well with, to take the case. He would be the kind to put two and two together in no time. He glanced at his watch; it was six o'clock and the afternoon had gone without as much as a goodbye. Once again he had gone all day with very little to eat, toast for breakfast and a light lunch, so he decided to have a bowl of chicken soup with a roll, talk to Harris then he would go to see his Charlotte. It was the big dinner party with his parents so he had to leave soon. 'He's in cell ten,' the desk sergeant stated, 'strange bugger he is, I would never have said he was a fighting man; he's not big enough for a start, didn't give me any bother signing in.' The desk sergeant asked how the old man was, referring to Inspector Ryan.

'Still an Oscar-holder for sarcasm and an Olympic medal-holder for swear words,' Rainbow replied.

Both cops laughed as Rainbow left and walked down the row of cells; he let himself into Harris's cell. He was sitting on the side of his bed looking at the floor.

'I didn't do anything, I was just standing there and the next thing I know I'm in the van, and I've been arrested for causing a breach of the peace, but I ain't done nothing. They say I was fighting, I never fought anyone in my life, I can't, I—'

Rainbow interrupted, 'Hold on, I'm not interested in why you're in here, it's another matter I'm interested in.'

He pulled up a chair and sat astride it, resting his hands on the back. 'I know you, Harris, I'm sure we have had dealings in the past,' he though for a moment, then said, 'yes, I remember interviewing you about the Church Town murders a few years ago; nobody was ever brought to justice, the case is ongoing.'

'Oh not that again,' Harris said with a sigh. 'It wasn't me; I told you over and over, you keep on and on and on. It wasn't me; for the last time, I've been clean for years, my mother and father need my help, so when my dad was told that he had only a year at the outside to live, I said that my days of being a naughty boy had come to an end. I'm clean now and have been for a while, if I got arrested for a crime now, it might kill the old man and I won't let that happen, I'm clean.' He was adamant, he got up and walked to the end of the cell, and for a moment looked at the barred window high up, just below the ceiling, and wondered if it was possible to squeeze through the bars. But it was just a fleeting thought; it came and went in a split second into the blackness of time, never ever to return.

'What I want to know is where you were last Monday night, at about six thirty?'

'Last Monday you mean, the night of the murder of Tommy in Baker Alley, is that what you're referring to? Don't try to pin that on me because he was a friend of mine, I saw him a few hours before it happened. He was with Tony Waybee outside the off-licence because Tony asked me for a pair of boots, and I told him that there was some in the big bin in the alley because I had put a pair in that very afternoon. If you're looking for Tommy's killer, I know who killed him,'

‘Oh you do, do you? Well that’s great, you cracked the case you should have been in the police force and all the crimes in this city would have been solved, you’re a bloody genius,’ Inspector Ryan’s sarcasm was rubbing off on Rainbow. ‘Who was it then?’

‘It was Waybee himself, he done it; everyone is talking about it, all the boys. I’m not grassing, it’s bound to come out sooner or later, and they were seen going in that direction at about that time.’

‘You seem to know a lot about this crime, maybe I should put you in charge of this murder enquiry, you are so much better at being a detective than a lot I know.’

‘Do you think so?’ Harris said with a wide smile on his face.

‘Of course I don’t, you fucking idiot, I wouldn’t put you in charge of a piss house. How do you know that the deceased, the man who was murdered on Monday night, was Tommy, when a name hasn’t been released yet? Even I don’t know the identity of the victim, even the press haven’t been told as of now.’ Rainbow stared at Harris with an intimidating look then said slowly, ‘You did it, didn’t you? You fucking killed this Tommy guy, admit it, you was in the bin like the rat you are, scavenging in the garbage, you jumped on him, killed him and then robbed him.’

‘No I didn’t, I was home with my mum and dad, go and ask them,’ Harris was feeling frightened, and shouted out in despair with a howl that a wolf would make.

Rainbow made to exit the cell when Harris pounced on him, pushing him into the door. His head was slightly cut; the blood seeped out and down his face, and a four-finger thrust sent Harris squealing like an injured dog back onto his bed just as two policemen entered the cell.

'All right, sarge?' The cop enquired; as they ushered him out of the cell.

'Yeah I'm OK, book him on the charge of assaulting me, and add it to the charge he's in here for now; I believe we may have the killer of the Baker Alley murder.'

Mrs Harris was handing in her son's medication as Rainbow came out of the cell and passed the front desk; she was heard to be telling the desk sergeant that her son was not a murderer and that three coppers had been to her house and searched it and she was sure that the ugly one they called Rainbow had planted some stuff in her son's room and she wanted to see the chief of police.

'That's him, that's him,' she repeated as Rainbow passed.

'See what your placid, non-violent boy has done to me? He just attacked me.' Rainbow pointed to his forehead and the trickle of blood coming down his face.

'Make sure it goes on his charge sheet, sergeant, and Mrs Harris, as for you seeing the chief, let me tell you, he's not available, so get yourself a lawyer.'

'He didn't do it, you're a liar,' she ranted. Rainbow ignored her and went to the restroom to clean up his face.

*

He didn't go to forensics; if he had he would have seen another policeman handing in some items that had come into his possession, and that policeman was Police Constable Charles Bright, the policeman who had been on duty around the crime scene the morning after the murder. He had been in the force for twenty-five years and was looking forward to his retirement day. He had a plot of land where he envisaged he would grow vegetables for the table, but just to get out of the rat race would be a blessing. His mind was on the week since the murder; he remembered how he came to be in the position he now found himself in, handing in the clothes that Detective Sergeant Rainbow had denied he had given to the bin man. Charlie's mind went back to that Tuesday morning when he had been on duty in Baker Alley. The bin man had returned later on in the day, still trying to do his job of moving the bins, and somehow the policeman and the bin man had developed a rapport and for the following days they would talk to pass the time away. It had really started when Mike the bin man had offered a cup of coffee from his Thermos flask.

Charlie had accepted gracefully, and the men in different uniforms discovered that they had lots in common. They would laugh together especially when Mike did his impressions of famous film stars, as he drove off with another load he would shout, 'I'll be back, hasta la vista, baby,' just like Arnold Schwarzenegger in a film that neither of them could recall. 'You want to fuck with me? You think you know best? Err… you're a fucken' choirboy compared to me, a choirboy,' that sent Charlie into fits of laughter. Another good impersonation of one of Arnold's films.

Mike would call at the bin alley at least twice a day and they would converse on every subject under the sun. Charles told of his life in the force and his forthcoming retirement, his love of the outdoors and gardening. Mike said that with a better education he might have been a policeman, or a film star or maybe a writer but being unable to read or write there was never any chance of him getting a Pulitzer Prize for the world's best novel writer; both men had roared with laughter at that suggestion.

'Don't you mean the Booker Prize for literature?' enquired Charlie.

'Pulitzer, Booker, means all the same to me, whatever. "You talking to me, you talking to me, it's only me, there's nobody else here, you talking to me?" Robert de Niro from the film *Taxi Driver*,' Mike said, laughing out loud.

'That's him, that's Robert de Niro, you got him to a tee,' Charlie said with delight in his voice, 'you certainly have got a talent there, Mike, great impersonation.'

'Thanks, Charlie, for your compliments, but I want to tell you one talent I've got and that's a brilliant memory. I remember every person I meet, even the last time we met, like if I saw someone, let's say, three years ago, and I met that person again, I would remember the last time we met, where we last met and sometimes the time of day almost to the minute, it's a wonder. I know it sounds complicated, but say I didn't see you for, say, five years, and we met again, I would be able to recall that the last time I met you was five years ago here in Baker Alley the sun was shining at the time and you were wearing a copper's uniform.' Both men laughed. 'I never put that talent into my reading and writing, who knows, I could have become a genius but here I am just a common bin man. I remember lots, that's why when your friend was talking to you yesterday morning at around eight forty, and he denied that he gave me a bundle of clothes just a few hours before, I couldn't help wondering why he would blatantly lie because he did give me the bundle of clothes. Maybe he didn't want you to know, Charlie, maybe he had something to hide?' That first conversation about the clothes had occurred on Wednesday afternoon, and forensics had covered the area with a fine toothcomb and concluded their work. Mike and his new-found friend shook hands and wished one another all the best before they went their separate ways.

Mike said as a farewell speech, 'I can only offer you toil, and sweat, and tears in the coming years, but we will fight in the fields, and on the beaches and on the bins, we will collect the garbage and we will never give in, we will never surrender,' in his best Winston Churchill impersonation. Once again Charlie curled up in fits of laughter.

PC Bright had been taken off the duty at the alley, and had resumed his duties as a beat copper, but what Mike had told him had played on his mind. What was the big deal in getting rid of a bundle of clothes? He had a hunch, and sometimes a hunch pays off, and sometimes it doesn't, but a hunch is a hunch. Charlie decided to go to the alley on Friday afternoon and wait for Mike the bin man to pick up another bin. He didn't have to wait long when the lorry came into the alley and Charlie approached. 'Do you still have that bundle of clothes at your house, Mike, the clothes you were telling me about? If you have I would like you to bring them to me, can you do that?'

'Sure can, I'll get them here tomorrow morning, Saturday at nine, or my name's not the one and only Michael J. Milford, bin man extraordinaire.' Once again laughter ensued.

Dead on nine the next day both men had met in the alley and Mike handed over the clothes as they drank tea in the cab of Mike's lorry.

'There's one thing I didn't tell you about, Charlie. Maybe your friend, your detective inspector, has a bad memory, because I saw him in a pub last night at six in the evening, and he sat with me and he didn't recognise me and yet he only spoke to me on Tuesday morning. I was talking about the bins and the job because I went to the pub to see some guy who is supposed to work for my boss. We sat there and he didn't say a word, it was as though he was avoiding me, then he bought a model boat that I had for sale, once again he showed no signs of ever meeting me, so as I have said, maybe he's got a poor memory. It's still hard to understand why someone would deny doing something that he did just two hours earlier, unless he didn't want you to know he had given me the clothes for reasons of his own.'

Mike explained that Saturday was his day off and he had to go because he had to visit his mother-in-law later in the day and had done his bit in helping the law. 'So all I've got to say to you is,' Mike put on a familiar look and shouted, 'GOOD MORNING VIETNAM,' exactly as Robin Williams said it in the film.

'Fantastic, bloody fantastic,' Charlie enthused. 'You even looked liked Robin Williams, you should take it up, you know, be an impersonator instead of driving a bin lorry. Anyhow I've got to go now, my friend, and by the way, he wasn't an inspector, he's a sergeant, that's all,' Charlie explained. They shook hands for the last time, and never met again.

Many years later Charlie heard that his friend Michael

J. Milford had found fame as a writer. And was living somewhere on a tropical island.

*

'Just check for blood and whatever you do, it's to do with the Baker murder, so it would be appreciated if you could get me some gen on them soon,' Charlie said, as he handed the clothes in to forensics.

'Didn't know you had been promoted to detective,' the pathologist said.

'No, just helping out, doing my bit, that's all,' Charlie replied.

'I'll have the results in a couple of days, got a load of stuff to get done.'

'Thanks a lot, as they say in America, have a nice day.' PC Charlie Bright left the station and went home, his duty done.

*

Rainbow was on his way to the dinner party but decided to pass the club to see if there was anyone there. It was open on Saturday evenings on occasions; there was something he had to sort out. The lights were on in the main part of the club; there was only one car in the car park and that belonged to Eddie Bail.

He was sitting behind his desk working on some figures and looked surprised at Rainbow's entrance.

'Hello Ray, I was expecting you to call in some time soon as we had arranged, pull up a chair and we can get down to business.'

'No Eddie, I want a workout first, so will you take me through a few moves, let's have a workout. I'll go and change, won't take a minute, you do the same then we can do the business OK?' Eddie agreed and within five minutes the men were facing one another on the mat. At first they went through the normal karate stances and blows, missing one another by fractions of an inch, then as Eddie turned for a split second, Rainbow struck with a blow that didn't stop but made contact, sending Eddie sprawling across the mat, and onto the wooden part of the club floor.

Rainbow ran forward and enquired if he was all right, apologising profusely for the uncontrolled blow, then helped him to his feet.

'Hell Ray, watch it, you were that much away from killing me,' he indicated with his fingers, 'remember what I taught you: control, have power over your thoughts.'

'Don't worry about that, I have power over my thoughts and actions.' With that he took up another stance, and hissing like a snake, he sent a blow straight toward Eddie's throat. Eddie blocked the blow and put his hands in the air.

'Whoa,' he said, 'what's happening here, are you trying to hurt me?' Rainbow threw another blow and followed with a drop kick that had Eddie shouting out in pain, flat on his back holding his throat.

'Sorry about that,' Rainbow spat out like the venom of the snake he had become, as he stood over him. 'I think you need a lesson, not in karate but in how to treat people. You think you can go around blackmailing? Well let me tell you, my dear friend, you fucking can't. I have to teach you something, and you must promise me that you will never do it again.' He kicked him in the ribs six times in quick succession, which seemed like it was only twice, he was like lightning.

'Your fault, Eddie, you shouldn't have been such a good teacher, and I wouldn't have been your number-one student. Now get up, and let's get this business you talked about over with, because after tonight we will not meet again, I've had enough of you.' One more kick concluded the workout. He bent down, pulled him to his feet, and pushed him into the office and sat him on the chair; Rainbow sat in the seat behind the desk. Eddie was still in pain, and as he got his breath back, opened his mouth.

'You're right, we won't be seeing one another again, because I'm going to call the police in on this, you're a fucking' disgrace to your profession, you're going to pay for this in more ways than one, believe me,' Eddie threatened. 'I'm not frightened of you. If you want to fight me for real, well that's OK by me. You are unsafe, I'm going to the board of directors of the karate federation, and I'll tell them of your animal-like conduct, you will be stripped of your status in the karate world; you'll lose your dans. You'll be nothing. I know what you did, remember,' he sneered.

Rainbow just sat back and listened to what his adversary had to say.

'Now there you go again, and so soon after I gave you a warning and your threatening attitude is rearing its ugly head again, will you never learn? Do you think I would tell you that I killed someone just like that? What I told you was a pack of lies; I was having you on, and you fell for it, hook, line and sinker. I thought you were brighter than that, now I'm wondering if I should read you your rights before I arrest you for blackmail, or would you rather call the station and report me? You get fuck all money out of me, do you understand now? I'm going to get my stuff out of the locker, and you won't see me again, unless it's in a court of law. You were lucky tonight I went easy on you, incidentally we arrested the killer today, and he's in custody now.'

'Sorry Ray,' Eddie spluttered, 'I don't know what came over me, I'm getting out of this game, I can't keep the club going any longer, the money's not there, I've been at my wits' end for a while now, been depressed more times than you've had hot dinners. I can't take this life anymore; do you know my wife left me, and took the kids? I'm alone in this world. I'll get the men who were going to do the roof to take down the scaffolding; I can't afford the thirty grand they wanted.'

'I bet you can't, it was my money that was going to pay for that, hard luck mate. You're a fucking' loser, I've never really liked you, you lost it all Eddie, you lost it all,' Rainbow said with a sneer as he left the office.

He went to the locker and got his things out and was about to leave when the shot rang out from the office and echoed through the club, over and over, tapering off into the silence again. He turned around and returned to the office, and saw the blood seeping into the carpet, and the hole in Eddie's right temple, his jawbone sticking out, giving him a smiling, hideous look in death. Rainbow bent over and felt his neck; there was no sign of life. He picked up the gun and slipped it into his pocket, then looked on the desk. *There's no suicide note*, Rainbow thought, *but what if he had written down what had been said a few days before when he had confessed? What if, in his files, there was something that might incriminate him?* Rainbow knew what to do; the place had to disappear from the face of the earth, and there was only one way: fire. He waited until the fire took hold, and the office was well ablaze, until he left the club car park. Within five minutes the whole wooden club was ablaze, and he was on his way to his dinner party, but now he could add another title to his name, that of an arsonist.

The old man in the darkness of the night outside the burning club struggled with his fear as he got on his bicycle and went home to decide what to do next; he had heard and seen it all.

*

They were all there to greet him as he entered the house. His father, who for years had been aloof, was this evening very cordial, and his mother her normal self, being warm and friendly to anybody she met. Everyone seemed to be in a good mood as they had a drink and sat down to dinner. Michelle was quiet and seemed sullen as though she was brooding about something; Charlotte was looking beautiful and had prepared herself to perfection for this special occasion.

Rainbow's father started the table talk as they finished the first course, 'Nasty murder in the city last Monday, I've been told, what? There's rumours going around that the detectives have blundered on the case, have no ideas or clues, an absolute shambles, and also that the lead detective is a nincompoop, and is going to be pulled off the case if nothing develops very soon. I call it Incompetents, what?'

'Father, I would be grateful if we didn't talk about work, not on this special night. I'm sure there are better subjects to discuss.' He looked around the table for support.

'Yes I agree,' said his mother, passing the bottle of wine over the table. 'Let's talk about that beautiful house that you are about to buy, and the venue, have you decided where you're going to have the wedding ding-dong? For the sake of better words, ho, ho, ho,' she chuckled. Everyone joined in apart from Raymond who was thinking of how, just a short while ago, he was looking at a dead man, and setting fire to a gym.

A week, just a week, and his whole world had turned upside down. To think, a detective sergeant with promotion on the horizon, a beautiful woman like Charlotte, everything going along just fine then bang, everything hanging on a thread now, it was unbelievable, but it was true. Raymond Rainbow had turned into a murderer, an arsonist, and was also trying to alter the course of justice by instigating someone to lie in court. These thoughts whirled around his head, flitting from one thought to another; he hardly listened to the chatter going on at the table.

'More wine, darling?' Charlotte asked three times before he came back from those deep thoughts. He smiled a half smile then surprised all by excusing himself for a moment. He went on to the veranda, sat down and buried his head in his hands.

Away in the distance thunder shouted out a warning, and lightning lit up the sky. For a moment he wished he could be hit by a bolt that would send him into another place, a place of peace, freedom from strife, away from the rigours of living. This was the first time that he had felt this way; the strain was beginning to tell.

'You OK, darling? You look pale, have you seen a ghost? I've got your wine.'

She placed it on the long coffee table, and put her arms around him.

'Tell me what's wrong, my darling. I'm sure I can help you, I'll certainly try.' She kissed him gently on the lips, and gave him a loving hug. 'You hurt yourself, how did you do that?' She pointed to the slight cut on his head where Harris had hit him.

'Oh it's nothing, just a scratch; there are worse things to worry about than that. Charlotte, there's a storm brewing, a big storm, and it's just over the horizon. There's been a lot of pressure at work, and the nincompoop my father mentioned before, unbeknown to him, is me.' He pointed to himself. 'There's been no clues in the murder case in Baker yet, the case may never be solved, and the inspector is on my back, I've got until Tuesday to get something otherwise he threatened to take me off the case, Tuesday afternoon at the latest; he can be a sarcastic bastard sometimes.' Rainbow shook his head from side to side.

The sky lit up once again, 'Is that the storm you were talking about?' she asked, pointing to the blackness in the sky.

'No, it's bigger than that; this one is life-threatening.'

'What do you mean, life-threatening? What can threaten us? We have got everything in perfect order, what could go wrong? I know something that will put you in a better mood,' she put her hand on his crotch and stroked it, laughing as she did it.

'Please, Charlotte, not now, can't you take anything seriously for a minute?' He pushed her hand away roughly. 'There's a time and place and that time's not now.'

'Sorry, I didn't realise you were such a misery, and on our special day, our party with your mother and father, they're here for our sakes, and all you can do is bring your work here. Why didn't you stay at the station then we wouldn't have such a misery to contend with? I'm going back in, and you better come in soon, you know your parents, they'll be going to bed soon. So get yourself out of your bad mood, and get in there, there's a lots of things to sort out, we have an appointment to go and pay the fifty thousand deposit for our house on Monday and don't say you can't make it because we will lose the chance of buying the house if we don't do it Monday. There are a lot of other people who would jump at the chance of getting our place, so we have to get in there now.'

He was surprised to see Charlotte so angry so suddenly, it was the first time he had seen her this way. He felt his own anger rising in the pit of his stomach, and he saw something in her eyes that was new; for a moment it looked like hatred.

She turned on her heels, which made a squeaking noise on the wooden floor, and went into the house. He shook his head; he had forgotten about the money, things had overtaken him. At times he felt he was heading for a nervous breakdown and at times very despondent and depressed. He sipped his wine; he realised that he had to make an effort although he really felt like hiding under a rock on his own. Laughter drifted through the doorway and he made to get up, and there she was, standing there. Her eyes rested on him, she lit a cigarette and blew the smoke out into the veranda, then appeared in front of it as though she was a magician's assistant about to do a trick.

'Don't you like your party? I've been told to come and get you to bring you out of the cold, as your mother put it, and I was happy to oblige because I want to ask you something that I couldn't do in there.' She pointed to inside the door.

'And what was that, what's so important that you can't ask me in front of the others?' Rainbow blurted out.

She walked towards him and sat down, and adjusted her dress around her knees.

'It's to do with me and you, Ray. I don't know if you are aware but it's been a while now,' she hesitated, 'yes it's been two years and it's been eating into me, but I guess this is the time to bring it out. I have lain on my bed at night not being able to sleep and thought about it over and over, again and again, and although I love my sister, I love you more, and I have decided that I can't go on like this any longer. I love you, Ray, and I have to have you in my life, more than as a sister-in-law, that just won't do for me. '

'Don't be so absurd, I'm very fond of you, you know that, but I'm in love with your sister and we are going to be married soon, and that's the end of it. Now come on, let's go into the party, and stop this nonsense.' He made to get up.

'You didn't say that when you were fucking me, or when I had your thing in my mouth did you? You didn't say it was ridiculous then, did you? Or to think of it as nonsense, you didn't think of my sister then did you? You just lay back and enjoyed my body. I do recall you said you loved me just before you came inside of me, well now, my darling Raymond, I have to tell you this, you're not going to marry Charlotte because you're going to be a…' She hesitated once more. 'I'm pregnant, and you're the father.'

*

It was pouring with rain on Sunday morning and after looking out of the window he felt like jumping back into his warm bed; he hadn't slept well. What Michelle had told him the night before had put the dampeners on a good sleep. He had tried his best to pretend to enjoy his party, and to avoid looking at Michelle, although he felt her eyes on him. He had made it up with Charlotte, and promised not to bring his work home again, but he also mentioned to his father, when the men were left alone, while the women were clearing up the dishes, that he was having thoughts of trying another profession and finishing with the police force. The old man made no comment, and after a last drink they had raised their glasses for one last time and drifted off to bed.

She had insisted on sex and he had done the business but it wasn't as long as they normally did it and at times his member started to flag; he blamed it on the amount of drink he had drunk, but the truth was he was thinking of what Michelle had told him. He had looked at Charlotte's lovely face as she was sleeping, and his guilt had risen up and broken like a wave on a beach, and a tear fell on to his pillow. He had promised to meet her at three in the afternoon at the high street bank the next day, but before that he would have to see Waybee, and retrieve his lost ten thousand pounds.

Breakfast was a quiet affair and he kissed his mother goodbye and shook his father's hand quite formally, and promised a house-warming party when contracts had been exchanged on the house sale, but before that of course there was the wedding where they would all meet again. He saw the tears in his mother's eyes as they drove off towards their home. He left shortly after; he wanted to get away before Michelle awoke. He could do without any more confrontations. Somehow he felt relieved as he hit the road; he decided to go a different way to the station, bypassing the club. He still had the watch and the wallet and boots in the Glove compartment of his car.

He put the wipers on as he drove through the downpour; the traffic was light on Sunday's at that time of the morning. He arrived at the station with Michelle's words ringing in his ears… 'You're the father.' After a brief 'Good morning' to the desk sergeant he went to the canteen and ordered a coffee, then sat down at a table with a red and white chequered tablecloth. His eyes looked over the canteen. It needed upgrading; it was showing signs of neglect. He felt cosy for a moment as he listened to the rain beating a rhythm on the window panes. He took some papers out of his briefcase and pretended to study them. This was the day that he would close the case with the crime pinned on Harris, and he would be in the clear, to continue his life.

'You won't be doing karate any more, Ray.' One of his colleagues pulled up a chair and sat down, putting sugar in his coffee and giving it a quick stir.

'Oh yeah, and why's that then? Do you reckon I'm too old and past it?' Rainbow said looking up from his papers with a disapproving look. He didn't need company.

'No club there any longer, went up in smoke last night, burned to the ground, not one piece of timber left, just ashes. Absolutely flattened, gone, kaput, as they say in German,' he said in a matter-of fact way.

Rainbow put on his surprised look, 'You're kidding me. Please, not on a Monday morning, you know "I don't like Mondays", like the song says, you know that song by the Rolling Stones. It's a bit early for jokes.'

'Monday? What are you on about, today is Sunday, you got your days mixed up, Ray. Like I was saying, the club's gone. It's no joke, the building's gone, the fire brigade just let it burn. It was burned down last night, when they got there it was too late to save it so they watched it go up in flames. The place was built of wood, all wood.'

'Of course it's Sunday, I'm not used to coming into work over the weekends, and this case is doing my head in. Burned to the ground, eh? Eddie the club owner won't be too happy. I don't think it was insured, he told me he was having money problems. So I guess I'll have to find another club, there's a few in the city. Poor old Eddie, he'll be unhappy this rainy morning, what a way to finish a week. I'll have to go around to see him, give him a bit of support. It happened last night, you say?'

'Yeah, about nine o'clock I was told, and going to see Eddie, there's no point in doing that because he don't care now, he died in the blaze. He was working in the back office apparently, so I was told, maybe he committed suicide, maybe the money worries you mentioned got to him. So he took that way out, setting fire to the place, there's a team working on it now.'

Rainbow put his best shocked look on, and put his hand to his face.

'Poor old Eddie, I didn't know it was that bad, if only he had asked me for help I would have helped him out. Anyhow, thanks for the info, just the right kind of news to start the week off, and this storm don't help, I wish I'd stayed in bed now.' He finished his coffee scooping the sugar from the bottom of the cup and putting the spoon in his mouth. 'Sweet tooth,' he pointed out with a smile. He picked his papers up and went to leave. 'See you later, got a meeting to go to.'

'Yeah see you Ray, incidentally, Boomtown Rats, not the Rolling Stones.'

'What're you on about, Boomtown who?' Rainbow said.

'You said something about the song, "I Don't Like Mondays", it was by the Boomtown Rats, not the Rolling Stones as you said, I'm just pointing it out, that's all.'

'Well thank you for that important information, I'm sorry I made that mistake, I'll make a note of it, anyhow whoever sang it, I agree with them, I don't like Mondays or Sundays for that matter.' He got up to leave.

Rainbow was informed that the pub fighters Waybee, Sims and Harris would be appearing in court on Monday morning, so feeling tired with his mind racing he decided to go to his apartment for a bit of solitude and thinking time.

FIFTEEN
MONDAY

Tony Waybee had finished his breakfast and was sitting on his bunk in his cell, waiting to go to the courts at ten o'clock on Monday morning. The night in the nick had gone fast; he had slept most of it. Now he wondered how he would fare in the law courts, he thought a small fine. He remembered the times he had been in custody in the past on more serious charges, so this time he wasn't worried at all, well, not about facing the judge that was the least of his worries. But he had had time to think, and something was not riding well on his conscience. He had to get the lost money back somehow, he hoped that some tramp hadn't stumbled on it, but then with the bad weather over the weekend he doubted if tramps were roaming around the park as they tended to do in the summertime. He and the boy might have retrieved the crashed helicopter and the money if it hadn't been for Rainbow coming across the park as he did.

Waybee decided he would go back to the park as soon as the weather improved; find the money, ten thousand smackers, that kind of money would keep his Ruby happy for a long time in sunny Spain. He would get himself a plane ticket and be away in no time, before Rainbow could say, 'Hello, hello, hello.' The thought made him laugh, and he glanced up at the camera looking down at him. He heard the cell door being unlocked, and a policeman walked in who he hadn't seen before.

'Harris,' the copper said as he looked at his board, then, realising he had made a mistake, immediately changed it, and said, 'Waybee, I meant Waybee. You're out of here. But before you go, Detective Sergeant Rainbow wants a word with you, and then you're going to court.'

Rainbow entered the cell and indicated that he wanted to be alone with the prisoner; the policeman left, closing the door. Waybee sat on his bunk and looked at Rainbow with apprehension in his head; he already knew that he wasn't going to like what he had decided over the weekend.

Rainbow stood near the cell door and looked down at Waybee with an expression that spelt disdain. 'Trust you to fuck things up, our plan was perfect, and you get into a fucking fight, you might go down for this, and what we talked about is all in vain, why don't you fucking wise up?'

'I didn't start the fight, it was that asshole Sims,' Waybee protested.

'Well let's move on. We all set then? I'm going to organise a line-up, and then you will pick Harris out like you said you would, then with the evidence that you supplied me with we can put this all behind us, and live happy ever after. Fancy getting arrested for fighting with him just before you finger him, he's going to be mad at you.'

'As I've just told you, I didn't start the fight, it was that bastard Sims who started it, Bootsy just got in the way of my fist, the whole time of the fight he was on his back out of it. Anyhow there something I have to tell you, last night I asked the desk sergeant if it was at all possible to see Harris because I wanted to apologise for what had happened in the pub, and the sergeant said although it wasn't what normally happens he would allow us five minutes as long as a copper was present, so when we had a bite to eat I told him. The sergeant thought it was a good gesture on my part, so I did, I told him I was sorry for what happened, and do you know what he did?

'No surprise me,' Rainbow said sarcastically, 'but make it fast.'

'He hugged me, that's what he did, fucken hugged me, then told me he held no grudge at all, then he went on to say that he had always admired me, then he showed me something that I've never seen—'

'Oh for fuck's sake don't tell me he showed you his cock,' Rainbow sneered.

'No need to be sarcastic, he showed me his hands. They're full of arthritis and there's no way he could fight or hit anyone with hands like his so—'

'Get to the point, do you think I'm here for an old boys' get-together, I've got things to do, I don't believe I'm hearing this after all we talked about what we agreed.'

Rainbow could sense that something not to his liking was about to develop.

'I can't do it,' Waybee said, 'I can't do it; I'm not going to lie in court, and put an innocent man behind bars. I couldn't live with myself, I've been a bastard in my time, but I'll not sink that low, so I'm sorry, I'm not doing it for you, or anyone. Do what you want, that's it.' He turned away and fidgeted on his bunk.

'Get my money back,' Rainbow sneered, 'you've just lost five thousand, and from now on, I'll be on your back, you won't see me, but I'll be there morning, noon and night, mark my words, you fucking moron.'

At that moment the cell door opened and Waybee was let out for his court appearance.

*

'Causing an affray by fighting in a public place, how do you plead?' the magistrate said with no feeling whatsoever; his disinterest in the case showed. Sims and Waybee pleaded guilty. Harris pleaded not guilty, but after hearing how Harris had spilled beer over Mr Waybee, as the magistrate called him, and evidence from Rainbow about the attack in his cell, the latter made the magistrate a little angry. 'You can't go around attacking police officers in the course of their duties, there's no excuse, and I'm not prepared to hear any of it.' He found Harris guilty and fined him five hundred pounds, and as he didn't have the money to pay he was remanded in custody until the fine was paid. Sims was fined the same amount but after swearing at the magistrate, was imprisoned for a further week for contempt of court. After that, Waybee explained how he was having a quiet drink when he was approached by Harris and Sims, who insisted on joining him at his table; an argument started then got out of hand, and a friendly tussle had ensued where others in The Black Kettle pub, who were waiting for a fight, joined in to cause the so-called affray.

'Sir I put it to you that the perpetrators of this crime have not been apprehended, and therefore a not-guilty verdict must be the outcome.'

Waybee looked around the court, saw where Rainbow was sitting in the gallery, and gave him a broad smile. Rainbow just looked down.

'Have you been watching television shows on the cases of Perry Mason, the wheelchair lawyer, Mr Waybee? Because I feel this is becoming a farce. You pleaded guilty, so are you telling me now that you want to change your plea to not guilty? Are you trying to waste the court's time? If so you may be in more trouble than you are in now,' the magistrate said, adjusting his glasses.

'No sir, I don't want to change my plea, but in mitigation I would want to put it to this court and to you, your learned honour, how much I feel sorrow for what I did.'

'Stop, stop now, Mr Waybee,' the magistrate interjected, 'I find you guilty and fine you five hundred pounds. And a bit of advice: stop thinking you're a lawyer. I remember having had dealings with you in the past you may have been a so-called prison lawyer, but it won't work in my court. I don't deal in sycophants or bullshitters excuse the vulgarity of the word.'

'I don't know the words you're saying, sir, so maybe you will understand me better. I won't pay, I can't pay, so do your worst, put me inside, I don't care I've been in before, do your fucken' worst.' The magistrate told him to refrain from swearing in court and said that he would stay in a detention centre until he had paid the fine.

DS Rainbow winced when he heard the swear word. He knew that Waybee was going to go inside, and his ideas of Waybee helping him out of his mess had now diminished. There was no way back. He wouldn't be searching the park for his money, it would have to go on hold for the duration, and the chances of someone else finding it had just increased. He shook his head in disbelief as he left the court, and gave Waybee a sour look, as he was led down to the cells to calm down.

Detective Chief Inspector Ryan also had the Monday morning blues. He had had difficulties with his car, it should have been in a garage but he hadn't had the time to take it there with the workload he was carrying, and he had just made it to the station through the morning storm. Now he was in his office on the phone arranging for it to be picked up by the garage to be repaired; he was, to say the least, in a bad mood.

It was ten thirty when the officers drifted in for the meeting. Briefcases and clipboards at hand, they took random seats, and talked among themselves about the weather and how their weekend had panned out. Rainbow slid next to Barns and told him that if he was asked if he had worked on the Baker case over the weekend, to say he had because he was sure it would come up. He was dreading this meeting, he had a bad feeling. The door opened and DI Ryan walked in, in a hurried sort of way. He took his seat and looked at his papers then looked up and said in a low tone, 'Yes gentlemen, I realise it's a terrible day to start a week, but we have a duty to the public to carry on, and try to make this city crime-free. It's a tall order, I know, but every time we get a result and put a criminal behind bars, it goes some way toward meeting our aims. My biggest concern at the moment is to get the Baker Alley killer in court, then in prison where he belongs. Now I know there must be some of you here this morning who think I may be going over the top when I push you for information, but I want to point out that the buck doesn't end with me, the top brass want to know how far we have got in solving this case. Remember, the victim was one of ours and the pressure is on me to find the killer. We have other crimes to solve as well, so I wanted you to put in every effort toward getting somewhere, and I'm sure you have tried your best. It's been one week today since one of our officers in the course of his duties was cut down in his prime, and I want to get it in the bag, and so although I acknowledge that the teams I put together last week have done their best,' he hesitated then continued, 'there have been no new leads in this case so far. So reluctantly I'm going to replace you all in new teams. I'll start with the leader of the teams, Detective Sergeant Rainbow; as from now, you are relieved of your duties on this case.' Rainbow felt immediate relief at the revelation and nodded.

The inspector continued, 'All the other teams will also be relieved, and by midday today the new teams will be in effect, led by Detective Sergeant Jones.' All eyes turned to DS Jones who smiled and muttered 'Thank you,' as though it was a promotion.

'You, Sergeant Jones, will confer with Sergeant Rainbow, and he will give you all the gen on the case so far; bring him up to date with what you told me.' The inspector looked at Rainbow who acknowledged once again with a nod. He had no intention of following these instructions; he was almost in the clear, now the pressure was off him there was no way that anyone could prove that he was the culprit. The only person who knew the truth was Waybee and he had him in his pocket; he would make sure he didn't talk as soon as he came out of prison.

'What do you have to say on the matter, Sergeant? Sergeant, wake up man, are you not taking this in, or has your mind gone on holiday?' the inspector said to Rainbow who had been deep in thought. 'Wake up, wake up!' he almost shouted.

Rainbow realised that the inspector was talking to him, and sat up in his chair. The other officers laughed, and muttered to themselves.

'Sorry sir I was thinking of the case; maybe we have been looking in the wrong places, at the local criminals, maybe this case is a contract killing. Maybe the drug cartel got wind of his underground activities and put a professional hit man on the job—'

'Lots of maybes,' the inspector said not allowing Rainbow to continue, 'but you may have something; put all your thoughts to Sergeant Jones when you meet with him; in the meantime, pay attention to this meeting. Today, gentlemen, is the funeral of our colleague Robert Jennet, and I have informed his brother Derek that we all here send our condolences to his family, because I believe he was married with two small children who have no father now, a crying shame, so please let's have one minute silence in his memory and for his devotion to duty.'

The officers bent their heads in reverence.

Rainbow felt really bad; he had been unaware of the fact that the man he had killed had been married. His brother hadn't mentioned it, and the knowledge that he had children made him feel worse. He hoped the meeting would come to an end soon. He wanted to get out of there, and go to his apartment just for a drink and a lie down for a while, he felt exhausted and it was only eleven in the morning.

The inspector concluded, 'that's it gentlemen, go and do your duties and with a bit of luck that's been avoiding us so far, will come our way, good luck.' The policemen gathered their papers together and streamed out of the room.

The inspector stopped to speak to Detective Jones, and Rainbow saw them shake hands. He overheard the word 'congratulations' as he walked by.

'Oh Rainbow, I want you to go to Hegging at High Croft to investigate a theft of some chickens from the farm; and a tray of eggs has been reported missing,' the inspector said with a shadow of a grin that stole across his face; the same look developed on Detective Sergeant Jones' face.

'Yes sir, I'll do my best, as I have always done, and let me also congratulate you, Mervin, on your promotion on my case and good luck. I've spent hours on it and it's certainly baffling, but with your permission, sir,' he glanced at the inspector, then back to Jones, 'try the karate clubs down in Dorston, it's been said that the blow was a karate blow, the sort that can kill, the pathologist told me.'

'Thanks for the advice,' Detective Jones said, 'I'll get on to it, as soon as the teams are chosen, and I don't mean to rub it in but this time I'm after the best men we have on the force.'

'With the help of top detectives from the Met, I've called them up to help solve this one,' the inspector said, butting in. 'The top man, Superintendent Perkins, the man who solved the Grimes murders a few years ago is coming in to help out, so it won't be long now. It's a week today and so far we haven't got a single clue apart from a dead body, and after today we won't have that after cremation, they don't mess around at the crematorium.'

'No sir, they don't, well I'll go and see what I can do about my new assignment; once again, good luck.'

Rainbow went to the door as the inspector said, 'you do karate, don't you, Rainbow, so I understand? So you should know all the places on the body, the pressure points. You would know their whereabouts. I'm sure you didn't need a pathologist to tell you that.'

'I do know, sir, he just volunteered the information when I was doing my enquiries. And for me doing karate, I gave up the sport when I injured my hand, good memory you have sir. I've got better things to do with my right hand than chop at dummies in the gym. Anyhow, my club was burned down last night, so I've been told, so I guess that's the end of that. And the owner was killed in the fire, sad case. I knew Eddie well.' The inspector and Sergeant Jones left the meeting room to go to the inspector's office for more discussion on the case.

'Fucking assholes,' Rainbow muttered under his breath as he made his way out of the police station. The storm had had a laugh, and was now on its way to play its game further afield. The sun was peeping out as though it wanted to make sure it was safe to come out to warm up the now-drenched land. He got in his car and sat there just looking out across the car park and watching other officers leaving to go to their various jobs. His mind went over the meeting he had just attended. It dawned on him that none of his former colleagues had given him any form of condolence for his losing his position as team leader; some hadn't even said good morning. It was as though he had been sent to Coventry; nobody was speaking to him, as though they blamed him for the lack of breakthrough in the case. That thought made him smile. He opened the glove compartment and saw the only bit of evidence he had: a wallet, a pair of boots and a watch, maybe it was time to get rid of them. He realised his plan to frame Harris was down the drain; Waybee had let him down. He started the car and drove to the river. There was no one around as he found a stone, and placed it in the bag with the items, tied the handles together, and threw it in the river. A certain satisfaction came over him as he saw it disappear into the depths to rest in the mud forever. The gun he had went into the river as well.

He arrived at his apartment and went up the steps. He looked out over the city and wondered what was going to become of his life. He felt drained and all he wanted to do was sleep; he had to have a bit of silence, to be on his own, the pressure on his mind was intense. He entered his flat and shouted, 'Pedro, Daddy's home.' There was no answer. He looked in the cage and Pedro his parrot looked back at him with unseeing eyes. At that moment he realised that a good companion he had had and loved for years was no longer in a position to talk or swear. He was dead, and the hard man who had seen terrible sights in his career sat down with the parrot on his lap. He remembered the time that he and Charlotte were in the city pet shop, and first set their eyes on the parrot, and Charlotte had talked to it. Her words were, 'Hello little man, you look nice,' and the parrot had spread his wings and squawked, 'Hello big tits, you're nice, squawk, big time.' Charlotte had burst out laughing, and wanted to buy it on the spot.

Over time she had taught the parrot all the swear words, and had had hours of fun with the bird. She, like him, would miss the 'little man' as she had called him. It would be hard to tell her that Pedro had flown off to the aviary in the sky. He placed the parrot back in the cage, covering it over with a tea towel, and put the cover over the birdcage, then noticed a tear in the corner of his eye.

This macho man had shed a few tears in the week that had just gone by. He lay down on the settee and closed his eyes; his head was throbbing.

Detective Constable Barns and Detective Constable Harris were sitting in their squad car on surveillance duty, looking out for a burglary suspect who had failed to turn up in court. Harris was munching into a meat pie, and his partner was drinking a soft drink. It was a boring job at times. They had been disappointed at being taken off the Baker Alley killing. They were shocked to hear that their ex-boss, Sergeant Rainbow, had been humiliated in being given the menial job of looking for lost chickens. In a way they felt a bit sorry for him, but one thing they couldn't understand was why, when the inspector had said that not one bit of evidence had been obtained, that Sergeant Rainbow didn't counter that statement. After all, it was in Harris's house on Fingle estate that the evidence was obtained. A wallet and a watch, the boots that the sergeant himself had found. They recalled that Sergeant Rainbow had punched the air with delight, had shouted, 'Got him at last, done and dusted,' yet none of these things were mentioned at the meeting. Something must have happened that they had not been told about.

DC Barns made a mental note that he would ask the sergeant what had become of the items that he had found when they next caught up with him at the station. The two detectives continued with their surveillance as the afternoon drifted on.

Meanwhile, after resting for a while, Rainbow rang Charlotte to tell her that he couldn't make the meeting at the bank, telling her that he was on a very important enquiry, and it was impossible to get time off, so asked her to get in touch with the bank for an extension to the deadline, another week would do, he had said. She wasn't too happy and asked him when he would be up to see her again. He had said that he was so busy on the Baker Alley murder case that it could be a few days. She was shocked to hear of Eddie Bail's death and the burning down of the club, she asked if he had retrieved the workout trousers with the big pockets that she had given him for a gift at Christmas. He lied and said that they had burned in the fire, but they were in fact the trousers that he had given to the bin man, which were now in forensics, but he didn't know that. She informed him that her sister was in a bad mood and had been crying, and had told her mother that she intended leaving home and that news had upset her mother.

'Sounds like it's not a nice place to be at this time; maybe I should keep away,' he had said. But the feeble joke passed on without a smile, let alone a laugh. He promised to take her to Norway when this busy time was all over. He replaced the phone, put his coat on, went to the birdcage, picked up the parrot, and put it in a shoe box he had in the bottom of his wardrobe, and left the flat. He was on his way to see Big Joe Bananas with a new plan in his head.

SIXTEEN
MONDAY

'Fly, fly,' the little man shouted out as he sat at his desk in the betting shop's back room. The butcher picked up the fly swat, and ran across the room to swat the fly as his boss swore that the bastards shit on the food, and moaned that he couldn't understand how God had made such filthy creatures and for what purpose. 'You know, Butch, if I had been God when flies applied for life, I would have denied it along with slugs and snails and coppers.' He laughed out loud at his ideas.

'Yeah and morons, who don't do as they're told', Buch remarked, 'eh boss?' 'I've told you before, you shouldn't talk about yourself like that, Butch, you're not quite a moron yet, I know you're getting there, but you're not there yet, an idiot maybe!'

'Oh come on, boss, I'm not that bad, I look after you, don't I?'

'Yeah, but I pay you well, don't I? Go fix me a drink before I slap you.'

The minder left the room to get the drink, muttering under his breath.

Five minutes had passed when he returned with the drink, and placed it on the table.

'There's a Detective Rainman out there,' he pointed to the door, 'said he wants to see you about something, boss.'

'Don't know any Rainman, he's not one of my cops, tell him to come in,' Joe ordered. Butcher left the room, and Joe lifted the phone and told his other henchman to come down.

Rainbow came to the door and looked around the flashily furnished room.

'Search him for a piece, Butcher,' Bananas ordered. The other bodyguard came in from a back door and walked across the room, and stood in front of Rainbow, blocking his view of the table. Butcher went to frisk him.

'Hey, hold on, be polite now,' Rainbow warned, 'show some courtesy to a member of the law, I haven't introduced myself, at least let me show you my warrant card, I could be anyone.'

'I don't know any Rainman, we've never met before, what do you want?' shouted Joe Bananas across the room from his desk.

'Well, if you get these gorillas out of my face, I'll tell you. I want to see you on a private matter.' He looked around the big man facing him who had the look of fury on his face.

'My men stay, search him,' Bananas ordered once again.

'Don't touch me, don't go down that road now, I'm warning you, back off.' Rainbow took a step back.

Butcher made his mistake in taking no notice of what Rainbow had just told him, and reached out to do his boss's wishes.

Blackness came instantly, no stars, just blackness, and all recollection gone. If he could have seen the way he catapulted across the room and landed on the desk knocking the glass into the air, and spilling the contents all over his wide-eyed boss, he would have been truly amazed, just as his friend was. He was crumpled on his knees holding his throbbing neck, he didn't even see the blow that sent him sprawling across the room, hitting his head on the door.

'Let's start again shall we?' Rainbow said with a stern look. He went outside and shut the door. Bananas sat in his chair transfixed, he had never seen anything like it in his lifetime of crime; he had met some nasty characters, but had never seen two of the hardest men he knew, dispatched in such a short time, a split second. He wanted someone like this stranger in his employ to be his bodyguard; he looked at Butcher still unconscious on the floor with his fat stomach showing and the other man moaning in a corner holding his head in his hands.

The door opened again and Rainbow entered and stood by the door slightly smiling.

'Good afternoon, Mr Joseph Bananas, I'm Detective Sergeant Rainbow and I would like to have a word with you in private, I'm sure it will be to your advantage.' He went to his inside pocket to show his warrant card, and Bananas ducked behind the table as though he was just about to get shot. Rainbow walked to the desk and peered over showing his card. My name is Rainbow not Rainman.' He pointed to the card.

Big Bananas stood up then flopped into his chair again. He bent down and went to a side drawer on his desk.

'Keep your hands on the desktop where I can see them, no funny business with me or you'll be going down the same road as your boys here,' he pointed at the men who were licking their wounds and moaning.

'Just wanted to get a tissue to clean up this mess,' Joe remarked as he pointed to the mess on his desk, his spilt drink.

'Forget about that for now, it's not important, what I've got to tell you is more important, but I want privacy, and that means me and you, just me and you,' Rainbow emphasised.

'Get the fuck out of here you fucking morons, now!' Bananas shrieked as he kicked Butcher, who came to and looked around the room not knowing what had happened.

'What happened, boss?' he enquired as he got up and tucked his shirt into his trousers.

'You were sleeping on the job, you lazy bastard; you're fired and take your boyfriend with you, fuck off. Get out of here,' he raged. The men held one another as they left the room by the back door.

'Pull up a chair Detective Rainbow, tell me, how I can help you?' Bananas said with a smile that showed a gold tooth. 'And I'm sorry we got off on the wrong foot.'

'Detective sergeant, I'm a detective sergeant; nice place you have here,' Rainbow said, sitting down and looking around the room. 'You must be doing well for yourself; it seems there's a lot of money to be made in this betting game, maybe I'm in the wrong business?'

There was wall-to-wall carpeting; a colourful, well-lit bar was neatly placed in the corner of the room, an Ami jukebox with rows of records stood opposite, there were some cosy settees with velvet covers, and in the middle of the room a chandelier hung down, which sparkled no matter from what angle it was looked at. A crystal glass bowl sat on the desk with a bunch of bananas spilling over, and looking out of place on the paper-cluttered desk.

'I do OK, I've had to work hard to get what I got,' He indicated around the room, 'It ain't been easy.'

Rainbow took his black book out of his inside pocket and opened it. 'Tell me, Mr Bananas, where you were on Monday last? At say,' he hesitated, 'six forty-five in the evening?'

A frown came over his face as he tried to remember.

'What a question, I can't remember where I was yesterday, let alone a week ago.'

'Well give it a try, I've got all day, nothing better to do.' Rainbow said sarcastically.

'You're not by any chance referring to the murder in Baker Alley are you?' Bananas replied, with mock surprise. 'Haven't you picked up the killers yet? Are you here for my help? Because I might know something, rumours, you know what I mean?' Bananas touched his nose and pointed his finger.

'OK, tell me where you were, and what you know, and then I'll tell you something that might interest you.'

'Monday I was here, I remember I was with a Mr Bootsy Harris, that's right, I sent him on a message for me, I instructed him to go to Bridgetown to pick up a parcel and he took the 8.30 bus, my staff will all vouch for me, they were all here when I was with Bootsy, you must know Bootsy, he's a local character. I help him out sometimes, he runs errands for me. Why, you're not trying to pin the killing on me, are you? Because it weren't me or Harris, that's for certain. Why would I kill someone I don't even know? Who was killed anyhow, was it that guy Tommy who hung around with Waybee? He ain't been seen for over a week.'

Rainbow was now aware that the framing of Harris had ended. But the main point was that Waybee was no longer needed in his plans. He was the only person living who knew the truth, and now another route had to be taken, a new plan had to be implemented, and the real reason for his visit to see Bananas had to be put in place.

'No Joe, you don't mind if I call you Joe, do you? I'm not trying to pin anything on you; the victim hasn't been named yet before his next-of-kin has been informed, you know the drill. And as far as the guy Tommy you're talking about is concerned, I don't know him. If he's missing, put a missing report in to the police station if you're worried about him. To get back to what we were talking about, you see there are also rumours going around, and your name has been thrown around. I don't know if you are aware but there's a certain person, no sorry, an asshole, called Tony Waybee, and he's been saying that you did the killing, because of a drug deal that went wrong. I've had so much trouble over the years with that reprobate; there was the murder of Randy Colbert in Churchtown four years ago. He even implicated that you were in on that one, not a nice guy, if you ask me. Now I'm not telling you what to do, far from it, but let me tell you this Joe, if I had someone telling tales of this nature about me I would do something about it. I would put a stop to it by any means at my disposal, I would stop his foul mouth once and for all. I never said this, by the way, because nobody would believe your word against mine, no offence, but a visit from your boys when you reinstate them might be warranted. It's not their fault, how were they to know that I'm a karate expert, second dan? They didn't have a chance, no matter how big they are, I let them off lightly,' Rainbow bragged.

'The bastard, I know who you're on about, I've been trying to get him to see me for a while now, and he won't come. In his own time, he told one of my messengers. He would see me when he felt like it, in his own time, cheeky bastard. He's implicated me in the murder of Colbert, has he? Well, that weren't me, that was nothing to do with me, sorry, but I feel riled up at the moment. If I had him here now I'd rip him apart, maybe I shouldn't say that in front of you, being the police, but I'm so mad.' It showed on his face, spittle coming out of his mouth and running down his chin. 'Let's have a drink, Sergeant Rainbow, are you allowed to have one? Or do you want a coffee?'

'I'm not ready for alcohol at the moment, but I'll have a coffee if you promise not to put poison in it,' Rainbow grinned at the suggestion.

'Now would I do that to someone who has come here to help me quell some bastard spreading malicious rumours about me? I doubt it. Come to think of it he's always had it in for me.' He lifted the phone and ordered two coffees, and told his two sidekicks to come in pronto.

'Anyhow I haven't come here today to talk about that punk Waybee, my real reason for seeing you is about this business of Maltese Joe, do you remember him? He operated around these parts then disappeared suddenly.'

Bananas hid his fear at the mention of the name he knew so well. Maltese Joe; he had disposed of him for trying to muscle in on the rackets on his so-called patch a few years back. He had warned him on several occasions, but to no avail, the last straw had been when Maltese Joe had said that he didn't talk to dwarfs and at one time he had pretended not to see him when he was talking. He remembered Maltese Joe saying 'Is there anybody there? I can hear a voice but I can't see anyone.' He had taken the piss too many times and was now lying at the bottom of the sea, in a concrete suit.

'Maybe he went back to Malta, real nice guy he was,' Joe mused, 'I miss him, we did a bit of business together.'

'He never went back to Malta; his relatives contacted us to find out what happened to him. We're still looking. Maybe someday, someone with information will come forward, like Waybee your friend; he's already intimated that you were involved in his disappearance.'

'The lying bastard, I had nothing to do with his killing…' Bananas stopped talking and corrected himself quickly, 'disappearance I mean, you see how mixed up I am, Sergeant Rainbow, the information you've given me today about Waybee has made my head go funny, I meant disappearance. If you meet Joe again give him my best.'

'I know what you mean, he did my head in as well, that bastard should be seen to, if I see the Maltese, I'll give him your love,' Rainbow smiled at his remark.

A knock on the door stopped the men talking. 'Come in,' shouted Joe. A very thin man stepped in, he had a visor on his head, and it was Joe's front-of-betting-shop teller. 'Whatever it is, not now Alex, can't you see I've got company?'

'You'll want to hear this boss, believe me, it's very important; you'll kill me if I don't tell you about this matter.'

'Oh come on Alex, I couldn't hurt a fly, you exaggerate.' He glanced over to Rainbow. 'It better be important, you know I'm a busy man just trying to make a decent living, so spill.'

'Its private, boss,'

'I've nothing to hide, I run a clean business, all legit and above board, so whatever it is you can tell me in front of my friend here,' Joe smiled and pointed to Rainbow.

Alex walked up to the desk, nodded hello to Rainbow, and gave Joe a docket. 'Excuse me a minute will you,' Joe said to Rainbow as he studied the docket.

'You haven't taken this bet have you?'

'No boss it's just come in a few minutes ago, I brought it straight to you.'

'Reject it, and place one thousand pounds to win on the horse through Jesse's.'

'I'll do that Right away boss, sorry to disturb you.' Alex left the room.

'You seemed distressed, something wrong?' Rainbow enquired.

Joe's face took on a severe look as he explained that a betting syndicate had just tried to put on a bet of £10,000 on a horse called Morning Glory, and the horse was an outsider at fifty-to-one.

'So what's the problem there? Don't know much about horse racing,' Rainbow declared.

'In this day and age there's a lot of knobbling, horse drugging, and it seems very suspicious to me; this is a case of insider knowledge, I always avoid bets of that nature, it could break me.'

At that moment Butcher came in with a tray of coffee

and placed it on the table, the other hood stood by the door looking sheepish. 'You,' Joe shouted to Bruiser, 'come in, here,' he pointed to the front of his desk. 'In future, have a little more respect for my friends,' he glanced at Rainbow who was picking up his cup. 'I am going to rescind your firing, and give you another chance; now get on your fucking knees, and say sorry to my guest.'

Both men got down on their knees, and said sorry in unison, their humility intact.

'There's no need for that, get up,' Rainbow instructed. Both men got to their feet.

'Now get ready, I have a very important job for you to do for me, to compensate for your bad behaviour, you have to visit someone and teach him a lesson but I'll give you the low-down later, now go, out, out, out.' The hoods scuttled away thanking their boss for giving them their jobs back, and shut the door.

'I'm too good to them really, they adore me, they would die for me,' Bananas bragged. They shook hands, although it wasn't meant from either of them.

'One last point, it's no good going after Waybee today, because he's in the nick at the moment, he got time for contempt of court with your friend Harris, along with a fine of five hundred pounds apiece. Most probably he'll be running you down in prison. Ah well, I must be off, got to put a few more bad men away where they belong, behind bars.' Rainbow shook hands with the gangster again and smiled as he left the backroom of the betting shop. Joe Bananas took out his ledger and noted the time of his meeting with Detective Rainbow. A habit of his, he kept ledgers for all his business dealings and meetings, especially with his police friends that were on his payroll. He watched the race on television and saw his horse, Morning Glory, romp home winning him £50,000.

Rainbow sat in his car as he tended to do before driving off, and smiled in his overhead mirror. He had been successful in planting the seeds of hate for Waybee in the head of Big Joe Bananas. He realised that his ability for lying was getting better, he had never had to lie so much in his whole life, but the last week lying was part and parcel of his world. He had lied to Charlotte, to his superiors, it seemed that every time he opened his mouth he would lie about something or other, but if it meant that he could extract himself from the trouble he was in, he would lie till the cows came home, as the saying went. With a bit of luck Banana's boys would go too far when they were sent to teach Waybee a lesson, and kill him. *Then I would be in the clear*, he thought as he put his seat belt on. A certain satisfaction settled in, and for the first time in a while a glint of happiness came over him as he drove home. There was no way he was going to any farm to enquire about some missing chickens.

*

A lot of events had taken place since Rainbow had been with the gangster Big Joe Bananas. The inspector had had his car returned, and after a nice lunch felt a lot better. The weather had got better as the day progressed, and the new detectives were arriving in dribs and drabs, and some were going over the files, and evidence that had been obtained thus far. The inspector had interviewed Mrs

Harris concerning her son, and going on what she had said, Inspector Ryan had ordered a doctor who verified that the suspect, the said Mr Harris, was not capable of delivering the blow that killed the deceased, that he had also been examined with the aid of the pathologist. Mr Harris, it was concluded, was not capable because of his acute arthritis in his hands plus a degenerative muscle disorder. Mrs Harris also complained that three policemen invaded her house and searched it without a search warrant although Detective Inspector Rainbow had said he had one. Inspector Ryan didn't rectify Rainbow's rank to Mrs Harris, he let it go. She continued to tell him that he had been in her son's room and found three items that she had never seen her son wear and denied that they belonged to him in the first place. He wouldn't put on boots that were that scruffy because she admitted that her son had a mental disorder in having a fetish for boots. The inspector changed his mind about Mrs Harris's intellect and her appearance, and the old adage came to his mind: you can't judge a book by its cover. She was believed, and the inspector instructed a policeman to go to the city jail where Mr Harris was incarcerated, to get an interview. In the meantime, he sent a detective down to forensics to find the items that he remembered Rainbow had told him about at their meeting on Sunday morning. The inspector had been surprised that no such items had been handed in so he wondered where the wallet, watch and boots had got to. He would have a word with Rainbow as soon as he came in from his farm inquiry. The policeman reported back from the city jail and told the inspector that Harris had been very cooperative, and had said that he had never owned a watch in his life and wallets were never his thing. He did suggest that these items must have been planted because he only liked well-made boots and he kept his boots in a special rack under his bed. And on the night of the murder he was on an errand in Bridgetown and there were people there who could verify that fact. The inspector had already dispelled the notion that Harris had anything to do with this crime, but he did wonder why Rainbow would go to all that trouble when it was blatantly obvious that he was innocent. The inspector was also aware of the attack he had made on Rainbow in his cell. He wanted to know what Rainbow had to say on the matter.

*

'Soil's a bit wet for gardening, surely?' Rainbow said to the gardener as he made his way up the path that led to the entrance to the apartments where he lived.

'Yes, it's just right for planting these few flowers I've got left, thought I'd get them in before it gets dark' the gardener replied.

'Do you think you could do me a favour, would you have a spare spot where you could bury my pet parrot? He was only small. If it's at all possible I would like a spot where the sun shines for most of the day, because he brought a lot of sunshine in my life, I can tell you. He died a day or so ago I think, I found him today. I called him Pedro, had him for years, the only trouble with him was he swore a lot. I've had some embarrassing times I can tell you.' Rainbow laughed, 'but he was a beautiful parrot and a good companion, we talked a lot together when I got lonely, now he's gone.' Rainbow sighed.

'Sure, I could put him over there.' the gardener pointed, 'near the rose bush, sun's there for most of the day, well not when it's raining of course,' both men laughed. He handed over the box with Pedro inside, and watched as the gardener dug a hole and buried the bird in the soil then covered it over, and patted it down. Rainbow gave the gardener a ten-pound note for his trouble saying, 'Get a drink on me and thank you very much for your trouble.'

The gardener said there was no need for payment, but put the money in his back pocket anyhow, and returned to his planting.

Rainbow opened his door to his apartment and had the shock of his life when he saw her sitting at the window table with a drink in her hand.

'Michelle, what are you doing here? You surprised me.' He glanced down and saw a small suitcase standing next to her on the floor.

'Remember, I've still got the key you gave me, you never asked for it back, did you?' She smiled and took a sip of her drink. He walked to the drinks cabinet and poured a double shot of bourbon and sat down opposite her, took a sip and looked at her. She was ravishingly beautiful and looked like her sister so much.

'Ray,' she started and added a sigh, 'my life has been fucked up, and although I don't want to start a row with you, it's got something to do with you; you did this to me.' She pointed to her stomach, 'It's yours and nobody else's, I've been with no one else, only you, the father. I know you love my sister and there's no room in your life for me so I've decided to go away. I might have an abortion or I might keep it, I haven't made up my mind yet.' He listened intently and saw her sorrow spilling out, her breasts heaving as she spoke; her eyes showed that she had been crying.

'It takes two to tango, so I can't take all the blame. I asked you if you were on the pill and remember what you said?' She looked down at her glass. 'You assured me you were, didn't you?'

'I did, Ray, but I forgot, the last time we made love, I couldn't resist it, you're so well endowed, I wanted you in me, Ray, I wanted you to fuck me, and you did didn't you? You fucked me good and proper, now I'm in the club, as the saying goes, and there's nothing we can do to alter that, we have to deal with it or should I say, I have to deal with it, and that's why I'm leaving for a place far away from here.'

He looked out of the window and across at the alley where one week ago his world changed so dramatically. In one week he had taken a man's life, started a fire, become a blatant liar, been unfaithful, and lost ten thousand pounds. It seemed that his chance of promotion had evaporated, and his karate days were over, all in a week. He shook his head in disbelief, and then looked at Michelle, who looked sad, her eyes red.

'Does Charlotte know about us? Have you said anything at all?'

'No she doesn't know anything, and I don't want her to know, it would break her heart. As it so happens I love my sister and I wish I had never started this affair.'

'Hardly an affair, a series of one night stands I'd say.'

‘Well you would say that, wouldn’t you? All those “I love yous”, now all forgotten,’ she said with a sneer.

‘These things happen in life, you came on to me in the first place, you’re making out that it’s all my fault, and you know that’s not the truth, you were just as guilty as me. What we should be dealing with is how to put things right now that the damage has been done.’ She stared at him over her glass, she wanted revenge now, she had realised that there was no future in continuing on this course, it had to end. He had used her to satisfy his sexual needs, and she realised that she had been stupid and naïve.

‘I have an idea how we could get out of this mess, but I’m afraid to say that it would cost money and as you know, my dear Ray, I haven’t got any money to speak of.’ She hesitated and went to fill her glass, then came back and sat down. She continued, ‘Abortion can be expensive so I’ve been told, then there’s my living costs and that’s high in London, but one good thing is that I would be out of your hair for you to get on with marrying my sister, you don’t want me to keep the baby do you?’

Rainbow pulled a face and found himself feeling uncomfortable at the question.

‘That’s a hard question to ask me but I can’t see any other way but to go for abortion, and what kind of money would solve this matter?’ He looked away as he felt embarrassed at the way he was discussing an unborn child.

‘How much are you offering to get rid of your child? How much is a life worth to you?’

‘Look, Michelle, I’ve had enough of this, this is getting us nowhere. If I gave you a thousand pounds now and see how it goes then when you find out the costs you could ask me again and I will see if—'

'No, no, no,' she interrupted, 'that's not enough. I was thinking more in the region of ten thousand, remember it's me who has to disrupt my life, it's me who has to leave my family and friends and my job in the salon, while you go on your merry way as though nothing has happened; no, I want ten thousand, or I'll have the baby at home and name you as the father.'

'That's bloody blackmail,' he exclaimed with a sneer.

'Yes it is,' she replied. 'And I want the money tonight, the sooner I'm gone the better for all concerned.'

'Ten thousand pounds are you fucking crazy? Where did that figure come from? Did it just appear from out of the blue, ten fucking thousand? You must be out of your tiny mind.'

He got up from the table, and paced the room.

'I told you I didn't come here for a row, so if that's going to be your attitude I'm off,' she said.

She picked up the remains of her drink, swallowed it in one go, and made to leave.

'Hold on, sit down, let's work this out,' he said demandingly, pointing to her chair. She sat down once again and he sat opposite.

'If I gave you the money, you say you will have an abortion, and the subject will never be brought up again. I need you to promise me that right here and now, because let me tell you this, if you do anything that jeopardises my or your sister's happiness, then you will see another part of me that's not as nice as you've seen in the past, do you understand that?'

'Don't treat me like one of your criminals, you don't scare me,' her nostrils flared. 'I already know that you have no concern for anyone but yourself, you betrayed my sister, and you've lied to me. I pity my sister in a way, but I would never hurt her, so you have my word. I promise I will keep this thing a secret and after tonight I will never speak of it again, but the way things are, I want the money to start a new life in London.' She fixed him with a steely look.

'I'll give you the money this time but never ask me for money again,' he snarled, 'you know what it's called, it's called blackmailing and it's a prisonable offence.' He left the room, went to his bedside table drawer and took out the wad of money that he had retrieved from Waybee. He remembered that it was two hundred pounds short of ten thousand, the money that Waybee had stolen off him. He took two hundred pounds out of his wallet and placed the cash in the envelope, and returned to his lounge.

'I didn't want it to be this way, Ray, you know what I wanted, after all, you went out with me first then when you met my sister you changed your mind. I thought we had a future together, you let me down, I did love you, big time.'

He handed her the envelope. She took the money and placed it in her handbag, then stood up to leave.

'Don't you want to count it?' he said sarcastically as he escorted her to the door.

'No, I trust you,' she said smiling. 'You let me down once, I'm sure you won't do it again; let's just say it's a pay-off for fucking up my life. One last thing before I leave. I want to know, what happened to Pedro the parrot? You know the sensible one that lived in this flat?'

'Have a good time in London and spend the money wisely. Pedro is no concern of yours,' he said with a sneer, then he gave a false smile, 'I do hope things work out for you, and to be honest with you I'm sorry it ended this way. Maybe one day we'll be friends again, after all you'll be my sister-in-law. One last thing: the key, the apartment key, you won't be needing it again, that's for sure.' She reached into her handbag and handed the key back. As she left she laughed out loud before disappearing down the stairs, and out into the night.

'Bitch, fucking bitch,' he muttered to himself as he shut out the evening chill with a slam of the door. He went to his trophy cabinet, opened a drawer and took out his bank statement. He studied it for a moment then poured another drink, returning to the window; he looked out into a dark world. Thoughts drifted through his head as he tried to get to grips with his situation. Where he was just a few days ago and now were worlds apart, his ideal world was crumbling around him, and he racked his brain to find a way out, to stop the decline. The deposit for the house was depleted, and the agent had already said that other clients were after it. Charlotte had set her mind on the house, how he was going to tell her that the money had gone, he had no idea.

*

Miss Butters seemed agitated as she examined the package that she had found in the locker tucked away behind some underpants and socks on a locker inspection she from time to time implemented. There was no address on the packet, but it felt bulky.

‘Come in,’ she commanded, in response to the slight tapping on the door.

Mr Jenkins entered the head teacher’s office, looking apprehensive as though his life was in danger of ending; he hated being summoned to the head teacher’s office. He wondered what the matter was.

He sat down on a chair opposite a desk full of papers and a mug with a grinning one-eyed pirate with a black patch over the other eye that held biro pens. Several fading photographs stood on the cluttered desk. Miss Butters, glasses at the end of her nose, was holding a package, sitting in a high-backed chair, looking intently as though she was a High Court judge about to sentence someone to life imprisonment.

‘Sorry to call you from whatever you were doing, Egbert, but this is the reason I wanted you to come to my office, have a guess what this is?’ She waved the package above her head. ‘You’re going to be very surprised what this package contains, I took a peek so I know, so have a guess, go on. You won’t believe it.’

‘I enjoy quiz games, let’s see.’ He frowned, then put his hand to his chin, and squinted. ‘Now let’s see, is it a manuscript? It looks like it could be one; you haven’t been writing a book have you? It’s a manuscript, that’s my first guess.’ he proclaimed.

‘No it’s not a manuscript, and this is not a game, its very serious.’ she exclaimed.

‘Where did you get this item that’s so important?’ he enquired.

‘I found it in a boy’s locker, when I was doing my random inspection. Benny Sparrow’s locker. As you know these inspections are very important as the boys and girls collect all sorts of things that this school will not tolerate. In the past I've found cigarettes, lighter fuel, and all sorts of things; remember that girl a few years ago had five kittens hidden away under her bed? Frogs, tadpoles, food, all sorts of things, beer and a half bottle of rum, remember that one, Egbert?'

'I sure do, it's coming back to me,' he shouted knowingly, throwing his hand in the air. 'I know what it is, something you really detest, it's those books that young boys like looking at, you know, girly magazines.'

'Oh, I'm not that straight-laced, you ought to know that, Egbert, but we can't have younger boys looking at scantily clad women, can we? It's not in keeping with the establishment I run. No, it's more serious than that, a lot more, believe me, and I have called you in for your input and good advice.' She placed the package on the desk momentarily, and adjusted her spectacles. 'I have taken the liberty of looking at the contents, only because the boy in question refused to tell me what was in the package. In fact he got very distressed when I questioned him about it. He actually struggled with me when I took it off him. Mrs Bates is in the day room as I speak, trying to console him. There are more questions I want to ask him when he settles down.'

'So what's in the mystery package, shall we look?' he said pointing.

She opened a drawer at the side of her desk and produced a pair of scissors and carefully opened the package fully. Surprise showed on their faces as the money fell on the table, with the note.

'Bloody hell,' muttered Mr Jenkins. He had never seen so much cash in his life.

'Language, Egbert,' admonished Miss Butters.

'Sorry, I'm shocked, where would the boy get that amount of money? There must be a few thousand there, that's a certainty, maybe four or five. I'll be buggered.'

'Egbert, please moderate, there's no call for that gutter talk, I realise you're in shock but no more than I am. What do we do now?'

'What does the note say? Is there an address on it?' he enquired.

She read the short note. 'No address. I can't understand it, all it says is, "make it the last time".'

'Count it,' Egbert said excitedly, 'that's the only thing to do, let's see what we are dealing with here.'

'Good idea, let's get to it.' They counted carefully and seemed to get enjoyment out of the task.

'£10, 000 exactly to the penny, wonder where he got it from. I hope he didn't steal It.' she said, looking amazed.

'I never ever thought the boy was a thief, a bit unruly at times but never a thief,' Egbert replied. 'I would say that if the boy doesn't tell us where he obtained the money then we must do the right thing and bring in the police. After all, that money could be the proceeds of a robbery, or some old person's life savings. Yes, this is a job for the police in my opinion, do you want me to phone them now, or are you going to question the boy again?' He looked at her, and waited for her response.

'Thanks for your input; I knew you would know what do, Egbert. I have never come across this kind of thing in the whole time I've been at this children's home. To tell you the truth, I'm a bit worried, I don't want to spoil my unblemished record by having would-be thieves and villains living amongst us, most of my charges have left here to go on to be good citizens. I'll have a talk to Benny and see if he can explain how he came to have this amount of money in his locker. All he has told me so far is that it was the mission, whatever that means, and if he refuses to tell me more I will have no alternative, the police will be called. Thank you, and remember, keep it under your hat, tell no one.' She smiled.

'Glad to be of help, I won't say a word.' He rose and left the office, as the head teacher collected the money and put it back in the cellophane wrapper.

Benny cried himself to sleep; he had refused to say how he had obtained the package that had been attached to the undercarriage of his destroyed helicopter. When he was asked by Miss Butters what it contained, he refused to answer because he didn't know, all he knew was that the package belonged to his new dad, and he wasn't going to tell anyone, he wasn't going to let his friend down, and maybe get him in trouble, after all, he might not get the new helicopter that he had been promised. He vowed to run away the next day to find his new dad, and tell him what had happened.

Miss Butters phoned the police.

SEVENTEEN
TUESDAY

The reflection in the mirror was of a tired-looking man, bad dreams and cold sweats had kept him awake for most of the night; he shaved, and had a light breakfast with coffee, then he would set off for another day of pretence and deceit at the police station. Rainbow had decided to go at last to the farm, a chore he had neglected to do. He felt degraded in doing this kind of work, and he was sure his colleagues were laughing behind his back, but then he was relieved in a sense, because his boss wouldn't be on his back as he had been in the last week. The loss of his deposit or part of it depressed him; he had to find a way of getting the money back before the house he intended to buy with Charlotte was sold. These thoughts filled his head as he drank down the last of his coffee. He jumped out of his skin as the phone rang; it was DS Mervin Jones, the detective who had taken over the Baker Alley murder case that Rainbow had relinquished. There was a meeting at the station and the inspector wanted everyone to attend. There had been a lead in the case.

'What lead?' Rainbow enquired.

'You'll find out at the meeting,' was the curt reply. 'Ten o'clock sharp.'

Lead, what fucking lead? Maybe that prick Waybee has opened his big mouth, he thought. He was not happy as he left his apartment for the station.

He drove into the police car park, and had a job to find a parking space. Someone had parked in the spot where he normally parked; it seemed that all the police were at the police station at the same time. He got out of his car just as DC Barns and Harris passed, making their way to the meeting.

'Hi there, sarge, where have you been? Haven't seen you about lately, we thought you were on holiday,' Barns said in a joking way. 'Did you solve the chicken and egg thefts down on the farm?'

'Trying to be funny, Barns? It's none of your business where I've been; telling me what you've been doing would be more to the point.'

'Sorry, sarge, I was only joking,'

'Don't worry about it; I'm never jokey at this time of day. Do you know what this meeting is all about?' Rainbow enquired.

'I think there's been a Breakthrough, in the murder case.' Barns replied, 'the one in the alley, so I believe, but it's only rumours, maybe Harris has admitted to it after the evidence we found at his place was analysed. You remember, the boots, watch, the stuff we picked up on the Fingle estate. Maybe forensics has come up with something.'

'Can't be that, I never handed that stuff in, it was stolen from my car, along with some other items, it's common knowledge, it's a wonder you didn't know, all the station knows,' Rainbow lied. 'Anyhow we'll soon find out, see you later.' 'I didn't hear that he had been robbed', Barns said to Harris, who shrugged. Rainbow went to see the desk sergeant, who had beckoned him as the men walked into the police station.

'Hi Ray, got a job for you after the meeting,' he looked at a worksheet. 'A Miss Butters from the Sunshine children's home in Bayfield Road has found a package with a good deal of money in one of the children's lockers, and when the child was confronted about it, the kid got upset and has ran away, so it's a missing child case, so look into it, will you? It's urgent; the kid is only ten years old. Take Barns and Harris with you, they have nothing on at the moment.'

Rainbow took out his black book, and wrote down the address, Bayfield Road.

'What's the gen on this meeting, do you know?' Rainbow asked.

'No, but what I do know is, there's a lot of top brass about, rumour has it that they may have a suspect, a local crook.'

'Anyone I know?' Rainbow said.

'Yeah, you know him well, we all do. They are giving him the third degree now before he's released from prison, that villain Tony Waybee, he was one of the last people to see him on the day he died, could be a result, let's hope so, eh, Ray?'

'Hope so,' Rainbow nodded. But the desk sergeant didn't see the look of horror that was on his face as he turned away to go to the meeting. What if Waybee succumbed to the pressure of interrogation? He knew that the questioning of a suspect could be persistent by some detectives, he had done it himself.

There were twenty or more cops in the small room as ten o'clock came. Inspector Ryan took his place behind a table, and sat down with a policeman alongside him; a few words were exchanged. The top brass was unknown to Rainbow.

'Gentlemen,' the inspector started, 'I have called this meeting to let you know in advance that a raid will soon take place on a drug cartel that has been operating in this area for several years, in the next week. We have gathered a great deal of information from informants and insiders over a long period. One of our informants is at this moment giving us information about the gang in question, we have him in custody, but this is the twist, he is due for release in a few hours. We don't want the gang to suspect that he is squealing, and that we are questioning him. He's in custody for a minor offence at the moment, fighting in a local public house and swearing at a magistrate.' Laughter broke out in the room. 'He will be under observation when he is released. He is also our number-one suspect in the murder of our underground operative Detective Robert Jennet but until this drug bust takes place I have decided to leave it in abeyance. But believe me he will be interrogated by the best men we have who used to work in the SAS to interrogate terrorist suspects in Afghanistan. So if they don't get the truth out of him, nothing will. So there you are gentlemen there is no need to tell you that this is top secret. Sergeant Rainbow you will be in charge of Tony Waybee's well-being when he is released. Make sure nothing happens to him, he's our top witness. Make sure that he is safe for the court appearance, it's no good if he ends up dead.'

'Yes sir,' said Rainbow, hiding his feelings.

The meeting broke up and the policemen went about their other duties. Rainbow beckoned to Detective Barns and Detective Harris and he instructed them that they had a job to investigate a missing boy. They all got in the same car and headed for the Sunshine home for children in Bayfield Road that Harris said he knew well, being a local man.

'Have you got an appointment?' said the woman behind the small desk in the foyer, not looking up from some paperwork.

'Police,' Rainbow volunteered showing his warrant card, 'you called us about a missing boy, I believe.'

'Oh yes, the Sparrow boy, excuse me.' She lifted the phone and said, 'The police are here,' then looked up and said that Miss Butters would be right along in a minute and to take a seat. The men declined the offer.

Miss Butters introduced herself and led the policemen to a boardroom, with a long table that was littered with papers and files. Books filled one wall, and the room smelled musty as though it was very rarely used.

'Pull up those chairs,' she said as though she was issuing an order to her children.

'I'm very worried, the boy has not come back, it's not the first time he's run away. He's changed a lot just lately since he met a man who once brought him back on another occasion when he ran away. The man put ideas in his head and promised to adopt him, that's all he talks about, his new friend, he now calls his dad. It's all very worrying.'

'Miss Butters,' Rainbow said looking at his black book, 'calm down, we are here to help, but let's start at the beginning. First thing, the boy's name and age, and most important, when did he abscond?' The two men got out their books and with pens in hands were poised for the answers.

'We are not sure when he left the home. Mr Jenkins reported him missing at breakfast this morning. Mr Jenkins is one of our teachers. It's not the first time the boy's done this, run away, but I'm worried this time because we had a bit of trouble with him yesterday, when we found a package in his locker and with further enquiries it was found to contain a large amount of money wrapped up in cellophane. He had hidden it behind a few books and clothes in his bedside locker. We do an inspection from time to time to make sure there's no contraband like cigs or alcohol; believe me you'll be surprised what we find sometimes. This is a good children's home and as the head carer I want it to remain that way.'

'Very commendable, Miss Butters, can I have a look at the package, please?' Rainbow asked.

She opened a side drawer then closed it again. 'How foolish of me, I remember I put it in the safe in my office, I'll go get it, won't be a minute.' She left the room.

'Glad she wasn't in charge of me, she seems full of herself,' Harris remarked.

'Yeah she's a bit doolally if you ask me,' Barns ventured.

'She seems caring to me; she looks very worried, I wouldn't want her job looking after all these kids day and night. She did the right thing bringing us in; the boy could be in a lot of danger out there.' Rainbow pointed to the window indicating the outside world. The door opened and she came back in the room waving the package, and

Rainbow knew at that moment that the package belonged to him.

She gave the package to Rainbow. 'There's exactly ten thousand pounds in there, Mr Jenkins and I counted it twice.' She returned to her chair.

'Do you know where the boy got this money from? This is serious money.' Detective Barns ventured as he wrote the details down in his black book.

'No idea, he wouldn't say, the package was unopened when I found it and he wouldn't say where he got it from; maybe he found it. We have been in the park in the last few days, he was looking for the remains of his helicopter that he crashed in the trees in the park, and maybe he found the package there.' She held out her hands in frustration. 'Ten thousand pounds could be money that thieves hid in the park to pick it up later, when the coast was clear. They could have been on the run, who knows where this money came from? The boy just wouldn't say where he got it from,' she said with a quizzical look on her face.

Rainbow asked, 'Have you got any photos of the boy that we can put out on posters?'

'As it happens I have some photos, I took them in the park, when we went there last week. I'll get them for you.' Once again she left the room. Rainbow hid his feelings well, it was obvious to him, the story was unfolding.

'How old is the boy?' asked DC Harris.

'Ten,' replied Rainbow, looking at his book.

'This is the boy, Benny Sparrow,' she pointed out to Rainbow, as she entered the room with the photos displayed. 'He's ten years old, an orphan and has been here at this home since he was born. A good lad generally but he always wanted a mother and father, don't we all, poor boy. He could never quite understand why he didn't have one. He was so happy to have this nice man as a friend,' she pointed to the photo, 'and was hoping that he could be his new dad. He was always on about him since they met on the river a while ago, last week in fact. This is the man,' she repeated, pointing at the photo once again. 'It was taken in the park just a few days ago, last Thursday I think.'

Rainbow's mind was working overtime and was putting the story together in his head. He recognised Tony Waybee immediately.

'This man here,' Rainbow pointed, 'you say they met down on the river, what were they doing there, do you know?'

'Sailing boats, I think. I've warned the boy not to go near the river, could be dangerous, but he took no notice. Benny can be headstrong at times, he loves remote control gadgets; he flew a model helicopter until he crashed it a few days ago in the trees in the park.'

Barns put out his hand intimating that he wanted to view the photos. Rainbow handed the camera over.

'I know this man,' said Barns, 'but I can't remember his name,' he looked at Rainbow.

'The man in the photo is Benny's friend,' Miss Butters exclaimed, 'Tony Brinks, they met at the river one day when he had absconded from here as he tended to do, and this man brought him back. He seemed to be a genial, kind man and offered to take Benny out on outings. I told him he would have to be vetted by the police first, and he agreed to that, he made out an application form that is still in the out-tray in my office. He told me he worked making furniture in a factory and was a foreman in the firm, and was married, but had never had any children, so that was the reason he had an interest in the boy. You don't think that he's kidnapped him do you?' she said, looking concerned.

'No I don't think that is likely, but we never rule anything out,' Rainbow said, in a matter-of-fact way. He knew damned well that Waybee hadn't kidnapped the kid, Waybee was in the nick. 'I'd like to see the form you say you have his application form, we will check him out. Now about the money, when we find the boy we'll find out where he got the money from, I will take it to the station. There could be fingerprints on the notes.'

'There are, mine and Mr Jenkins', we counted it, remember?' she said, looking alarmed.

'Oh don't worry about that, it's just a formality, a police formality,' he repeated. She left the room for the third time to get the application form, and the detectives rose from their seats.

'We got all the info we need, that wraps it up then, don't worry about making the report, I'll do the necessary. There's no need for three reports, continue with whatever you were doing, there's too much paperwork anyhow, give the desk sergeant the boy's details, and set up a search for him and get his photo out to every copper on the beat now' Rainbow said, and both men nodded. They left the room.

Miss Butters handed Rainbow the application form and a photo of Benny that she had kept in a drawer in her desk. He promised her that the boy would be found, and urged her not to worry. The policemen left the home, for the station and lunch. Rainbow sat in his car and studied the application form that Waybee had filled in and laughed at the contents. False name Mr Brinks, a foreman in a factory that made Rainbow smile. *Waybee had never done a day's work in his life*, he thought, but a picture was forming in his mind. It was quite obvious that Waybee had used the boy's talent and expertise in flying a model helicopter in his blackmail ploy, and in a way Rainbow admired his adversary for his ingenuity and cunning.

He looked at the money that was rightfully his, but wondered how he could keep it. Barns and Harris knew it was in his possession; they might enquire at any time if he didn't hand it in. He had to think of a way to keep the money. In the meantime, he would go to see Charlotte and see what she had to say about her sister leaving home for London.

*

She was in the garden pruning roses, her little basket with cuttings laid on the grass next to her. She had a sun hat on that made him think of a film he had seen with Audrey Hepburn doing the very same thing, pruning roses. The film's title escaped him momentarily; she was beautiful, just like the film star. He wondered how she would take the news of his decision not to take the house that was on offer. He knew that deception would be involved, and hated lying to her, but he could see no other way out of this dire situation. The house deposit was gone, or part of it, and they would have to wait for the next opportunity to come along.

'Charlotte, time for a tea break, we must have a talk, it's important,' he said as he approached her. She had been lost in her thoughts of her wedding day and old school friends she would invite when she heard his voice, which brought her back to reality.

'Ray, what are you doing here? Aren't you supposed to be out there catching the naughty men of this world, the crims as you call them?' She put her secateurs in the basket and put her arms around him and kissed him. He kissed her back passionately; they linked arms and went up to the house. Her mother and father had gone out for a drive, so it was swiftly decided to make the most of an empty house, and they had an hour of sex, the kind you only read about in certain books or what some people may watch on certain channels on the internet. It was passionate, and oral intercourse was very prominent, and very tiring, so much so that when Charlotte was in the shower, Rainbow fell asleep.

Charlotte woke him in late afternoon, with a gentle tickle on his nose. He awoke with a start, and for a moment wondered where he was; it had been a deep sleep.

'You were snoring, darling,' she whispered, 'and I thought I'd let you have a rest, you've looked so tired just lately, but you've been asleep for almost three hours, so I thought I'd wake you, haven't you work to do?'

'Bloody hell, Charlotte, you should have woken me earlier, I have things to do.' He jumped up and got dressed; glancing out of the window he saw the sun backing away towards the far horizon across the fields.

'Sorry, darling, you looked so contented when I came back from my shower, I just let you rest. You're overworking yourself, it's about time you had a holiday,' she made for the door. 'I'll make some tea, and then we can have that talk you mentioned.'

His mobile phone buzzed. Something important had come up concerning the boy Benny Sparrow. He had been found under the jetty down on the river, he had drowned, it appeared, the desk sergeant said. All hell was breaking loose and he was advised to report back at the station.

'Has the boy been identified? Are you sure it's the boy who absconded this morning?' Rainbow enquired. Details were sketchy at the moment, but a body had been recovered from the river and the boy's name had been mentioned, the desk sergeant said.

'I've got to go, they want me down at the station,' Rainbow said to Charlotte, 'a boy went missing and he has been found in the river. The boy ran away this morning, I went to the home for children where he lived just before I came here, so I must go.'

'Have your tea first, I've just poured,' she ordered, 'surely you've got time to drink it, now they've found the boy, and everything's fine then?'

'Well, not really, dear, he was floating in the river, he drowned, and he was only ten years old. A sad case of a wasted life,' Rainbow explained, 'of an orphan lad from a children's home.' He sipped his hot tea.

'Do you miss your sister at all?' he enquired.

'No, and why should I?' She looked puzzled.

'Oh it's just that she did mention that she may go away to London to try out her acting ability, when I last saw her when we had our family party last week, if I remember rightly.'

'Yeah, wishful thinking, she's been saying that for years. She'll never leave home, she's too much of a mummy's girl, and a daddy's girl too. She's been utterly spoilt if the truth be known.' Charlotte laughed out loud. 'You can ask her about it if you want, she'll be back soon, she's only gone into town to have lunch with a school friend.'

'Sorry, I've got no time to talk to her today.'

Rainbow finished his tea, kissed her goodbye and they went to his car.

'What is it you wanted to talk to me about? It can't be that important, you preferred sex than talking it seemed,' she laughed once again.

'It can wait, see you soon,' he said then he drove towards the police station.

He wondered what game Michelle was playing. He had expected her to be far away up in the smoke in London town, spending his money. Maybe she was going to leave soon, before the baby began to show. He shook his head in disbelief at the bad luck that had overwhelmed him in the last week or so. He wondered where it would all end. What he didn't know was his luck wasn't going to get any better; in fact it was going downhill as fast as a train whose brakes had failed.

The police station was busy as Rainbow walked in; the desk sergeant looked up from his papers, and indicated that the inspector was in the next room. The sergeant looked strained. Detective Sergeant Rainbow saw a familiar bag on the desk and a scruffy-looking individual standing in front of the desk that he vaguely recognised as the fisherman he had spoken to the day of the cash drop near the jetty on the river.

'Thought I'd caught a shark at first,' said the fisherman enthusing, 'but it turned out to be a rock on the river bed; bent my hook almost straight, it was then this bag came up. I was shocked what I found in it, a rock a pair of boots, a watch, and this wallet, no money in it though, now I wonder who would throw a good pair of boots and a perfectly good watch in the river. Anyhow, I being a good person thought I would bring it in, and claim the reward if there is one?'

'I doubt there's a reward on a pair of boots, and an imitation Rolex watch, but I'll check,' the desk sergeant muttered, holding the watch and looking at the back of it.

At that moment DC Barns and DC Harris came in the station door and approached the desk, immediately recognising the items that they had picked up on the Fingle estate at Barry Harris's house, the very stuff that Sergeant Rainbow had said had been stolen from his car.

'I fished it out of the river this morning, the same time as the body was found,' the fisherman said, when asked by Barns how he had acquired it.

'These items were stolen from a car last week,' Barns informed the desk sergeant, 'they were stolen from DS Rainbow's car.'

'I fished this bag out of the river this morning, I don't know nothing about stolen goods,' the fisherman protested.

'This is the evidence that was stolen from your car, isn't it, sarge,' Barns said, holding up the boots.

'Looks like them, you fished this lot out of the river you say?' Rainbow asked the fisherman.

'Yeah, this morning, I've just explained to the desk sergeant three times.'

The desk sergeant nodded, pen poised.

Rainbow picked up the bag and explained to the desk sergeant how these items were stolen from his car, and could be evidence in the Alley murder. He led the fisherman to an interview room to get a statement. He had to keep up the pretence; nothing he did seemed to go right; he thought he had seen the end of these items when he ditched them in the river. He thanked DC Barns for his observational skills as he led the frustrated fisherman to the small interview room.

Ten minutes later the fisherman left, moaning that this would be the last time he handed anything he found to the police when there was no reward, not even a thank you. 'No gratitude,' he muttered as he went back to the river. When he had left, Rainbow tore up the phoney report and stuffed it in his pocket for disposal later. Now he had the things back that he had tried to dispose of when his plan to frame Barry Harris had come to nothing. He needed to think and think hard because Waybee would be out soon, he was soon to be released from the clink, and he had been given the responsibility of looking after him and making sure no harm came to the main witness in the drug bust. He had to see Big Joe Bananas to warn him off, because he had put bad thoughts in the gangster's head and Rainbow knew that Waybee was in line for a beating, but now, with the change of circumstances, he could not allow that to happen. Waybee might break, and spill the beans when being tortured by Joe Banana's hoods. No, that could not happen, and he would make sure it didn't. Rainbow left the interview room and returned to the desk.

'I got that sorted, it's not what I first thought,' Rainbow said to the desk sergeant. 'The bag contained a pair of old boots as you saw, but there's no point in even giving them in to forensics now after they've been in the river for who knows how long,' Rainbow pointed out.

The desk sergeant frowned as he listened to the person on the other end of the phone. 'Two men you say with balaclavas on their heads? Running out of the house five minutes ago, Mr Waybee's place, hold on a minute will you.' He put his hand over the receiver, 'listen to this Ray? It seems like two hooded men have just run out of Waybee's flat and sped away in a car. Better go down there to see if he's OK, he was only released this morning.'

'I'm on my way,' Rainbow shouted over his shoulder as he went out of the station door. Whether the body in the river was little Benny had been forgotten, and there had been no mention of it.

'Did I see DS Rainbow just walk out of the station?' Inspector Ryan enquired as he walk passed the desk.

'Yes sir he just left, some trouble at Waybee's house I've just been informed.'

'Well, when he gets back send him to my office, I want a word with him. I've had no reports from him in the last few days, and get that empty tea mug off the desk, not good for police image, the public will think all we do all day is drink tea.'

'Sorry sir,' the desk sergeant said, as he removed the offending mug.

*

The ambulance was at the house with the paramedics inside; a policeman on the door looked bored. Rainbow flashed his identity card, and walked into the flat. The place was in disarray, the table had been overturned, models had been smashed and were scattered all over the place, and there were bloodstains on the walls. Waybee was lying on the floor, and the medics were putting him on the stretcher. He had a deep wound to the side of his head with blood over his shirt; he had been stabbed several times, it appeared. He was unconscious.

'Might not make it,' Rainbow heard a medic say to his colleague as they did their best for their patient, and lifted him carefully on to the stretcher.

'Looks like he's been beaten up by someone with a big, big grudge, if you ask me,' muttered the constable to Rainbow. 'They hit him with that hammer over there in the corner, there's blood on it, and nothing's been touched. Two blokes with balaclavas over their heads sped away in a blue car, the lady over the road said. A Mr Waybee, well known to us, sarge, had just been released from the nick this morning. Someone in the gang got their revenge, it appears, but I don't know for sure.'

'Thanks, I've got it covered now, go get a statement from the witness,' Rainbow ordered the constable, who nodded and left the room. The medics had put Waybee in the ambulance, and were on their way to the hospital, as Rainbow pretended to look for clues. Inwardly he was happy with Waybee's downfall, at least he wouldn't have the job of looking after him anymore, and in his state he wasn't going to do any talking to anyone. He hadn't meant for Banana's boys to do this amount of damage to Waybee, a smack, a few smacks, but certainly not with a hammer, that was too far, those criminals had no morals.

Other police arrived and Rainbow left the scene after letting another CID officer take charge. He told him he had another important case he was investigating. That certainly wasn't true. He was now living in a world of deceit.

He drove to the Sunshine home in Bayfield to see how everyone was bearing up after the bad news about the boy. He met Miss Butters in the front of the home; she was checking the locks on the main gates. He parked his car and she approached the vehicle before he could get out. He wound down the window.

'I'm sorry to hear about the boy, its bad news, I've been on another case so I don't know the details, when was he found? Was it in the river? That's the information I got.'

'Thomas Street, near the park, climbing over a wall, the constable said,' she replied.

'Thomas Street? Climbing over a wall – who? Who was climbing over a wall?' Rainbow looked baffled for a moment.

'The boy who ran away this morning, the boy we called you about, Benny Sparrow. The policeman saw him climbing over the wall in Thomas Street, and with the photograph he had of the boy, a copy of the one I gave you, he recognised him and brought him back. He's confined to his room as we talk, he's not so hyper now, he's calming down, he's a good boy really,' she explained with a smile. 'Your men did a good job in finding him; he was back here two hours after you left. Maybe it was just a bit of luck that the constable was walking along that street, so everything is all right again until the next time he runs away. We just have to find out where he got the package from with all that money in it, and then I hope we can get back to normal.'

That was a relief, and Rainbow felt it. He was very happy that he didn't have to impart the bad, sad news of someone's demise, especially when the person was as young as ten years old. The information he had received was false, a mistake had been made, he would find out later in the day. But in the meantime this was his opportunity to get the full story from the boy.

Tea and biscuits were served in the head's office as Rainbow interviewed the boy in a way that was more like a game, with the detective talking about the boy's likes and dislikes. At one stage he promised to buy a replacement helicopter.

The full story unfolded slowly but surely, as the boy began to trust, and even like, the way this new man was taking an interest in him, and what he did. He told how he met this man called Tony, who was sailing a model boat, on the river, and how friendly he had been. He even admitted that he was hoping that he would be adopted by Tony, and pointed out that he had put in an application to take him out on outings and days in the park flying his new helicopter. He reluctantly admitted that he had crashed his helicopter, but blamed it all on the high winds and bad weather on the day. He went on to tell the story of how he had climbed the trees in the park to look for his crashed helicopter. And the package, he said, he had found in the hollow of the tree attached to the undercarriage. He didn't open it, and hid it in his locker to give to Tony when they met up again; it was all part of the mission, the boy said. Rainbow was satisfied that now he had the full story of how he and his money were parted.

He thanked the boy for being so truthful and promised to get a new model helicopter within a few days. The boy beamed with delight, and he promised not to run away again.

'I'm going to be a police helicopter pilot in the police force when I grow up,' were the boy's parting words as Rainbow left the children's home. Rainbow wondered who had been found in the river, but was pleased that it wasn't the boy he had just met.

It was proving to be a very busy day for Rainbow as he pulled in to the hospital car park. 'Just checking on Mr Waybee,' he told the nurse on the main desk, 'he was admitted this afternoon. Police,' he flashed a card.

'There's a doctor with him now, he's on the intensive ward, take the lift over there,' she pointed to the lift.

'Thanks,' he mouthed, and walked to the lift. He was met at the intensive ward by a young doctor who looked strained and tired.

Rainbow found out the patient was in a bad way, and in a coma.

'Fractured skull, its touch and go, whoever did this meant business, a vicious attack. I hope the perpetrators are apprehended, sergeant. You did say you were a sergeant, didn't you?'

'Yes, Detective Sergeant Rainbow, CID. Here's my personal number, give me a ring if there is any change will you?' As he left the hospital a pang of hunger flashed through his head and he realised that he hadn't even had a coffee since leaving Charlotte at lunchtime. The afternoon had left and evening time was in place. Rainbow shuddered; a nip was in the air as he decided to go to his café for a bite to eat and a hot cup of coffee.

*

Across the city, Big Joe Bananas was feeling happy when his hoods had reported back to say they had 'done over' Waybee. 'That'll teach him not to bad-mouth me, the bastard,' he had said to his boys after they told their boss the gory details of the beating. He had left the office early and had come home to plan the get-together of the gang top dogs on the forthcoming drug importation. The meeting was only a week away now. He sat in his big lounge on a velvet sofa opposite a gold coffee table with a world atlas opened at the South America page. With a magnifying glass he studied the route of the ship that would bring in his drugs and fortune; he smiled. The house was quiet; nothing stirred; outside there was only blackness, the blackness of the night. He pressed the electric switch by his sofa that was inside a book on a small pedestal, and the heavy curtains closed with a soft buzzing sound. A different switch switched on the record player, and a classical record started to play. He loved his electrical gadgets that he had devised himself, he admired his Charles Dickens book that lay on the top of the metre-high pedestal; with a flick of the cover it exposed an array of six switches that operated the music, the curtains, the lights, and the water fountain; it took him ages to cut out all the pages of the book to fit in the switches.

He laid back, contented with his life, a little man who had done well against all the odds. He had had to fight at times to build up his empire, and at times had to put down some people that got in his way. Maltese Joe was one gang boss who he had disposed of, and was now at the bottom of the sea, feeding the fish. He leant forward and took a sip of his expensive wine, and went back to his thoughts. It had certainly been a long road to get to the position he now found himself in: nice house, money in the bank, and a new fortune just a short while away. Not bad for a boy from nowhere; he had been ruthless at times but it had been worth it in the long run. A gentle contentment overcame him. The music filled the room and a crescendo was building; he was unaware that he wasn't alone, and behind the sofa the door was closed slowly and gently.

The coldness of a muzzle touched the side of his neck, which made him jump.

'Don't turn around, don't turn around,' the man repeated.

'What the fuck's going on?' Joe spluttered, easing forward on the sofa.

'Stay where you are, don't move.' the intruder said

'I'm not moving, what do you want with me, if it's money, I have plenty in the safe, there's no need for any violence, I'm not into any trouble, you can have all I've got, it's in the safe. I can get it in a minute.'

'Shut up, I don't want your money; I get very well paid for what I do.'

'What do you do? I will pay you more,' spluttered the now very frightened Joe.

'I have a question for you; do you remember a man called Maltese Joe lived on the east side of the city? A beloved father, brother and Uncle a caring man who worked hard to look after his family, a dedicated man.'

'Yeah, I remember him, a friend of mine, nice man, haven't seen him lately, why do you ask?' Joe mumbled.

‘So, you miss your old friend, do you? Would you like to meet up with him again?’

‘Sure I would, is that possible?’ Joe was now sweating profusely.

‘To answer your question on what I do for a living, I’ll tell you now. Because you won’t tell anyone will you?’

‘No I won’t tell a soul,’ Joe promised.

‘I’m a hit man, an assassin, and you have your wish, you’re going to meet your friend Maltese Joe. And that time is right now.’

Blackness, just like the night, was instant as the bullet entered the brain, blood shot forward onto the coffee table and into the wine glass, splattering the atlas. Joe slid off his settee onto the carpet, a grotesque smile on his pocked face. The hit man took the silencer off his gun and slid it into a pouch then placed it into his inside pocket. He walked up to the record player took the needle off the record, and calmly walked out of the room. In the hallway to the front door he passed the body laying in a pool of blood, he bent over and felt the neck of a man he had only met a short while ago, very briefly, but life had departed, the bullet had gone right through his heart. The other hood he had encountered was in the hallway, the mask of death on his face. Both men hadn’t put up much of a fight. Surprise made this assassin one of the best. He felt no remorse, there was no empathy, and he was just doing his job. He walked away to pick up his car that he had parked many streets away, and disappeared into the darkness of the night.

Revenge is sweet and the killing of Maltese Joe had been avenged.

*

Rainbow was still in the café drinking his second cup of coffee; he had had time to think about things, and felt a little better than he had done over the last few days. Waybee wasn't going to say much in his condition, the doctor had said that he may not pull through and he was the only threat, the only witness. He had resolved the trouble with Michelle, and now all that was left was finding a way to keep hold of his ten thousand pounds that he had got back from the home, rightfully his money.

Rainbow's thoughts were brought to an abrupt end as a man sat opposite him and plonked a cup of steaming coffee on the table. It was Brian Stevens who he always called Steve, one of his karate colleagues, whom he had seen the last time he had trained that fateful night as he was just leaving the club. Rainbow looked surprised for a moment.

'Hiya Ray, haven't seen you since the club. I was hoping to see you around, it was sad to hear what happened to Eddie Bail. Fancy him committing hara-Kiri, so the boys have said; but what do they know? He may have been sleeping when the club caught fire; we may never know the truth of what really happened. I didn't think Eddie was in that much trouble, I was shocked when I read about it in the papers. Never ever thought it would come to that. Remember I told you at the club last Monday night that Eddie had money problems? But to die like he did, it's beyond belief.'

'Steve, this is a surprise, you're right, I haven't seen you around for a while and like you I was shocked to hear about Eddie's death. It was investigated by officers in another department so I only know about it from the talk in the station, and from the papers. I've been very busy with other things, certainly a sad time for his friends and family, I don't even know when his funeral is. I've been out of it, way out.'

Steve took a sip of his coffee, and leant forward slightly as though sharing a secret, 'It's been the opposite for me, and I've been in it up to here.' Steve indicated with his hand to his forehead, 'that's why I wanted to see you to ask you, how long does the questioning go on for?'

'Questioning? What do you mean questioning?' Rainbow enquired.

'Well I've had at least six detectives coming to see me at different times, asking about the people who used the club, not all six at one time, you understand, but two maybe in the morning, then two the next day then they came back, time and time again. Questions, questions, when will it end? That's the reason I wanted to see you.'

'What detectives, who were the detectives?'

Steve thought for a moment then said, 'There were Detectives Smith and Jones, no, correction, that was James, then there were the two Ws, Willis and Weston, they are the most persistent, but the worst is a cop called Derek Jennet, he asked me a hell of a lot of questions on karate guys I know. He said he was investigating the murder in Baker Alley last Monday night, eight days ago; he wanted to know every member of the club. He even asked about you, Ray.'

'And what did you tell him?'

'He wanted to know what you were like and had I ever seen you lose your temper? Of course I told him that we've always got on well, and I've never seen you angry. He asked about your hand.'

'My hand?' Rainbow said looking at his hands 'What about my hand?'

'He wanted to know about the injury to your hand, and did I see you do it? Well I told him that I didn't see you injure your hand but you mentioned it to me and Dave.'

Rainbow sat listening intently then Steve asked him if he would like another coffee. Rainbow replied in the affirmative, and then indicated to the proprietor of the café in sign language by sticking two fingers up and mouthing the word coffee. The café owner put his thumb up to indicate that the coffees were on the way.

'What else did he ask you?'

'Loads, he wanted to know if I knew that you were in the police force, how you came to the club last Monday night, if you walked or if you came by car, what time did you leave the club. I told him you always walked to the club, and you left at six thirty.'

'Six thirty? Who told you it was six thirty when I left the club?' Rainbow asked.

'You did, I remember distinctly, you pointed out it was six thirty, and had to go home for a special event, you were running late, if I remember rightly.'

'Coffee coming,' Rainbow warned Steve as the café boss brought over the drinks and placed them on the table.

'Closing in half an hour, Ray,' said the boss.

'Yeah, we're going soon,' Rainbow acknowledged.

'You know, this copper even asked if I knew the way you went home, what route you took. I told him I had no idea. It was at that point I suggested that he ask you personally, after all, you work for the same firm. Anybody would have believed you were a suspect. Then after he went, the next day, two more detectives came to question me. To tell you the truth, Ray, I'm getting a bit fed up with it all, that's why I was glad to see you today; maybe you can put a stop to it.' Steve took a slurp of his drink.

'Thanks for telling me, Steve, I'll see to it that you won't be bothered again. It's just routine, just police work; don't let it spoil your day. Are you still doing karate and what club do you use now?'

'I go to Eric Sternson's gym, he's got all the top gear there, and there's a good crowd. Why don't you join us Ray, or are you training elsewhere?'

'No not at the moment I'm having a rest since I injured my hand on that dummy, no more training for now,' He finished his coffee and went to the counter to pay, he shook hands with his old friend Brian Stevens or Steve as he called him and wished him well, then made his way home. His mind was full of thoughts. Fancy Derek Jennet asking questions about him. He wondered if they were on to him, maybe the game was up. He slept fitfully that night, with vivid dreams disturbing his mind.

EIGHTEEN
WEDNESDAY

Police Constable Charlie Bright was sitting in the office belonging to Chief Inspector Ryan along with Detective Sergeant Mervin Jones and Detective Constable Derek Jennet, who had just come back from his brother's funeral.

The atmosphere was, to say the least, not conducive to a good time, and if seriousness could be measured in length, then this was a mile long.

It had started when PC Charlie Bright had reported for duty and was told that forensics had some information on the items that he had handed in a few days previously. After getting the information from forensics Charlie had reported the findings to the chief inspector, explaining how he came to have the items. The constable explained how he came to have the clothing, and what the bin man had told him; how he had handed them in to the forensics department, and the missing button from the ripped shirt of the victim had been found in the trouser pocket. It was identical to the other buttons found on the ground near the body. The inspector had summoned the other detectives to his office. Shock and surprise were evident as the constable explained the situation for a second time. The inspector thanked Constable Bright for his good work, and dismissed him back to his beat duties. The constable smiled and left the office feeling satisfied at the praise he had just received.

'Why would Sergeant Rainbow deny giving a bundle of clothes to the bin man who clearly remembers the incident, now there's a question? I want this cleared up as soon as possible. Where is Sergeant Rainbow at the moment, does anyone know what case he's on?' the inspector inquired.

'I was told that yesterday he was on the missing boy inquiry,' said DC Jennet.

The inspector lifted the phone on his desk, rang the front desk and asked the desk sergeant if he knew where Sergeant Rainbow was. He was informed that Sergeant Rainbow had not reported in yet, and that the last job he went on was yesterday when he left the station to inquire about the Waybee beating incident. The only information that had been obtained was that Waybee was in intensive care and in a coma, but that information had come from other sources, not from Rainbow. The desk sergeant could only assume that Rainbow would be in soon.

'Send him straight up to my office as soon as he comes in,' the inspector ordered.

'Sergeant Rainbow did a good job in looking after Waybee,' the inspector said mockingly, 'our number-one witness to the drug cartel, and the only witness to the murder of your brother, and he fucked that up. It seems that our Sergeant Rainbow is falling apart. I told him to look after the man, and within a couple of hours of being released from the nick he's in intensive care, and in a coma; it beggars belief.' The inspector shuffled some papers on his desk till he came to a file that said in big letters, 'Anthony Waybee statement'.

'This statement I got when I interviewed him when he was in custody,' he pointed to the statement. 'He was with your brother all day on the day of your brother's demise. He was in the skip, he said, looking for a pair of boots of all things. He said he heard talking, and a thud; it was all over in a few seconds, it seems; he heard a ripping sound and a pinging noise like ping, ping, ping, like a machine gun. He didn't know what it was, he says he heard a man talk but didn't catch what was said. He looked out from the garbage bin and saw his friend lying on his back; he jumped out and landed on the body by accident. He gave mouth-to-mouth, but there was no response; he said he was scared so ran away from the scene. This all took place at approximately six forty-five. Now you've told me that it's fifteen minutes' walk to the karate club that our Sergeant Rainbow was in on the night in question. Now with this new evidence it seems to me there's a possibility that we have to see what Rainbow has to say, do you agree Mervin?'

'Yes sir, it's now all coming together, how would that button get into the trouser pocket? One chance in a million. I would say, it flew through the air, bounced off the nearby bin, that's the pinging sound Waybee said he heard, and landed in the pocket of the sports trousers. Only three buttons were found near the body; there was one still on the deceased's shirt, and now the missing button turns up in these sports pants that allegedly belong to Sergeant Rainbow. He gets rid of his clothes by giving them to the bin man for disposal, never realising that the incriminating button had landed in his pocket. It's an incredible idea, I hope it's not true, but it all sounds plausible. If it's proved the clothes belong to Rainbow then he's got a lot of explaining to do.' A knock on the door stopped the discussion.

'Come in,' shouted the inspector. It was the desk sergeant who looked strained.

'Sorry to disturb you, sir, but something big has just been reported. A lady, a cleaning lady called, she's just phoned in saying that she went up to the house where she works and the front door was open, so she walks in, and there's blood everywhere and three dead bodies; she's very distraught, it's the house that belongs to that gangster we all know as Big Joe Bananas.'

'Joe Barnsom, Big Bananas, dead?' the inspector said in surprise. 'When? What happened? Joe Barnsom, the mobster from the manor house?'

'Yes sir, him and two of his henchmen shot in the head, she thinks. She was hysterical, I've sent a squad up there but I thought I'd let you know straight away; she said nothing has been taken so at the moment it seems like another gangland killing.'

'Thanks, sergeant, better get up there right away, things are getting worse every day,' he said as he slipped the parcel of clothes in a side drawer, and put on his coat then left the office with the two detectives in tow.

*

Rainbow, unaware of the developments in the case, was buying a model helicopter. He still hadn't worked out how to keep the money that rightly belonged to him, but he felt a little better due to the fact that Waybee was in a coma and wasn't talking to anyone at the moment. He would go up to the hospital later to see how he was faring. He did wonder what he had said in the interview that he believed the inspector had conducted at the station.

He paid for the helicopter and put the package into the boot of his car then drove to see the boy at the children's home. He had made a promise and he was keeping it. The model helicopter had been on the expensive side, but it would be worth the expense to see the boy's face light up. After all, little Benny had been forthcoming with the truth and Rainbow had admired that in the boy.

Mavis was at her reception desk reading a romantic novel as Rainbow went in to the main entrance; she slipped the book in a side desk drawer as though she was hiding it, and her smile was false. Rainbow could tell straight away, he had dealt with people of her calibre, a person who had little time for life's pleasantries. Maybe she had been let down too many times in her mundane life, he mused, as he walked towards her desk with the package in his hand.

'I've come to see the boy Benny Sparrow. I've got a gift for him,' Rainbow said as a matter of fact, 'could you let the head know I'm here?'

'Do you realise that you need an appointment to see any of the personnel who work in this establishment, and without one there's no way that I can allow you to see anyone, I have my job to do, and I might add I do it to the best of my ability. If you want to leave the gift, I will make sure it gets to the appropriate recipient.' She gave her false smile once more, and went to a file, and started to go through it.

‘Don’t need one,’ Rainbow said in a stern manner, ‘I don’t have to have an appointment when it’s the kind of business I’m in.’

‘And may I enquire into the business you profess to be in, because if you’re selling something you need to have an appointment.’

‘Don’t you recognise me? Take a good look at me, madam; surely your memory’s not that bad. I’ve seen you twice in as many days. Don’t say, please, that you have never seen me before.’

‘We see lots of people, am I expected to remember them all?’ she said bluntly.

‘No, I don’t expect you to remember everyone, but you should remember when it’s a police matter.’ He placed the package at the foot of the desk, and fumbled for his police identity card, and held it in front of her face. ‘Police,’ he said aloud.

‘You don’t have to shout, officer, why didn’t you say so when I asked you for your appointment? It would have saved time, and any misunderstanding. I’ll let Miss Butters know you’re here, take a seat.’ She pointed to an area away from her desk.

Rainbow looked hard and tried to remember where he had seen this woman, whom he now had a dislike for, before, apart from behind her desk.

‘Haven’t we met before, apart from here? I seem to recognise your face; did you ever have anything to do with someone I arrested a few years ago, a local man called Ted Sims? If I remember, you had to be escorted out of the court for bad conduct, shouting and causing a fuss. I’m sure it was you, or am I mistaken?’

'I don't think I'm obliged to answer that,' she said sternly.

Her face contorted in anger, she said, 'I didn't think you had come here today to question me. Am I a suspect in your enquiries, whatever they may be? Or do you just want to chat? Because may I say that I don't have time for any talking, I've got work to do, so if you'll excuse me I need to get on with my work.'

'Look, lady, I'm here to deliver a gift and that's all, I'm sorry if you have any problems with talking to policemen, I've tried to be friendly but given your belligerent attitude I must warn you to moderate your tone of voice and answer my questions, or we will have to take a different route, so let's start again and do the right thing.'

She looked up from her desk and sat back in her chair, arms akimbo.

'What do you want to know officer?' a sneer still on her face.

'Your name would be a start.'

'Mavis Sims, yes I'm the sister of Ted whom *you*,' put in prison for something he didn't do. He served time in jail because of you, and your false allegations. On the night of the robbery that you said he was involved with, he was with me, and didn't go out of the house. We were playing cards but you wouldn't believe me when I told you, you put him inside, an innocent man. I know my brother is no goody-goody, but he's no robber and never has been. A bit of a fighter, admittedly, his scarred face will tell you that, but never a thief.'

'Calm down, calm down,' Rainbow demanded.

'I am calm, you lot have never frightened me, so if it's at all possible I would like to get back to my work,' her face wasn't a pretty one.

'Well do it, then.'

'Do what?'

'Tell Miss Butters I'm here, that's what I came in here for in the first place.'

She picked up the phone, and Rainbow walked to the window that looked over the front lawns of the home. He glanced over his shoulder and saw Mavis put down the receiver and get up from her desk; she then left the room.

His mind wandered back to the time he had put Ted Sims away and had met his sister in court. She had caused a bit of a rumpus and had to be escorted out of the court; he never forgot faces. He tried to remember the circumstances of the case; it had been a few years back and the details had escaped him. He glanced at his watch, the morning was slipping away and he hadn't reported into the station yet. He paced up and down, looked at a few pictures that were on the wall, portraits of men and women who had worked at the home in years gone by, now long dead, or gone off to do other things. There were no sounds at all; it seemed that he was the only person in the home. He wondered where that woman Mavis had disappeared to; he had been alone for fifteen minutes and was beginning to get restless. He wandered outside and stood for a minute on the edge of the lawn. He saw a man walking towards him across the courtyard. He recognised him as Mr Jenkins, who was carrying a big cardboard box, with some difficulty. He stopped and placed the box on the lawn's edge.

'Hello, detective, and May I ask what brings you here again? Have you found out who owns that money that the boy Sparrow found? I was hoping that maybe the home might benefit from that money if no one claims it; you know, finder keepers, as the saying goes.' He laughed out loud.

'I have a good idea where the money came from but I doubt it will ever make its way into the home's coffers, unfortunately.' Rainbow said firmly.

'Only joking, don't take any offence, can I help you in any way?' Jenkins said with a smile, flexing his painful arms.

'Yes I have popped round with a gift for the Sparrow boy, he was so helpful in the enquiries, and he broke his model helicopter in the park, so he told me, so I promised that I would get him a new one, I have it here,' he indicated the package.

'I'm afraid to tell you that he's not here today. Periodically we let the boys stay for a few days with prospective foster parents, and if successful the boys and girls leave with their new mothers and fathers for a new life, and that's where Benny Sparrow is today. May I point out we did have a bit of trouble with him, he didn't want to go because he had set his mind on Mr Brinks being his new father; apparently they had a strong bond together.'

'Mr Brinks?' Rainbow said in a surprised manner.

'Yes, the man who filled in the application form that Miss Butters gave you.'

'Yeah I remember it, we are checking it out,' Rainbow lied.

'I better get on, got a lot to do this afternoon,' Mr Jenkins said as he mopped his brow, 'got to get out of this sun, I overheat you know.' He bent down to pick up his box.

'Before you go, could you do me a favour and give this gift to the boy when he gets back? I'm busy today so I can't come back. I promised him I would get him a new model helicopter, and I've kept my promise, he was so truthful when I questioned him and I do feel sorry for children who have no family to love them.'

'Oh they are loved, don't make that assumption, that wonderful Miss Butters loves all the children in her care, she's a very caring, loving woman. But I also know what you mean; you can leave the gift in my office if you follow me.' Both men walked across the courtyard and into a side door, down a narrow corridor and into a neat office. Jenkins placed his box in a corner of the room and said, 'Would you like a cup of coffee? I'm just going to make one for me, will you join me? I have some ginger biscuits as well.'

Rainbow glanced at his watch; it was midday. The morning had slipped away.

'Yeah thanks, I'm a bit dry so I will join you, thanks very much.'

'Take a seat; I'll put the kettle on, milk and sugar?'

'Two sugars please and milk, that'll be great.' Rainbow placed his package on the desk and made himself comfortable in a softly padded seat on the left of the desk.

'How long have you worked here?' Rainbow enquired not really caring one way or another. A smile crept over Jenkins's face, as though he was glad that that question had been asked and he was happy to answer it.

'Twenty years or thereabout, and I will tell you a little secret, the day I arrived I fell in love, and to this very day I'm still in love and with the same woman, every day the same as the day before I wake up in love and when I go to bed I'm still in love with her, it never alters, day in and day out, never-ending.' He made the coffee and placed it on the table, opened the tin of biscuits and offered them.

'So you're happily married? That's lovely for you,' Rainbow ventured.

'No I'm not married, never have been, wish I was, but it will never be, I'm afraid, too damn shy, that's always been my trouble, to damn shy,' He shook his head, then sipped his coffee. Rainbow did the same.

'So you mean to say you are in love with this woman yet you're not married to her? Have you ever asked her to marry you?'

'Good heavens no, she doesn't even know how I feel. I've never told her, too shy as I have said, but I'm happy because she's like me, hasn't got a partner. She's unmarried as well, and we get on as though we were a married couple anyhow, but without,' he hesitated, 'you know... the sex part.' He smiled broadly.

'Don't tell me, Miss Butters, is it Miss Butters?'

'Who else?' he smiled, 'she's the only one I've ever loved and I've never told her, but I guess she knows deep down. One day I might pluck up the courage and ask her, but to be honest with you, I couldn't take the rejection. I would just die if she said no, so I guess I'll carry on just loving her, I'm happy this way.'

Jenkins stood up and collected the cups and took them to the sink then turned around.

'You know, you are the first person in my life I've told that secret to, you're a very easy man to speak to; you're not a counsellor are you?' Jenkins burst out laughing.

Rainbow rose from his seat and said, 'Your secret is safe with me, but if you want my advice, I would make my feelings known to the lady. She may be as shy as you are. Anyhow, my friend, I must get on my way, I've overstayed my welcome. Thanks for the coffee and the bikkies, make sure the boy Benny gets his helicopter, will you?'

'I'll do that for you, it's safe where it is, I'll make sure the boy gets it when he gets back here.' The men shook hands, and Rainbow left the home. As he passed the main entrance he saw Mavis sitting at her desk, head down, oblivious of anything around her, deep in her romantic novel.

*

Rainbow was happy with what he had done for the boy; now he had other things to attend to. He drove to the hospital to see how his charge Waybee was faring. There was no change, he was still unconscious in a coma, and the doctor informed him once again that the prognosis was not good, and that he should be prepared for the worst news. The doctor had said that they had tried to inform his next of kin, but so far no one had come forward. Maybe the police could shed some light on who Mr Waybee's relatives were, and give them the bad news? Rainbow said he would look into the matter. He continued on to have a bit of lunch with his fiancée.

There was no one at Charlotte's home, so he let himself in with the key that she had given him, and made a ham sandwich and a cup of tea. He sat in the quietness of the downstairs room at the kitchen table. His mind wandered to the parties that had taken place in the past, in happier times. He saw the faces of the people, and remembered the drinks and laughter that had taken place over the years since he had been going out with Charlotte. He remembered how Michelle had first brought him to meet her family unit and her sister. He thought of the first time he had laid his eyes on his now fiancée Charlotte, how he had fallen in love with her beauty the very first time he had come to the house. The difficulty of telling Michelle that it was her sister he wanted and how she had reacted at first. He thought Michelle had accepted it. He wasn't to know that Michelle never gave up, and kept on coming on to him. At first he had thought that he could have his cake and also eat it, but as time went by he realised he had to make a choice, and he had chosen Charlotte. There was no way he wanted to be in the position he now found himself in with Michelle having his baby, but at least that had been resolved with Michelle going off to London to have an abortion.

He munched his sandwich as his thoughts ran amok; he glanced over to the mantelpiece and saw the gold-framed photo of Charlotte and himself laughing on a beautiful summer's day on holiday, just the year before. He also saw the red plastic flower in a vase that he had held in his teeth the night he had proposed to her; she had kept it and put it in a vase and there it was on the mantelpiece for her to remember the happiest day of her life so far, she had said. *To think, one mistake, just one mistake and the whole world could come tumbling down on you*, he thought. He drank his tea and refilled the cup, added milk and sugar. So much trouble, Waybee beaten up so badly that he had almost died. He would have a go at Big Bananas and his boys; he didn't mean them to be that brutal.

The grandfather clock in the hallway chimed twice, it was time he reported in to the station. He picked up the now empty cup and rinsed it out in the kitchen. He tidied up, replacing the sugar bowl and teapot in their places; he did wonder where everyone had got to as he switched on the kitchen radio. The two o'clock news had just come on. Rainbow stood there at the kitchen sink shocked as he heard the newsreader announce that police were hunting for a killer, or killers, of three males at the mansion in the Claiborne area of the city. 'Police believe it's another gangland killing,' the announcer said. '"The killings happened late last night," said Inspector Ryan in an interview this morning. "All leave has been cancelled and every effort will be made to bring the perpetrators to justice." Some roadblocks have been set up, and raids on some addresses are now taking place. Mr Joseph Barnsom, alias Big Bananas, it was reported, was one of the deceased, the other two males have yet to be identified and next of kin have yet to be informed. Police are asking the public to contact them if they saw anything suspicious last night in the area of the mansion or in the Claiborne area. The weather forecast for the next few days is overcast,' said the newsreader.

Rainbow switched the radio off and hurried to the door. As he was getting into his car, Michelle's car pulled in next to his. She got out, opened the boot, took out two carrier bags of shopping and, ignoring Rainbow, walked to the front door.

'I thought you were going to London, Michelle,' he shouted.

She turned around and shouted back, 'London, why would I go to London? There's nothing I want in London.' She turned the key and without another word went in and shut the door with a bang.

'Where's everyone?' he wanted to ask but the words never came out of his mouth. He shrugged and wondered for a moment what she meant by that statement about London, but decided to leave the matter for the time being. He would find out what game Michelle was playing at later, he had other things to attend to that took priority.

He drove towards the police station.

*

Across town, Chief Inspector Ryan, along with a number of detectives, had the mansion sealed off as tight as Fort Knox, with the police photographer taking pictures of the bodies and the crime scene generally. Fingerprint experts were powdering items of interest to them all over the house. It was plain to see that no struggle or fighting had occurred as everything was spick and span, no upturned tables or chairs. No disruption in any respect, it was as though the killers or killer had been invited in, and decided to kill everyone in the place. 'According to the cleaning lady there was nothing missing so the motive wasn't robbery,' the inspector declared without much debate.

The other detectives just nodded in agreement. It was Detective Barns who found the diary, and came across an entry that he thought the inspector might want to see.

The orange-coloured ledger was laid on the table and the inspector put on his spectacles and studied the book, turning it over and over again and flicking the pages.

'A diary belonging to Joe Barnsom,' the inspector pointed out, 'it says so on the front page.'

'Yes sir,' said Detective Barns 'but I just wanted to point out an entry on Monday the tenth, page sixty-four.'

'SAW RAINBOW THIS AFTERNOON WAYBEE IS SQUEALING GOT TO BE SEEN TO. PIGS WILL BE SQUEALING SOON WHEN THINGS TAKE OFF,' it read.

'So what's your take on this, what's the significance?' the chief inspector said.

'I don't know sir, just a thought, is the reference to do with our Sergeant Rainbow? I believe he had meant to see Big Joe at some time, I think it was mentioned at the station one day last week.'

'Or it might be that he saw a rainbow in the sky and wrote it down, some people will write anything down, just for something to do, these gangsters have crazy minds.' the chief surmised.

'Waybee is also mentioned, it seems to me that just after this entry Mr Waybee gets beaten to a pulp; on his death bed in hospital I understand, as I speak.' Detective Barns placed the diary in a plastic envelope.

'Looks like a professional hit job to me or maybe a disgruntled employee, whoever did this could be in another country by now, we have our work cut out, that's a certainty,' the chief mused.

'I agree with that one, sir,' said Barns.

'After we've wrapped it up here track down our reclusive Sergeant Rainbow, he might shed some light on the situation, he's been involved with Waybee and the deceased and there's other matters I want to have a word with him about.' The chief made for the door, he certainly wasn't looking too happy.

'And make sure the atlas that was on the coffee table gets to my desk, along with the diary, I'm going back to the office; look after things here will you, Barns?'

'Yes sir, will do,' Detective Barns said, feeling important as he walked into the main room just as the body of Big Joe Bananas, big time gangster, was being carried out, on his way to hell via the city morgue.

Rainbow arrived at the crime scene when most of the work had been done, and got all of the information about what had happened from a constable who had been posted on the main gate. He was told that the only detective in the house was Detective Barns, and that the chief and Detective Jennet had gone back to the station. The three bodies had gone downtown to the city morgue.

Rainbow thanked the constable and left; he had decided that he didn't want to see Barns, and there was no point in going up to the mansion. For a moment he was at a loss as to what to do; he had a sense of foreboding, he didn't feel right, and he felt nausea welling up in his stomach. He decided to go home to rest. He would report in sick, he decided, after all he had been under a lot of stress, and now it was beginning to tell. He realised he hadn't been eating or sleeping in the last few days, he needed time off, time to think.

NINETEEN
THURSDAY

A tanned woman left the hospital after finishing her vigil. It had been a long night and most of the time she had been taking notes from a patient who had come out of a coma and wanted to get 'things out in the open.'

Some of the statements made were indeed startling, but the patient was very fluent with the information, and when the woman asked certain questions, they were answered without hesitation. She had even read out some of her writings and they were confirmed to be true and correct, and at the end a signature was obtained. It had been an unusual time, and although she was tired and wanted to go home to bed, she felt compelled to do what she was doing, and that was a morning visit to the address she had in her pocket along with the copy of the statement she had obtained at the man's bedside in the early hours of the morning.

The woman's long coat hid her nurse's uniform. As she stepped out of the taxi, she looked at her watch; it was 8.23. A bit early for a visit to someone she had never met, but the information she had obtained was not the kind that could wait and be put away in a drawer, it needed immediate attention. She found the apartment easily, and gave the door a lusty knock, then went to the veranda and saw the storm clouds in the distance approaching the city; the forecast looked grim in more ways than one. Not the weather she was used to where she lived.

Rainbow was just drifting off to sleep again; he had been up early and had phoned in to say that he wouldn't be coming in on duty because he felt unwell. Just a brief call, he didn't go into any detail of what his ailments were, the night desk sergeant said he would pass the message on and wished him a speedy recovery. He had a drink of water, looked out of the window, saw what the weather was like and decided to go back to bed. He felt safe and warm as he lay there away from his world, a world that was slowly eroding, decaying, and unknown to him was about to get worse.

The knock at the door awoke his sleeping brain, and made him jump. He got out of bed reluctantly and walked down the hallway in his pyjamas and looked through the spy hole in the door. There was no one there; he turned to go back to bed when there was a second knock.

'Yes,' he said in a brusque manner, as he held the door just slightly ajar. He was in no mood for callers, especially at this time of the morning, and before she could answer added, 'I'm not buying anything.'

'And I'm not selling anything, you are Detective Rainbow, I believe,' she answered, looking at a slip of paper that she produced from her pocket.

'Detective Sergeant Rainbow and you are...?'

'Sister Susan Dipper from the city hospital, and I have come to see you this morning on a very serious matter, something that has to be attended to without delay. Can

I come in out of this cold and I'll explain everything.' She glanced up to the grey sky, as if to prove that the weather was not ideal for talking on a doorstep.

'Look, lady, I'm busy at the moment, can't it wait? Come back later on, maybe in a few days' time.'

'I'm sorry but I'm busy as well, I've just done a full night shift and I should be in bed myself, but I thought I would see you first to see what you had to say about the information I've obtained before I take it to the police station. So can I come in, or am I to go to the police station now?'

Information? What information? And police station, what did this all mean? Flashed across his mind. He opened the door and invited her in reluctantly. He indicated where she could sit on the couch and switched on the electric fire.

'I will get this out of the way as soon as I can. Do you mind if I take my coat off? I believe I'm having a hot flush, time of life,' she said flippantly.

'Be my guest, I hope this won't take too long, excuse my pyjamas, I'm officially on sick leave, and you have come at the worst possible time. Now what's all this about?' He sat down next to her.

She explained her position at the hospital, and told him how she was in charge of the intensive care ward and one particular patient, a Mr Waybee, who was in a coma. And at one thirty this morning he had come out of his coma, and after an hour he started to talk although he was very poorly, and some of what he was trying to say was unintelligible. 'But as time went by his speech got better and then he whispered, "I know I'm going to die," so he asked me to get a pen and paper as he wanted to make a statement, stating that he wanted to get things "off his chest".'

Rainbow listened intently, as she reached into her handbag and produced a foolscap sheet of paper. 'This is what Mr Waybee told me to write down, I'll read it to you, but before I do, let me warn you that this document contains some damning evidence, and you may be shocked, and this is the reason I came to you first, before I do anything further.' She gave him a look that for a moment had a frightening aspect to it.

'Continue, please read it out,' he said with a puzzled look on his face. She put on her reading spectacles and started to read the document.

'This is what Mr Waybee asked me to write down, word for word and we went over it at least twice,' she pointed out.

'"I saw Detective Sergeant Rainbow kill my friend Tommy Crawly in Baker Alley on Monday evening, with one blow to the neck. He ripped open his shirt as he lay on the ground. I was in the skip bin, and saw it all through a crack in it. Rainbow tried to make a deal with me when we met, and I tried to get money from him, I confronted him and he admitted the killing to me. I was going to keep strum, keep my mouth shut, but he had me beaten up, and between every blow they accused me of squealing. Banana's hoods told me that Rainbow had told their boss that I had been spreading rumours implicating the gang boss in a killing and I never did grass on anyone in my life. I've killed, that I admit to doing. Now Rainbow must pay for his crime, he's a disgrace to the police force and to the human race."'

She looked up from the page and said. 'This is his statement, I read it out to him twice, I asked him if it was all true, and he smiled and said that as God was his witness it was the absolute truth. See, he even signed it.' She showed him the signature. 'May I add at times he was very distraught, and his statement upset me as well, I was already having a busy night with other patients.'

Rainbow was in shock once again. *He would go to the hospital at once to see Waybee to get him to withdraw his statement*, he thought.

'You're right, Susan. May I call you that?'

'That's fine,' she said with a smile.

'You're right, it is a shocking statement but in a way it doesn't surprised me because we get that kind of thing all the time, some villains never give up trying to get their own back on the cops who nick them. It's happened to me before, believe me this isn't the first time I've seen this kind of accusation and I don't know if you're aware but this man Waybee is a right villain, and a liar.'

'So you're denying it outright, are you? That's OK then, I don't know what to do now, it's not often I get a bedside confession like this.' She went to put the document into her handbag.

'Can I have the so-called confession? I would like to study the allegations, when I have more time.'

'Sure,' she replied, 'it's only a copy.' She handed it over.

'A copy, you mean to tell me you have other copies?'

'Yes, the original is in the safe at the hospital.'

'In the safe!' he exclaimed. 'Why would you make more than the original?'

'It's what we do, we always duplicate, in case a copy is lost, or gets into the wrong hands. Everything that goes on in the ward has to be documented,' she gestured with open palms and shrugged her shoulders.

'Look Susan, I will come to the hospital with you and I'll talk to Mr Waybee and get to the bottom of this pack of lies, then you can give me the other copy you have in the safe, then we can get back to normal, is that OK with you?'

'That won't be possible I'm afraid,' she said shaking her head, 'for two reasons, first I've just done a ten-hour night shift, and I have things to do at home and that's before I go to bed, I'm pooped. And the second reason is that you can't talk to Mr Waybee because—'

'Don't tell me he's gone into a coma again,' Rainbow interrupted.

'No, Detective Rainbow, worse than that, he died at five twenty-eight this morning.' The shock was as sudden as an express train going through a station at full speed. He tried to suppress the surprise but failed; she saw it as plain as the nose on his face.

'I'm sorry to hear that, that's bad news,' he blurted out.

'Yeah, it is, so now I hope you can see the importance of the deceased's statement, you could say, his last will and testament, so I had to let you know. I considered it my duty to let you know, maybe to give you the chance to take it all in before your superiors, you know, look into the matter.' She made as though she was preparing to curtail this meeting.

'It's just the ramblings of a crook, a villain,' he said in a raised voice. She was startled for a moment. 'It's just a piece of paper, with a drugged-up man who's out for revenge, I knew him well, I put him away many times over the years, he held a grudge, a grudge against me. If these lies got to the police chief there would have to be an inquiry, it could go on for months and who can tell the outcome. My career could be ruined all because of lies. It's happened before, where innocent men have been condemned because of deceit; this statement isn't worth the paper it's written on.' He tore it in half and threw it on the coffee table.

'Sorry you feel that way, but I take a different view,' she said, 'a dying man's last wishes must be adhered too, so if that's all you have to say on this matter, I'll be on my way. As I have said, I have things to attend to.'

'No wait Susan, maybe there's another way this matter can be resolved, I just want to say to you right now, and I can see you're a reasonable woman, that there's no truth in these allegations, there's no shred of evidence that would hold up in a court of law. It would only cause trouble for you, and for me, you would have to be interviewed over and over again. I could get suspended until they went into every aspect of it all, and in the end I would be vindicated; all this trouble for nothing. Susan I've been in the force for fifteen years, and I'm up for promotion soon, and I can't risk all that just because a lowlife writes a load of bollocks about me, excuse my language.'

'So what do I do? I believe what you say, how do we resolve it?' she said, now really wanting to leave, and feeling slightly apprehensive.

'Money,' he hesitated and smiled for the first time, 'money is the answer to most things in life, and I think maybe if you could forget this unfortunate incident and let me have the other copy then a reward would be in order.'

'Money, that never dawned on me, it never came into it, my intention was never to extract money from you, and I was only doing what I thought any decent citizen would do. I'm not a blackmailer, you know, but if that is what you want to do I guess you know best. And we are going on holiday soon, that's my husband and me and of course the kids, so a reward might come in handy, for a few ice creams.' She laughed for the first time. 'And maybe a few drinks for me and Len, my other half.'

'Good I'm glad you could see sense, how does a thousand sound, a good morning's work if you ask me? A one-off reward for your silence; there's no need for this to get out, it could alter our lives in many ways, and lies have brought down many a good man and woman throughout history, it's a fact.' He smiled, and nodded.

'Whatever you think is fine with me. But once again I didn't come here for money, I was only looking for justice, you know, doing the right thing for Tony,' she hesitated, 'eh, Mr Waybee.'

'You're doing the right thing, believe me.' He got up and put his hand on her shoulder to reassure her.

'OK I'll get the money from the bedroom, I won't be a minute, help yourself to a coffee, I'll switch the kettle on, and you can bring the copy of the letter in when you're passing. I trust you, after all, we made a deal.'

He went into the bedroom and counted out the money as she made the coffee.

He felt relieved, he had pulled it off. That bastard Waybee could have been his downfall, the downfall of Raymond Rainbow. Now with his death he was off the hook, now there were no witnesses to his misadventure and now maybe there was a chance he could pick up the threads once more and put his life back together again. These thoughts made him smile. He returned to the couch and sat down opposite the woman whom he had just taken a liking to, and across the table he handed her the thousand pounds, and smiled broadly.

'It's been a pleasure doing business with you, Susan; hope to see you again very soon, and I hope I've satisfied you in every way, this is not goodbye, hope the holiday is a good one.'

His smile soon faded as he glanced up and saw his fiancée Charlotte standing near the hallway, at the corner of the room, her face like thunder.

'Charlotte,' he spluttered, 'what are you doing here? I didn't hear you come in.'

'Obviously not, did you forget that I have my key?' she held the key in the air.

'I think I'd better go,' Susan said picking up her coat and bag.

'Hold on, this is not what you're thinking, Charlotte, I'll explain, Susan here is a nurse, and—'

'Save it,' Charlotte walked past both of them straight into the bathroom, and picked up her toothbrush and a few items that belonged to her, then on into the bedroom. She noticed the unmade bed that seemed more ruffled than she had ever seen it before, her mind working overtime.

He followed her into the bedroom as she gathered things that were hers, photo frames, nightgowns and a few clothes. She threw them in a bag, which had been on top of the wardrobe. She was livid. 'How could you do this to me when I trusted you with all my heart? How long has this been going on for? How long have you been two-timing me?' She started to cry.

He approached her and tried to console her by putting his hands around her shoulders, but she pushed him away.

'Charlotte, please let me explain, it's all innocent, and it's not what you're thinking.' he pleaded. She turned around to face him, her arms akimbo, her face now devoid of any beauty and almost sneering.

'I arrived here unexpected, and find you in your pyjamas, with your dick trying to get out. Look at yourself, you can see the outline of everything you've got between your legs, giving money to a woman sitting on your sofa, thanking her for her services, and I'm supposed to say "Hello how are things?" am I?'

'Charlotte please, just calm down and I'll tell you what this is all about, please darling just listen to me, it's not what you're thinking.'

'Don't darling me, get rid of that woman,' she pointed to the other room with her finger that jabbed forward like the muzzle of a gun. He left the bedroom to ask the nurse to leave but she had left already, and was on her way through the rain-drenched streets to her next assignment. Her head was full of laughter as she thought of her encounter that morning with Tony's mortal enemy.

He went back into the bedroom. 'She's gone,' he said in a low voice.

'And I'll be out of your hair in a few minutes, just getting what belongs to me, I should have known better,' she said to herself as she continued to gather her bits and pieces, throwing them in the small case she had on the bed.

'Don't do this, Charlotte, you're chucking away your future, our future, all the time we've been together will have been wasted on something that I can explain only if you let me, just hold on please just a few minutes.'

She stopped packing and turned around to face him. 'What future are you talking about? You know that house we were going to buy, you remember, the one in the country, the one with the lawns and the flowers, and beams in the ceilings, the one you said we would bring up our children in, our dream, you remember that one Ray? The house I fell in love with, our house, you said.'

'Of course I do, it's still our dream Charlotte, and it's still ongoing if you want it to, all you have to do is listen to me.'

'No Ray,' she shouted, 'that dream has gone, it's fucking gone, it's been lost because of you and your indecisions, I don't know what you think I am but I know when something comes to an end, and our relationship is over, over,' she screeched.

'Please give me a chance, we will get our dream, it's still here, it never went away,' he pleaded.

'Yes it did Ray, the agent phoned to tell me that the time limit we both agreed to, remember, had run out, and the house has been sold. We lost the dream, because of you, so excuse me if I'm a little unhappy at this moment,' the sarcasm showed.

'We can get another house, there's plenty on the market,' he said feebly.

'Not for us there's not, there's nothing left for me in this relationship.'

She closed the case and left the bedroom, with him following.

'Blackmail,' he shouted, 'I was being blackmailed,' and she stopped at the door and turned around.

'Blackmailed, you've been blackmailed? What do you mean?'

'Look, let's sit down and I'll explain everything to you, come on, for old times' sake,' he pleaded. She returned to the lounge and sat at the table by the window.

'Go and get dressed, I'll give you fifteen minutes, and that's all. I'm meeting my sister Michelle at the Bedford Hotel for lunch in town, your explanation better be good.'

Rainbow went into the bedroom to get out of his pyjamas; he stood in front of the mirror for a moment and saw for himself what Charlotte had meant about his bulge in his pyjamas trousers, the flimsy material did make his tackle show. As he changed he couldn't believe his bad luck, his fiancée coming in just on the point as Susan was going to leave, his mind was on overtime as he tried to concoct a story that Charlotte would swallow. He didn't want to lose her, he needed her.

'Thank you, darling, for agreeing to listen to my explanation, it won't take long, I promise,' he said as he sat opposite her, her normally beautiful face was now etched in anger and a certain sadness was denoted in her eyes. The rain pittered and pattered on the windowpane, and the dullness of the day cast a shadow of gloom over the pair as he tried to cling on to the happiness that he once knew.

'No promises, Ray, just get to the point, what's this all about, this blackmail?'

Rainbow didn't know quite where to start; he wasn't going to admit everything to her. How can you say to someone that you killed a man, hid evidence, tried to frame an innocent man of a crime he didn't commit and burnt down a gym?

'The woman who was here,' he began, 'was from the hospital, she's a night nurse and came round to warn me that a crook, a local villain, has lied and implicated me in a murder.'

'A murder, a murder?' she repeated.

'Yeah, he told her, this liar, that he saw me hit a man who died; he said he was hiding in a skip bin when he saw me.'

'A what, a bloody dustbin?'

'A skip bin, he said he saw me hit this guy, and said that I killed him,'

'And did you? Did you kill someone, and when were you supposed to have done this?' she enquired.

'The Baker Alley killing, a couple of weeks ago, and I certainly didn't kill anyone, I'm a policeman not a lowlife, but this asshole has said that he saw me do it, and he told the nurse about it, and she came here to warn me, so to speak.'

'So why were you giving her money, what was the point in that?'

'She said she felt it her duty to go to the higher authorities with this information. I can't let that happen, as I told her there would be an investigation into the matter, I could get suspended while all this was going on, the top brass always investigate all accusations no matter what.'

'You mean to tell me that the top brass would believe a crook, before the good word of a detective sergeant who's up for promotion, with years of dedicated service under his belt? Pull the other one, Ray, you have to do better than that.' she sneered. 'First off, were you in Baker Street at the time of the murder?'

'Alley, it's Alley not Street, it runs behind the high street, behind the shops. The shopkeepers use the alley to dispose of all the garbage and the packing. What's all this, you're questioning me like a fully fledged detective at the station.'

'Answer the questions, Ray; is there any truth in what this man has said about you? If not, then you have nothing to worry about, have you?'

'OK, I was never in Baker Alley,' he lied, 'I was here with you and we were celebrating our engagement, remember?'

'Once again, why were you giving her money? After all it's only hearsay, as they say in court.'

'No Charlotte, that's the main point, she had this document with the statement written down and duly signed, may I say. She said he dictated it to her throughout the night as he lay dying. His last will and testament,' she said.

'The man was dying, has he died?' She looked shocked.

'Yeah he died, so I persuaded the nurse—'

'Susan,' Charlotte pointed out.

'Yes, Susan, not to go to the station with the document, and if she would leave it in my court I would deal with it. After all, it was just some villain trying to get even with the law, it's been done before, and I'm sure it won't be the last time. So I gave her a reward, that's all. That's when you came in, so you see, it's not what you thought at all. I hope that clears it up.'

'How much did you give her, to keep her mouth shut and for the document?'

'I gave her a couple of hundred pounds for the document, she seemed to be happy with that, so that should be the end of that,' he lied once again.

'Let's see that document, I deal with documents every day of my working life, it may not be genuine.'

'I tore it up, what do you mean, it may not be genuine?'

'Raymond, just let me see the fucking thing, stop wasting my time.'

He got up from his chair and went over to the coffee table where he had thrown the document, then looked on the carpet near the settee, then behind the settee.

'Well let's see it, let's see this document that you tore up.'

'It's not here, it's gone,' he declared, 'there's only one explanation, she took it with her, the bitch,' he muttered to himself.

'Or it never existed; it's been just one big lie, like the rest of your lies. And Two hundred pounds? I saw you count out a thousand, and you mean to tell me that in a murder case that you're investigating, it turns out that the culprit is you? Or some two-bit crook says it was you? You must have been reading too many second-rate detective novels, the kind you pick up in seedy second-hand bookshops. It amazes me to think that you expect me to believe all your bullshit. We have been drifting apart for a while, I've seen you flirting with my sister on more than one occasion, and I believed you when you told me that the short fling you had with her was just that, a short fling; we haven't had sex for ages either.'

'We could have sex now if you wanted,' he interjected.

'You must be joking, haven't you had enough sex for today with Susan? Excuse me, I need the toilet.' She went into the bathroom.

He didn't know what had happened to him. He felt like he had just been hit by an avalanche, his head hurt badly, her words were tumbling like a washing machine in his mind.

Fighting with his confusion, and not understanding why his life had taken this direction and was now heading for oblivion, he felt he was losing everything, he felt lost. She came out of the bathroom, walked across the room, picked up her case and made her way to the door. He wanted to shout out to her to stop, to turn around, to take him in her arms, and to kiss him, but the words lay dormant, they wouldn't come out, although his mind was shouting from the highest mountain.

She turned as she opened the door, 'You know, Ray, you didn't even tell me what happened to Pedro, the parrot I loved, you just didn't take the time.'

She shook her head in disgust and slammed the door.

Rainbow was sure of one thing, he would get the document back, and the hospital was the place to start. He would get Susan's home address and pay her a visit. He went to the bathroom and there on the washbasin was Charlotte's engagement ring.

TWENTY

Rainbow was very distraught as he left his apartment, and to make matters worse, soon he would have to vacate his apartment for good in the next month; the letter in his hand said so. He had heard rumours to this effect but had put the matter on the back burner, his mind had been on the new house he was going to get with his new wife, that house in the country, with flower beds, and timber beams, the dream that had gone up in smoke, just that very morning.

The rain had eased as he drove to the hospital on the other side of the city. The morning traffic was heavy. He pulled into the hospital car park and went into reception; a pretty female looked up from her file she was looking at and smiled.

'Good morning, can I help you sir?' she said, putting the file to one side.

'Yes, and good morning to you, the weather's not so good today,' he remarked as though it really mattered. She didn't answer but just nodded as though she already knew, but wasn't that interested.

'Can I help you?' she repeated.

'Yeah, I'm looking for an address, it's a night nurse who works at this hospital, it's very important that I see this lady, and before you say that you can't divulge this information, may I tell you that this is police work.' Rainbow flashed his identification. The smile disappeared from her face as though someone had just told her that her pet dog had just been killed. She disliked his manner, and he seemed abrupt for no apparent reason.

'I wasn't going to say anything of the kind; I'm here to help not hinder, what's this nurse's name?' the receptionist said in a matter-of-fact way.

'Her name is Susan Dipper; she's on night duty, I believe.'

'Don't recognise the name, but I'll check the employee's list, there's a lot of people working in this hospital, I know a lot of them but they come and go as in any job.' She went to the filing cabinet and brought out a black ledger and flicked to the D index, then fingered the page with a downward movement. 'What was the name again?' she inquired.

'Susan Dipper, D I P P E R,' he spelled it out with emphasis.

'Sorry, there's no one of that name who works on night shift, in fact there's no one of that name who works in this hospital,' she closed the book.

'Let me see for myself,' he demanded.

'OK, if you don't believe me, have a look for yourself,' she handed him the book.

He satisfied himself that her name wasn't in there, and handed the book back.

'That's strange,' he muttered to himself. 'Can you tell me who was on duty last night, to be more precise the nurse who was looking after a Mr Waybee, a patient in intensive care?'

'That would be Sister Trembull, I know because I saw her when she came off duty this morning, in fact we had a cup of coffee in the canteen, and a chat before I came on duty and she went home.' The telephone rang behind the desk.

'Excuse me; I must answer this, is that all?'

'Answer it, there's just one more thing.' He moved away from the desk as the receptionist answered the phone. What was this unknown woman's motive in pretending to be a nurse? It was mystifying and perplexing, he thought, as the telephone was put down.

'I just want to say thank you for your help, I realise you're busy, all hospitals are, but you must realise that this is also important to me as an upholder of the law,' He smiled a false smile, but she didn't know that. 'Can you tell me what you talked about as you had your coffee this morning? I mean did she tell you how her shift went? Were there any incidents, apart from the main one, I mean?'

'She did say that Mr Waybee had a visitor who spent a good few hours at his bedside writing down things that he was dictating to her.'

'Visitor? I thought there were only visiting hours during the daytime?'

'If you are close family you can visit at any time if the patient is in a grave condition, at any time. I believe it was his wife, who lives in another country. She didn't say where that is, her name was Ruby, I was told. What main incident do you refer to?'

'Mr Waybee's death, he died at five twenty-eight didn't he?' he said quizzingly.

'Where did you get that information from? Mr Waybee came out of his coma. He was in a very bad way, but suddenly he improved. Maybe it was seeing his wife that brought him round. He's improving as I speak to you, in fact he's being interviewed by the police at this very minute, but I guess you already knew that. I'm sorry, detective, but I must get on with my duties. I hope I've been of some help to you, and by the way when you find this Ruby woman, charge her with stealing a nurse's uniform.' She left reception to attend to other duties.

Rainbow left the hospital, his mind racing. It seemed he had been conned again, everybody he was coming into contact with was taking his money. First there was Waybee, twice, then Eddie Bail at the gym, Michelle for her trip to London and now Waybee's wife. At this rate he would be bankrupt in no time at all; something had to break. He walked through the car park and got in his car, he automatically switched on the radio, and the song that wafted through the car was Roy Orbison's song 'It's over.' 'It's over, you won't be seeing Rainbows anymore, it's over, it's over.' Charlotte was listening to the same record, as she waited in her car for her sister to come out of the hairdressing salon.

*

Meanwhile Ruby had visited another address that her estranged husband had given her, as he lay on his bed thinking he was on the way out. She promised to give the money that he knew she would get from his arch-enemy Rainbow to his new-found son, whom he had taken a shine to, the son he had never had. Ruby felt she owed it to her ex 'for old times' sake,' to remember the good times they had once had together, before he took the wrong road and ended up in prison leaving her for years waiting for him to change, but he never did. She had left for a new life in Spain, and was in a loving relationship with a Spanish baker, but when she heard through the grapevine that her ex-husband was nearing the end, she took the time to fly over to say her goodbyes. She was flying back to Spain later in the day.

'Sunshine home for children on Bayfield Road,' Ruby said to the taxi driver, 'then I will want you to take me to the airport; got a plane to catch out of this weather to a warmer climate.'

'Sure thing,' the driver answered, 'going somewhere nice and hot?'

'Yeah, going back home to Spain, back to the sun.'

'Nice one, wish I could join you, always wanted to go abroad but with a misses and four kids to support, its hard going you know.'

'I know, that's the way of the world,' she surmised. It was strange how many taxi drivers all had four kids to look after; maybe it was a good ploy in getting bigger tips, she pondered. The rest of the journey was spent in silence, with Ruby thinking of her ex-husband dying in hospital, not wanting to accept that their marriage had ended years ago. He had been a good man in many ways, but his upbringing had made him a crook, there were no two ways about it, but a lovable rogue all the same. As a final farewell and for the good times he had once given her she was doing his bidding, her love for him hadn't completely died.

'Sunshine home for children,' the driver said as he pulled up outside the establishment.

‘Thank you, will you wait? I will only be fifteen minutes at the outside.’

‘I’ll be right here, ma’am, right here,’ he pointed down and switched the engine off. ‘Got a good magazine here,’ he said smiling

‘Have you got an appointment?’ Mavis said, in a matter-of-fact way, to the request to see the boy called Benny Sparrow.

‘Mavis, are you Mavis Sims?’ Ruby said with surprise and pleasure in her voice.

‘Yes I am, and you’re Ruby Waybee, we went to school together, haven’t seen you in years, how are you? Well what a surprise to see you again, didn’t you go overseas a while ago? Well I’ll be blessed, fancy that, meeting you again here of all places.’

The two old friends talked for a few minutes about old times, and the fun they had had together years ago when they were young and carefree. The atmosphere changed when the men in their lives were mentioned, and the fact that they had fallen out with one another, and had fought, on many occasions, Mavis recollected.

‘That’s men for you, friends one minute, enemies the next. You know I divorced Tony years ago,’ Ruby volunteered. ‘You wouldn’t recognise Tony now, he’s changed so much, I suppose we all change with time, you know as we get older.’ Mavis hadn’t recognised him when he had visited the home just a week or so before, to fill out the forms for the police check. But he had recognised her. Ruby explained that this was just a flying visit as she was in town just for a short time and was leaving to go back to Spain later that day, where she now lived.

And the reason for her visit at the children's home was that she wanted to give the boy a sum of money.

'The boy's in the day room playing games I believe, I'll check with Miss Butters, she's the head of this home,' Mavis hesitated then added, 'this home's for orphaned children, so because I know you from old, Ruby, I'm going to waver the need for an appointment, and as you have a plane to get, I will allow it in this instance,' she felt flushed with power as she lifted the phone to enquire as to whether the meeting would be allowed. Ruby stood at the desk and looked at the woman who had once been her school friend, and saw how time can do so much damage to body and mind. She deduced by her attitude that the woman at the desk was now a bitter and unhappy person who had nothing in life to hope for; she felt sorry for her.

Benny Sparrow was surprised to have a visitor, his little face lit up as he was told that his friend had given him the money to get a new helicopter that he had been promised; the boy didn't mention that he already had a new helicopter. But he did ask if he would be seeing his friend, or as he preferred to say, his new dad, again.

'I don't think that will be possible,' she explained to the boy, and to Miss Butters who was in attendance throughout the meeting. 'He is a very sick man and he's in hospital, he wants you to have this money, and he did say that he thought you were a very talented boy, and said you will do well in life as a helicopter pilot one day. And he thanked you for the good company you were.'

Miss Butters took the envelope with the five hundred pounds, promising to let the boy have it when he needed to buy things. Ruby kissed the boy on the cheek as she was leaving, to the boy's embarrassment; he wiped his cheek with the back of his hand, and then ran off to continue his game with the other children.

'Goodbye Mavis, it was nice to catch up with you again, all the best for the future,' Ruby said as she walked out of the home. She didn't stop, everything had been said, and she had done her bit, she felt that keeping five hundred pounds for herself was justified as she had to pay for her taxi, plus her time, she was satisfied with herself, she had said her final farewell to her ex-husband and it was time for her to go to the airport. The taxi driver was fast asleep with the magazine over his head. He jumped as he heard her open the rear door.

'Sorry I was a little longer than I said I would be, but I met an old friend who happens to work here, someone from years ago when I was at school, we were school friends, and it was a surprise to have met her, hadn't seen her in years.'

'That's nice,' the driver said disinterested, 'where to now, the airport didn't you say?'

'Yeah, but I need to stop at a post office. I need a local stamp and a big envelope.'

'That's not a problem, the post office is on the way to the airport,' he said casually.

She paid the taxi fare with a ten-pound tip that made the driver smile broadly, and thanked him for being so patient with her. Just before she went into the departure area she posted her envelope, she checked the address as she put it in the slot and was satisfied. 'Done,' she said to herself. It would arrive at the police station the next day, first thing.

*

The two detectives looked at one another from time to time in disbelief as they sat by the bedside taking statements. Tony Waybee was making a fine recovery to the surprise of the doctors and the nursing staff. Just a day before, it had been touch and go as to whether he would survive his trauma, but his demeanour had changed dramatically when his wife uttered those first words to him as he lay in a dream that was way back in time, when he was just a young lad, and before he took the path to crime. That time when he had first set eyes on her. She had whispered, 'Hello darling, now what trouble have you been getting into this time?'

He had slowly opened his eyes and as her face came out of the fuzziness of his unconsciousness and came into focus, his lost world took on a different slant and was suddenly renewed like a battery being charged. He had smiled broadly.

'Hi there sweetheart, long time no see, how've you been?' Needless to say, from that moment on he started to improve. She had gone now with his best wishes and no hard feelings to do his bidding, to get even with his arch-enemy, Detective Sergeant Raymond Rainbow, the man who had done this to him indirectly, nearly cost him his life. It was, in his mind, payback time.

'Iron bar, a fucken' iron bar the bastards used on me.' He lifted his hand slowly to point at his heavily bandaged head. 'Tied me to a chair and beat the shit out of me they did.'

'Did you know these people who did this to you?' the detective asked.

'Course I know them, it was Big Bananas' boys, big Butcher and that other asshole, the ugly one, they said that your Sergeant Rainbow had told Big Joe that I had squealed on him in the murder of Maltese Joe. And I never did.'

The detectives looked at each other and continued to take notes.

'Serious allegations, you've implicated a member of the police force, remember you will have to reiterate them in a court of law,' the detective warned.

'I'll do that, once I get out of this bed, I've learned my lesson this time. It's the straight and narrow for me after this lot, look at the state of me; I'm on the edge of death, fucken' death. No more, I can't take it, I'm going to get out of this city and go to a sunny country to live in peace away from the scum that I've associated with all my life. I'm going to find her, my Ruby, make it up, start anew. Big Bananas and his gang belong behind bars, and I will have to be protected from their brutality, go on your protection plan, or whatever it is your lot do, they'll kill me for sure next time, there's no second chance with that lot.' He hesitated for ten seconds then mumbled 'Fucken' lowlife, the lot of them.'

Waybee closed his eyes and laid still, a tear showed and slid down his face.

The detectives were concerned for a moment and thought he had passed away and caught the attention of a nurse passing the room.

'That's enough for today, gentlemen, he needs to rest now,' the nurse said as she adjusted the pillows. The detectives closed their notebooks and were preparing to go when Waybee opened his eyes and blurted out, 'Bananas did murder Maltese Joe, I know because he recruited me for the job, I refused to do it and I'll say that in court, you know what they did, the wankers?' The nurse blushed and looked away. 'They smashed up all my model boats, smashed them to smithereens, every one of them, and I spent weeks and months putting them together, all my boats gone beyond repair, the bastards.'

'Thanks for your cooperation, we will pass on your statement to the higher authorities and go from there; we will be in touch, oh and by the way, get better soon.' The detectives left the bedside. Waybee didn't see the smiles on the officers' faces as they left the room. Outside the hospital the detectives decided that morning coffee was in order before they decided what their next course of action would be.

*

The Copper Kettle coffee shop was a nice place where a lot of passing policemen would stop for their coffee breaks, and it was just a stone's throw from the hospital. The detectives chose a window table and ordered a latte each. They got out their notebooks and compared them. 'What do you reckon then?' Willis said to his partner, Weston.

'Bullshit, a load of bollocks, it's obvious that that scum Waybee has got it in for our Sergeant Rainbow, we have both worked with him and I've always found him to be a good cop, he was up for promotion if I'm not mistaken, yeah, first class if you ask me.'

'Yeah, the sarge put him away a few times over the years, and I know sometimes some villains hold a grudge, and this is a classic case,' Weston put three spoons of sugar in his coffee and stirred it slowly.

'Hey, you're fat enough already, watch your intake,' Willis joked. They sipped the hot coffee, and for a moment looked out to the people going about their business in the dull cloudy morning, lost in their own thoughts.

'He's sick, isn't he? Ray's off sick, I believe I heard the desk sergeant say this morning,' Weston ventured.

'Well I certainly haven't seen him around for a while now, maybe we should pay him a visit, he will be home, maybe we should put this to him, see what he has to say on the matter.' He picked up his black book and lightly threw it back on the table. 'I think we owe it to him, after all, he always treated us the right way, he's never given me a hard time, what do you say, are we both in agreement?'

'Let's face it, these allegations are very serious, I agree we owe it to the sarge to hear what he makes of it, before we submit them, let's go and see him. One more thing,' Weston said.

'What's that? As if I didn't know. Don't worry I have already paid, your round next, I've already made a note of it,' both cops laughed as Willis lifted his black book in the air, and left the coffee shop en route to see their sergeant and colleague.

*

What the good-intentioned detectives didn't know was that Rainbow wasn't in his sick bed at home, but was spying on his ex-girlfriend who was having lunch with her sister at the Bedford Hotel. He had parked his car in the hotel's car park and gone to the reception, and for a change he found out that indeed a table for two had been booked, and the ladies were in fact now taking lunch; for a change he didn't have to show his police identity card and the receptionist was polite and petite he noticed. He declined a table saying that one of the ladies was his fiancée and she had forgotten her keys. He found that lying came easily to him now.

'No problem,' the nice receptionist responded, 'the head waiter will show you to the table, and if there's anything else you require I will be more than happy to oblige.' Rainbow thanked her, his dirty mind working overtime. There's a lot he would have liked to have done to her. He smiled and followed the waiter to the table that Charlotte and Michelle were sitting at, eating a prawn cocktail.

Surprise took a running jump at both the ladies' faces, as they looked up from the cocktails.

'Ray, what are you doing here?' Charlotte said with a mouth full of food. 'What part of "we're finished" didn't you understand?'

'Charlotte, please, just listen, I've been to the hospital and there's a lot more to what happened this morning, you just have to hear me out, and if I don't convince you this time then I promise you I won't bother you ever again,' he pleaded. 'Can I sit down?' She looked at her sister who knew the full story of what had happened in the apartment, of the woman she found there, of him in his pyjamas, of his bulge between his legs showing, how mad she had been with him, and of her breaking off their engagement, the whole story.

Michelle had sympathised with her sister, and tried to console her at one time, when she was a little tearful, but inwardly Michelle was happy that her sister had got rid of the rat that she knew him to be. Her feelings had now fully fled the scene; she no longer cared a hell for him. She had had her revenge, and had been paid for her trouble. She certainly wasn't going to sell her hairdressing shop to go to London, there was no need at all, she wasn't and never had been pregnant, and she had learnt a valuable lesson: never trust a man who was full of themselves and Raymond Rainbow was certainly that kind of a man.

'Sit down,' she said reluctantly. 'But Ray, make it quick, we were enjoying ourselves weren't we Mish?' Michelle said nothing and looked away; she really wanted to escape.

'This thing is between me and you,' he began, 'so Michelle would you mind if I have privacy, while I have a talk with Charlotte?'

Charlotte was still very angry. 'She stays, she's not going anywhere or I don't want to hear what you have to say, so it's up to you. Can't you wait and tell me later, what makes it that important?' She fiddled with her prawn cocktail.

'It's a private matter, what I have to say is private, it's between me and you and not for her ears and I insist that—'

'Is there anything wrong with the cocktails, madam?' the waiter said as he passed the table and hovered between the two women.

Rainbow looked up at the waiter and said, 'Disappear, vanish,' very abruptly.

'I'm sorry, sir, I was only doing my job, I don't like rude people, I was only asking if the meal was all right.'

'Yeah well, go do your job elsewhere, and leave us alone, so withdraw.'

'Don't be so offhand, who the hell do you think you are, barging in on our lunch? Go now, Ray, before I lose my temper,' Charlotte sneered.

People from other tables were beginning to realise that a confrontation was taking place and fidgeted uncomfortably in their seats.

'Is there a problem here?' the hotel manager said as he approached the table, followed by the waiter who had just reported the incident.

'Yeah,' Rainbow said with anger in his voice, 'we do not want to be disturbed continually by him.' He pointed to the waiter, who looked surprised.

'He's only doing his job, sir, the ladies have their main course ready to be served, we are very busy, there's not only this table in here to tend to, so with the greatest of respect, please allow him to continue with his duties.'

Charlotte was embarrassed and said, 'Sorry.' The manager ushered the waiter away. Other diners returned to their lunches, mumbling among themselves.

'You have a lot to answer to, fancy showing us up like that, you're not with your underlings now and I won't be treated like this. I'm not listening to you so you can sling your hook,' Charlotte said with anger in her voice. Michelle looked most uncomfortable.

'Didn't you say you were going up to London? I believe there was something said on the matter,' he said directly to Michelle. He knew he was treading on dangerous ground, but why she hadn't gone when he had paid her all that money had been on his mind.

Michelle looked surprised at the question and was just about to answer when the waiter approached again. 'Can I take it that you are ready for your main course?' he said sheepishly.

'No, sorry, we wish to cancel our reservation, there will be nothing more, thank you.' Charlotte picked up her handbag and gave the waiter a ten-pound note. 'Thanks for your patience, we're finished with these,' she pointed to the half-eaten prawn cocktails.

'There's no need for that,' Rainbow shouted, 'there's no need to not have your lunch. I only wanted a talk with you. Always were a bit of a drama queen, getting your own way, sometimes I wonder why I put up with you for so long, you and your bloody family.' He knew all was lost; this was the end of the road, goodbyes were written all over her face.

'Fuck off, get out of my face you two-bit bastard,' she screamed as she threw a glass of water in his face. The waiter scuttled away, as people got up from their seats to seek out the manager to complain about the conduct in their lunch break, the likes that none of them could ever remember happening before.

Rainbow grabbed a napkin and wiped the water off his face and felt a hand on his shoulder. He half turned and two burly men stood there with security armbands. 'Please sir, please leave the premises at once, you've caused a commotion that I've never seen in here before, and I've worked here for five years, please leave now or we will have no option but to escort you off the property.'

Rainbow stood up, the chair he had been sitting on fell over making a cracking noise that made the diners gasp;

people had abandoned their lunch now, some enjoying the unusual excitement that mundane days can sometimes produce. A sense of excitement filled the dining room. Charlotte and her sister hurriedly left, paying for the food that had been ordered but not eaten, and apologised profusely.

'Take that hand off me now,' Rainbow roared, 'that's not a request it's a warning, you don't know who, or what, you are dealing with, I hope you are not trying to be a hero in front of this lot.' He pointed to the gathered diners. 'Let my arm go, or you will be having your tea in the general hospital,' he warned.

'Now there's no need for this behaviour, just leave, and that will be the end of the matter,' the restaurant manager said, almost pleading.

'I suggest that you tell your bouncers to withdraw now, or they will be going down a road that will be very frightening to them, it's the last time I'm going to say this, you have been warned.'

'Let's not get too dramatic, just leave please, look at the chaos you've caused in my hotel; it's a disgrace, are you leaving peacefully or do we have to eject you ourselves?'

'I'm a policeman,' Rainbow blurted out.

'And I'm the King of Arabia,' said one of the security men.

At that moment Rainbow's hand went to his inside pocket to get his identity card out. Like lightning both the security men pounced on him and with his arms forced up behind his back, he was marched out of the hotel restaurant to the cheers and applause of the watching diners. Rainbow now knew how it felt to be frogmarched, powerless, as he had done to countless people he had arrested over the years; he felt humiliated as they took him out to the front door and threw him out of the hotel.

'Bloody idiots, you don't realise what you have just done,' Rainbow said as he smoothed himself down, tucking his shirt back into his trousers.

'You were lucky we didn't call the police, our receptionist was on the verge of calling them, so go on your way, and don't ever set foot in here again,' the manager replied.

Rainbow was just about to show his warrant card but had second thoughts, he had failed in getting his fiancée back, completely fucked it up, and so as the door shut, head down, he shuffled to his car.

'Well done, James, your SAS time came in handy there, and you Harry, your boxing experience, you haven't lost it, good job lads, go and get yourselves a hot cup of tea, you deserve it. You have more guts than me, let's face it, he could have been a karate expert for all we know.' They all laughed as they walked away, and James winked at the smiling receptionist.

Rainbow sat in his car for a moment to try to get his thoughts together; he knew his and Charlotte's time together had come to an end. He saw it in her face as he said what he had said about her family; he regretted it but it was too late now. He still couldn't understand what Michelle's game was, and somehow he didn't care. Things were now beyond his control; he felt he had lost, there was only one thing to do and that was end it all. But how, he wondered? He could hand himself in, come clean, knowing that his career would be over. Running away popped into his mind as he sat in his car deep in thought. Or he could end his trouble and kill himself.

A knock on his window brought him back to his senses, two policemen indicating to him to pull the window down. He slid the car window down.

'What's the problem, officer?' Rainbow said; he didn't recognise the officers.

'Could you step out of the car, sir?' the first officer demanded.

Rainbow knew the procedure. 'And why would I do that?' he sneered.

'We had a call of a disturbance from a member of the public, a diner in fact, and you have been pointed out as the perpetrator of the disturbance, so will you hand me your keys, and get out of the car.' The officer went to his belt checking out his taser gun, and Rainbow saw him.

'There's no need for that, constable, you've got no trouble here,' Rainbow said as he got out of his car, and went to his inside pocket.

'Keep your hands down where I can see them, sir,' the officer commanded.

Rainbow said, 'Look before you make a mistake here, I want to tell you—'

'You don't tell me anything,' the cop interrupted, 'I do the talking here, do you understand?' He said the last three words slowly emphasising them. 'I'm going to search you, have you anything on you that could hurt me? Like Knives, syringes or things of that nature?'

'I have something in my inside pocket that might interest you,' he went to his pocket.

'Keep your hands in front of you where I can see them, sir, I've warned you, or I will take you to the ground, this is your last warning, now behave yourself.'

Rainbow had seen cops of this calibre before in his career, policing by the book kind, jobsworths, no leeway; he felt anger rising in him, but controlled his temper.

'You, officer, with the greatest respect for you, and your position as a law man, may I say in all modesty that it would need more than you and your colleague there to take me to the ground. I have a black belt in the greatest art in the world, karate. So let's not waste your time or mine and go to my inside pocket for something that might interest you.'

'Calm down, calm down, you don't want to kick off now, do you? Don't make a move, I'm going to your inside pocket.'

The officer looked at the identity card, with the other officer looking over his shoulder, and Rainbow saw the blood drain out of his face as he read it out.

'Detective Sergeant Raymond James Rainbow, homicide division.'

He looked at the photograph, then at Rainbow and said, 'Sorry, sarge, just doing my job,' he tried a smile but it was an embarrassed one. 'Sometimes we get things wrong in this game, it isn't easy being a copper, as you well know.'

'No I don't know,' Rainbow ventured, taking his card back, and slipping it in his pocket, 'I love my job, and I find it easy, maybe you should pull your head in a bit, not everyone you stop is a crim, you know there's a lot of innocent ones out there, remember that. This incident was just an argument between two people, and it was blown out of all proportion by people who take their jobs too seriously, so take my advice, sonny boy, take a step back and look at yourself and calm down. Now off you go, there's real villains out there who should be behind bars, go to it.' Rainbow felt better after his avalanche of advice and philosophy, and was sure he had gained the upper hand after the threat of being taken to the ground. He didn't mind doing the threatening but hated it when the tables were turned, when the shoe was on the other foot, as the saying goes. He smiled as he got back into his car, and drove out of the hotel car park.

He arrived home in the middle of the afternoon and after a shower put his pyjamas on and settled down to watch the world snooker, after all he was off work and was on a 'sicky'. He had decided to give the doctor a visit the next day. He felt he needed some medication for depression at least. He was trying to get over a love affair, a broken romance, a lost promotion at work, the house had gone, he had lost money, and his pet parrot was dead, he would soon lose his home, he was under a lot of stress, more than most men could cope with. *Where would it all end?* He thought, as he sat on his settee and the afternoon drifted away.

A crucial game was being played, and the black ball would decide the game, when Rainbow's concentration was disturbed by the knock on the door.

'Fucking hell,' he muttered as he slipped on his gown and went to the door. He wasn't very happy to see the two police detectives' contorted faces through the spy hole, waiting outside the door. If he had known what was on their minds he would have kept the door shut. This was the second visit for the police; they had knocked in vain the first time, then left for the coffee shop, and had returned to the station.

They had had an encounter with Inspector Ryan who was not very pleasant; in fact he was almost obnoxious. They had spent an hour in the chief's office, and the questions were coming thick and fast. The main questions concerned the whereabouts of Sergeant Rainbow; he had been missing for most of the week. Where were the items that were retrieved from the river? He wanted to know where the money from the children's home had got to, and why it hadn't been handed in, and many more questions, which the detectives just didn't know the answers to.

'I'm going to start calling him the Pimpernel, he's as elusive,' said the chief.

'Who is, sir?' Weston had said.

'The Scarlet Pimpernel, that French geezer who was hard to pin down, haven't you read the book?' The chief's face was flushed, his blood pressure rising.

'No sir,' both men said in unison.

'I want some answers today, so go to his home address and tell him to report in. I don't care how sick he is, unless he's been struck down with the Black Plague,' he said, his sarcasm in full flow.

The detectives were pleased to be released; they knew from old that when the chief inspector was in that kind of mood it was best to be away on a case.

On the return run, Detective Weston had had a change of mind on the Waybee statement. He had said it was a load of bollocks at first, but with time to think he had realised that there's no smoke without fire, and he wondered why Waybee would implicate a detective sergeant in a killing. What was his point? The revenge thing just didn't stack up, he was sure that the allegations made by Waybee were true, and that he had witnessed the incident in the alley. He had discussed all his thoughts with his partner, Willis, and he had also agreed. It had dawned on them as they were driving towards the apartment that Sergeant Rainbow had had them running around on wild goose chases just wasting time most days, achieving nothing, solving not one case when he was in charge.

The door opened and Rainbow smiled a warm welcome that was false; he wanted to see them like he wanted a hole in his head.

'Hi there lads, now there's a nice thing, coming to see your sergeant when he's sick. Come in, excuse the untidy state of affairs, haven't had much time to clean up. I was just about to make some coffee, want some?' He led them into the lounge, and pointed out the settee, 'Take a seat there,' he ordered.

The snooker game he had been watching had ended, and another game was on with two new players that he had never heard of. He switched the set off, and made the coffee.

The two detectives looked at one another and Weston spoke first.

'How have you been, sarge? Haven't seen you since last Wednesday, by the river, remember? The guy who accused you of hitting him by the old pier, remember him? He's still walking the river daily hoping to see his assailant again, says he's going to kill him when he sees him again, a real nutter. Anyhow that's neither here nor there, the reason we've popped around is to see if you're all right. Hope you're not too ill, because the rumours down at the station are running rife, some say you're on your last legs,' they all laughed.

'I'll survive, a bad cold won't kill me,' he lied. He didn't have a cold. He placed the coffee on the table and a bowl of sugar. 'Help yourselves, if you need sugar.'

He plonked himself down on the armchair facing the two detectives.

'Now,' he said, 'tell me what the real reason is for your visit. And please don't tell me you were worried about me, I'm a big boy now.'

Weston looked at his colleague and he indicated with a nod of his head that he should do the talking.

'Waybee's statement, sarge, we were with him this morning at the hospital, he's made a good recovery after coming out of the coma, and getting stronger as we speak, it was touch and go for a while. The doctors didn't hold much hope, he took a severe beating, and we were instructed to get a statement from him, if and when he came out of it. And we've done that, we got a statement, we thought that we would come to see you first before we submit, because the statement is shocking, in as much as he implicates you in the Baker Alley fatality ten days ago, and also in his beating.'

'I didn't beat him up, did he say I did?' Rainbow blurted out.

'No, but he told us that the Banana boys told him as they beat him, that you had instigated it by trying to say he had been spreading rumours, and bad-mouthing their boss Big Joe Bananas.'

'Now that's a fucking laugh, have you ever met Waybee, he's one of the biggest liars I've every met. Tom Pepper was truthful compared to him. What else did he say?' Rainbow laughed at his comparison.

Weston took a sip of his coffee and looked at his sergeant straight in his eyes and said, 'He said you hit his friend and killed him in the alley, it's all written down.'

'What a load of bullshit, the man's delirious, confused, he most probably got a head injury and is hallucinating. Its revenge, I put the bastard away many times over the years, not worth the paper it's written on, he's got no proof that I was in the alley at all, it's his word against mine, and I'm sure the judge in court would take my word against a villain like him. Anyhow on Monday night I was with my fiancée in this very place celebrating our engagement, it's all rubbish, seems I'm always being accused of hitting someone, on river walks even, no matter where I roam over land, or sea, or foam. Fucking hell, I'm a professional black belt in karate and ju-jitsu, my control is precise on the point of perfection, and is controlled through years of dedicated training. I don't need to hit anyone, I only have to touch them to make them cry out for mercy, fucking moron. Waybee's a fucking moron.' The detectives were feeling uncomfortable at the sergeant's outburst and fidgeted slightly as if they were preparing to leave.

'So should we hand in his statement?' Weston enquired.

'Now Detective Weston, that really is a stupid question, you're an officer of the law, and you must do your duty, of course you've got to hand it in. Now gentlemen when you've finished your coffee I want to rest a while, I'm sick remember, so thank you for taking the time to come and see me first, that was decent of you.' Rainbow drank the remains of his coffee and took the cup to the sink as the two detectives did the same.

'The inspector wants to see you tomorrow, he's raving mad, he's certainly got a bee in his bonnet, he reckons you're the Scarlet Pimpernel, that Frenchman who was never around. He even asked us if we had read the book, he was fuming. We had an hour with him this afternoon, really sarcastic he was, wasn't he, Jim?'

The detective, who had said nothing so far, just made a face in acknowledgement and nodded.

'He was asking where's the evidence that you had, and why hasn't it been handed in, and wants to know what happened to the money that was handed to you from that kid at that children's home, wasn't it twenty thousand pounds?'

'No, it wasn't that much and I still have the money. What does he think I'm going to do, keep the money and go on holiday with it? As for the other evidence, it's useless, it's been in the river for three days, and all fingerprints would be gone.'

'How do you know how long it had been in the river, sarge?' Willis said for the first time, surprised at himself for asking such a forthright question.

Rainbow knew he had made a mistake immediately. 'Just a figure of speech; what's this? Are you going to give me the third degree? Do you suspect me, Detective Constable Willis? Are you going to read me my rights? Will I have to be handcuffed or can I go to the station on my own accord?'

Willis wished he hadn't asked the question now and felt intimidated. 'Sorry, sarge, didn't mean anything by it, I just wondered, that's all.'

'We all know that the chief can get het up for most things, and its common knowledge that he's a very sarcastic man, always has been, and always will be. Before you ask, I haven't read the book either but I do know that the book was written by Baroness Orczy, I'm hardly the Scarlet Pimpernel, the chief must be having a laugh. Right gentlemen, I'll try to get in tomorrow morning, you can tell the chief that, and as far as the evidence I have in my possession, everything is in order, and it will be handed in when I have finished my lines of investigations, have a nice day.' He led them to the door.

'Sorry we disturbed you, sarge, hope you get better soon,' was the parting shot from Weston. Willis nodded in agreement as the detectives went back to the station.

In the car they had a giggle over the question that Willis had asked about the time the sergeant had said the items had been in the river. And Willis talked non-stop about the guilt that he believed his Sergeant Rainbow was concealing from them. He felt elated that he and his partner had found the killer of one of their colleagues, there certainly would be promotion on the cards. He could see the headlines in the city newspaper: DETECTIVE WILLIS AND HIS PARTNER SOLVE ALLEY MURDER. It made him smile.

Rainbow made himself a stiff drink and switched the television back on, although his mind was on other things.

TWENTY-ONE

Friday dawned, a beautiful day, there was not a cloud in the sky, and people felt well as they arose from their beds to face another day. For some, the rewards they had been waiting for, for working hard at their jobs, achieving the heights they had hankered after, and others their just rewards for doing the wrong things. Detective Sergeant Raymond James Rainbow was in the latter group. He had drunk a lot the previous evening, to the point that he had nearly lost his life. He had at one stage, after many whisky shots, gone onto his balcony and contemplated ending it all with the one step off; in a few seconds all his torment would have been over. He had looked at the concrete pathway below his apartment where Pedro had been buried, and for a moment wondered if he would join him in his everlasting sleep. Charlotte, Michelle, Eddie, Waybee, Bootsy Harris, his mother and father had all popped into his mind. He had talked to them in his drunken state, and argued with some of them. He had smashed up his television set by throwing his empty bottles at it when something came on he disagreed with.

He vaguely remembered phoning Charlotte, and the abuse she had thrown back at him concerning the debacle that occurred at the hotel. He was hazy on that matter, and told her so. He had trashed the photographs of himself and Charlotte, torn up the old love letters she had sent him in more loving times. His apartment now looked like a bomb had gone off in it. He had slept on the floor where he had collapsed, and had thrown up over his pyjamas. He was, to say the least, in a sorry state; he woke up at ten thirty.

*

At the station, the chief inspector had read the two documents; one statement that Waybee had signed, the one that had been delivered by post, plus the statement that detective Weston and Willis had obtained, and was having a meeting with DS Melvin Jones, and DC Derek Jennet in his office. The air was tense as the unsmiling policemen talked about the seriousness of the situation that they found themselves in. The chief passed the documents around. 'As you can see someone must have had second thoughts when they tore it in half, and sellotaped it together again,' the chief pointed out.

The men read the document and returned it to the inspector.

'I know of this character, this crim, a blatant liar, if I remember right,' DS Jones proclaimed. 'It could be sour grapes, Rainbow did arrest him on many occasions, and he was a suspect on the murder investigation concerning that Maltese Joe, or should I say his disappearance. Its common knowledge that the underworld believe that Maltese Joe was got rid of, nobody has ever solved that case. It's still on the books.'

'But there's no smoke without fire, sir,' DC Derek Jennet ventured, 'maybe Sergeant Rainbow was at the scene, it's possible.' He referred to his notebook. 'I've interviewed his training partners at his club, his karate club, and a witness, Stevens, a Brian Stevens, told me that on that Monday night our sergeant left the club to walk home at roughly six thirty, twenty to thirty minutes' walk away, and that's the time it takes to get to Baker Alley. I have walked that route, sir, it took me thirty minutes along the high street, and I believe that he came into contact with my brother that night. I'm sure that Waybee didn't just pull this accusation out of the air.'

'Well, thanks for your input,' the inspector said, 'but you know, all we're doing is going over old ground, all this has been said before. I have to take the bull by the horns now and get Sergeant Rainbow in, and see what he has to say on this matter.' The inspector picked up the phone and spoke to the desk sergeant. The two other detectives spoke in soft tones to one another.

'What? I hope you're not joking with me, sergeant, I'm not in the mood,' Chief Inspector Ryan said on the phone, then covering the phone with one hand, whispered, 'Rainbow just came in, he's downstairs now.' He went back on the phone. 'Tell him to go to the interview room and wait, I'll be down in ten minutes, and get someone to pick up that witness I was telling you about, yes bring him in right away, yes and make it quick, thanks, get him some coffee.' The chief put the phone down.

'Rainbow just walked in, as you heard,' the chief said to the detectives. 'I've sent him to the interview room so I will do the interview and I want you with me, Mervin, see what he's got to say on this matter once and for all. I suggest that you, Detective Constable Jennet, go and do your packing; I believe you're going back up north tomorrow; your bosses up there want you back. Remember, you were only on loan to us and don't worry you will be fully informed about the outcome of the interview.'

'Thank you, sir; it's been a privilege to have worked with you. I have to a certain extent enjoyed trying to get to the bottom of my brother's demise, and now it seems to be coming together, with the new evidence we got from the pathologist, it switched a new light on it all.' He shook hands with the policemen and left the room.

Downstairs, Rainbow sat in the interview room sipping his coffee, and waiting for the shit to hit the fan. He felt like death warmed up as his thoughts flashed through his mind. The drinking he had done the night before was taking its toll. Hazily he remembered once again phoning Charlotte and her anger at him; strange how love can quickly die; he had had it all, and now he was on the edge of a precipice.

Earlier that morning he had walked down Baker Alley on the way to the station; it had been cleaned up in the last ten days and most of the skip bins had been moved to a different location. There were new lighting fixtures at several spots, some doorways had been boarded up, and flower boxes made the once infamous drug alley a much nicer place to shortcut the high street. He had stood on the very spot that was the beginning of his downfall; he had sensed that his running was over. He remembered talking to the police constable who had been on duty the morning after, he could see his face but his name now escaped him.

He had walked to the station after going to the bank and drawing out ten thousand pounds to hand in, as he should have done earlier after getting the money from the school; galling, as the money belonged to him. An implausible situation for anyone to get into but it had happened to him; it was unbelievable but it had happened. A lot of his fellow policemen had not acknowledged him as he arrived at the station; his good mornings had gone unanswered by a few. The rumours and station gossip was at a high, he felt alone. He handed the ten thousand pounds reluctantly to the desk sergeant, and got a receipt. Michelle had the original money, the money from the school, the money that the boy had had in his possession. He handed in the bag containing the wallet, watch and boots, remarking that the reason he hadn't done so earlier was because he had felt that there was no worth in items that had been fished out of the river.

'Next of kin might want the items,' the desk sergeant had grunted, and had got on the telephone to the inspector. 'The chief said you're to wait in the interview room, he'll be down shortly.'

'The interview room? You're joking. The interview room?' He repeated, 'Christ am I a fucking criminal now?' Rainbow half laughed.

'That's what he said, the interview room, sorry Ray.' The desk sergeant handed over the receipt, and then pretended to look for something behind the desk; he felt embarrassed. It had been obvious to Rainbow that although the desk sergeant wasn't unfriendly, he wasn't his normal self. Something had been said, he hadn't even asked about his illness. 'Are you feeling better now?' would have been nice. Rainbow sat alone staring at the wall and waited.

*

Detectives Barns and Harris came in the station door, and after instructions from the desk sergeant, went to the side room next to the interview room.

They instructed the man who was with them to sit down at a small table, and invited him to have a coffee. The man accepted, and Barns went to get one from the canteen. On returning he was met by the chief and DS Mervin Jones in the corridor.

'He's in the interview viewing room, sir, just getting him a coffee, there was no trouble in picking him up, we were in the vicinity of the man's home, he lives close by.'

'Good work,' the chief said as they went into the side room.

The man got to his feet as the inspector went in, and the men shook hands.

'Thanks for your time, don't be concerned, he won't be able to see you through the one-way mirrors. All I want you to do is tell me if you recognise the man sitting in the other room. If you are not sure you must say so, you are obliged to tell the gospel truth here, a man's life is in jeopardy. The blinds on this wall will be parted,' he pointed to the wall, 'then tell me what you see, and if you recognise the man in the next room.'

'Detective Barns,' the chief indicated. Barns switched out the main lights and opened the blinds of the one-way mirror wall.

Rainbow was pacing the room; his coffee had been drunk.

The man nodded immediately, 'That's him,' he exclaimed in a whisper. 'I would recognise him anywhere, that's the man in question.'

'Now you are positive that the story that you have told me is the truth, the whole truth and nothing but the truth so help you God and this is the person you saw that night?'

'Yes sir, I swear to God it is, and to go further, I would go to court and say the same to the magistrate.'

'OK Barns, do the lights and the blinds, then take this gentleman home, after he's had his coffee of course, then get him,' he pointed to Rainbow, 'in my office, Mervin.' Detective Mervin Jones nodded and did the inspector's bidding.

'What's this all about, Mervin? I'm being treated like a criminal, fucking interview room, what's the big deal?' Rainbow said as the detective walked into the room.

'Just go with it, Ray, the chief wants a word. After all, you've been missing for days, and a few things have gone down since you were around. Let's go to the chief's office.'

Rainbow picked up the receipt that he had been looking at, thinking of how his money had soon diminished.

As the men walked upstairs and into the chief inspector's office, a certain depression descended the room, a tense atmosphere hung in the air.

'Sit down, Ray, there'll be no formalities today, we have a lot of things to get through, and time is ticking by. The chief constable is up in arms so let's get started.' The chief sat behind his desk with pen poised. Detective Jones sat next to him with his beady eyes firmly fixed on Rainbow.

'In your own words, Ray, tell us where you were on the evening of Monday the sixth of October. Although I already have the picture, I want the bits filled in.'

'Monday the sixth of October, that was the day that our undercover man went down, was it not?' Rainbow said.

'One thing I forgot to tell you,' and the chief hesitated, 'and that's I'm in no mood for any kind of shit, whether it is bull, horse, or camel shit, you know very well that is the day I'm referring to, so let's start again.'

'No bullshit, sir, I left my club, karate club, at six thirty and walked home along the high street, and arrived home at about seven o'clock, where I spent the evening with my fiancée. '

The chief glared at Rainbow. 'Already you have lied, Ray, for fuck's sake, in just two minutes of talking and you have already lied. You were in the alley that night, we know you were.' The chief opened his side drawer and took out a bundle of clothes and placed them in front of him on his desk. 'Do you recognise these training trousers and this designer sports shirt?' Rainbow looked at the trousers and realised that they were the ones he had given to the bin man in the early hours of the morning on the seventh of October.

'Never seen them before,' Rainbow declared, 'why, who said that I should recognise them? What's this to do with anything, what's the point?' Rainbow spluttered.

The chief came up with his first bombshell, 'Charlotte, your ex-girlfriend, has said that she gave these items to you as a birthday gift, she has identified them this very morning. Detective Jennet got this evidence this morning before he finished his duties here at this station. You have already denied owning these items in front of Constable Bright, so it says here,' he pointed to his notes.

'A colleague of yours, Brian Stevens, also identifies these clothes as the same ones you wore on the sixth of October when you were at the club. He said that he spoke to you about the quality of the garment and the big pockets in them, do you remember that? Ray, now come on, tell us the truth, get this out of the way because we already know you were in Baker Alley that night and we also know that you met with the deceased man Robert Jennet, so come on, Ray, come clean, for your sake in all decency, for your own conscience.'

Rainbow was quiet and looked down at the carpet; he knew this was the time to admit the truth. 'First off, sir, I'm sorry but I did something wrong; it was a moment of madness, I wish I could rewind like a video, and if I could go back to that night, I would. I made a mistake and I guess the piper must be paid… ' He stopped talking and took a drink of water.

'Go on, tell it as it was,' the chief implored.

'The clothes are not mine, and the reason that different people have said they are is because I have identical sets at home. I don't deny that I spoke to Stevens about the clothes I was wearing at the club on the night you've mentioned, but these are not the ones. I didn't give that bin driver any clothes, he was mistaken, and I told him so in front of Constable Bright. I do remember having a word with him on the way here to the station. Yeah, it was on the morning of the seventh. As far as my ex-girlfriend is concerned, I would take whatever she said with a pinch of salt.'

'So you're saying that these clothes don't belong to you?' the chief concluded, writing it down, and glancing over to DS Jones.

'No, sir, they are not my clothes.'

'Let's move on, tell us what happened when you left the club.'

'I left the club at six thirty or thereabout and took a shortcut through the alley. Sorry, sir, I did take the shortcut that night; all will be revealed in due course; I'm sorry I wasn't truthful about that. It was a dark night and as I walked between the bins that were on either side of the alley, I could hear a confrontation ahead of me; at first I believed that there was a fight taking place. I saw at least two figures but I may have been mistaken; as I approached, a man jumped out at me. He jumped out from behind the skip bin, he was staggering, talking in ways I didn't understand, he lunged at me, he had his hands around my throat, he was choking me, I tried to push him away, then he fell to the ground, hit his neck on a bit of wood sticking out from a skip bin. I tried to give him resuscitation, I ripped open his shirt and gave heart massage, but it was in vain. The man died as I was attending to him. I know I was wrong but I left the scene. I left the dead man lying there amongst the garbage of the bins. It was dereliction of duty, I know, but my mind was in turmoil, my hand was hurting me, throbbing like hell, I had injured it in the club. Believe me, sir, I was in a state, wasn't in my right mind, and that's the reason I have never admitted to going that way on the night in question. I went home, knowing that the man would soon be found, there was nothing more that I could have done,

I admit that in leaving the scene I failed in my duty, and I apologise for that, sir.'

'So you didn't hit back when he attacked you?' DC Jones asked for the first time.

'No, I was in no fit state,' Rainbow lied again.

'When you ripped his shirt off, did all the buttons come off the shirt, do you remember?'

'Yes, sir, they flew all over the place, rattling on the side of the bin.'

'And all the buttons were found apart from one, *this one*,' the inspector emphasised, holding it up between his finger and thumb. 'This one was found in this trouser pocket, it seems to have flown through the air, bounced off the side of the bin as you have just described, and landed in the open pocket of these sports pants, a chance in a million, and that's how we know that you were in the alley on that fateful night because these clothes belong to you, admit it, you might as well, as you just admitted that you were at the scene.'

A button in the pocket of his sports trousers, a flying button had given him away and put him right there at the scene. It was unbelievable, there was nothing for it, he had already admitted to being in the alley, now was the time to try to get out of the lie he had told.

'Let me see the clothes again,' Rainbow asked. The inspector pushed the parcel over across the table. Rainbow pretended to examine them, first the shirt then the pants. 'Yeah, now I remember these, they are the ones I wore at the club but I can't remember giving them away to that bin man that was on the site the morning I saw Constable Bright. Why would I do that, I ask myself? They are perfectly good gear, there is no need to throw this stuff away, I was having a spring clean. I may have given them away without realising it, my mind was troubled that morning with what I had been through, it was a mistake, I didn't remember because they were not meant to be thrown out.' He knew it was a feeble excuse but it was the best he could do, he returned the parcel to the chief.

'I'm glad that at long last you have come clean and admitted to something, there is also a witness who said that it was you who hit the deceased man. This document was delivered to me this morning; are you aware of it?' The chief held the paper in the air. 'Because it was brought to my attention by… The inspector glanced at his notes, 'by Detectives Weston and Willis, two good men, if I say so myself. Make a note of that, Sergeant Jones,' Mervin nodded and wrote the names down. 'Yesterday afternoon, you must remember that surely, Ray?'

Rainbow could see that the chief's sarcasm was starting to creep in once again.

'Yes, sir, I am aware of the document, it's not worth the paper it's written on. It's obvious to me that he was the one who was fighting, and as he saw me approaching, jumped in the skip bin to hide. He said he saw me hit his friend, and that is a blatant lie. He's a legendary liar, he is, and it's purely revenge; as you may be aware, sir, I've put him away many times in the past. Waybee is an out-and-out baddy, and it's my word against his. Can I point out, sir that I've got fifteen years in the force? Not one blemish on my records so far. We are all human and I made a mistake in leaving a dead man to phone for an ambulance at my apartment that's only a few minutes away. I'm sorry once again for that mistake. If I had known that the killer was in the skip I would have arrested him there and then, but I didn't know. I did search the area before I left.'

Sergeant Jones pointed out, 'But not in the skip?'

'No not in the skip, Mervin.'

Rainbow fidgeted in his chair, he considered his lies were working and with a bit of luck he thought he might get away with it. It was wishful thinking; the inspector had a few more things he wanted answered.

'The money that was found at the school, it seems it has gone missing again. I was wondering if the fairies had succumbed to the temptation and secreted it for their treasure trove down in the woods somewhere, to be shared out among the elves, and the Irish leprechauns.'

Jones burst out laughing, but Rainbow didn't see the funny side, and kept a straight face.

'That money has been handed in, sir, it's in the safe, I have the receipt for it. I personally handed it in after I had conducted my investigations; the boy found it in the park, he told me, in the tree area, on the outskirts of the park.'

'That's fine then, it's most probably drug money, and I will ask the chief constable if it can be confiscated, and put in the police fund. Make a note of that one as well, Mervin.'

'There was no evidence that it was drug money, no evidence at all,' Rainbow said with disdain in his voice.

'Well, where do you think the money came from then? Normal people don't just lose that amount of money in the park, unless they are morons or mentally deficient, certainly not anyone with an intelligence of any worth. No, it must be drug money, a drop-off that for some reason went wrong,' the chief was certain of his convictions and beliefs.

Rainbow wanted to shout out, 'It's my fucking money! The Money that I earned; and money towards a new home for me and my new wife; money that Waybee conned me out of; money now lost forever.' Instead he lowered his head and said nothing.

'Whatever happened to the items that you alleged you found at that criminal's house on the… ' he glanced down at his notes once again, '… Fingle estate, where Barry Harris lives? Wasn't there a watch, wallet and a pair of boots? Are you aware that Harris has indicated that those items were planted in his house, and he insisted that you, Ray, did the planting? I remember warning him that allegations towards a member of the police would not be tolerated, and he could go to prison for a long time, but he was adamant in his accusations, really adamant.' The chief frowned as he shuffled his papers and sat back in his chair.

'I'm not at all surprised, that lowlife would say anything to get off of any charge that was brought against him. The day I paid him a visit I was with Detectives Barns and Harris and they will say I had no such items on my person when we all went into his house, in fact it was Detective Constable Barns who found the boots and he also found the watch in the bedroom. What would be my motive to set him up? I have no idea. I'm sure Waybee put him up to say this about me, they were inside together just last week,' Rainbow said, convincingly, he thought.

'And what happened to the said evidence? I believe it was in your possession, then the next thing I hear it was handed in at the desk by a river fisherman who fished it out of the river, then you took it into your possession again, next there will be a report that the stuff will be discovered on the moon on the next moon mission. It's a load of make-believe to me, a bloody fairy story.' Rainbow could see a hint of anger creeping into the interrogations; the chief's face was starting to redden.

'It was in my possession, sir, but somehow it was mislaid. I thought it had been stolen and the next thing I knew it was being handed in after being fished, as you say, out of the river. A mistake on my part, but the items have now been handed in.' The atmosphere in the office was about to explode, even Mervin Jones looked uncomfortable as he shook his head from side to side.

'Another mistake, that's three you've admitted to so far, it seems to me that trouble follows you around, Sergeant Rainbow. You go to see the big crime boys and put ideas in their heads, so it's been alleged, and so they go around and beat Mr Waybee to a pulp, nearly kill him. Then somehow three of them take leave of this earth with shots in the heads, Waybee's in intensive care, and to crown it all, the gym you train at mysteriously burns down with the owner in it, with a hole in his body. Now forgive me if I'm wrong, that's a hell of a coincidence, a hell of a record.'

'I'm sorry, sir, but are you suggesting that I shot Big Joe Bananas—?'

'No Rainbow,' shouted the chief inspector, all goodwill suddenly gone, 'but I'm arresting you for murder, and anything you say will be taken down in evidence,'

The chief continued to read out his rights, as Rainbow stood up in shock and bewilderment, his mind in panic mode.

'Murder, Bloody Murder? Who the fuck have I murdered? I've already told you, I didn't lay a hand on him. My hand was injured, I've already told you, I did it at the gym, and I never touched the man. Waybee's a fucking liar, after all I've done in this force and you treat me like a criminal,' Rainbow protested.

'Cuffs, Mervin,' ordered the chief.

'Sorry about this,' said Mervin as he put the handcuffs on his former colleague, and sat him down in his chair.

The chief got on the phone and spoke to the desk sergeant, ordering some coffee and a charge form to be delivered as soon as was possible.

'Your warrant card will be handed in as soon as this interview is over, but let's see how this goes first. This is now formal: I have arrested you for the murder of Edward William Bail on the eleventh of October at Bloomfield Road and further, a charge of arson will also stand.'

Rainbow looked at his hands, and he lifted them in front of him. 'Is this really necessary? I don't understand what you have just charged me with. I haven't killed anyone, the report on Eddie Bail was out, and it was in the local paper. He killed himself after he burned down his gymnasium; it's nothing to do with me. You're not going to pin this on me just because I went to his gym, are you? It's well known, its common knowledge that he was in debt and a depressive, he did himself in—'

The chief interrupted Rainbow's outburst in mid flow, 'When was the last time you saw Edward Bail?'

Rainbow thought for a few seconds then said, 'Last week. I went to the club to pick up my gear; I cleared my locker out. I'd found out that the club may fold up, he was up to his neck in debt, he owed money all over the place. I only saw him briefly, maybe a few minutes, I collected my stuff and left, that was the last time I saw him.'

'Were you alone in the club, or was any other member there who can verify what you have just said?' the chief inquired.

'Just me and Eddie, there was no one else there.'

'Do you remember a gentleman paying a visit when you were at the club, a Mr Turnbull, the husband of the cleaning lady who works at the club for Mr Bail?'

Rainbow had forgotten the incident; his mind raced as his memory searched his brain. 'My mistake, sir, yeah, I do remember him, he popped in to sort out his wife's wages; he was only there in the office for a short while, my mistake, I forgot him.'

'Well, he didn't forget you, he picked you out in an identification just today, when you were in the interview room, and as far as Edward Bail being financially embarrassed as you have pointed out, it's strange that he could afford to have extensive repairs done to his club, with all the scaffolding up around the place. Not consistent with a man with money troubles, if you ask me. And why would he commit suicide with all that going on, answer that one?' The chief looked at Mervin, who with a nod agreed with his boss. 'It seems to me that your memory is in severe trouble, and mistakes are flying around like a sky full of jumbo jets.' Chief Ryan's sarcasm was in full flow.

'I've had a lot on my mind just lately,' mumbled Rainbow unconvincingly.

'I bet you have,' the chief sneered, 'you have let yourself down, and may I say the good name of the force.

It's hard enough to get the public on our side without all this, Rainbow. You're the rotten apple in the barrel, and I'm going to extract you. You were in the club on the night of the fire; it was you who killed Edward Bail. We have witnesses to say you disliked him and had had your differences. You killed him, and then you tried to hide your deed by burning the place down. On Saturday evening you were seen at the club; you were heard to argue with the deceased, and after the argument you killed him. Ten minutes later you were seen to vacate the premises by our witness, a Mr Roy Turnbull, who came to the club that very night, because there had been a shortage in his wife's wages, which had been given to him a few days earlier by Eddie Bail, the time you met him, remember? He was short of ten pounds, he saw and heard everything that went on, and he picked you out today as the man who committed this crime. You and Mr Bail just didn't get on. The incident at the club wasn't the first time you and Eddie almost came to blows. Explain to us what the trouble was on Monday night, the night you left the club at six thirty. As you have already stated, it is known that after you left the club, the late Eddie Bail followed you to return something you had forgotten, an engagement ring. He left the club to return the ring to you; on returning to the club a little later his mood had changed somewhat, so witnesses have said. He told Brian Stevens and others at the club that you had threatened him with severe violence; he was in a distressed state.'

The men sat staring at one another for what seemed like eternity, then Rainbow stated, 'Eddie Bail was a wimp, a weak man, I admit he wasn't my cup of tea, but I didn't kill him, and no one can prove otherwise. All this is a load of bollocks. I need to get a lawyer at this stage because, to be honest with you, you're barking up the wrong tree. Eddie Bail shot himself through the right temple with one shot, with a Smith and Wesson, obviously suicide. He told me on many occasions that he was fed up with running the club, and that's the reason I had decided to move out and find another place to do my training.'

'That's it!' the chief inspector shouted. 'It was never disclosed how Mr Bail died, the newspaper headline said, "Club owner dies in club fire", it was never disclosed how the man died. Nothing so far has been said of any shooting, only the investigating team know this information and the investigation is still ongoing. How would you know the make of the gun? Do you know what happened to the said gun, no weapon was found at the scene?'

'I don't know what happened to the gun, maybe—'

'Well, let me tell you a story,' the inspector interrupted. 'Do you remember when it was reported that a body was spotted in the river near the rickety pier this week, they thought it was a little boy that had gone missing from a children's home? Well, it turned out to be a mistake; it was a dead swan with head injuries floating around. I personally sent a diving team down that part of the river and have a guess what they found in the river.' the inspector opened his desk drawer and took out the Smith and Wesson gun. 'This,' he held the gun up. 'So you see, Mr Bail committed suicide in the gym, set fire to it, then went to the river and disposed of his gun, very clever thing to do when you're dead.' The inspector stared at Rainbow then said, 'You disposed of the gun, didn't you? You must have been there on the night in question to know this information. You need that lawyer, Mr Rainbow. Take him away, Sergeant Jones, fill in the arrest form and sort out my coffee, will you?'

Rainbow was put in a cell before being carted off to prison, to await the court's decision on his future. The police station was buzzing with almost every policeman talking about Sergeant Rainbow's downfall.

'I knew he was guilty of something,' said the desk sergeant as he was sipping his coffee in the station canteen. 'On many occasions he seemed very cagey, and he would never look you in the face when he talked.'

'I never liked him,' Detective Barns replied.

'Well done, sir,' Detective Sergeant Jones said, 'if you don't mind me saying so, you caught him out, he certainly slipped up on that one. Good idea of yours to keep the full details of Edward Bail's death secret, only a few of us knew the full facts. The head wound in the right temple, I mean.'

'Thank you, Mervin, but the real breakthrough came with our witness, Mr Turnbull, who only came forward because he felt aggrieved at his wife losing her job at the club when it burned down. That was his main motive for coming forward; it had nothing to do with the death of poor old Mr Bail. Let's just assume that Rainbow didn't kill or burn down the club. The one thing we know is that he was on the premises when the fire started. Why did he not call the ambulance and the fire brigade? He just walked away. If that's not guilt, I don't know what is. Put it this way, it's not consistent with the duties of a high-ranking police detective sergeant, no sir, it was blatant dereliction of his duty, he's quite obviously guilty of the crimes, what his motives were may come out in court.'

TWENTY-TWO

In the weeks that followed there were a lot of shocks and surprises for lots of people who had once had dealings with ex-Detective Sergeant Raymond Rainbow.

Nurses had rushed to the bed of Mr Waybee as he screamed in mid morning at the end of the trial. They had been very concerned, because the patient was on the verge of being discharged from hospital after, at one time, facing death fully in the face. The nurses had thought he had taken a turn for the worse before finding out he was hysterical as he was reading the newspapers with big headlines on the front page.

'Listen to this,' he said excitedly. He read out loud as the nurses gathered around his bed. 'Thirty years in prison for a corrupt sergeant in the city police. The murder of Edward Bail solved. Chief Inspector George Ryan made a statement at six o'clock after a unanimous verdict from the jury. "It's not often that you get a case of this severity within our ranks, this was an exceptional one of abuse of his position. I, with my team of dedicated officers, worked tirelessly night and day to bring this perpetrator to justice for the murder of a hard-working man just trying to get on in life." When asked a question by a reporter from the *City*

Times, the inspector replied to the effect that the Baker Alley death case was ongoing and that enquiries were continuing and an arrest was expected very soon.'

Waybee whooped with joy after reading it, to the nurse's amusement as they returned to their duties. 'Mr Waybee must have disliked that sergeant,' remarked a nurse to her colleague.

'Seems like it,' came the reply.

Mr Rainbow Senior was kept from the truth about his only son because of his fragility after a heart attack, and the beginnings of senile dementia. 'It would destroy him if he knew,' his wife said, so their son's name was never uttered in the house again. Over the years the old man forgot he ever had a son, and eventually died in peace.

Charlotte was soon going out with Rupert who, incidentally, was her boss's son, and with her mind set on living in a country house with beams, was soon engaged to be married. Her police boyfriend long forgotten in the mists of time, she very rarely mentioned her past, and never in the company of Rupert. Her sister Michelle slowly spent the money she had obtained from Rainbow under false pretences to fulfil the revenge she felt when he had spurned her, not only on herself but also on her sister, who enjoyed a romantic holiday with Rupert that Michelle paid for, saying that her hairdressing salon had been doing well in an upturn of new clients. After all, she felt she owed it to her beloved sister for the things she had done behind her back, and still had pangs of guilt sometimes. She had had her revenge, and he had paid the price. She felt no guilt whatsoever as time went by and all because of a film she had seen, called *Fatal Attraction*, which set her on that course of action. She had never been pregnant; as the years went by, he was put to the back of her mind, and she never spoke of him again.

His mother was asked by the owners of his apartment to collect his clothes and other things before the block was demolished, which she did with a sad heart, and apart from keeping a few photographs, dumped the rest in a skip that a bin man dumped on the city refuge tip, Including Pedro's empty cage.

*

The first few weeks of his sentence were hard, as Rainbow tried to adapt to his new strange world. At first he kept to himself, not talking to anyone at all. He tried to hide the fact that he was an ex-member of the police, and a sergeant detective at that, but that didn't last long. You can't hide this kind of information in a prison. Tittle tattle and gossip galore spreads like an Australian wildfire, and soon he was being called 'Sergeant' by the inmates, and one day one inmate called him 'Colours' and that nickname stuck; he was known as 'Colours' from then on. He did ask why the name and the inmates told him it was after the colours of the rainbow.

'That's fucking' ridiculous,' he had protested, but it had made no difference and although at first he wouldn't answer to his new name, in time he accepted it, so 'Colours' he became. Earlier on in his sentence, he made no friends at all, but the gym changed all that. He was soon mixing with big hard men, some with bigger muscles than he had ever seen on the outside, and so made friends with the bodybuilders. What the convicts liked about him was his fearless attitude; nobody fazed him, and he would stand his ground to any man, and was soon on the side of the underdog. He stopped any sort of bullying in its tracks.

Colours was getting to be a named inmate, one to be looked up to by screws and inmates alike. His demonstration of his fitness and speed impressed the men in the gym. He knew that no one would dare to challenge him, and his prowess and skill in the art of karate was second to none. He enjoyed the sessions, and got involved in all sorts of activities including weightlifting and helping newcomers in turning over a new leaf when they were eventually released. Colours had become a good egg until Waybee turned up on a three-year stretch for burglary. Then the crook Sims, known as Scarface, appeared on a charge of grievous bodily harm. He was followed by some of the Animal Gang who had caused a lot of trouble in the city when they tried to take over the dives and places of prostitution left over by the demise of mobster Big Joe Bananas. Chief Inspector Ryan and his force had had their hands full in dealing with this new outbreak of crime since Rainbow had been incarcerated.

'I need your help, lads,' Rainbow said to the boys at the next training session, as the inmate muscle-men gathered around. 'You will all agree, I'm sure, that I have done my best to help you all achieve your utmost in our chosen sport, and I will continue to help all of you at all times. We have all come a long way.'

'We sure have,' ventured big Jason, who flexed his muscles and made a karate hand movement and hissed like a snake, taught to him by his new friend Colours. All the men laughed in agreement. The guards seemed to find it funny as well, and joined in the laughter.

'This is serious, so thanks for your vote of confidence. As you know I have a court appeal pending, and I don't want any trouble of any sort; you know my history by now.' He hesitated, smiled, and then went on, 'When I was in that gang of blue, the fuzz, that load of bastards, my old life, I put away a few villains. It was my job at the time, and I've regretted some I put inside, but you can't put the clock back unfortunately, and sometimes the past catches up with you and that's what's happened now. That's why I want your help, your backing, so to speak. I could deal with this on my own, but I wouldn't be able to control myself—'

'For fuck's sake, Colours, get on with it, my fucking' muscles are flagging and the session will be over,' shouted Ratface Ralph. Once again, all the men laughed.

'Sorry Ratface, I'm digressing and pontificating and time is getting on, so I'll come to the point. If you don't understand my big words, ask someone with a bit of intelligence, OK Ratface?' All the men curled up with laughter, including Ratface Ralph. Rainbow knew he could get away with this abuse because he had had one altercation with Ralph on his first day in the gym. Rainbow had smelled Ralph's bad breath as Ralph had tried to intimidate him with his swearing and bullying ways. Rainbow had focused on a pressure point, and within a second had Ralph squealing like a rat, crying out for mercy. Suddenly a change of heart had come over the bully and he had decided that a friendly disposition was the way to go with the new prisoner. They had shaken hands and were now training companions.

Rainbow continued, 'As I was saying, I need your backing. Three new inmates have arrived at this establishment only yesterday, and I know from the grapevine that they hold some grudge against me. They wouldn't worry me in normal circumstances, but I can't afford any grief, not at the moment, not with my appeal outstanding.'

'So you want us to have a word with them, is that what you're trying to say?' said Big Dog Reggie Bradshaw.

'That's exactly what I want you to do.'

'Well why the fuck didn't you say instead of prevaricating, or should I say procrastinating? You carry on like a big girl's blouse,' Big Dog stated, picking up heavy weights and pushing them above his head.

'Been reading your dictionary again, big man?' said another inmate, to more laughter. I didn't know you could read.'

'Waybee, and Sims, are the ones I want you to have a word with, just put the word out that no trouble at all will be tolerated, you understand.'

'We're with you, Colours, you have no worries, and it will be done. Now can we get some work done? My fucking' muscles have turned to flab, and we've only half an hour left.' The inmates returned to their workouts, mumbling to one another.

Rainbow was happy to have the full support of his new friends. It seemed he had more friendships in prison than he had ever had on the outside. There was a common bond, it seemed, that held them together. As long as you didn't grass, and you hadn't been convicted of child offences, your crimes were of no significance. Nobody gave a shit about robbery or arson; even murder was warranted in some cases.

It wasn't long before Big Dog and his boys put their promise into practice. There was no escaping in the exercise yard, so when Waybee and Sims were pointed out by a passing inmate – he pointed to them sitting deep in conversation on some steps on the other side of the yard – the boys spread out and Big Dog was the first to approach the talking men.

'You're Waybee, yeah?' he said to Sims.

'Why, who's asking?' Sims said.

'Look, let's get this right from the start, I'm not here to just make your acquaintance, you mean fuck all to me, so just answer me straight: are you Waybee, or is this ugly fucker him?,' he pointed his fat finger at Waybee.

Waybee looked up to the big man and, unafraid, said, 'Yeah, I am, and if you call me ugly again, then I will have competition because your fucken' face will certainly be worse than it is now, so fuck off while you can still walk, your muscles don't frighten me.' Sims looked on in admiration at his friend's daring.

'Is that so you fucking' moron?' Big Dog sneered. 'We can arrange to meet up any time you like, but in the meantime; you keep away from a friend of mine. He doesn't want your smell around him, understand me now, I'm doing you a favour, a big one, his name is Colours.'

'I don't know anyone by that name, and I don't need your favours, so once again, fuck off.'

'It seems you didn't get what I was saying,' Big Dog sneered more aggressively, as he made a sign behind his back, and two brutes of men slid up and stood either side of him.

'Fucking hell,' Sims said, 'you bringing your army out now, are you?'

'Yeah, and it's a big one as well, I've got to make you understand how serious this is for your own well-being if nothing else.' He flicked his fingers in the air and twenty more big weightlifting muscle-bound monsters gathered around him.

Waybee swallowed, as his brain told him it was the time to back off. He considered he was a hard man, but this was plain suicide.

'Who's the asshole you're talking about, what was his name again?'

'Colours, Rainbow, you had dealings with the man when he was on the other side, when he was a member of the filth. But that was then, and now is now. He's changed, he's a much better person since he left the pigs, so *we*,' he emphasised the word 'we', and made a circular movement with his hand over his gang of giants, 'want you to keep away from him, no contact at all; do I make myself clear?'

'I knew that wanker was in here, but that's the last thing I want is to mix with a killer like him. He killed five men to my knowledge, Big Joe Bananas and his two boys, Eddie Bail from his own club, his gym he used to go to, and also my friend Tommy Crawly, in Baker Alley; so why would I want to mix with the likes of him? Rest assured, there'll be no contact,' Waybee said with conviction.

'What's happening here?' two guards demanded. 'Move along, you have the whole yard, no meetings, move on, no congregating.' The men dispersed immediately.

At dinner break the same day Big Dog reported to his friend Colours, what had gone down in the yard, and was repaid with an extra pork chop that was placed on his plate, with two roast potatoes. 'Thanks for that you're a very nice man', Big Dog mocked. Then continued,

'You have a hell of a reputation, according to this Waybee guy. He reckons you are a serial killer; you killed five men and all in keeping the peace and upholding the law of the land. Hell of a career, I don't know if I should be mixing with you really.'

'Give me back my fucking chop then,' Rainbow said, making a move to take back the chop, and the Dog moved the plate away laughing.

'You know, Reggie, everyone in here is innocent, there's not one con here who says he's guilty. And so nobody believes the innocent, because there are guys in this prison who are innocent but they are not believed, because as I have said nobody will take the blame for things they did, wrong things in society. The truly innocent are put in the same category as the guilty. As for me, I have never killed anyone in my life; do you believe me, Reg?'

Reg stopped eating, looked into Rainbow's eyes for twenty seconds and said, 'of course I don't, you're as guilty as we all are, but five is hard to believe, don't think it was five.'

'See what I mean? It's all the same, that's the reason inmates don't talk a lot about their criminal activity, and the innocents must fight for their rights through the law courts sometimes for years to get justice. Remember the Birmingham Five who did years in prison for a bombing they didn't do? They were innocent but nobody believed them.' Rainbow felt he had made his point and mopped up his gravy with a piece of bread.

'You know, Colours, you've got a point there, but I still believe you're not in here just because you're an ugly fucker, you must have done summit they don't give you thirty years for noffink.'

'And that's why I've got an appeal pending. I left the scene of a fire and a dead man without reporting it, he committed suicide and set fire to the club as I just happened to be on the premises, getting my gear from my locker, that's when he set the place on fire, and then shot himself. OK we didn't get on, and we had had a bust-up, but I didn't do him in. I was seen leaving the burning club, so they put two and two together and made a big mistake and that's why I'm here. My only mistake was to pick up the gun he shot himself with, and I disposed of it; why I did that I have no idea. I should have left it where it was in his hand. I must have been in shock. I'm in here an innocent man, unlike most. Nobody believes me, but I'm fighting it, and I hope it will all come out in my appeal.'

'On second thoughts, now I've got your full story, I believe you, my friend,' Reggie said with a doubting nod of his head. The whistle blew for the meal's end and the men returned to their cells.

'Thanks for your help, Reg; see you tomorrow in the gym.' Rainbow tapped him on his shoulders as they walked away from the mess hall.

Waybee got the message and didn't go anywhere near his adversary. He mixed with Sims and Freddy the forger whom he had known for years, and did his time quietly, keeping his nose clean. Most times, thinking that one day he would be with Ruby in Spain laying on the beach drinking rum and Coke, he lived in a dream world. What he didn't know was that he was dying slowly inside.

Rainbow spent his time training in a routine that was persistent, days in relentless and unremitting monotony, and waiting for the day he hoped he would get in court, on his appeal. As time went by he caught the eye of the prison governor and with good reports coming in at regular intervals, was called into the office, and was praised for his work with young offenders, and the good job he was doing in the gym. Trouble in the prison had decreased since his induction and the governor offered him a job in the infirmary as a reward for his good work, and being a model prisoner, with a chance of becoming a trustee on the cards. Rainbow accepted this opportunity with open arms as it was considered a choice position in the nick, and there were extra privileges to go with the job.

Days turned into weeks, months slipped by, with spring, summer and winter coming and going. Sometimes it seemed at a slow pace, at other times time just flicked by as it tends to do when you live a busy life, and Rainbow kept busy as he tried to make the most of the disastrous time he had experienced. Somehow he felt relieved that it was all over, that two weeks of his life had taken its toll. Sure he felt angry at times when he thought of how he was doing time for some murder he hadn't committed, and the one he had done, he had got away with. It was ironic. It was in his second year of his sentence that he heard something that disturbed him, and kept him awake for nights.

Alf 'Fatso' Feldman, who worked mostly on the night shift, sidled up to Rainbow as he came on his morning shift. Alf was twenty-two stone and was a supervisor in the infirmary. Both men got on amicably and often played chess in the middle of the night when all inmate patients were away with the fairies.

Alf had killed his wife one night after years of her abusing him with taunts and jibes about the size of his penis, which was just three inches long on erection.

'Seen bigger on a spider, you fat bastard,' she would laugh. She was always mocking him, and one night he stopped her abuse by stabbing her forty-three times. He only told his story once, and told Rainbow never to mention it again. Rainbow never did. Alf advised his only friend, as he now claimed, of a new addition to the ward that had come in overnight.

'He's in 4C, he's very ill, the big C, with a T attached,' Alf said with a sigh. 'Cancer, Terminal, he's being moved out to a civvy hospital, that's if he survives the night. Make sure you keep an eye out, because no matter what my patients have done in life, while they are in my department they have to have that respect that all human beings deserve whatever has gone down in the past. It's my way of making amends for what I did, if you understand me, Colours.'

'Don't worry, Alf, I understand, and you're dead right I agree with you, hundred per cent. No matter who it is that comes in here, I'll look after him like the professional nurse that I am,' he smiled broadly. 'Who is the patient in question?'

'Go see, 4C,' Alf said as he went to the office to sign off.

It was his old enemy Tony Waybee. He had been admitted into the prison hospital and it was Rainbow's job to care for his patients, no matter who they were, as Alf had just reminded him. Rainbow was surprised at his appearance: he was frail, thin and obviously dying. As he approached his bed, Waybee held out his hand in a goodwill gesture. Rainbow took it and both men shook hands. His weak hand came up to his face and removed the oxygen mask.

'Bygones, eh, Ray,' Waybee said weakly, as he recognised his old enemy coming towards his bed. 'Let's put our past to rest, I want to tell you something before I go, something I lied about and something you should know, I have been thinking about it for a while now and I have to clear my conscience, so please listen to me. I ain't got too long.'

Rainbow pulled up a chair and sat near the bed. He poured a glass of water and offered it; Waybee took a sip and pulled himself up on his pillows.

'Hi Tony, it's been a while since I saw you, I guess it's no good me asking you how you are, you don't look too good to me, but as far as our feud goes, I agree it's time to call it a day, it's time to call a truce,' Rainbow said, meaning it. 'And let's not talk about going anywhere. You'll survive, you always have, you've done it before and you'll do it again; anyhow, you're too fucking' wicked to die.'

Waybee smiled a faint smile, and talked in a soft tone. 'Do you remember the night in Baker Alley?'

'Can I ever forget it?' Rainbow replied. 'That night still haunts me to this day.'

'I know, but it won't after I tell you the truth about that night.'

'The truth, what truth are you on about?'

Waybee began to talk before he had a coughing bout. When he had recovered he began again. 'Tommy was with me, and I told him I wanted to get in the skip bin, but it was too high for me to get up, so I asked him to give us a bunk up. He lifted me up but with my weight he had difficulty. He heaved me and as I got over the top, he shouted out that he had a pain shoot across his chest. I looked at him over the top of the bin; he was in agony, he said he couldn't breathe, he didn't know what to do. He cried out in pain, and then he said to me words I'll never forget. He said that he was having a heart attack; he stumbled around holding his chest. I tried to get out of the skip, but the more I tried the more I sank in the garbage of the bin, then I fell down. By the time I stood up I heard him talking to someone, and that someone was you. I saw you through the crack in the skip, you see, *I killed him*, it was me who caused him to have the heart attack by asking him to lift me up. Yes, I did it, and all for a pair of fucken' boots that Harris had told me he had dumped in there, a pair of boots,' he shook his head in disgust. 'And one more thing, I lied, because I saw you through the crack but I didn't see you hit him, I made that up. I heard a crack, an almighty crack, and I just assumed you know… you do, don't you? I'm sorry but I had to do this, tell you, please forgive me will you, Ray? I put you through a lot of grief I know, sorry I couldn't get your money back, I just didn't get the time. I got a beating, but you know that don't you?' His eyes lifted up as though he was expecting an explanation.

'Yeah I was told by a couple of my ex-colleagues that those hoods, Butcher and that other idiot Bruiser, had told you as they gave you a slapping that it had something to do with me, and that was a load of bollocks. They were born liars, and they died liars.' Rainbow got up from the chair as he saw the prison doctor with his entourage come into the ward. 'I'll see you later, the doctor's on his way; you need to take your medication. I'll come back after lunch so have a little sleep, rest after you've seen the doctor.' He gripped his hand, 'you'll be OK, Tony just rest,' Rainbow said reassuringly.

The revelation of what had happened in the alley played on Rainbow's mind as he ate his lunch on his own in the small side room that the staff used as a rest room and where a rest was taken from time to time, apart from the numerous tea breaks that were taken every two hours. Deep in thought once again, he went over that Monday evening. It had all come together now; all the pieces were fitting into place. His part in the death was next to nothing, a blow that did nothing more than stopped the attacker in his tracks, if at all. He was being attacked. That man had died of a heart attack. Now he realised why, within a week of meetings and high-brow top cops on the scene, they soon disappeared, but no one told him of the final pathologist's report. If only he had been aware then, there would not have been all that trouble with the blackmailing that had marred his life. Eddie Bail may still be alive.

Rainbow continued with his duties during the afternoon but was made aware of inmate Waybee's deteriorating condition. As Rainbow approached with a new glass of water, Waybee's eyes seemed to light up. 'Did you see her? She was here, just over there,' he lifted his thin finger and pointed to the end of the ward. 'Ruby came to take me home, my wife wants me back, we're going to start a new life away from all this, all this,' he gave a slow smile and sighed.

'That's good news, Tony, real good news.'

'You know they smashed up my boats, all my models, every one of them, them bastards, and you know what I would do if I could get my hands on them? I would fucken' smash them up, like they did my models.'

'Too late, Tony, they're dead.'

'Who's dead, who died?' Waybee said feebly.

'Butcher and Bruiser, they're both gone, they're both dead; so is Joe Bananas, their boss, they all died the same time, brutal as they were.'

'Are you sure, Ray? Are you really sure? Who are they anyhow?'

'Look, Tony, you need to rest, don't worry about these things, they're not important anyhow.' Rainbow could see that Tony was hallucinating, the heavy drugs he was on were kicking in and taking over the mind and confusing it.

'You know I have a secret, I never told anyone, ever in my life.'

'What's your secret? Are you going to tell me, Tony?'

'Yeah, I never had the ability to love anyone, not my mother or father, I only loved two persons in the world and that was my wife Ruby and little Benny. Yeah, Benny, he was going to be my son, but it never happened. I loved him, I'm going to go and get him and show him to you,' Tony made to get out of bed.

'No you can't do that, Tone, stay where you are,' he reached out to restrain him and pushed him gently back on his pillows.

'Will you go and see him for me, Ray? Bring him to see me, I need to tell him that I love him,' he implored.

'Can't do that my friend, if I could I would but it's not possible. In fact it's impossible, so rest now.'

'Why can't you do this little thing for me, after all we are friends now?'

'Prison, Tony, we're in fucking prison, don't you remember? Fucking prison.'

'Prison,' Waybee muttered to himself as he went quiet, trying to remember why he was inside. He lay there for five minutes as Rainbow attended to another task then he returned and studied Waybee and remembered a younger, unlined face that he had met many years before, and now death's ugliness was in place just waiting for the word, it seemed. Waybee's eyes opened, he struggled to speak.

'Tommy, I didn't love him but I came close to it, he was a great guy, we did everything together apart from sex,' Waybee laughed weakly at the idea. 'But we did eat, laugh, slept in the same bed twice when we had had too much booze,' he laughed again. He seemed to perk up as he spoke, 'We were good buddies, and he was one of the best people I ever came across in my life.'

'You never liked cops, did you, Tony? You had no time at all for the likes of us, did you?' Rainbow pointed out.

'To be honest, Ray, I never met a decent copper in the whole time I did my work as a criminal, if you excuse my bad language they are a bunch of bar—'

Waybee jerked back and had a coughing fit.

'You did meet a good copper once, Tony, and don't worry, it wasn't me, it was… now this will surprise you.' Tony lay back waiting, it seemed, in anticipation.

'Detective Sergeant Robert Jennet was a good friend of yours, but you knew him by another name, by the name of Tommy Crawley. He was with you for several months, he was undercover, now he was a good friend and a good cop, wasn't he?'

'Yeah, Tommy was a good cop, one of the best, and he was my friend. I always knew there was something different about him, something unique, something exceptional, now the games are over, the last dice has been cast. Goodbye, Sergeant Rainbow. Please forgive me,' he closed his eyes and smiled. The men held hands as Tony Waybee passed away.

Ted Sims was released and went back to his life, but he was a changed man. He had found religion, and moved in with his sister Mavis, and got a job with a security firm doing night duties on premises that at one time he might have robbed. His criminal activities were at an end. He managed to say goodbye to 'Colours' on his last day in the exercise yard.

Rainbow's appeal was rejected, and as time went on he just accepted his fate and put his mind on his work in the prison hospital, eventually becoming head orderly when Alf got too heavy to continue with the job. On Alf's last night on duty, both men talked more than they had ever done. Alf had already been warned of a transfer to another prison.

In the early hours of the morning, in the small room they used for coffee breaks, with all the hospital inmates fast asleep, Rainbow opened up to his friend.

'Sleep, that's the best thing to escape this drudgery. I just sleep as much as I can and dream. Yeah, just dream of what could have been. You know what my trouble was, Alf? I was too big-headed, being the chief's blue-eyed boy, I could do no wrong, I thought I was the bee's knees.'

'Yeah I know what you mean, Colours, I was like that once myself before I became this fat lump,' Alf said interjecting.

'My world was full; I was self-righteous,' Rainbow continued, 'another way of putting it is complacent. Too bloody complacent, then one day I left my gym that I used to train in when I did karate, to go home. I had done the same thing on many occasions but on this night I took a different turning into a dark alley and made a mistake. My whole life changed in a split second, and took a different path that has led to this,' he pointed. 'But Alf, I won't go on because I've told this story before, it's time to sleep, time to dream, but if I could only turn the clock back, I would,' he paused and then with sadness in his face repeated, 'I would, I would.'

THE END

FINAL

The retirement party in the police canteen was in progress, and Inspector Edward Sims had just sat down on a table at the top corner of the room. He was with his colleague Chief Inspector Tony Waybee. Other officers arrived in ones and twos, and took their places at the bar, but the main man had yet to arrive.

'Have you read his book yet? I've been informed we have all got parts in it, I'm a villain, I believe,' remarked Inspector Sims, 'a scarred one at that,' he laughed out loud as he took a sip of his whisky.

'He cast me as the top criminal, I believe, and I come to a nasty end. I always wondered if he liked me or not,' Inspector Waybee said with a nod.

'Yes he gave me a free copy when the book was published, and I believe he's bringing more copies tonight to hand out to all his friends and colleagues whom he's worked with all these years. There's one sure thing, he won't be bored in his retirement, I think he'll do well in the world of writing; damned good book. The idea of casting all of us as the criminals, and the gang of baddies as the law officers, now that's original and creative if you ask me. Fancy having that cop with a name like Raymond

Rainbow as the main character who was he based on?' Detective Inspector Waybee asked as he looked around the room that had been set up for this retirement party.

'I have wondered that,' Inspector Sims replied, 'well it can't have been himself, because he was a bin man in the book, a small part, so who can it have been? Who was Raymond Rainbow based on? I'll ask him when he comes in.'

Charlotte and Michelle, police section vice squad, laughed at some joke that came from bulky Joe Barnsom who had been in the force, on the beat for twenty years or more, and Constable Barry Harris wondered if his farewell party would be that well attended. All the police had agreed that the writer could use their names in the book, many going along with it thinking a book would never come out, but now the book was published and those who had read it thought it was a good effort from a cop with a vivid imagination, and a well-liked member of the force. No one took any offence at their characters in the book; on the contrary, some thought it was hilarious. Charlotte and Michelle just smiled at the sex parts in the story, and denied knowing what it all meant, amid laugher from fellow officers.

There was a round of applause as the policeman who everyone was there for walked into the room. His wife Ruby on his arm, he made his way to a table that had been reserved for his party. Drinks were ordered, and then the chief constable stood up to make the retirement speech.

'Ladies and gentlemen, we are all here to say farewell to one of our colleagues who has served in the force for twenty-five years and won two medals in the process. I'm sure everyone here will wish Detective Sergeant Michael J. Milford a long and fruitful new career in being an author. I look forward to reading my copy of his book. We will miss him, I'm sure you will all agree. Put your hands together in a round of applause,'

The chief constable left the small stage and shook hands with the now retired detective. 'Speech, speech,' shouted someone in the crowd.

Mike took to the little stage.

'Fellow colleagues, thanks for coming tonight, I have enjoyed my time in the force. There have been good times, and some bad ones. Cases that have been solved, cases unsolved, have all been part of my time. Now that time has come to an end, and I will have to find something else to fill my life. My biggest regret is that whoever killed our undercover operative years ago in the alley was never apprehended and brought to task; also the arsonist and killer of the owner at the gym in the city is also still at large. In my book the culprit was my fictional character Raymond Rainbow, based on nobody I know, but the real killers are still out there somewhere. Who knows, one day they might slip up and we'll nab them and bring them to justice? Thank you for your support over the years, I will miss you all as my wife and I lay on the beach outside our villa in Spain. Thanks for coming tonight. Whoever wants one of my books is welcome to a copy, thanks once again and goodbye.'

He returned to his table and a young smart policeman placed a drink on the table and smiled. 'You don't remember me do you, sarge? Do you remember I once told you years ago that one day I would become a police helicopter pilot and here I am just qualified, and when I got the word that you were retiring I took it upon myself to come tonight to wish you a good retirement. I lived in a children's home.'

Sergeant Milford just shook his head and said, 'What's your name?'

'Kenny Barrows, sir, from Garfield Road children's home,'

'Sorry, I don't remember you at all, but there's a strange thing because there's a character in my book that lived in a home for children, and he wanted to be a helicopter pilot. Have you read my book yet?'

'No, but I'll make a note of it, have a good retirement and a good life.' The young policeman shook hands and joined his colleagues at another table.

'He seemed a nice person,' said Ruby, 'pity you didn't remember him, he looked a little hurt; you could have said you remembered him even if you didn't, poor boy.'

'No dear, some things are best forgotten. I mean, I don't remember him.' He gave a knowing, wary smile. He left the party with applause ringing in his ears. The pain had gone, and so had the guilt he had carried with him in his mind and heart for so long. He was free at last.

THE END (AGAIN)